JEREMY IS STUCK

ALSO BY RICH NEVILLE

CATBIN FEVER

JEREMY IS STUCK

by Rich Neville

Sometimes, if you put enough effort into ignoring a problem,
it goes away all by itself.

WEDNESDAY

CONTROL

1

BUSINESS AS USUAL

Jeremy sank back in the chair and felt his stomach sink further still in anticipation of the questions to come. He distracted himself by focusing on the dust particles sparkling in the shafts of afternoon sunlight, and despising them for their apparent carefree abandon.

'Robert, close that, would you please,' said Ray, having concluded that no-one else was going to turn up.

He swung his legs onto the oval table as Robert reached back to push the meeting room door shut. The other attendees were all sat in chairs, as one might traditionally expect in such circumstances, but Ray considered that his senior position in the company behoved him to perch in a vaguely yogic cross-legged position at the head of the table. It was part of the quirky managerial style he was doing his best to foster, and it meant that everyone had to physically look up to him.

'Right,' he said, shuffling the wrong pieces of paper, which he had hurriedly grabbed on his way into the meeting, 'who's doing the minutes?'

'It's Martin's turn,' smirked Jem, clutching printouts from the previous week, which clearly credited her as the last minute-taker. Strictly speaking, they had begun as Keith's work, but they had proved sufficiently erratic to require a complete rewrite. Sadly, Keith had been unavailable for congratulations, or to perform his own edit.

'Snitch,' said Jeremy, under the comedic disguise of a cough. She smiled at him mischievously, and he flushed a little.

Martin sighed and accepted the pad Ray had just slid over to him. He noted down the date.

'Present,' he said as he looked around the table, intending to announce the names as he wrote them.

'Martin Priest,' he began, getting himself out of the way first.

'Ray Ciscombe.'

With this one he followed the grand tradition of always pronouncing Ray's name as 'racist scum'. Ray knew nothing of this tradition, and had always assumed that the snorts and exhalations which followed the announcement of his name simply reflected the fact that it was obvious he would be present. His attendance had always been exemplary. He couldn't remember the last time he had been ill, and only broken bones had ever led to actual absence.

'Jeremy Starwars.'

Jeremy was of Polish extraction, and, as was often the case with more difficult pronunciations, his parents had adopted a westernised version of their family name when they had come to settle in the UK in the mid seventies.

'Jemima Pepper.'

Jem stuck her tongue out at Martin. He was fully aware that she wasn't fond of the unabridged version of her name.

'Guy Mange.'

'*Ghee Mondge*,' said Guy Mange, correcting Martin with a pronunciation that sounded considerably less like a gentleman's disease than Martin's effort.

Guy was visiting from Paris for a few weeks to perform translation and design work. He was by far the best dressed person in the room, in an immaculate linen suit that spoke of a positively alien level of professionalism. He also elected to coat himself in a layer of aftershave that was stronger than any scent to which the others present were accustomed. Martin shrugged and wrote 'French Guy' on his pad.

'Ian Gerald Peterson.'

Ian very much did like the unabridged version of his name, and he might have smiled at its proper use at this juncture had his mouth not been busy, as it so often was, dangling open for breathing purposes. There was another Ian Peterson working in the storeroom, and Ian

Gerald Peterson didn't want him taking credit for any of his ideas. In the pad, as usual, Martin skipped the identifying middle name and wrote 'Stores' in parentheses, while Ian sat obliviously scratching at his patchy facial hair. Thus far, the Ian Peterson in Stores remained unrewarded for his sparkling performance in the Programming meetings.

'Robert Smith.'

Robert was Chinese, and a Goth. It was generally suspected that he was not going by his birth name.

'Will Simons.'

Will was quite reserved in his manner, and there could be few in the office who hadn't at some point taken the time to offer a hushed amateur estimation of his position on the autistic spectrum. However, their whispers were unnecessary, as Will was far from sensitive. He was, in fact, a self-diagnosed sociopath who happened to devote his cold analytical nature to software, and he considered his freedom from the shackles of emotion to be something of a superpower.

'And who is this?' Martin asked of Ray, motioning with his pen to the entity stood in the corner, away from the table, looking for all the world like a highly polished mirror in the vague, blurry shape of a man. As Martin pointed, he watched the reflection of his pen distorting across the surface of the figure's torso, and he waved it back and forth in a subtle effort to better make out their unnaturally fuzzy edges. He then noticed upon the shiny stranger's chest the reflection of his own puzzled frown. He lowered the pen and attempted a smile, for fear of causing offence.

'That's Manny,' said Ray. 'He's just going to be sitting in and seeing how we do things around here. Don't mind him.'

'Manny,' said Martin, seemingly happy with this explanation, and he added their guest to the list of attendees before taking one further theatrical look around the room. 'I assume Keith is still absent?'

'Keith is still upstairs, yes,' said Ray solemnly.

There was a moment of silence as the attendees considered the information. Ray broke this with a brief whistled rendition of a descending bomb.

'OK,' he continued. 'What's new from last week? I appear to have brought the wrong minutes with me, as per usual.'

Jem reluctantly slid her printouts across to Ray. He mouthed a 'ta' and filled the otherwise silent moment with an oddly random tune composed of 'do do doos' as he scanned the first page. Ray often did this, and the general assumption was that he was too afraid of copyright infringement to produce a recognisable, or indeed pleasant, sequence of notes.

'All right, then. Birmingham. You all know by now that we just lost Birmingham. So we don't need to talk about points one to three any more.'

Ray looked up from the sheets spread out in front of his crossed legs.

'Don't think this means you can sit around twiddling your thumbs. If anything, it means we need to work harder. The people upstairs are watching, remember that.'

As Martin wrote down this warning, Jem and Jeremy stole quick glances at Manny, sat silently in the corner, the sunlight glinting off what they took to be his face.

Ray continued to scan the minutes of the last meeting.

'Do do do do doo... the custom layout generator Keith was suggesting...' Ray paused to pull his best pained concentration face. 'I think we're going to stick that on the back burner for now. I'm worried about function creep.'

'Will's fine, he's just over there,' said Martin. Jeremy chuckled and Jem suppressed a giggle. Will looked nonplussed.

'Ooh. You'll cut yourself, Mister Priest,' observed Ray without a smile, before returning to the minutes. 'The dripping ceiling. The ceiling has been looked at, and the CEO has come to the conclusion that the leaks are manageable.'

'So she's not going to do anything,' said Ian, flabbergasted. 'I wouldn't mind if it was just water.'

'That guy who came on... what was yesterday? Tuesday. That guy said it would take months for it to burn through to the next storey, so Barbara says it's just not high priority,' explained Ray.

'False economy, as always,' tutted Ian.

'Said Ian coquettishly,' wrote Martin. The one fun thing about taking the minutes was the embellishment. Martin would always attempt to portray every exchange between Ian and Ray as flirtation. Jeremy would do the same. Little things helped people get through the day at the office, and more so since the people upstairs had taken over.

'What about the blinds?' asked Jem, in the monotone reserved for questions to which people already know the answer.

'Aren't you being blinded enough?' responded Ray, and Jem mimed the words as he spoke. The old blinds had been taken down long enough ago that no-one could remember what colour they had been, but the long-promised new ones had never materialised. Everyone had to simply rotate the equipment and trays on their desks throughout the day to shield either themselves or their screens from the glare of the sun.

'It's like being in the presence of Wilde,' mused Jem.

Martin whistled part of the chorus to 'Kids in America', and grinned at her.

'You tit,' smiled Jem, rolling her eyes.

'Tit. Good one,' said Martin, continuing to minute everything. A sub-table kick was foiled by the central leg support, shaking the contents of several mugs, and Ray decided to re-establish some order.

'All right, let's move on, gentlemen. And lady. I don't know about you, but I don't want to join Keith upstairs any time soon. Does anyone have anything work related to add to what was discussed last week?'

Everyone fell silent and tried to look like they were thinking. Here, the minute-taker had an advantage, as they had a pad to stare at and pretend to be writing in during such moments.

'OK, anything since the last meeting that anyone wants to raise? Have any of you come up with anything new and exciting?'

These silent intervals were excruciating. Of course, there were always new ideas and problems during the week, but they were either talked about immediately or only relevant to the person they occurred to, so nothing interesting was ever raised during a weekly meeting.

'Nope? I suppose we'll have a quick round table then.'

The round tables were when everyone would try desperately to remember anything worth speaking about that they had accomplished during the seemingly fleeting period between meetings. The only people who would pay the slightest attention to what was actually said were Ray and the minute-taker. Ray would forget the vast bulk of it within seconds of leaving the room, while the minute-taker would catch snatches of what was mumbled, scribbling as quickly as possible. They would then go away and type up a Chinese Whispers version of proceedings. The inaccuracies were irrelevant, as nobody ever bothered reading terribly far into the minutes.

Today, however, was different. Today another pair of ears or their equivalent was paying close attention; everyone was very much aware of the silent shimmering presence of Manny in the corner of the room.

Jeremy had always been of the opinion that it was better to get this bit out of the way quickly, as it meant that firstly it wouldn't build up in his mind into some kind of traumatic episode while everyone else was taking their turn, and secondly that the lack of progress on his project could quickly be forgotten as others related their own woes. To this end, Jeremy always sat closest to Ray. And Ray would, almost without fail, go the other way round the table, resulting in Jeremy having to go last.

'Let's hear from Martin first. What have you been up to?'

'I've been finishing the changes for Coventry. I'm assuming the fallout from Birmingham isn't going to affect the Coventry contract?' Martin felt a little ashamed to be using Birmingham as a diversionary tactic like this, but getting a question in quickly probably meant not having to say anything else, and as minute-taker he could make himself appear to have been very productive later, when he did the typing up.

'You know as much as I do about Birmingham, if you've been watching the news. As far as I'm aware, Coventry is still go. I've not heard anything to the contrary, anyway.'

Martin turned his full attention to writing up this response, and Ray moved on. This was just the sort of quick exchange Jeremy Starwars had hoped for.

'Ian?'

'Drawing up the test cases, some documentation… I can't do the layouts until the parser's finished.'

'Said Ian, with a wink,' wrote Martin.

Jeremy felt a little light-headed. His parser was no closer to completion than it had been a fortnight ago, when he had declared it to be 'nearly ready,' and last week he had called it 'almost there,' through a fixed smile.

'Right, well, we'll get round to Jeremy in a moment, and come back to that,' decided Ray. 'Robert?'

'I've been ill,' Robert Smith reminded Ray from beneath a shock of spiky hair.

'Good. Will?'

'I've been optimising the transaction layer. I'm sure Keith would have spotted all these bottlenecks eventually, but I've increased the throughput by a factor of ten. I've also dramatically reduced the number of round trips to the server. I'm just waiting for Jeremy's parser now, so I can integrate the reporting code.'

Jeremy felt his brain begin to throb.

'I'm sure Jeremy will have some good news on that front in a moment,' suggested Ray.

Jeremy raised his head, squeezed out a weak smile, and returned to examining the yellow knuckles of his tightly clasped hands.

'I do think we should put some time aside to discuss naming conventions, though,' said Will, apparently not finished. 'They're a mess.'

'We should, we should,' said Ray unconvincingly. 'Not right now, though.'

He turned to the translator. 'Guy?'

'Ghee,' said Guy Mange.

'Ghee,' Ray corrected himself. 'Ghee?'

'The documentation is nearly finished, and the French version of all the menus and message boxes is complete. I still need to translate all the reports and apply the correct logos, of course, but I cannot do this without the generator.'

Jeremy stared with feverish intensity at the patterns in the pine effect veneer, convinced that his face was by now giving off light as well as heat. The repetition in the fake knots seemed unnecessarily frequent to him, and he tried to concentrate on finding this annoying, although it was very much an insufficient distraction from the conversation that was encircling him ever more tightly.

'I can correct the spelling and grammar in the English versions of all the menus and message boxes while I am waiting, if you would like,' added Guy, pointedly.

'Good. Thank you, Guy.'

'Ghee.'

'Ghee. Who's next? Ah, the lovely Jem.'

Jem rolled her eyes, stinging though they were from Guy's pungent aftershave.

'My loveliness notwithstanding, no serious help desk problems to report.'

'The children are behaving themselves?'

'Thom and Ollii are manning the phones even as we speak.'

Considering Jem's two testers-cum-support-staff to have been cursed from birth with ludicrously affected names, Martin generally noted them as 'Thumb' and 'Olliii' in the minutes whenever they arose. Today, however, he found that he had given Ollii seven 'i's before he stopped himself.

'And the testing?'

'The release candidate is looking OK, some small bugs. But we can't test half of it without the layouts.'

Ray breathed in through clenched teeth and slid himself round on the table to face Jeremy Starwars, who just had time to glance across at Jem wincing apologetically at him.

'So, Jeremy, speak to me.'

'I can see the light at the end of the tunnel,' said Jeremy falteringly.

'When? Later today? Tomorrow? These folk are waiting.'

Jeremy could feel his heart pounding.

'The day after tomorrow?'

Ray groaned.

'What still needs to be done?'

Jeremy felt his head getting hotter. It was way too late to respond with 'working out how to do it.'

'Tidying up, some documentation.'

It wasn't a complete lie. Those things would certainly need doing, once the actual code was working.

'Right, fair enough,' said Ray. 'We'll all meet again on Friday and you can give everyone a demonstration then.'

'Sounds good,' said Jeremy, to whom this sounded far from good. At

16

least it wasn't now, that was the main thing. By Friday he, or preferably everyone else, could easily have gone under a bus and the dread demonstration of nothing would be cancelled.

'Good stuff, Mister Starwars,' said Ray as he eased himself back round to address the whole group, polishing one portion of the table with the seat of his trousers even as his shoes squeakily deposited black marks elsewhere. 'Any other business?'

Martin focused on scribbling in his pad and everyone else stared quietly into the middle distance. Ray made a couple of bubble-popping noises with his mouth and was preparing to wrap things up when Manny addressed the room.

'We will speak now.'

Everyone turned to face their unusual invigilator. Manny reflected his surroundings cleanly, and his edges were so strangely blurred, it was difficult to see where he ended and the room began. They all looked at each other's reflections in him, finding it easiest to try to focus somewhere in the centre of his torso.

'Firstly, we are pleased with your acceptance of the new order in this workplace. Everyone must get on with their lives. Nobody wants another Birmingham.'

All present could see the tasteless responses forming behind each other's eyes, but there was no way the words were going to be given houseroom in the presence of Manny.

'Secondly, Keith has stopped working. We need a replacement. One of you will accompany Manny upstairs. Racist Scum must choose.'

The moment of delight that should have accompanied the realisation that the people upstairs had accepted their pronunciation of Ray's name as fact, as Guy Mange had done before them, was sadly absent, as abject terror gripped the attendees.

'Do do doo. Do I have to chose right now?' asked Ray, climbing down from the table.

'Now. Who can you best continue without in the short term?'

Ray winced and pointed, and all at once Jem hated him.

2

WE'RE ALL IN THIS TOGETHER

Jeremy Starwars sat down at his desk, feeling nauseated. He was sure that his colleagues were all staring at him, thinking *he* should have been the one to go upstairs instead of Martin. He was convinced that Ray was the only one who was fooled in the meetings when he claimed to be on top of his project, and that they all secretly considered him a fraud. And now they were all sat there, thinking about who had truly been the most expendable person in that room.

Jeremy glanced over at Jem, looking small in one of the few decent office armchairs in the building, tufts of jet black pixie cut hair haloed in the bright afternoon sun. Surely she would hate him most of all. Everyone had either heard or actively spread the rumours about her and Martin, and whether or not they were true, she had certainly been upset in the meeting room. And with good reason; nobody knew precisely what the new owners were doing upstairs or the direction in which they planned to steer the company, but everyone was firmly united in having a bad feeling about it, and Keith's disappearance suggested that they were willing to dismiss people at the drop of a hat.

There Jem sat, sniffing, and typing up Martin's minutes. Despite everything, Jeremy found himself feeling jealousy toward her, not just for her superior chair, but for having this mundane activity to carry out. It required little thought and made it very easy to appear busy. Typing the weekly minutes was like stepping into a time machine that made half the afternoon disappear. He always found that appearing to be concentrating gave him more of a headache than actually being productive, at least from what he could remember of being productive. He took this as a sign that there might be something to the visualisation techniques that some sportspersons practised, and he would occasionally go for a jog in his head to keep fit while sat at his desk. Jeremy was not, however, greatly gifted with sporting aptitude or inclination beyond the confines of his own mind. Not like the young testers, or Martin, who, thanks to two overlooked spell-checking alterations during the creation of a company newsletter, had become known for having the best goat-scaring record in the company's interdepartmental football tournament the previous year. That was all before the people upstairs had taken over; football was rarely mentioned in the office these days, nor the many important goats that Martin had scared.

'Martin is leaving with us now,' announced Manny from the far end of the office. 'We will contact you again shortly, Racist Scum.'

Ray Ciscombe waved timidly at the impossibly reflective humanoid shape from the safety of his desk. Regardless of distance, Manny's voice was no different subjectively in volume or timbre than if he had been stood right in front of anyone in the office who heard it, and the effect was deeply unnerving.

Jem craned her neck and stared down the office, but Martin was nowhere to be seen, presumably waiting somewhere around the corner by the door to the stairwell. She watched as Manny moved out of sight and turned back to her monitor.

'I'm sure he'll be fine,' suggested Will, who sat opposite Jem. He was sure of no such thing, as he considered Martin to be technically incompetent, but he was already sick of the sniffing sounds that had been coming out of his coworker, who even now was blowing her nose. Jem forced a weak smile in response and sniffed again. Will clenched his fists and returned the smile as best he could, knowing that he would be sailing close to looking deeply sarcastic. He could do the mouth, but no matter how much he practised in the mirror, he could never quite get the eyes right.

He returned to reading a news website. Will had answered a phone call that had been work-related during his lunch hour, and the call had taken nine and a half minutes. For time sheet purposes, he had no option but to round this up to a quarter of an hour, that being the minimum unit, and he had every intention of reclaiming those minutes. Ray knew that this was the case, as Will had made the situation very clear just before the start of the meeting, to ensure that there would be no confusion. The last thing he needed now, was to complicate matters by taking time out to comfort a work colleague during what was already time off in lieu. He snorted at a political cartoon on the website. It depicted the Prime Minister sat in a nest, on an enormous egg. He knew it was the Prime Minister, as it was clearly labelled as such. The egg had 'ANGLO-FRENCH RELATIONS' written on it. He had no idea what any of it was supposed to mean, and he would normally have found this intensely annoying, but the idea of the Prime Minister having passed an egg that was clearly so much larger than himself had tickled him. And him a man. Ridiculous, and exquisitely painful, he imagined. The next story was about three children who had been killed by a falling tree house. 'That's awful,' he forced himself to think, after some considerable deliberation. He thought it again, mouthing it as he did so, in order to get it properly ingrained. Satisfied, he determined that this would be his position on the matter, were anyone to raise it in conversation, and that his expression would be one of respectful solemnity. That was a look he was convinced he could pull off with aplomb. 'That's awful,' he thought for a third time, just to make sure.

***

Martin walked slowly up the stairs behind Manny, spellbound by the manner of his motion. Manny's limbs didn't seem to pivot, and the transferral of whatever weight he had was imperceptible. He seemed to be altering his physical shape to proffer the appearance of putting one foot in front of the other, while his upper body simply glided diagonally up the flight. All of which was very difficult to make out while, however hard he tried, Martin's eyes kept focusing back on his own worried reflection staring back at him from Manny's utterly smooth surface and blurred edges. Martin was just shy of six foot and in reasonable shape, he thought, for a man in his late twenties, but distorted across this weird mirrored skin he looked thin and childlike.

'So, Keith isn't working out, you say?' he inquired, finding the silence hard to bear.

'Keith isn't working,' corrected Manny.

'He's normally pretty cooperative. Are you sure you're not just being fooled by the tattoos? He's a bit of a conspiracy nut, but he's quite smart, really.'

'We hope you will work for longer,' said Manny flatly, seemingly ignoring Martin's babbling.

As they turned to mount the next flight, Martin sneaked a peek through the windows of the doors onto the fourth floor. He could see many empty desks in the unlit office, but no employees that might sit at them.

'What is it you're actually doing up there?' asked Martin as he caught back up with Manny. He wasn't sure he wanted an answer, but felt certain he should be asking the question.

'We are getting to know people.'

As they headed further up, the large window in the front entrance no longer provided a great deal of natural light in the stairwell.

'Jesus,' exclaimed Martin, having bruised his shin on a discarded vacuum cleaner between flights of stairs. 'Have you lot forgotten to pay the electric? I can't see a bloody thing.'

'Apologies. Please wait there,' said Manny, as he easily negotiated the trailing hose of the cleaner.

'You must eat a lot of carrots,' noted Martin, as he rubbed his leg and watched Manny make his way to a push-button light switch.

'I don't. Come, we must hurry.'

Martin rose and looked around, searching for the newly illuminated cause of this apparent panic.

'The switch is on a timer,' explained Manny.

'Cheapskates,' Martin mumbled to himself, shaking his head.

From then on, they followed the same routine on each landing, with Manny activating the next timed light switch just as the previous one went out, and Martin snatching brief glimpses of the darkness and inactivity beyond the doors on each floor. Martin fell silent for several flights, before the lack of any sign of life prompted him to speak once more.

'Manny?'

'Martin.'

'Where did Birmingham go?'

***

Jeremy Starwars had been aware that there was someone sat behind him waiting for him to look up from his monitor and take his headphones off, for at least two agonising minutes. His temples throbbed as he stared intently at the screen, flipping between two code windows and scrolling up and down a bit. It was becoming increasingly apparent that they weren't going to give up and go away. He hoped it wasn't obvious that his music had long since stopped playing.

Jem lost patience and tapped on Jeremy's headphones, causing him to jump. In gentler times, this would have amused her greatly, but less so now. Jeremy scrambled to remove the oversized headphones and brazened out the miming of clicking 'pause' before turning to face her. He braced himself for what would surely be a colossal attack on his fragile psyche.

'Jeremy, I need your help,' said Jem, taking him completely by surprise.

His mouth managed to use the air he exhaled at this point to form a few words. The ones it chose formed the question, 'what fresh hell is this?'

'I think we should offer to help Martin,' she said.

Jeremy was so relieved that Jem wasn't insisting on seeing his non-existent work that before he knew what was happening, he'd nodded.

'What—What are you thinking?' He spoke the words with a squeaky interrogative inflection, but as Jem responded, he was playing it back in his head repeatedly as shouted rhetoric.

'Whatever the people upstairs are trying to do, they don't seem that fussy about who they get to do it. No offence, Martin.' She looked to the ceiling while she added the apology, and this reminded Jeremy of a bereaved individual looking to the presumed location of a lost loved one.

'Surely several heads would be better than one?' Jem continued. 'Maybe we could get the job done quicker all together, whatever it is, rather than Martin being stuck up there for God knows how long, or getting fired. I think we should go and see Barbara and suggest you and me go upstairs.'

Jeremy snorted only briefly at this choice of words, as this clearly wasn't the time.

'You think we should go over Ray's head?'

Jem, in turn, sniggered at this choice of words, but quickly regained her composure as this definitely wasn't the time.

'We'd have to. Ray would never go for it. Barbara might see the big picture.'

'I'm not sure *I* see the big picture,' countered Jeremy, in a small voice.

'Come on, Jeremy, we're all in this together. We're a family.'

'Of course we are,' he muttered, nodding. 'And you think of me like a brother. That figures.'

'What?'

'Nothing. I'm sure you're right. We're a family. One big, weird, dysfunctional family.'

'All families are weird and dysfunctional. My Gran ran my Auntie Jean over in her own Fiesta and just drove off once, never even apologised. It doesn't mean we don't all look out for each other. And maybe if we get the job done, the people upstairs will bugger off and leave us alone, and we can all just get back to normal. Come on Jeremy, we can do this. We can at least try. You're nearly finished with what you're working on anyway, right?'

Jem fixed Jeremy with a big doe-eyed stare throughout her plea. This was partially wasted on him, as he could only look into people's eyes fleetingly during conversations, but it had a subliminal effect at the very least. Perhaps she was right. More importantly, perhaps it would get him away from the project. Perhaps forever. Maybe they'd all be killed, skinned and eaten, and he wouldn't have to demonstrate nothing on Friday. And if he survived, perhaps there would at least be fewer people to demonstrate nothing to. Actually, he reasoned, it might simply be a valid excuse for not being ready to demonstrate nothing.

Most importantly, he had to avoid answering her question about being nearly finished; she was looking right at him, her round expectant face not two feet away, and she would see straight through him.

'All right, let's go and see Barbara Pappa,' he said at last, and Jem smiled broadly.

'Hooray. That's brilliant, Jeremy. And I don't think of you like a brother.'

'What? No?'

'No. You're more like a weird uncle.'

'Cheers. You're not too old to go over my knee, you know.'

'There it is. Weird, creepy uncle.' She grinned.

'What's she broken, Mister Starwars?' boomed Ray.

Both Jeremy and Jem jumped at this interjection, and immediately set about worrying how long had he been standing behind them. Ray's question was in itself a relatively harmless and traditional piece of passive aggressive rhetoric. He would ask something similar whenever he saw two or more of his team talking instead of working. Ray would then pretend to listen to what he would always assume to be a couple of minutes of technically phrased bullshit before walking away, happy in the knowledge that he had successfully made people squirm, and that those people would most likely wrap up their conversation quickly and get on with some work. This was a key part of his job.

Jem and Jeremy exchanged glances. They could only gamble that he had heard nothing.

'Nothing,' averred Jeremy, 'Jem was just confirming what I'd said in the meeting. For the minutes.'

Of course nothing was broken. Nothing was pretty much what he had written at this point. Whilst Jem furtively scanned Ray's face for signs that he might be aware of any plotting going on, an entirely unrelated mantra was being chanted loudly in the mind of Jeremy Starwars. *Please don't ask to see anything. Please don't ask to see anything. Please don't ask to see anything.*

'Well that shouldn't take more than a few seconds.'

Sarcasm from Ray. Would this be enough for him, or would he now change tack and ask far more probing and dangerous questions? Starwars could feel all moisture leaving his head as the fight-or-flight instinct began to grip the most primal portions of his brain. Ray paused for a moment, stony-faced, then turned and wandered back to his desk smiling in triumph at his skillful put-down. Jeremy was happy to be able to breath a sigh of relief over Ray's departure without Jem thinking it strange, and the screaming in his brain receded, allowing him to once more focus upon the problem at hand. Plotting was quietly resumed.

3

ORDEAL

The company of Ian Gerald Peterson was generally considered to be very much an acquired taste. He was in fact responsible for several people in the office giving up smoking, back when it was still permitted in the rear stairwell. Committed nicotine addicts had decided that it simply wasn't worth the risk of him following them out there and talking about his hobbies. It was possible that he had inadvertently saved lives.

He was extremely capable at his job, and the team found him easy enough to work with when kept on-topic, but given free rein to discuss those things which interested him most, his low, monotone voice was for some akin to the probing of a dentist's drill. Minutes could seem like weeks. People would feel themselves ageing, and begin to panic.

Ray found Ian particularly difficult to cope with, and he had once been seen climbing out of a window and hiding on the fire escape to avoid him. He had strenuously denied this, until Jem had shown him the photos on her camera. Ray had failed to consider that the fire escape was fully visible from the kitchen. The quiet deletion of the photos had earned Jem two days extra leave.

Now Ian was to be Jem's secret weapon. The plan was to set Ian on Ray in order to provide the distraction Jem and Jeremy required to sneak off and talk to Barbara Pappa. Ray would not be happy, were he to see them wasting further time, and would almost certainly object to them seeing Barbara without a complete explanation. Said explanation would doubtless be met with a request to return to their desks. Ray wouldn't countenance any plan that involved the rocking of boats. Of that, Jem at least was certain, and Jeremy had reluctantly been forced to take it as read. As for the idea of him being bypassed altogether, both plotters knew that Ray would find this unacceptable. A former Drill Sergeant in the Territorial Army, he was very much a believer in the chain of command, and without it, his very position in middle management would crumble. Therefore, Ray had to be distracted, and if possible be driven from the room altogether. If anyone could achieve this, it was Ian Gerald Peterson.

A coin was tossed, and then a brief but heated mumbled squabble had ensued, during which Jeremy was called a baby, and a 'best of three' decision was arrived at. Jem had subsequently lost, which left Jeremy Starwars feeling positively euphoric, as it meant that he didn't have to speak to Ian Gerald Peterson in a way that would *definitely* have invoked talk of his hobbies. Jem was to 'light the blue touch Ian', as Jeremy had put it, by means of a perfectly innocent reference to a clause in the employee's handbook. Jeremy and Martin had happened upon this clause some months before, and had chuckled over what might happen were Ian to spot it. They had thought it through and solemnly agreed not to show it to him, as it would probably only have been briefly funny before becoming unpleasant. Circumstances had, however, changed fairly substantially since that pact had been made, and now it seemed to Jeremy that Martin would probably have approved the deployment of the Ian clause. As he watched Jem sidle over to Ian, handbook in hand, Jeremy wondered what proportion of the fireworks he would get to see before Jem dragged him off to meet with Barbara Pappa.

***

Ian Gerald Peterson was positively apoplectic. Ray had time to spot that he was headed in his direction, but not enough time to flee his desk. He was still working his way round the side, cursing its awkward L-shaped executive styling, when Ian reached him. Ray looked ruefully back at his phone, upon which he realised it was now too late to pretend to be having an important conversation.

'I'm just paying a quick visit to the little boys' room, Ian. I'll be back in a moment if you want to wait at my desk.'

Ray cursed himself for not being better at thinking on his feet. He'd only bought himself a few minutes, unless he could come up with something that would demand his immediate attention on his way back from the toilet. Also, he was suddenly aware that he was moving at an entirely inappropriate pace in his bid to pass Ian before he could be challenged. Was he actually running? Was he actually, in front of all his underlings, running to hide in the toilet now? He had to slow it down a little. Keep his cool in front of his team. Keep it managerial. As he made his way down the aisle between the desks in the open-plan office, trying not to waddle like an Olympic sprint walker, he became acutely aware that Ian was still close behind him. Following. Following him to the toilet. Was Ian actually going to start talking at him in the toilet? This was making a bad situation worse, but there was no turning back now. Nobody sprints halfway to the toilet, then changes their mind and walks back to their desk, without assumptions being made as to their having simply not made it in time. When all is said and done, one cannot effectively manage people who think that one has soiled oneself.

Jem and Jeremy watched as Ray walked away at a strangely varying speed with the furious Ian in dogged pursuit, wondering whether it was yet safe to head for Barbara Pappa's office. This apparent opportunity had arisen far more quickly than either of them had anticipated. As first Ray, then Ian, disappeared around the corner into the narrow corridor that lead to the toilets, the plotters looked to one another, their expressions tinged with guilt, all at once aware that they had used a most fearsome sledgehammer to crack a nut.

A little relieved not to have been forced to slow down by meeting anyone in the corridor, Ray reached the bathroom door, still pretending to be unaware that there was someone right behind him. Opening the door without turning was easy enough, but now as he entered the bathroom, Ray reached a tricky juncture; all his social graces demanded that he look back before releasing the door and allowing it to slam shut, in case there was someone directly behind him, which there most unquestionably and dreadfully was. Another reason Ray would ordinarily look back, related to the close proximity of the door to that of the ladies' bathroom, which stood at a right angle to that of the Gents. There had been several toe-curling incidents in the past where he had heard someone walking behind him down the corridor and had held the door open for them automatically, only to turn and see the *female* member of staff behind him head into the Ladies with a look of revulsion on her face at his apparent invitation to join him in the Gents. Did he dare follow through with his feigned ignorance of his this-time-definitely-male pursuer to the brutal extent of actually slamming a door in his face? It turned out that dare he did. Ian was already in the doorway, however, and caught the rapidly closing door against his shoulder. Ray bravely continued his pretence, but he knew the game was almost up. Ian would know that he couldn't fail to have heard the door partially closing, squeaking back open and then slamming again so close behind him. Also, he could actually see Ian in the mirror now. He could see Ian seeing him seeing Ian in the mirror. The gig was up. *Please let there be a stall. Please let there be a stall. Please let there be a stall.* To Ray's delight, he saw that all three stalls were available. He opted for the end one, colloquially known as 'Trap Three.' Ray walked briskly to it and sealed himself in.

In less high-pressure conditions, Ray would have boldly announced his arrival in the toilets with the phrase 'get back to work.' He knew full well that at least one of his staff would be sat in a cubicle passing nothing but time on any given visit, and even if the Gents was filled entirely with sincere and genuine users of the facilities, it never hurt to unnerve them a little. These, however, were not normal circumstances, and here he was, hiding in Trap Three.

He could hear Ian tread slowly over to one of the urinals. Perhaps he really only wanted to relieve himself. Perhaps he would vacate his bladder at the urinal, wash his hands, and go back and wait at Ray's desk as had been suggested. Ray quickly realised that he was essentially standing in a cubicle listening to another man urinate. This wasn't managerial behaviour. He quickly dropped his trousers and sat down on a toilet seat that he wished was colder than it felt. Momentarily Ray heard the onomatopoeia of Ian's zip and listened for the running of a tap. The hiss of the water didn't come, but it was possible that it could have been too quiet for him to hear, so he carried on listening for the roar of the hot air drier. There would be no missing that. He heard no such thing. This came as little surprise to Ray, although he was always appalled when he saw anyone leave without washing their hands, but he was more concerned to listen for the blissful sound of the door opening and closing behind Ian. That noise didn't come either. Ray realised with mounting horror that there was a pair of shoes visible at base of the cubicle door. Ian was standing right outside, waiting for him.

'It's about my contract.'

No. Not waiting. Ian was actually going to talk at Ray through a toilet cubicle door. *What next? Will he try to climb in?* Ray was beginning to panic a little. This 'trap' had suddenly acquired a terrible new connotation. Still, at least he wanted to discuss his contract. That was something managers should be able to handle, if not actually do anything about. At least he wasn't talking about his hobbies.

'Actually it's about how it relates to my home-brew software.'

Shit. Shit Shit Shit Shit Shit.

'Shit. I—I'm having a shit,' said Ray before he could stop himself, in a slightly strangled voice that ascended in pitch. *Not managerial enough. Fix it.* He cleared his throat. 'Grab a coffee and wait for me in the kitchen, Ian.'

Better. Ray heard an annoyed exhalation from outside the cubicle, and then punched the air as he listened to Ian's fading footsteps and the sweet, sweet, squeak-and-slam of the bathroom door.

Ray sat on the toilet wondering how long he should wait before leaving. After ten minutes or so had passed, he started to get up, but then he heard someone else come in, and deemed it prudent to wait until they had gone. Then yet a third person entered the bathroom and began chatting to the second. It sounded like Robert Smith and Thom, one of the testers. After a while Ray became aware that he'd been in the toilet for something approaching the runtime of an American sitcom, and those beyond the cubicle door were in no hurry to leave.

Instinct kicked in.

'What's he broken?'

Probably-Robert-Smith and perhaps-Thom broke off from their conversation.

'Sorry?'

'What's he broken?' repeated Ray. 'It must be something big for you to be in here so long.'

Ray listened to them leave, tutting. One of them muttered 'weirdo' between the squeak and the slam. There was a seed of doubt in the back of Ray's mind as to their identities now, but that was something he could dwell on later. Right now, he had to vacate the bathroom before any more people came in. He'd been in there for a statistically improbable length of time. He pulled up his trousers, tucked himself in and opened the stall door. He decided there was just time for a quick sink visit. The cool water was refreshing and calming on his hands. Then he looked up and emitted a small shriek, as he could see Ian Gerald Peterson in the mirror, stood near the door, holding a mug and staring blankly at him.

'I wondered if you were all right. I've been waiting a while.'

Ray quickly moved to square up to his gangly nemesis, hoping to regain the initiative. As he moved closer, however, he found himself looking up at him. The manager was a good eight or nine inches shorter than his subordinate, and a few years older. In the event that they were to come to blows, Ray was confident that his stocky physique and army training would quickly overpower the shambling stick insect before him, but standing face to face was clearly not the way to conduct verbal combat with this foe.

'I need a coffee. Kitchen,' he asserted and left the bathroom with Ian in tow. After a few steps he realised that he hadn't done a pretend flush. He would just have to hope Ian would think that he was a filthy non-flusher, rather than realising that his manager had been hiding from him in a toilet cubicle for nearly half an hour. Filthy non-flusher was the better option. At least he had seen him wash his hands.

4

DIVERSIONS

While Ray's toilet exile was in progress, Jem and Jeremy had made their way down the dark tongue-and-groove-clad corridor to Barbara Pappa's office. Its woody finish served to distinguish the area from the white-walled drabness of the rest of the floor, and to remind its visitors that they were headed somewhere special. Receptionist Tracy Ireland was sat outside doing some admin for Barbara. Tracy was Barbara's confidante, and P.A. in all but name. Her days of answering the phone were coming quickly to an end, and everyone knew it. Not that her phone downstairs rang terribly often any more, as she had a tendency to hand out direct line numbers at every opportunity. Befriending Tracy was on Jem's to-do list, in the hope of getting into her fast-track slipstream. Today however, she was the last obstacle between them and Barbara Pappa. The gatekeeper.

'Hi Tracy. Is Barbara in?'

Straight to business. Jeremy Starwars admired this. He knew that left to his own devices he would be trapped in stilted small talk for anything up to an hour in this situation. Tracy Ireland held up her left hand momentarily, whilst continuing to type with the right. Then she swapped over hand duties in order to press the 'Control' and 'S' keys and save whatever she had been doing. Finally both hands were brought to rest.

'Hello Jem,' she said, seeming to Jeremy to be ignoring his presence entirely. 'I think she's free, I'll just check, chuck.'

Tracy tittered at her alliteration. Jem just smiled politely, having heard her use it on many previous occasions. As Tracy waited for Barbara Pappa to answer her phone, Jeremy stood and dwelt on the manner in which he had just been slighted. Perhaps it was just because he hadn't said anything. This sort of thing happened a lot; he'd wait too long to enter a conversation and would then be left awkwardly orbiting it.

'Hello,' he hazarded, with a wave.

Tracy returned the gesture with a puzzled look. Her face morphed into a smile as the receiver squeaked into life.

'Hi Barbara. Jemima and …' the blank look returned as she stared up at Jeremy.

'Jeremy,' he offered. More for him to dwell on. They had spoken many times. All those self-certification sick forms he'd handed her; had they meant nothing? The notion that she might have been faking all the sympathy she had appeared to offer him over the years for his many pretend illnesses, sickened him.

'…and *Jeremy* would like to see you, if you have a moment.'

Tracy listened to some further squeaking from the receiver.

'What's it in reference to?'

'The project upstairs,' said Jem, and Tracy passed this on.

After a moment, she thanked Barbara and told Jem that she could go on in. With some quiet bitterness, Jeremy inferred his own inclusion in the invitation.

Barbara Pappa sat smiling in a fashion that was both friendly and professional as Jem and Jeremy filed into her expansive office. Barbara Pappa was also expansive, with a tiny face that had for whatever reason elected not to spread like the rest of her head and body. Jeremy remembered the svelte young P.A. who had joined the company all those years ago, and pondered the many cakes success had brought in its wake.

'What can I do for you today, Jemima?'

Jeremy decided that he must actually be invisible now, and considered stealing some things from Barbara's desk. He thought the Newton's Cradle looked nice.

'Well, as you're no doubt aware, Martin has gone upstairs to help them with whatever it is they're doing.'

Barbara nodded, to the extent that the spare tyres around her neck would allow. She was aware of no such thing, and would be having words with Ray on the matter later, but for now she would bluff it out.

'They've already tried having Keith help them, and apparently that hasn't worked out, so we don't think one person is enough to get the job done and get us back concentrating on the paying jobs. Put simply, we want to suggest throwing some more manpower at the problem. We're offering to go up there and help Martin get whatever it is that needs doing done.'

'We, as in you and...' Barbara trailed off and gestured at Jeremy Starwars, who released the Newton's Cradle ball he was studying in reaction to the sudden attention.

'Jeremy. Jeremy Starwars,' he said, while trying to stop the clacking of the executive toy as quickly as possible.

***

Ray stood waiting for the kettle to boil, saying 'let me just get a coffee' over and over again as Ian attempted to start their meeting. He had also said it in the corridor. And on the way back to his desk to get his mug, during which journey he had failed to notice the absence of Jem and Jeremy from their desks. And on the way back to the kitchen. Ray didn't suppose for one moment that coffee would make this all better, but at least it was delaying things. As the smell from either the gentlemen's or ladies' lavatories drifted into the kitchen, he began to regret his choice of meeting place. Health and safety regulations stipulated that there should always be two doors between a toilet and a place where food was prepared. The Gents and Ladies of course both had doors, and the kitchen had the other one to bring things up to code, but this was almost never closed owing to separate time and motion issues. In addition, in warm weather there would be windows open in both the bathrooms and the directly neighbouring kitchen. Consequently a miasma would gather and settle in the kitchen throughout the day from both directions. Once a stench like the one that was currently assaulting Ray's nostrils had established itself, it was too late to shut door and window. That would simply mean sealing oneself in with the smell. Better to leave things be and hope that the effluvium would eventually dissipate. Finally the kettle boiled, and Ray poured with a sigh. He stirred mournfully and sat down at the table in the smelly kitchen opposite Ian, allowing himself another louder sigh as he descended into the chair.

'Speak to me.'

***

Barbara looked doubtfully at Jeremy, as he carefully withdrew his hands from the Newton's Cradle, having successfully dampened its movement to a gentle unified rocking.

'I'd have to consult with Ray, see how he feels about this.'

Jeremy looked to Jem for a solution to the Ray conundrum. It had seemed obvious to him that they would arrive at this impasse from the beginning. His approval would be necessary whoever they spoke to.

'Ray will say no,' said Jem.

Barbara raised her eyebrows and Jeremy slowly turned his head to stare sceptically at his co-conspirator. This didn't sound like an ideal footing for their side of the argument.

'So why come to me?' asked Barbara.

'Frankly, because you're further up the ladder. You've spoken to *them*. Ray isn't in a position to see the big picture. You're better placed to know whether it's a better use of my time to be helping to finish off whatever the big project is upstairs, or to be typing up minutes, which is what Ray has me doing.'

'I'd hope your job entails more than that.'

'Well, we've hit a bottleneck waiting for the layouts. Until the new report engine's finished, the layouts can't be done and there's nothing new to organise for my testers.'

Jeremy's blood ran cold and Jem realised that she'd taken a bad misstep. Mentioning a bottleneck to a manager was to invite them to rain their management down upon it.

'So who's doing the report engine?' asked Barbara.

'I am,' said Jeremy, uncrossing his legs and leaning forward in an

35

effort to appear attentive and on top of things.

Barbara looked to the ceiling and shook her head. She took a moment to gather her thoughts.

'Here's what we'll do. Jemima, you head upstairs first thing tomorrow morning. I'll let Ray know.' She turned and looked blankly at Jeremy.

'Jeremy,' suggested Jeremy Starwars.

'Jeremy, you need to get that report engine finished, and when you do, you can replace Jemima upstairs. How much time is left on that?'

Jeremy could feel the final vestiges of hope leaving his body through his feet.

'I'm supposed to have something ready to demonstrate on Friday,' he said.

This was the most non-committal sentence he felt he could muster at this point. It included an actual date, which would hopefully avoid follow-up questions, while leaving open the very real prospect of complete failure to meet the deadline mentioned. Even in this darkest moment, he drew some small personal pride from the way he was holding up under pressure, all the while knowing that running screaming from room, floor and building was still an option.

'All right then. I might come and sit in on that demonstration. I'll see how I'm fixed.'

'Great,' said Jeremy Starwars.

***

Ray sat trying to remember his old life; the one he had lived before Ian had started talking. He strained to picture the faces of his family. He attempted to tot up all the bad things he had done, but no matter how he worked the figures, he couldn't see how they amounted to any kind of justification for what was happening to him right at that moment. He had done all he could to truncate the lengthy history of Ian's home brewing software and its associated website. Ian had asked questions like 'you know my *HomeBrew-HomeBrew* software, right?' and Ray had given clear and positive responses each time, but no matter how loudly he shouted 'yes,' and pleaded that he knew all this, Ian had ignored him and painstakingly taken him once again through every stage in its development, including quotes of the various testimonials his customers had provided. Ray's fingers itched for the cigarettes he had long since given up, that he had held for comfort on the previous thirty or so occasions he had heard this information. On reflection, this had all been so much easier to cope with when he had had the nicotine to distract him, and the window to stare out of and pretend that he was alone. Oh, for the stairwell window, with its glorious view of the car park, and the tyre yard beyond. How he missed it now. He looked down at the table separating him from his tormentor, speculating upon what was most likely a low density chipboard beneath that thin veneer. He imagined the kind of impression that might be made, were a forehead to be driven directly into it.

'Please, for the love of all that's holy, get to the point,' he suggested.

Ian concluded his opening statement by explaining that *HomeBrew-HomeBrew* was entirely produced outside the office and then an indeterminate number of additional sentences followed. Ray wasn't sure if he had blacked out, or for how long, but the next thing he was aware of was Ian thrusting the employee's handbook toward him, tapping at a clause that had been angrily circled several times in red ballpoint pen. Ray scanned the paragraph in question, repeatedly shouting 'let me read it' while Ian provided commentary. It related to the company claiming sole ownership of all work produced by the employee while in their employment.

'Listen, Ian, whatever you do that we don't pay you for, that's yours. Don't worry about it,' said Ray. The paragraph he had just read suggested otherwise, but he was pretty sure that the acquisition of *HomeBrew-HomeBrew* would be low on the company's list of priorities. This was bad, though, he thought. Ian was going to be difficult to placate, because he had a perfectly valid concern that would probably end up requiring something in writing to resolve, after an interminable back and forth. Ray passed the handbook back, and in doing so, knocked over his almost-full second mug of coffee of the meeting, shooting half a litre of the hot beverage into the lap of Ian Gerald Peterson. *That looked like an accident, didn't it?* Ray was reasonably confident that it had. Without further delay or consideration for his own safety, he selflessly grabbed the now-empty mug and righted it, to ensure that nothing more could spring from it to further soak his valued team member.

The legs of Ian's chair barked against the kitchen floor as he rose from the table, stunned and stained.

'Are you all right? I don't know how that happened,' said Ray, fixing Ian with his best look of concern. 'You're not scalded, are you?'

Ian stared down at his groin and pulled at the warm sodden material clinging to his thighs.

'Just warm and wet.'

'You need to go and get changed. Get off home early. There's not much of the afternoon left anyway. We can talk more about this later, if we need to.'

Ian nodded. Ray watched Ian waddle bow-legged from the kitchen. Coffee had made it all better, after all.

***

Manny had led Martin into what felt to him like an office built for endeavours of a scientific nature, which had been constructed on the top floor. The main limb of the storey was mostly open plan, like downstairs, but some areas had been divided off. To their right stood an impressive glass-walled server room filled with rack after rack of processor boards and storage units. Next door to that was another glass-walled room housing a large boardroom-style table. Beyond the meeting room a white plastered wall ran the rest of the length of the right hand side of the office-cum-laboratory, with three further doors spaced out far enough along it to allow for what Martin supposed to be three generously proportioned offices. At the far end was what appeared to be some kind of aseptic chamber. Two figures clad in white were visible through the windows of this enclosed area, but they had their backs to Martin. The partition walls had clearly been completed recently, as toolboxes were still present and several long portions of skirting board were leaning in a corner, waiting to be added. The main area had multiple terminals, each with three large screens, with a power and networking block embedded neatly in each desk.

Almost everything had a gleaming white finish. On a trolley to the far left lay Keith, covered by what looked like a sneeze guard from a delicatessen.

'Keith isn't working,' reaffirmed Manny, as Martin stared in disbelief at the lifeless body of his colleague.

Keith's left wrist appeared to have a hole through it, and his right was badly scratched. There were a series of what looked like ink blots on his trousers, above the left knee. His socks and lower trouser legs were caked in blood, and the right side of his skull was caved in. The eye socket was broken, leaving that eye loose and staring askance at Martin, while the other eye was closed and peaceful. Unready for the rest, Martin tried to focus on the ink blots. As alternative as Keith liked to appear, Martin knew that he would nevertheless be annoyed about getting that ink on his best cargo trousers. He'd be beside himself when he saw those stains. Martin's eyes wandered to Keith's shirt; that seemed safe to look at, as long as he stayed low, away from the red area. Blood aside though, the shirt appeared to hold other stains, fringed with odd yellowing watermarks. It also struck Martin that Keith seemed to have piled on an awful lot of weight since last he had seen him. Looking closer, he realised that this wasn't the case, but that in fact the shirt was heavily padded. Was that toilet paper sticking out at the neck? It was soaked in blood, but… Martin became aware that he was back looking directly at the blood, and then that dreadful unblinking eye was glaring back at him once more. That *was* toilet paper.

'What,' Martin began, finding it suddenly difficult to construct whole sentences.

'What,' he began again. 'The *fuck.*'

He was frustratingly close to a fully expressed thought, but he stumbled now.

'Fuh,' he managed next. He turned to stare directly at Manny, who was barely visible in this gleaming environment, but for Martin's own baffled and disgusted reflection.

'What the fuck did you sick bastards do?' Martin exhaled sharply, relieved to have pushed out a question that more or less covered it.

'Keith ended himself,' said Manny. 'With the hammer. We found him in the bathroom.'

Martin took a moment to let this information sink in.

'Why? What? Why?'

'We think he became frustrated when he realised he couldn't get the last nail in. Do you still want to talk about Birmingham?'

Martin stood dumbfounded, one hand to his forehead, as though in fear that it might pop open.

Eventually, he responded, asking with no detectable interest in his voice, 'what's Birmingham?'

5

HOMETIME

Jem and Jeremy came back in plenty of time to witness Ian return to his desk to switch off his computer and collect his bag. Various looks were exchanged. Ian said 'it's coffee' to a few people, with a sheepish grin. Jem felt terribly guilty and hushed her giggling testers.

'Everything all right?' she enquired, eyebrows raised and focusing demonstratively on his upper half.

'Yep. Yep.' Ian looked down at the vast stain radiating from the crotch of his beige trousers and pondered whether he actually had anything clean to change into at home. 'I showed Ray the clause and he threw his coffee at me.'

'Oh dear.'

'It was just an accident, I *think*,' Ian snorted, and he gathered up his rucksack. 'Round two tomorrow. See ya.'

'Cheers then,' said Jem, biting her lip as Ian waddled away. As he disappeared around the corner he could be heard saying 'it's coffee' once more before the door to their floor swung shut with a squeak and a click.

Jeremy sat idly wondering whether he could just come in, pour a jug of coffee on himself and head off home again on a regular basis. He imagined that after the second or third day Ray would probably bring in an embarrassing assortment of second hand clothes for him to change into, but it was certainly something to stick a pin in. He realised the same bit of code had been on his screen for some considerable time, so he scrolled up and down a bit as he took stock of his situation. Things had somehow become worse as the day had progressed. He now had to sit in front of the monitor staring sternly at the space where his code should be until Friday, while worrying about having to then demonstrate nothing to the entire team plus Barbara Pappa. At least, the entire team minus Jem, Martin and Keith. If, by some miracle, he actually managed to knock together something that merely looked like it might work, his worries would still be far from over; the greater task would be to flannel his way through the demonstration in such a way that he appeared to know what he was talking about, while somehow avoiding awkward questions regarding how it might be deployed. And the prize for vaulting these seemingly insurmountable hurdles was now a trip upstairs to an uncertain fate. In this preposterous fantasy scenario of a successfully accomplished demonstration of a seemingly competent piece of usable code, Jeremy vaguely supposed that he might actually want to live afterwards. Still, he thought, perhaps Martin and Jem might be safely back by then, boasting about how quickly they'd cracked the problem upstairs. Maybe everything would just all work out, as sometimes things did. He clicked the 'build' button on his unaltered code so that his computer could look busy, and he went to get some coffee with which to see out the day.

***

'I'm sorry he was so desperate to leave us. I think we gave him too much to think about without giving him the time to let it sink in. We'll try to do better by you, Martin.'

Martin wheeled round, trying to locate the source of the mellifluous female voice that was hugging his head. A woman dressed in a white lab coat emerged from the aseptic chamber at the far end of the floor.

'Sorry. I startled you,' she said as she walked toward Martin. She stopped in front of him, removed a latex glove, and presented a slim, dark hand for shaking. 'You can call me Denver. I'm pleased to meet you.'

Trembling, Martin took and shook the extended hand, and found himself fighting an inexplicable urge to fall to his knees and kiss it. He released his grip with a start, and the impulse was gone as quickly as it had arisen. She smiled. Martin could only stare at her. He estimated her appearance to be North African, guessing at Moroccan for no reason that he would be able to adequately articulate; he wasn't great on matters geographical. Martin estimated her to be younger than himself, but with a bearing that made her seem far more mature. Most importantly, she was beautiful *so beautiful and you can trust me trust me I will never lie to you* – Martin shook his head to clear it and looked away.

'Sorry again. I genuinely forgot,' said Denver, donning some particularly dark glasses that she had been carrying in the pen pocket of her lab coat. 'There. Safe now. That wasn't deliberate, I promise. We want you to be able to think clearly here.'

Martin looked back. She seemed somehow more *normal* now, despite the fact that she was wearing sunglasses indoors, like the worst kind of human being that he could imagine. She smiled again, and he noticed that the blue smudge he had seen on her forehead from a distance was in fact a tattoo, featuring what he recognised to be an ankh symbol, with the number 23 next to it.

'You really can trust me, though.'

Martin remembered why he had been angry and scared.

'Did Keith trust you?'

Denver nodded.

'But I think Augustine had a stronger effect on him.'

'Is that Augustine?' Martin nodded toward the remaining figure standing in the aseptic chamber.

'I am Marlowe.'

This new, deep voice barked from a public address system, and made Martin jump.

'It's rude to eavesdrop,' said Denver.

'Sorry,' came the muffled singsong reply from behind the glass at the other end of the floor. Denver smiled and shook her head.

'That is indeed Marlowe. You'll meet Augustine tomorrow. When you do, try not to get too swept away. He can be terribly earnest, but...'

'He means well?'

Denver considered this.

'No.'

Martin decided to put that to one side for the moment.

'Can you please tell me why Keith was putting nails in himself?'

'I think Augustine might be of more help to you there. I'll sit in while he talks this time, though. You'll be fine.'

Martin looked over at his fallen workmate and thought this unlikely.

'We should show you to your quarters. You can stay where Keith did. You won't mind that, will you?'

'I'm not going home tonight then.'

'No, you're not going home.'

They followed Manny into the other limb of the floor, L-shaped like the rest of the building. Martin was shown into a room he estimated to be above the kitchen on his own floor. Through the window he could see the fire escape, snaking down the wall. He could also see that they were on the top floor, and that the storeys below were unlit, much as they had appeared from the stairwell. He briefly thought that he could see a pale white figure looking up at him from the floor below, but he scanned the whole row of windows and couldn't find it again.

His room, *Keith's* room, was sparsely furnished. It looked like the cheapest possible implementation of a bedroom; if his company were suddenly to become a hotel, this was just the sort of thing Martin would have expected to be on offer. Three tidily constructed flatpack units adorned the room: bed, cabinet and chest of drawers.

'Did you furnish this yourself, Manny?'

'I did,' he said, and Martin thought he detected some pride in his voice. 'It all came in kit form. I had some pieces left over. I still have them, if you would like them.'

'I'm all right, thanks. Maybe later.'

There was a moment's silence, during which it was possible that Manny might have been considering something, but his vague edges defined an inscrutable reflective interior, which betrayed nothing.

'Keith asked to see the pieces. He said they were too small, though.'

Martin thought about the pin-like nails and tiny screws that tended to accompany flatpack furniture, and then about the holes in his departed colleague. A wave of nausea hit him.

'I think I need to go to the bathroom now,' he said.

44

'You're not unwell, I trust?' Denver looked genuinely concerned as she waved him to turn right out of the door.

'No, no, I'll be fine in a minute,' he managed as he headed past her.

The bathroom was just around the corner from his room. Keith's room. Same layout as downstairs, apart from downstairs not having a bedroom, unless there was one in the Ladies. Martin always pictured there being comfy sofas in there, and possibly a coffee table. Perhaps a standard lamp. Bedding seemed a long shot though. Martin closed himself into a stall and retched a few times. Once his lunchtime pasty and crisps were gone and his stomach had made sure it was absolutely empty with a couple of additional dry heaves, he flushed and leaned against the wall with both palms while his breathing returned to normal. Feeling weakened but strangely refreshed he left the stall and rinsed his mouth out a few times. It was only as he turned from the sink that the strong smell of bleach hit him, coming not from the stalls or the urinals, but from the far end of the bathroom, where nothing lay but a hand dryer at one end of an otherwise unadorned, discoloured wall. The plaster seemed damaged in a few areas, and there appeared to be several deep holes, one just above Martin's eye level, and more closer to the skirting board. As Martin was moving in for a closer look, a tall blond man in a lab coat and sunglasses entered the bathroom. On his forehead, the man had a tattoo in blue ink, very similar to that worn by Denver. Next to his ankh, though, he had the number 35.

'Hello, Martin. Are you all right in here?' he enquired.

'Better, thank you.'

'I'm Marlowe. We haven't met properly,' said Marlowe, extending his hand in greeting.

Martin declined the handshake.

'I haven't washed my hands yet,' he explained, thinking on his feet.

'I see you've noticed the holes. Manny hasn't had a chance to fill those in yet. Keith made quite a mess in here. At least it was the bathroom I suppose. Mostly wipeable surfaces. Of course, he couldn't have used his own room.'

'What do you mean?' Martin asked cautiously.

'They're only partition walls. The masonry nails would just tear through them, and they certainly wouldn't have supported his weight.'

'You're telling me Keith crucified himself.'

'Well, sort of, yes. *Ish*. Nailed himself to a wall, anyway. He tried, poor thing. Not really a one man job, though.'

'No. No, it wouldn't be,' Martin stepped back and leaned against a sink for support.

'And Manny was never going to put the last nail in for him, no matter how much he screamed and swore at him.'

'What?'

'Yes. The language was awful, apparently.'

'Manny just stood by and watched him?'

'Yes, it was all he *could* do. Just awful language.'

'And he didn't try to stop him?'

'Oh, I see. No. He'd certainly have helped him down, of course. But Keith decided to go another way with things and took himself out with a couple of strokes of the old hammer. *Pow*. *Pow*.' In an apparent bid to be helpful, Marlowe was miming the hammer blows for Martin using both hands, complete with eye leaving socket on first strike, skull popping on the second. They stood in silence for a moment, Martin stunned, Marlowe patiently awaiting his response.

'I'm finding this all a little difficult to take in,' Martin said at last.

'Augustine will make sense of it all for you tomorrow, I'm sure. Come on, let's get you something to eat. You'll feel better on a full belly.'

'I'll feel better when I know what it is you actually want. What are you doing up here?'

'We're looking for something.'

'All right. When did you last see it?'

Marlowe smiled.

'I don't know if we have, yet. I'm afraid this is an altogether more existential problem.'

Martin sighed, feeling slightly numb.

'What is it, then? Love? Happiness?'

'We might have a chance at both if we find what we're after. We've been promised, you see. And it's here, somewhere. All three of us can feel it. What we've been searching for, what we've been waiting for, it's never been stronger. It's at work in this building.'

46

'That should narrow it down. Hardly anything works here. Or anyone.'

Vaguely mystified by his own sudden candour, Martin watched Marlowe's eyebrows rise.

'Interesting.'

'I'm sorry, what is?'

'I say we're looking for some *thing*, and you talk about any *one*.'

'Sorry, I was just being facetious.'

'Does anyone in the building seem strange to you?'

A small laugh coughed its way out of Martin's mouth before he could stop it.

'I think you've got your work cut out. It's a person, then, that you're after?'

Marlowe paused for a moment, a pained expression on his face. He screwed his eyes shut and lifted his sunglasses a little to pinch the bridge of his nose.

'Martin,' he said with a sigh as his glasses dropped back into place, 'I think we're trying to find God.'

THURSDAY

ALTERNATE

6

HOLE

Great Birmingham: The Year of Unity 452

Having battled their way through trees and nettles following the sound of running water, the three students made their way carefully out onto a muddy slope that fell sharply away to the rocky stream which had led them there. The stream ambled obliviously onward into the mouth of a large cavern, and it was at this that the trio stood gaping, as they caught their breath in the light afternoon drizzle. Talisha Designer pulled the hood back on her anorak and looked up to where the limestone met the sky, squinting as the water ran into her eyes. She tipped her head down once more to stare into the blackness of the enormous hole set into the cliff.

'This is it,' she said. 'Welcome to the Bull's Arse, boys.'

The moment was marred only slightly by her need to repeatedly spit out strands of her long black hair, as the wind flattened it against her wet face.

'Big,' said Graham Bakersdaughter, deliberately leaving some mystery hanging in the air as to whether or not he thought this was a good thing. There seemed little sense in committing to positivity this early on, and leaving no option to moan later. He had sufficient cause for complaint as it was, though, as he stared at the reddened weals that nettle stings had left on the backs of his hands.

'Imagine how the first people must have felt, finding all this stuff.

The rivers, the hills, the caves. Amazing,' said Jim Driversmate.

'And realising that the maps they already had were right. Can't imagine how freaked out they must have been over that,' added Talisha, still gazing into the shadows, and beginning to make out some of the shapes within.

'Some of the maps,' Graham corrected her, as he surveyed the vegetation crowding the base of the trees behind them, in a quest for dock leaves with which to treat his newly acquired skin condition.

'The pair of you really believe all that stuff, don't you?' Jim rolled his eyes and smiled.

'It's no more crazy than what you believe,' said Talisha. 'Anyway, I've seen pages of them. The true maps and the apocrypha both. My father took me to see the archive when I was a little girl.'

'You're still a little girl,' Jim observed. This was enough to make her turn and cock a threatening eyebrow at him, which in turn was sufficient to make him take a cautious step backward.

'I may be small,' she conceded, 'but I'm wiry.'

Graham nodded, chewing at half a dock leaf he had just torn from a plant, hoping that it had been high up enough to be free from urine. 'She could kick your arse, mate, to be fair.'

Jim took a moment of chin stroking to consider this. He was a good foot taller than Talisha, and his dreadlocks added several further inches. Planting her feet more firmly, she narrowed her eyes, presenting him with an upturned palm and beckoning him on.

'OK, OK. Don't hit me. I'm a bleeder,' he said, pouting. 'It *is* all bollocks though, isn't it? I've seen dupes of those pages. The so-called true maps, the ones with the contour lines, they're clearly just drafts for the terrain charts the first people made. And the other stuff is just from some fantasy book, or role-playing game, or just an outright hoax. If those cities existed, all those roads, where are they? It's not like there haven't been digs. They never found anything man-made, not once.'

'All I'm saying,' said Talisha, fully aware that she was going to say other things as well, 'is that the city makes a lot more sense in the world the other maps show. The one the apocrypha describes.'

'Well, of course the city didn't make sense,' said Jim, tapping at his temple. 'That's why so many of them died in the first years.'

'The first years.' Graham shook his head. 'Listen to yourself.'

He spat the dock pulp into his palms and began to rub the backs of his hands, feeling the painful itch begin to recede.

'What?' Jim feigned incredulity. 'I'm just talking about what *is*. The city where we all started out is real, right? We know roughly how old it is, and we know everyone came from there. We know the Dark Ages were about 500 years ago. We know we grew out of war, famine and pestilence, all of that, and most importantly we know we're alone. I don't know why you people can't just accept things for what they are, and move on. There's enough to discover in this world, without making shit up and then wondering why you can't find it.'

Talisha blinked at him in disbelief. 'You talk about what we know. What about what *they* knew? It doesn't pique your curiosity at all that the establishment was able to locate things like cotton and sugar so easily, or oil, for that matter? It's a big world out there. I'm telling you, they knew where to look, because they already had the maps. Not just for this island, for the whole planet. Maps almost as accurate as the ones the satellites gave us.'

Jim shook his head. 'The founders were smart people. Just because we're run by inbred idiots now, doesn't mean they couldn't have done what they did back then all by themselves.'

'So you don't believe there were machines in the city, either, I suppose? Because what's left of the original ruins suggests otherwise. You think the founders invented everything from scratch?'

'It makes more sense than the alternative. If there were these ancient vehicles and computers for them to just turn on or reverse engineer, who built them? The theory answers nothing.'

Talisha sighed.

'I'm not saying it provides all the answers, I just think it points us towards asking the right questions. I mean, have you heard of the Hancock recordings?'

Jim shrugged. 'The three kids? I saw the documentaries when the guy died. I don't know. Maybe we all share dreams, and we just don't know about it. I don't see what that has to do with anything.'

Talisha grabbed at her hair in frustration, but once her fingers were at her scalp, she indulged in a satisfying scratch at some of her itchier insect bites.

'All right, You're not ready for that. I don't want to blow your mind, or anything.'

'Please don't,' Jim deadpanned. 'And rest in peace and everything, but that guy seemed like a proper dick.'

'All right,' she said, scratching once more. 'All right. I'll start smaller. How about the junction? All those weird, twisty, massive, raised roads on the edge of the old city, that snake over each other and don't go anywhere? What were they for, if not to link us to the other places on the old maps?'

He shrugged again. 'Who really knows? I mean, were they even roads? They were probably built to worship the sun, or something. Maybe they make ancient symbols when you view them from above.'

'So you believe in spacemen, then,' said Graham, as he clambered down to investigate the river at the base of the cave entrance.

'No, I'm saying maybe *they* did,' Jim shouted after him. He watched as Graham struggled to maintain his footing. 'Is it slippery?' he asked, skidding as he followed him.

Graham turned to see that the question had already become redundant as Jim slid toward him with gathering speed. Rather than answering, he elected instead to howl and swear for a bit, just as soon as Jim's hiking boots had come to an abrupt rest against his thigh, halting his friend's descent.

'Careful,' advised Talisha.

'Yep. Thanks, Tal,' Graham called up to her through gritted teeth as he gripped his stricken leg. Jim gave her a thumbs-up from his freshly seated position. They waited as she zigzagged her way gingerly down to join them, without incident.

After a brief break for mint cake, Talisha surveyed the dark clouds on the horizon.

'If we want to have a look today, we'd better get a move on. I don't want to be too far in if it pisses down. It could fill up pretty quickly in there.'

The trio strapped on their helmets. All three quickly blinded one another while checking that the built-in lamps were working.

'Good gravy, that's brighter than the sun,' said Graham.

While he waited for his sight to return, he struggled in vain to make his helmet straps comfortable against his shaven head. He was still getting used to having a bare scalp, having recently decided that the look, in combination with a small beard, would serve to deflect attention from his cruelly premature male pattern baldness as it worsened. Unprepared for such exposure, the skin on his head had suffered during the hike: sunburnt, insect-bitten, and scratched by various branches. He settled upon the strategy of tightening the straps as far as possible, in the hope that the helmet would at least not rub too much against his various bumps and abrasions.

'Best if we try not to look directly at each other while we're lit up,' suggested Jim, eyes screwed up and pinching his nose.

'You think?' Talisha smiled and gripped the rock for balance, as she gazed at the purple trail now obscuring her vision.

After they had stood admiring the cathedral-sized entrance chamber for a good few minutes, they squeezed their way through a narrow gap to a smaller and darker antechamber.

'This is the best place to hear it,' she assured Jim and Graham.

She massaged the back of her neck, already sore from scanning her surroundings, as she cast her lamplight around the cave.

'Come on then, Bully. Let's be having you.' Jim's call echoed off the rock walls, and, finding this pleasing, he followed it up with some animal impressions.

'I must be off my bloody rocker,' muttered Graham, while taking this latest opportunity to rub his bruised thigh as conspicuously as might be possible in the near-complete darkness. He dipped his head to better light the afflicted area, keen for Jim to feel as guilty as possible.

'Stop playing with yourself, Gray,' Jim tutted. 'I know it's dark, but there are other people here.'

Graham decided that this was as close to an act of contrition as he was going to get, and offered a brightly back-lit middle finger to Jim, who squinted as though studying the digit in detail, before chuckling in response.

Talisha shushed them, and the trio stood in silence listening to the syncopated rhythms of the dripping water.

'Maybe it hasn't rained enough,' she said at last.

'I can't believe we've walked all this way to hear a cave make sounds like an arse, and it's not even going to bloody do that,' moaned Graham.

'Never mind mate, we're still sharing a tent tonight. You may yet hear those sounds,' Jim consoled him.

Talisha shushed them again. 'I thought I heard something.'

'Was it an annoying shushing sound? I think it might have been you,' said Jim.

Talisha shushed yet a third time.

'There it is again,' whispered Jim, and she punched him on the arm.

'OH COME ON,' said the cave.

The three jerked their heads rapidly in all directions, alternately illuminating small sections of the cave and dazzling each other as they did so. They stood for a moment listening to their own thumping hearts, and each other's breathing.

'FOR FUCK'S SAKE,' said the cave.

'Right, I definitely heard it that time. What the hell's going on?' asked Graham in a panicked whisper.

'Assuming we make it out of here, are we going to tell people about this verbatim? A talking cave is probably enough to get us locked up as it is, without it being a swearing cave,' hissed Jim.

'It's got to be a trick. There's a speaker somewhere. You know, for tourists,' suggested Graham.

'Tourists? We're in a fucking damp hole in the middle of nowhere,' Jim reminded him.

'It's coming straight out of the air,' said a wide-eyed and barely audible Talisha, 'from somewhere else.'

'BUILD,' said the cave.

'What?' breathed Talisha, stretching the word far beyond its traditionally accepted length.

'FUCKING BUILD,' insisted the cave, now louder and squeakier than before.

Talisha stared in wonder at the stalactites as the voice echoed around her.

Rising to a faltering stage whisper, she promised the cave, 'I will.'

***

Thom clambered out of his car, and heard the greeting 'Good morning, Thom-arse,' from somewhere behind him. He turned as he closed the door to see a grinning Ollii walking across the parking lot towards him.

'Good morning Wally,' he responded. 'It's getting harder to find a place in this bloody car park every day.'

'Mental, isn't it? I had to park right up against the security shed again.'

'Frankie won't like that.'

'I'd like to see him stop me,' said Ollii, as he surveyed the full parking lot.

'He'll mess you up, mate. Who do all these cars belong to, anyway?' he asked, as he did most mornings.

'No idea. I swear most of them never move. We should clamp the bastards.' This was Thom's standard counterintuitive suggestion.

He performed a cursory visual inspection of his workmate.

'Your Internet date didn't kill and skin you, then.'

'Not yet, no. Actually, it went really well. She's so funny. Really great personality,' insisted Ollii.

'Right. Is that a clinically great personality or a morbidly great personality?'

'Shut up. She's not fat. She's...' Ollii considered this, '...fit. We're going out again at the weekend. And it's not an Internet date, we just happened to meet on-line, granddad. It's not that bloody unusual.'

'Fair play, man. At least she turned out to be female. Don't think I'd risk that whole business though. You don't know what kind of freak is wanking away behind those avatars.'

They reluctantly began to head for the entrance to the office.

'When the Black Widow eventually finishes you off, I'm having your window desk,' said Thom, after some further thought.

They trudged up the stairs, after quickly waving in at Tracy, who was checking the morning mail in reception. Tracy had a soft spot for Thom and Ollii, which they did their best to foster. Apart from anything else, it was her they phoned whenever either of them threw a sickie. A call upstairs would involve direct conversation with Jem, or in her absence Ray, and that would mean a far stronger performance was required, and the day off would be soured slightly by the certain knowledge that they wouldn't have believed a word of it, and would be impatiently awaiting their return. With Tracy, on the other hand, they would receive sympathy and soothing assurances that things would tick over just fine without them for the day, albeit from someone in no position to make such assurances, and the knowledge that she would pass on notice of their absence in a manner that would make them sound like they were at death's door.

'There was one weird thing last night,' said Ollii, pausing on the landing between flights.

'I know, you went on a date with it.'

'Shut your face, you tit. No, listen, right, I asked Janice what she thought about Birmingham. You know, what her theories were. Nothing. Blank.'

'What, she hadn't heard about it? Maybe she was too busy lurking for victims on-line.'

'Not just *it*. She hadn't heard of *Birmingham*. Is that a bit mental?'

'Wow.'

'I know, right?'

'Sounds like a right ignoramus.'

'She's really well-read, though, honestly.'

'Really well fed, more like.'

'Seriously, leave it. She's not fat.'

'Oh, seriously? OK. Seriously,' said Thom, pulling a deeply grave face. 'Actually, now you mention it, there was nothing about it on telly last night. Everyone seems to have got over it pretty quickly.'

'Funny.'

'Funny peculiar. You'd think they'd put some kind of documentary on, or something. I don't have a clue what happened, if I'm being brutally honest. I mean, obviously I know basically what Birmingham was, but I don't know where it went, or anything.'

'That's your story, and you're sticking to it.'

Thom tapped in the key code and they entered their office.

'She is fit, though,' Ollii asserted once more.

'OK, OK, don't make me throw up,' sighed Thom, and they hung up their coats and took their seats in the small island of desks designated as the Test Department.

'She's late,' he added, nodding toward Jem's empty chair.

***

Martin was trying a new tack this morning. He would build up to the bigger questions like 'what do you want' more slowly this time. Almost everything he'd asked up to this point had resulted in measured, tiresomely enigmatic responses. So far, he'd learnt that the people upstairs had been following the fortunes of the company for some years prior to acquiring it. He'd learnt that the rack system in the server room was principally being used as an Internet proxy and cache. He was informed that it was useful, as it remembered things longer than people did, and he had let this apparent truism pass with a polite nod. He'd also learnt that Manny had moved Keith during the night, and that he was not to worry about that. Now, he pondered how he would work up to asking about that aseptic chamber he hadn't been invited to look at yet.

'Marlowe, there's this weird liquid leaking onto our floor downstairs,' he said, looking around at the gleaming surfaces. 'I don't know if Barbara has mentioned it? It's sort of melted the ceiling tiles. I just wondered if you might have spilt something, or left a tap running that you didn't know about, maybe.'

'Yeah, I know what that is,' said Marlowe, smiling sheepishly, 'and no, darling Babs said nothing to us. You guys should get something plastic under that. We were working a couple of floors down. What a mess. I don't know what we were thinking, really.'

'Working on what?'

He hesitated for a moment before beckoning Martin conspiratorially towards him.

'We were trying to remember how we made Manny,' he said in a more hushed tone, glancing across the room at the blurry original. 'It's the damnedest thing, and I'm embarrassed to even tell you this, but none of us have the first inkling how we did it.'

'You're telling me those buckets have been full of Manny Mark

Two?'

'Sounds like it. Don't worry, it isn't sentient.' Marlowe paused. 'I do hope it's not sentient. It's all over the walls down on nine. That's no life. That's no life at all.'

He shook his head mournfully before snapping out of his reverie to draw himself to full tiptoe height and stare, meerkat-like, at the main door for the floor. Martin followed his eye line, but couldn't see what had drawn his attention. Then the door buzzer went, and following that, through the small reinforced glass pane he saw pixie cut black hair and a familiar round face rise into view.

'See what she wants, Manny,' said an intrigued Marlowe, his voice back at its regular, more confident volume, and Manny performed his eerie approximation of walking to reach the door; faster than Martin had seen him move before, but still smooth and unhurried. Martin wondered just how quick Manny might actually be, and hoped that he wouldn't need to find out. Manny operated the keypad and opened the door to reveal Jem easing down from tiptoes. As she spotted Martin she smiled nervously and offered a small wave. He returned the favour and stared at her with a mixture of surprise and delight.

'What do you want, Jemima Pepper?' asked Manny brusquely.

'I've been sent up to help Martin,' replied Jem, before correcting herself, 'to assist you in your work.'

'Racist Scum didn't inform us.'

'No, Barbara Pappa sent me. Because two heads are better than one, you know? Can I come in please?' asked Jem. A part of her still wanted to be told to go away, but she was reassured somewhat by the presence in the room of Martin, apparently still alive and well.

'Oh, you can most *definitely* come in, Jemima,' said Marlowe, walking over and enthusiastically beckoning her into the room. 'The more the merrier. Manny, you'll need to make up the second guest room.'

Manny headed dutifully off down the corridor.

'Guest room? Is this where you've been all night?' Jem asked Martin, who nodded from across the room. 'I tried to text.'

'It's a pleasure to meet you. You can call me Marlowe.' He removed a glove and offered a hand for Jem to shake. She saw Martin shaking his head vigorously in the background the instant before their palms met. The next thing she knew, she was on her knees looking up in loving admiration at this sculptured colossus of a man who seemed simultaneously to be a teen pin-up and a wise father figure and *trust me trust me trust me*. She pulled her hand away, or was released. She drew breath with a gasp and struggled back to her feet, registering that this man was now casually putting her mobile phone into his pocket, but feeling unable to protest. Marlowe turned to Martin with a mischievous smile that chilled him. He'd wanted to punch Marlowe, but now he felt frozen to the spot, as if every bone in his body had just been given a stern piece of advice to which he wasn't party. *I wouldn't.*

'Ah, that never gets old,' he said, and chuckled as one might at a private joke. 'Tell me, Jemima, how are things going downstairs?'

'Please call me Jem. It's fine. I mean, things are ticking over, I suppose.'

'I'm not actually interested in the work, you understand. We're proud of what you all do here, of course, in the way a parent might stick their children's drawings to the fridge, but we didn't buy the place for that. It's people that matter to us. The people. How is everyone? Tikai babu?'

'Erm. I guess everyone's, sort of, you know, normal.' Jem considered the response she'd just given and realised for the first time just how abnormal everyone's normality seemed.

Marlowe smiled.

'Good, good. That's what I like to hear. Everyone taking things in their stride. Excellent.' He gestured to Martin. 'Why don't you take Jem into the kitchen and the pair of you grab a coffee. Augustine will be up in a little while.'

***

Jeremy Starwars sat down at his desk bang on twenty minutes late, as usual. You could set your clock by him, and this was something in which he took some measure of pride. He now had one day in which to produce the work that he had been pretending to do for the last two months. He recognised that it was probably a little late now to ask for advice. He mused that he might have a little more than a day, that perhaps the meeting wouldn't be until late afternoon on the Friday. That would give him almost a day for each month's worth of work, and if he took a laptop home, like he'd thought about maybe doing yesterday, who knows what he could accomplish? That would mean asking Ray though. Ray might want to know why he needed to do overtime on this ready-to-be-demonstrated project. Jeremy considered sneaking a laptop out and doing overtime without claiming for it, before dismissing the idea as ludicrous. Perhaps he could just disappear. People disappeared all the time. He could start a new life somewhere else.

Jeremy began to wonder whether his passport was still valid. He looked across the room at Guy Mange, who would probably have had his passport about his person at all times, and thought about stealing that. He sized up their physical differences. He and Guy were of a similar height, and both in their early 30s. Jeremy was perhaps slighter of build, though he wondered how much padding there was in the Frenchman's suits. It was clear, however, even to a man as straight as Jeremy presumed himself to be, that Guy Mange was handsome. This was something that Jeremy had decided while still at school that he himself was not, and few in the intervening years had attempted to convince him otherwise. Guy had dark and luxuriant salon-styled hair, whereas Jeremy's own was mousy, thinning, and had grown out to collar length through inattention, rather than by design. Still, although he might not have looked that much like Guy, armed with enough of his cologne, Jeremy fancied that he might have been able to blind the customs officials sufficiently to simply wave him through.

Jeremy had thus far given Guy Mange lifts back to his temporary accommodation on two occasions during his visit. Each had been a claustrophobic encounter, featuring the near-constant deflection of enquiries on Guy's part with regard to how close to completion Jeremy's project was, and each had required Jeremy to drive with blurred vision, as the tears streamed from his burning eyes in reaction to the intensity of the toilet water with which Guy elected to constantly slather himself.

Jeremy studied the poise of Guy Mange, straight-backed and tapping away busily, and tried to replicate it by sitting up a bit.

'Mister Starwars,' said Ray, slapping his palms onto Jeremy's shoulders, having successfully crept up on him. Jeremy leapt in his seat, to the delight of a chuckling Ray. 'I've booked the big meeting room at ten thirty tomorrow for your demonstration. OK?'

'Yep,' said Jeremy Starwars, now realising that his computer monitor still bore witness solely to his desktop background picture of the cartoon character *Hong Kong Phooey,* an hour into the working day.

'Any chance of a sneak preview?' asked Ray.

'No spoilers,' said Jeremy, itching to open the development environment on his PC but keen not to do anything to draw attention to the pyjama-wearing canine martial artist who was currently adorning his screen to the exclusion of any actual work. Ray laughed and walked away. Sometimes a little joke seemed to be sufficient to satisfy him that everything was going according to plan. Starwars had adopted the light-hearted approach with Ray on numerous occasions, with a fair degree of success, when wanting to appear on top of things. Lately he had been adopting this strategy more frequently, whenever the anxiety of not progressing with the project had become too much, and he had wanted to take afternoons off with no notice. He watched Ray return to his desk and idly thought about asking for that afternoon off, given that there was about as much chance of him doing two month's work before lunchtime as there was of getting it done in the one day he apparently now had. Perhaps, he thought, he had better see how he got on for a bit first. He opened the development environment, hit the 'build' button to make the computer look busy once more, and went off to get a coffee.

Jeremy could tell that the kettle had recently been boiled, but the kitchen was empty, so it was a simple matter to dispose of the inconveniently almost ready water. He refilled the kettle to capacity. This was, he convinced himself, a service to those who would come after him. It would also take a nice long time to boil. Jeremy gazed out of the window, across to the tyre yard, and tried to work out whether any of the tyres had moved since his last inspection. None had, but it was still early. As the kettle clicked off behind him, it occurred to Jeremy that before going very much further with the process of making coffee, he should perhaps pay a visit to the toilet. It was, after all, just around the corner, so this would make perfect sense, were it to be proposed to an expert in the field of time and motion studies. He left his mug next to the kettle and headed onward, knowing that it would be safe from theft, as the interior was so densely stained with tannin from a recent and prolonged phase of tea drinking, as to suggest that a small and particularly accurate dirty protest had taken place within.

Jeremy passed a quiet quarter of an hour sitting in Trap Two. He did not, as it transpired, need to go, having opened his bowels as part of his morning routine before leaving the house. To Jeremy's mind, however, the clinical efficiency he displayed outside office hours was not something he ought to be punished for. Others would save their defecation for the working day, he reasoned, and it was only fair that he should be entitled to a similar amount of toilet break time. He further reasoned that others would, in all probability, take pretend toilet breaks in addition to their genuine ones, and he tried to ensure that he made sufficient visits to cover himself for these as well.

It was calm in the cubicle, away from all the code that taunted him with its inappropriateness and unanticipated complexity, but Jeremy Starwars knew that his strong work ethic wouldn't allow him to stay in there forever. Careful to flush the entirely empty bowl before vacating his pod of serenity, he made his way to the sink. Jeremy had become fastidious in his hand-cleansing, not through any deep-seated regard for hygiene, at least not directly, but because he had long since realised that, much like his many faked bowel movements, it ate up time for which he was being paid. This was time he could spend just standing there, in public, doing very little and knowing that nobody could say a thing about it. There he stood, patently and inarguably doing something that he was supposed to be doing. It was probably the only time during his working day when he could truly feel at ease. The only thing that could have made it better would have been a comfortable chair in front of the hot air drier. It also enabled him to shake his head solemnly and feel superior to those he watched walking straight from urinal to door as he stood repeatedly activating the drier. The dirty men of Europe, he called them. He was aware, from the many scientific journals he read on-line while searching for new diseases to realise he must have, that he was holding his hands in more or less the perfect conditions for bacterial growth, and so never dried his hands more than three times per visit.

Jeremy sniffed his hands as he withdrew them from the germ hothousing machine. This was the final, bittersweet moment of his ritual. He had grown to enjoy the smell left by the scented liquid soaps Tracy had been ordering in recent months, particularly the nice coconut one, but the odour was always tinged with melancholy, for he knew it indicated that his special time was drawing to a close. Now would come the twenty-odd paces to the kitchen. At any point between the toilet door and the kettle, he might be intercepted, and asked to do something, or worse still, asked for something he had already been asked to do.

In the event, he made it back to his mug unchallenged, emptied and refilled the kettle, and was back at his desk in what seemed like no time at all.

***

With no furniture in the kitchen, Jem lifted herself onto what seemed from a cursory inspection to be a clean area of the work surface, and sat swinging her legs as Martin searched through the drawers for spoons.

'You look knackered, sweet,' she pointed out cheerily.

'I think I slept for about ten minutes,' said Martin, forcing a yawn and putting a hand through the tuftier areas of his ginger-brown crew cut, and in the process making it look more like he had just got up. 'Does it show?'

'Well, you know those bits in American shows, where someone goes, "you look so tired," and they totally don't? I mean, they look exactly the same, like basically amazing?'

'Yeah,' he said slowly, 'of course I do. I was the one who pointed that out to you.'

'Bollocks, did you. Shut your face. Anyway, this isn't like that at all. You totally look like hammered shit.'

He fixed her with a bloodshot stare.

'Thanks, babe. Don't know what I'd do without you. Actually, how did Big Pappa come to be sending you up here, anyway?' he asked as he put the kettle on and spooned instant coffee into a couple of mugs.

'My idea,' she answered proudly. 'I thought maybe we could get whatever needs doing up here done quicker together. Jeremy was supposed to come up too, but Barbara made him stay to finish his project first.'

'We won't be seeing him in a hurry then,' smiled Martin.

'No, probably not,' grinned Jem. 'So, are you pleased to see me?'

She slid back down from the work surface and held out her palms in a 'ta-dah' gesture.

'Very much so,' said Martin, and went in for a hug. 'That's definitely not a gun in my pocket.'

'Don't harass me in the workplace, Priest. I'll have you in front of a tribunal.'

'Kinky. You'll have to catch me first.'

'Being smutty is not big, and it's not clever.'

'Like you, then.'

Jem feigned a wounded look while she considered her response. 'Like… your tiny willy.'

'Do you? Thanks. I grew it myself.'

'Smartarse. I hope for your sake it's a work in progress.'

They nuzzled foreheads and made faces at one another until Martin settled on a mildly puzzled expression and pulled his head back to properly regard her.

'So what are you going to do up here? Our skill sets don't overlap much.'

'I don't know. What are *you* doing?'

'I don't know.'

'Well, then. They didn't ask for anyone in particular in the meeting, did they?'

'That's true.'

'And they did seem genuinely glad to have me, didn't they?'

'Yes. Fair enough. And who wouldn't be. I'm glad to have you, too. Always.' After a moment, his leery smile dropped, and he murmured, 'I wish I did have a gun in my pocket, though.'

'Beg pardon?'

66

'Keith's dead,' he said in a whisper that he managed to combine with a sigh. He'd gone through a hundred acceptable ways of saying those two words in his head beforehand, and recognised immediately that he had hit upon none of them.

'What?' gasped Jem, pulling out of the embrace.

'He killed himself, they're saying. They won't tell me why.'

'Jesus. Oh my God.'

Martin told Jem about seeing the body, and how entirely unlike the result of a suicide it had appeared, and then gave her a few moments to process this. She leaned on the counter, staring at the boiling kettle. She waited for its click like it was the terminating signal for a minute's silence, thinking about the contents of her fridge, visualising *Tetris* pieces falling into place, anything but the information she'd just been given. That was too big. It was going to have to be dealt with later.

'What? Who are they?' she asked as the kettle's red light went out.

'Christ knows. I think there are three of them. Chuckles out there, a woman called Denver, and this Augustine guy who's coming to talk to me, well us, I suppose, in a bit. I think he's supposed to explain everything. I still don't know why I'm even up here yet, after all the bloody rush yesterday.'

'Arseholes.' Jem decided to focus on the inconvenience for the moment, and perhaps work her way up to the whole possible murder thing as and when she felt ready.

'Oh, and then there's Manny, of course. They say they made him. If that's true, they're the smartest idiots I ever met. Apparently, they don't remember how they did it. They mainly seem to use him like a walking P.A. system. He seems friendly enough, but don't trust him. There's something about that mirrored bastard. He's got his own agenda.'

'Don't trust the shiny, blurry, man-shaped thing. Got it.'

Jem forced a little smile and bit her lip. Martin shook his head.

'Do you ever think that we should be finding all this a lot more strange?'

'We're great copers, Martin,' suggested Jem. 'It's what we do. We cope.'

'Is that what it is? They made us use coping saws in woodwork when I was at school. The blades always snapped on me. Then I'd pick up the bits and they'd be stupidly hot. It was an absolute minefield.'

'Now you mention it, there was a weird question going through my mind as I was struggling up all those bloody stairs just now,' said Jem, ignoring Martin's retreat into nostalgia.

'Why *are* there so many bloody stairs? It's out of all proportion with how many people there are.'

'Yes! Exactly. Why is our building so stupidly tall? I just kept thinking it as I went past all those empty floors.'

'I'll give you another.'

'Goody.'

'You know how full our car park always is?'

'Yes. It's a pain in the arse. Who are all these bastards who park in our car park every bloody day?'

'I stayed here last night. Most of those cars never moved. I think they're just parked here permanently. What's that all about?'

Before Jem could respond, Marlowe poked his head into the kitchen.

'Augustine is on his way, kids. See you in the meeting room.'

7

AUGUSTINE

Great Birmingham: The Year of Unity 473

'Are you excited?'

Talisha Designer broke off from staring through the open hatch to pull a nervous face at a beaming Sevita Minister.

'I guess. I just can't believe we're finally going to turn it on.'

The other three walls that surrounded them were smooth, featureless plaster on breezeblock and concrete, but the wall containing the hatch through which their attention was focused was rough, weathered limestone. Beyond the hatch, and the metres-thick rock into which it was embedded, a suspended walkway lead to an opening in the shell of a large metal sphere, which at first glance appeared to hang in midair. This giant grey ball, similar in scale to a small family home and wrapped almost entirely in thick glistening coils of cabling, was positioned in the horizontal and vertical centre of the vast cave that had once spoken so insistently to Talisha. It sat atop a thin column rising from the bed of the stream far below, and was also supported and stabilised by numerous metal rods protruding from the surrounding cave walls, all combining to make the globe seem as though it were attempting to lift itself free from a huge yet delicate web.

'What is it, fifteen years since you did the first sketches?'

'I suppose it must be, near enough.'

'From napkins in a canteen to this. I'm so proud of you, babbee.'

Sevita pulled her in for one of her hugs. She was fuller of figure and a good bit taller than the slender Talisha, who pulled the same 'don't snap me' face she always did.

'Napkins. Please, you sound like the journalists,' Talisha said with a snort, as Sevita loosened her hold. 'I was doing a doctorate, and I used computers, like everyone else. Anyway, you're the one that'll be getting in the thing, Birmingham's poster girl.'

'Stop. That stuff is so embarrassing. I can't wait to get in there, and away from the interviews. It's ridiculous. I've not done anything. I must come across like some insipid bimbo.'

'Oh, you could talk to them about toilet cleaner. They'd still want pictures of you.'

'Thanks. That doesn't make me feel vapid at all.'

'You know what I mean, gorgeous.'

'Oh, shut up. They always ask about *us*. It's really awkward, Tal. I wish you'd come out of the lab and do one of those press things with me some time.'

'You're not making them sound too inviting. Kush is there normally, though, isn't he?'

'When he is, the subject just comes up quicker. They never see him with the same girl twice, so there's no story for them to latch onto there.'

'All right. If it'll make you happy, when you make your triumphant return, I'll greet the reporters with you.'

'Humph.' Sevita nudged her, and smiled. 'They'll have plenty else to talk about then. And if the whole thing's a failure, you still get a win out of it.'

'Oh, I think if it turns out I've wasted everyone's time and money, they'll *really* want to talk to me. What do you think, Gray?'

She turned to look at the visiting Graham Bakersdaughter, who had been waiting patiently behind them.

'It's great that you've found someone,' he mumbled.

'What?' Talisha squinted at him. 'I mean, what do you think about the project?'

Graham's face flushed visibly through the gaps in his bandages. Talisha hoped that she was successfully concealing her alarm at his

70

appearance; people generally healed quickly and completely, but Graham was one of those rare and unlucky cases whose bodies violently rejected nanobot treatment.

'Oh. Yes. Incredible,' he blustered. 'I can't believe it's the same place.'

'I know,' Talisha grinned, 'the weird thing is, it's always felt the same to me, right from the start with you and Jim. Like the cave was just waiting for this stuff the whole time.'

She looked him up and down demonstratively. 'Anyway, you must be exhausted. Let's head for the canteen. You're fine with liquids, right? They have some quite good soups.'

'That sounds lovely, yes,' said Graham, looking down at his remaining hand. 'I'm still a little slower with the left, but I can do spoons.'

***

Talisha scrunched her toes inside her shoes. Despite having never fainted in her life, she was suddenly nervous that she might do so now, and miss everything. She had been so calm, almost blasé, about everything for so long, but in the days since Graham's visit, this moment had built up in her mind to a staggering significance. Seeing him again, or what could be seen of him, seemed to have thrown all the work of the intervening years, all that gradual progress, into sharp relief. She took a deep breath, and it felt like an eternity before she spoke again.

'OK, Harry. Pull out the probes.'

'Check, boss. Probes withdrawn. We have a complete seal now,' Harrington Barber assured her from beneath a thick mop of blond hair.

'Confirm power to coils.'

'Power to coils… confirmed.'

Harrington was having to project his voice to be heard above the now loud hum of the enormous and quite obviously powered electromagnetic coils mounted one storey above them. As he turned his head in her direction, Talisha caught sight of the engineer's spotty chin, and marvelled afresh at how he managed to even see the equipment through a fringe that almost covered his nose.

Several meters beyond the hatch, in the cave beyond the thick limestone wall in front of them, the team knew that the coils wrapped around the exterior wall of the probe would be resonating in sympathy, charging it up for the pulses that would knock at the door of the other world Talisha had long known to be waiting.

'Deep Zero return set for one-zero seconds,' she asserted.

'Ten second cut-off confirmed,' confirmed Sandeep Programmersdaughter. Eye contact accompanied this confirmation, a pair of spectacles the only visual barrier to his angular face. Sandeep had short, sensible hair of which Talisha quietly approved.

'Deep Zero is a-go.'

'Deep Zero is a-go,' echoed Harrington.

Sandeep observed that the light was working on the big red button, and that this was 'a good start'. Talisha's hand hovered over the big red button. The whole thing could have been triggered by a word or gesture. Thought-based activation had technically been a further option, although problems were still being ironed out with false positives from people thinking about what they were going to have to think. Early on, though, the team had insisted on a big red button. It was mounted all by itself on a narrow plinth that had annoyed Talisha on a daily basis as she continually walked around, or, just as often, straight into it. She was glad of it now though, as she was trembling with excitement, and wasn't entirely sure that she had complete control of either mouth or fingers. She slapped her palm onto the button.

There was little to indicate that anything had happened, other than the sound of the deep-voiced Commander Kush Accountantson shouting 'boom' from somewhere behind her. The hum from the coils was the only operating noise, and that remained constant. Talisha cursed the decision to set the journey time for the probe at ten seconds. It now seemed a stupidly long time.

***

The team waited in hushed reverence, like audiophiles in closed-eyed anticipation of the run-out groove on a treasured piece of vinyl, until the coils had completely powered down, the already low frequency of their throb dropping further as the volume faded. Soon, the only sound louder than their own breathing was from the low rumble of the running water far beneath the floor on which they were standing, at the base of the cave system into which their facility had been built.

Talisha examined the readings on the display panels before her, taking a moment for her heart rate to slow.

'This… this all looks OK at my end. Harry?' She hoped that she hadn't sounded too surprised, with both prospective pilots in the room.

'Everything looks like it checks out. It seems to be back in one piece,' said Harrington. He blew through pursed lips. 'Fuck me, I think we've done it.'

'That's the sound bite for the media, right there.' Kush stretched and cracked his knuckles behind his lantern-jawed head.

'3:15. All external telemetry looks normal,' said Talisha, addressing the operational recorder. 'I'm preparing to unseal the chamber.'

'Good,' said Kush, 'I'm glad we're having a shufti inside. Because, you know, if the whole thing's burnt to a crisp in there, I might not be up for taking the next trip.'

'Well, it is a couple of degrees warmer.' Talisha frowned. 'The oxygen level looks near-identical to the departure reading though, and no elevation above background radiation. I'm pretty sure nothing's been fried. Gravimeters are fine, so no gaping black hole on the other side of the hatch either.'

'Oh, gaping black hole was an option too, was it? Fine. I don't remember any mention of that on the papers I signed.'

'Calm down, Tinkerbell. There's not much that could happen to you in there that the nanobots couldn't fix,' Sevita reassured her assigned co-pilot.

'Yeah, well. I can't help thinking that whatever the bots might need to fix, might just sting a bit in the first place, you know what I mean?'

'Settle, petal,' suggested Sevita.

Ignoring this suggestion, Kush continued. 'Anyway, don't you ever read up on bot reconstructions? Big ones, I mean, like decapitations. When is it not the same person anymore?'

'If you don't keep banging on, we won't have to find out, will we?'

Talisha was struggling to know what to do with her face, as the hatch began to slowly swing open. She slapped her palms to her cheeks. 'Bull's ring. Bull's ring and balls, I'm shaking, but I can't stop grinning.'

Breaking off from glaring at Kush, Sevita offered her a calming rub of the shoulder. 'It's all working. We're just going to pop in there, check the clocks, and the chamber will be exactly how much older you said it would be.'

Talisha exhaled slowly.

'Right. Let's have a look.'

Sevita and Kush exchanged glances and watched as she walked forwards and stepped through the hatch.

'Looks like we might be going on a bit of a trip soon, Veet.'

Sevita nodded. 'I suppose we'll find out how long when she checks the clocks.'

'What if her calculations are wrong? What if we need to be gone years?'

'Probe seems fine,' Talisha was hollering from the airlock, 'the door's not even warm. I'm going in.'

'We'll have to pack a few more toilet rolls,' Sevita suggested to Kush with a shrug.

'You're a riot.'

'Um,' called Talisha.

The team peered through the hatchway to see her stood silhouetted against the opening in the probe.

'Tal? What's wrong?'

Talisha disappeared into the probe, calling after her, 'we cleared the chamber, right? There was a security sweep.'

'They swept through the whole place, then swept right out,' shouted Kush. 'We're in a complete lockdown. Nobody here but us chickens.'

'Erm. Why?' asked Sevita, as she headed down the walkway towards the probe to see Talisha emerge once more, wide-eyed.

'Because there's some…' She swallowed. 'There's someone lying in there.'

***

'Ian, I thought we settled this yesterday,' said Ray, head in hands. He had been cornered at his desk for some minutes now.

Ian sat before Ray, resplendent in his only clean spare trousers, half of a burgundy crushed velvet suit he had once purchased from a second-hand shop. They seemed to have become considerably tighter than when he had bought them, so he had been unable to do them up that morning. Rather than go back to the beige pair with the heavily stained crotch, he had decided to just hold the red ones up with a belt and hope that the gaping fly would go unnoticed. Nobody had said anything yet, so he thought he had probably gotten away with it.

'Well, I've been developing *HomeBrew-HomeBrew* for five years now. It all started when...'

'NO!' screamed Ray before he could stop himself. Realising that everyone else in the office had now redirected their attention from Ian Gerald Peterson's trousers to him, he lowered his voice and continued. 'I'm fully aware of the history of *HomeBrew-HomeBrew*. God help me, I think I know it better than I know my children. If you shut...'

'I just think it's important that you understand the chronology, and how...'

'Let me finish.'

'...how it's been conceived and developed entirely...'

'Let me finish.'

'...outside working hours. The code involved...'

'Let. Me. Finish.' growled Ray. Ian saw that he had picked up his coffee mug and tailed off. Ray gradually lowered the mug and continued, speaking now entirely through clenched teeth. 'If you promise to never speak to me about your software or your website again, I will go to Barbara Pappa right now and get her to sign a waiver covering both those things. How does that sound?'

'Erm. Great,' said Ian.

'Fantastic,' said Ray, exhaling. He waited for a moment. 'Well?'

'Hmm?'

'Promise,' hissed Ray.

***

Jem and Martin sat at the large, cheap, pine effect MDF table with Denver and Marlowe. They had all been sat there saying nothing for several minutes. Jem broke the silence with a throat-clearing cough. Denver's benign smile began to incorporate just a hint of concern, and perhaps embarrassment.

'He's definitely coming, is he?' she asked at last, without turning her head from her guests.

'Patience, dear,' suggested Marlowe, 'you know how he is.'

'I'm not so very sure that I do any more.'

Marlowe drummed the desk with his fingers.

'Lazy bastard, is what he is.'

'Well, we all like a sleep,' sighed Denver.

Marlowe sniggered. Jem and Martin exchanged looks of bemusement.

'Are there really no normal chairs we could be sitting in?' asked Martin. He and Jem were half-sat, half-kneeling in posture-improving backless seating, at a markedly lower eye level than that of Marlowe or Denver. They were barely peeping over the table.

'There are a couple of stools in the lab, but they're much too high for this table. You'd look silly. Honestly, you'll be fine,' Denver assured her, 'those kneeling chairs are good for the back. They're ergonomic.'

'Maybe we should get a refill. Is anyone else low on coffee?' suggested Martin, slapping his hands onto his thighs.

As Denver opened her mouth to respond, Marlowe raised his index finger sharply.

'He's here,' he pronounced.

Jem and Martin felt obliged to pay attention as silently as possible, staring up at the tiles to which he appeared to be pointing. Within seconds they could all hear the beeping of the entry code being typed into the keypad on the office door. Having now ruled out the ceiling as an area of interest, Martin leaned back further than he had initially intended, thanks to his unusual chair. Quickly overcoming the initial swell of panic his unanticipated horizontality had caused, he craned his neck to see the figure rounding the server room corner. A fat, bald, bearded man in sunglasses was sauntering toward the meeting room. He was wearing what appeared to be a fluffy white bathrobe over some frayed blue jeans, and as he stopped, framed in the doorway, it became clear that the ensemble was completed by a pair of fluorescent green moulded plastic sandals. Becoming suddenly aware of the proximity of the lurid footwear to his head, Martin quickly heaved himself back into an upright position, and turned as best he could to look the newcomer in his unkempt face. Augustine offered him a cursory half-smile in return, nodded blankly at Jem, and then shifted his attention to Denver and Marlowe, sat at the far side of the table.

'Augie,' said Denver, by way of greeting.

'Which of you fuckers has a straight?' asked Augustine, by way of no greeting at all.

Marlowe produced a sealed packet of cigarettes from his pocket and tossed it across the room to him. Augustine proceeded to unwrap the pack, and run a fingernail across each filter before making a selection, which he then plucked out, inverted, and returned to its companions. Marlowe crossed his arms and shook his head at this, smiling.

'Something to say, Mar?' Augustine pulled out a second cigarette and lit it, dragging deeply as he pocketed the pack in his robe.

'Go for your life,' said Marlowe, shaking his head ruefully.

Augustine scanned the room, frowning. Denver was trying to direct his gaze to a vacant chair at the head of the table. Upon seeing it, he took the chair and dragged it round behind Jem and Martin.

'Part,' he said, exhaling a large quantity of smoke as he did so.

He sat, moving his chair between Jem and Martin as they shuffled awkwardly aside.

'There. Nice and cosy.'

He patted them both on the knee, the cigarette bouncing on his bottom lip. He then removed his sunglasses and placed them on the table, revealing the plain white orbs that were resident in his eye sockets. He turned his head to face Jem, who did her best not to look like she was staring. She tried to focus instead on the tattoo the man bore on his forehead. He had an ankh, much like that worn by Denver and Marlowe, and next to his was the number 88.

'Yeah,' he said, after Jem had been staring alternately at his forehead and his peculiar eyes for about a minute, 'these are working.'

'Wow. It's like I'm looking at *Mekhenty-er-irty* again,' said

Marlowe. 'Maybe I could paint some irises and pupils on them?'

'If we do, it'll be Den doing it, not you, dick-pipe. You'd deliberately make me look cross-eyed.'

'You know me too well.'

'I should do by now, fucker. I should do by now.'

Marlowe and Denver were still wearing their sunglasses, but appeared to Jem and Martin to be deep in thought after this exchange, as Augustine relaxed in his seat and finished his cigarette. Finally, he stubbed it out on the table and gently cleared his throat.

'What are these bitches called?'

'Our guests are Martin Priest and Jemima Pepper,' said Denver.

'Pepper. Priest. P—P—P—Perfect,' he said, momentarily adopting an approximation of received pronunciation. 'Well, Marty, Jemmy, I'm going to talk for a bit now, and then there will be questions at the end, which I most likely won't answer. OK?'

Martin and Jem both nodded nervously.

'My name is Augustine, but I've used others. I try not to, but you know how complicated things can get once money is involved. Myself and my friends here have been in this hole for around seven thousand years, on and off, and frankly we're pretty fucking sick of it.'

'Seven thou...' began Jem.

'Questions at the end. Hush now, Daddy's talking. And try to take it all in without popping your little skulls like your wacky pal did. *There* was a weird kid. Nice tats, though. Anyhow, unlike my shitty, shitty life, my patience is not unlimited. You've no idea how many times I've —Whatever, where was I? Oh yeah, we're old. Except we're not. You know how you can dream and dream and dream, and it seems like forever, and then you wake up and find out you were only asleep a few minutes?'

He paused, eyebrows raised, his blank eyes seemingly staring at Jem. She assumed his question to be rhetorical, and wasn't keen to interrupt again.

'DO YOU KNOW HOW YOU CAN DREAM AND—' he leaned towards her and shouted, enunciating his words as though conversing with a lipreader.

'Yes. Yes. Sorry, I do know, yes,' said Jem quickly, nodding, and blinking nervously. Her eyes flitted between the flecks of unknown foodstuff lodged in Augustine's untidy and uncomfortably close beard, and Martin's concerned face, peering around the dishevelled and apparently angry man's shoulder.

'All right,' said Augustine, immediately calm once more, if he had ever been otherwise. 'As long as I'm not wasting my breath.'

Jem was struggling not to react to the breath in question, and held hers as she shook her head. She felt engulfed in a cloud of warm halitosis, swirling in a whiskey mist.

'Well, we've been in your stupid nightmare for a really long time,' he continued. 'I've had it worse than these two, though. They've at least been home occasionally. All I've had are brief, tantalising glimpses of bright lights, just maybe enough time to burst into tears, and then it's straight back to you… people, in some new body, in some new place, trying to make sense of another life. And I've not always had the ready charm you see today. It wasn't always so easy to make friends and influence people, if you can believe that. Can you believe it?'

Jem shook her head, and, relieved to see him turn to Martin, breathed out. She quickly put her hand over her mouth before inhaling once more.

'No, that's unbelievable,' said Martin, blankly.

'Unbelievable. Unbelievable. You know how I got so instantly likable? So lovable I can't even turn it off and I have to hide my eyes?'

He turned his plain white eyeballs on each of them in turn for far longer than was necessary to merely witness their shrugs, and they did their best to pull faces that conveyed bafflement and wonder.

'Monks. Some monks taught me. Monks up a mountain,' he chuckled. 'Monks who only talked to other monks, when they talked at all, and they had the secret of making anyone love them. And get this, they'd only teach it to other monks. Folk who'd stay with them forever. And they could make you stay, too, 'cause they had the charm, you understand. They'd teach it for their own defence, but those guys didn't want anyone going out in the world using that gift.'

He studied them both again, seemingly pleased with their genuine confusion this time, having not asked them any question.

'But I beat the system,' he said proudly, tapping his nose. 'I stayed. I learnt from them. I died. And then I came back, and I did it again. Well, what else did I have going on? I spent the best part of five lifetimes there, until I could charm the charmers. You know what I did then?'

Neither Martin nor Jem knew what he had done then, and they silently expressed this to the best of their abilities.

'I went back one last time, and I told them to jump off their mountain,' he grinned. 'And one by one, meek as lambs, they did.'

He giggled as he looked at their reactions, and drummed at the table with his fingers in delight.

'That was a dick move,' said Marlowe, visibly unamused. 'We were only on our second go around.'

'Oh yeah.' Augustine looked upward, as though dimly remembering something inconsequential. 'That was when I met these two. I couldn't work out why they hadn't killed themselves, and we got to talking. Turned out we had a whole lot in common.'

'Bullshit. You knew about us before,' asserted Marlowe. 'You knew, and you felt threatened.'

'I'm sorry you're not as powerful as me, Mar, but you need to get over it. It's ancient history. Be cool, like Den.'

Denver looked on, impassive, and Augustine faked a little shiver.

'Anyway, being able to make friends and influence people is no use when you can't find any people worth influencing,' he said, seemingly addressing the whole room, before turning his attention back to Jem and Martin. 'It wasn't always a bed of roses. Who I came back as each time, or where, was pot luck. You've no idea what it was like before you people got to grips with transport, and navigation. Do you know what it's like to just dehydrate? To have goitres? Lesions? To be really, truly, hungry? For months? To have your digestive organs swell inside you?'

Martin and Jem shook their heads as he looked to each of them in turn. He held up a hand and smiled faintly.

'No. Why would you? But these are the kinds of things that you get when you find yourself suddenly a thousand miles from the nearest human being. And then it's not much better when you finally find some people, and they're all suffering from the same things you are. You tell them to give you everything they have, and like lambs they do, and it's still barely enough to last you until the next settlement. Sometimes I'd kill myself out of convenience, just hoping to come back as someone nearer where I wanted to be. Still. I've got a feeling that's all behind me, now.'

He put his arms around Martin's and Jem's shoulders. Neither of them particularly wanted to make eye contact with him, but found themselves turning their heads regardless. They peeped past his nose to see each other frowning in bafflement.

'This is nice,' he insisted.

'Is the talk over? Can we ask questions yet?' asked Jem. She quickly focused past Augustine's nose to see Martin shaking his head.

'No, and no,' said Augustine firmly. 'And think long and hard before you make me answer a third question.'

His face became stern, and Jem felt his grip tighten on her shoulder. She made a quick zipping gesture across her now-tightly-closed lips. Jem was still trying to determine an appropriate level of fear for this situation, but she suspected that if she were able to see beyond Augustine's blank contact lenses, she would currently be sat in a pool of urine. Considering the logistics further, and having become suddenly aware of the fullness of her bladder, she entertained the notion that her and Martin's unconventional sloped seating might deliberately have been selected for its superior drainage.

'This is where we've been headed, all this time. What we've been waiting for, is here. I can almost smell it,' said Augustine, and Jem closed her lips even tighter. The body odour of the man with his arm around her was close to overpowering, and she could feel the stiffly matted fluff of his bathrobe scraping against the back of her neck.

'You see, there's a doctor Den and Mar know, and he says we're here for a reason. We've been following a path this whole time, and it's finally lead us to you.'

'To us?' Martin only realised he was speaking when he heard his voice. He immediately felt Augustine pull him closer.

'Shh. Shh. Not you specifically. You guys are fine. You're golden. No, your building. We had to buy it, because there's somebody powerful here. Somebody of interest. Someone here is changing things around. Is any of that sounding familiar at all?'

'Ray made me move my desk so he could put the printers right next to me,' offered Jem.

'That's right. And now I have to walk about six more paces to get to the kitchen,' said Martin, by way of backing her up. 'He just messes with people's quality of life for no reason.'

'That's nice. It'll come as little surprise that I want you to think bigger. Think ripping things out of this reality. And maybe don't speak for a bit, while you're thinking. We've been watching the effects since we've been here, but we haven't caught the cause yet. When we do, we can leave, Den and Mar can tell the doctor, and he can make it so we don't have to come back here any more.'

'That's right, Augie,' said Marlowe, 'that's the deal.'

'It's been so long, I don't even remember what my life was like there, or what my family's like. I can't wait to go home and find out.' Augustine seemed to be becoming wistful.

'Not long now, man.'

Ignoring Marlowe as he spoke, and choosing instead to look across at a taciturn Denver, Jem caught her in what appeared to be an unguarded moment of melancholia, before she joined her friend in what seemed a comparatively weak version of his reassuring smile. Jem prided herself on her ability to spot dishonesty, despite evidence to the contrary from several failed relationships. She would practice on her testing team, often allowing Thom and Ollii to get away with little white lies just to learn their tells, and hone her skills. In any case, the detached perspective afforded her by not being the person to whom lies were being told made matters far more straightforward. Almost everything that came out of Marlowe's mouth reeked of bullshit anyway, but Denver seemed decidedly uneasy with whatever story they had told Augustine. She wondered why he couldn't see it, and guessed it was simply that he assumed in his arrogance that these people wouldn't dare to cross him.

'Yes, Martin.' Augustine had felt Martin nervously raising his hand before he had seen it.

'Um. What are we here for?'

82

***

Finally freed from his conversation with Ian Gerald Peterson, Ray strode triumphantly around the office, surveying his staff. He entertained himself by walking past Jeremy Starwars three times, with Jeremy focusing ever more furiously on nothing but his monitor on each occasion. Allowing himself a chuckle, Ray finally moved on, past Will, to the Test and Support Department, where Robert Smith was currently sat chatting to Thom and Ollii. All three fell silent upon his approach and followed his gaze. The fact that the managerial structure meant Thom and Ollii weren't directly under his control was a constant source of annoyance to Ray. If he wanted to get at them, he had to go through Jem, and didn't they just know it.

'Feeling better, I see, Robert,' he said. He was in charge of him, at least.

'What?'

'You're not feeling ill any more.'

'What are you—Oh, yeah. Much better, thanks.'

Thom and Ollii sat grinning at Robert. This was exactly the sort of thing that annoyed Ray the most. People he couldn't bring his management down upon, clearly knowing things that he only suspected. Restrictions upon who he could and couldn't manage were also a source of immense frustration in his everyday life outside the office. People far below his pay grade could question his signature at the bank, or keep him waiting at the supermarket while they checked the price of something worth a few pence, or tell him that they were taking a year off before university to go interrailing with their boyfriend. Too many people in this world just didn't recognise how much they needed to be managed.

'You've probably got a lot to be catching up with, then,' he suggested to Robert.

'I don't know. Maybe. I've not got through all my emails yet.'

'Well, if you wouldn't mind doing that, and then coming to see me to bring me up to date, that would be great.'

'Yeah, sure.'

'You're too good to me, Mister Smith,' said Ray to the still-motionless Goth.

He folded his arms and waited until Robert eventually got up and wandered back to his desk. Ray shook his head. He was looking forward to Robert's appraisal of his workload, as he was sure it would, at the very least, be creative. It wasn't until he looked at the chair he had vacated that Jem's absence struck him.

'Where's your headmistress?' he asked the two testers, motioning to her chair.

They both shrugged their shoulders.

'She's gone AWOL,' suggested Thom.

'She hasn't phoned in?'

They both shrugged their shoulders again. Something felt very wrong here to Ray. Still, he thought he should probably resolve the Ian situation first. He frowned and turned to go. The testers had the briefest of instants to relax before they realised Ray was executing a full three hundred and sixty degree turn, now waving his index finger to indicate that a thought had occurred to him. They both looked up with the special blank expression they reserved just for him.

'Any support calls coming in?'

'None,' said Ollii.

This also made Ray uneasy. It felt like the eye of a storm. With the gibbons he had coding here, there should always be support calls. There was plenty wrong with every release that went out the door. Ray knew this just from the bugs the two testers before him had bothered to find. Only a fraction of those problems that were found were ever fixed, and those that were found were just a fraction of what the end users had to deal with. He leaned over and peered under Ollii's desk. Ollii wheeled back in his chair, with a disturbed look on his face.

'Just checking you haven't unplugged the phones,' explained Ray, straightening back up. 'Again.'

One thing at a time. He turned once more, and headed off to see Barbara Pappa.

'He was totally trying to check you out under the desk just then,' noted Thom.

'He's only human,' said Ollii, putting his feet up on the spare chair.

8

AUTHORITY

Great Birmingham: The Year of Unity 474

'And you're sure that's it?' Sevita half sat, half fell back onto the sofa.

'As sure as I can be.' Talisha explained breathlessly as she sat down beside her. The maglev had been quiet, and she'd had some time to process things on the way home, and to calm down a little. But even now, everything felt slightly unreal, as though someone had been round and fitted slightly brighter bulbs everywhere. The world was just a little different now.

'How did they miss it this whole time? How many bloody years have they been looking at them?'

'I don't know. I suppose they've had hundreds of lifetimes to go through. There's so much else for them to study. Obviously, I've told them time and again to look for the inexplicable, but that doesn't really narrow things down all that much when it comes to the Hancock recordings.'

'I guess, but I mean to say, if it's right there at the end of Augie's dream…'

'Well, I had to go in twice before I saw it, even after they'd hinted at what to look out for. And I can understand why they don't keep going back there. The endings aren't exactly fun to experience.'

Sevita grimaced. 'I didn't think. Are you OK?'

'I am now, but it bloody stung a bit at the time.'

'What was it like? Dying, I mean.'

Talisha shrugged. 'Who knows whether the recordings give you that? I can tell you about the pain, and I can tell you about feeling like you're in a lift, and the cable's just snapped, but then you're just suddenly out of it. I don't know what happens next.'

'Look at me nodding, like I know anything about it.'

'We all will, and too soon, love,' Talisha sighed.

'Dark.'

'I cried after. Just thinking what they let him go through, so many times. So many of his lives ended like that.'

'He always knew he was coming back, though, and he did have all those lives. What would he have had here, if they'd even been able to wake him?'

'I suppose. Putting it that way, he had a pretty good innings, didn't he? And he did act the twat a lot.' She craned her neck over the top of the sofa to follow Sevita as she rose and walked to the kitchen area. 'I need one too,' she said.

'You don't know what I'm getting.'

'As long as it's drunk, I don't really care.'

'Lucky guess.' Sevita poured gin into the two glasses she had already retrieved from the cabinet, adding barely enough tonic water to each for it to be considered functional rather than decorative. Talisha hungrily gathered her glass as Sevita passed it to her from behind the sofa on her way round to sit once more.

They spent a few minutes trying not to think, in the guise of quiet contemplation. Sevita broke the silence first.

'So what happens now?'

'Now we push on with Deep Probe Two and see if we can actually get there,' Talisha replied between sips. 'Then we prep the room for Lucky. And if she comes back OK...'

'The pig comes out and me and Kush go in.' Sevita bit her lip.

'You're ready, Veet, we just need to know that the room is. One of you is going to need to play Augie's ending, though, so you can see the guy's face. Are you up to that? If I've put you off, I'll just make Kush do it.'

'No. No, it's OK. Are you kidding? I want to see him. Is he

handsome?'

Talisha pulled a face that made Sevita snort.

'Nondescript would be putting it kindly. He can change reality, though. I'm guessing he does all right for himself, one way or another.'

'And I'll get to see this gun trick of his.'

'Well, Augustine's whipping his head around a bit, but yes. It's under a table, and then he sees it just appear in the guy's hand, and there's no table any more when he looks over again. You need to concentrate, because he's getting hit a lot, but you feel like Augie knows right away, like he knows all his lives have been leading up to this.'

'Sounds like kind of a rush.'

'It'll put some adrenaline through you, all right.'

Sevita considered this as she studied Talisha's expression. Happy that she saw no obvious trauma there, she sipped her almost neat gin and continued to look deep into her big hazel eyes. A sparked memory snapped her back into the moment.

'Oh, Graham called round a little while ago. He was sorry to miss you.'

'Gray? How was he? Why didn't he stay?'

'We only spoke in the corridor, really. He didn't want to scrape the door with his chair. It's quite a big one.'

'Chair?'

'Yes, he's in a chair now. Just while they're making him some legs.'

'Bull's balls. That's all four limbs now, then.'

'Yes, he didn't seem to have any arms with him either, for some reason. Perhaps he left them at home. I didn't like to ask.'

'What did he do this time, to lose the legs?'

Sevita shrugged. 'He didn't say. I expect he fell off something, or into something. You know Graham.'

Talisha nodded sagely. 'How did he seem, though, in himself?'

'He was quite heavily bandaged, but his eyes seemed, I don't know, alert? It was hard to make out what he was saying a lot of the time. His tongue seemed really swollen up. He mentioned something about a bad reaction, I don't know.'

Talisha took this news in, frowning all the while. 'Poor Gray.'

'He wasn't at all pleased to see me, as usual. He's still carrying a torch for you, you know, Tal.'

'How?' Talisha asked before she could stop herself.

Sevita burst into laughter, which only intensified as she watched Talisha cover her mouth, mortified at having joked at the expense of her unfortunate old friend. The very thought of how inappropriate it would be to join Sevita in this laughter then caused Talisha to do exactly that. Soon they were both shaking in helpless hysterics.

'Bloody Dudley, I needed that,' Talisha admitted as the power of speech returned, and she dabbed the tears from her cheeks.

'Yep. Thanks, Graham,' offered a sniffing Sevita in agreement, 'although I think I've wet myself.'

'So,' she added, clearing her throat.

'So,' said Talisha, sitting up with a serious face.

'So how long until we actually go?'

Talisha took a breath. 'If everything goes according to plan? A month. Six weeks on the outside.'

'It's actually going to happen, isn't it? All this time, I've had it in the back of my mind that I'd end up old, and bore people at dinner parties, anyone who'd listen, that I was once attached to this project. I'd be really proud, but they'd only vaguely remember reading about it, and smile politely.'

'You'll still get old and boring, beautiful,' Talisha reassured her, while holding out her glass to be chinked, 'but those people are going to totally lose their shit when you tell them how you were the one who stopped the Axis.'

Sevita was hesitant, and withheld her chink.

'It is the right thing to do, right?'

Talisha took a swig as she considered her response.

'I think we've seen enough of that world from the recordings to know we wouldn't want to live in it. The Axis could bring all that down on us. I mean, global warping isn't a theory anymore, it's a fact. Who knows how much it's corrupting our history right now. It put us here, it could end us altogether, just like that.'

'The Axis giveth, and the Axis taketh away.'

'Well, we're going to make it leaveth us alone. We're living next to a volcano the whole time, and you, my girl, are going to plug it.'

Sevita nodded firmly, increasingly bolstered by gin.

'With your big fat arse,' added Talisha.

'And now I must kill you,' said a grinning Sevita, putting down her glass and picking up a cushion.

***

Martin leaned back and watched between the blinds as Augustine ambled off through the office, before straightening up and rubbing first his neck and then the base of his back. His spine was not yet fully appreciating the ergonomic benefits of the kneeling chair. He looked at Jem, who was by now achieving an admirably upright posture, and marvelled at the ease with which she had taken to the unorthodox seating.

'He's a one, eh?' he said to her, nodding in the general direction in which Augustine had headed.

'Oh, don't mind him. I think he liked you both,' said Denver, sat across the meeting room table from them with Marlowe. Martin noted that they looked considerably more comfortable in their traditional office chairs.

'Was any of that true? I mean, he was pretty drunk, right?' asked Jem.

Denver shook her head.

'You don't want to see him drunk. But yes, that was more or less all true.'

She turned to Marlowe for confirmation, and he nodded accordingly, adding a mumbled, 'all true as he sees it, anyway.'

Trying to ignore this, Jem ploughed on. 'So you're saying those aren't, you know, your bodies?'

'They are now, sweetheart, said Marlowe with a smile. 'It's life, Jem, but not as we know it.'

'Really? *Star Trek*?' she pulled a face at him.

He shrugged. 'I watch a lot of television. And excuse my language, but thank fuck you people finally invented it. Anything that helps pass the time is a massive deal to us. Huge.'

'I suppose I can see that.'

'Kirk's my favourite captain. I watched his whole run on its original transmission in the States,' he said proudly.

Jem looked doubtful. 'You don't look old enough.'

Marlowe looked down to appraise himself, appearing pleased, and seemingly about to take this as a compliment, before his face dropped a little, and he said, 'oh, yeah. Not in this body.'

'They never said it on the show anyway, the "it's life" thing. It's a myth,' said Martin.

Instantly aware of the other three staring at him, he added 'apparently,' in an attempt to recover the situation.

Jem shook her head and slowly mouthed the word 'geek' at him. Martin responded by making a play of fumbling in his pocket for something, before producing his middle finger to show her with a playful sneer.

'Nice, Doctor Spuck.'

'What did you call me?'

'Oh, I'm terribly sorry, Trekko. *Mister* Spuck.'

'*Spuck*?' Martin shook his head in disbelief, and Jem beamed at how easy it was to bait him.

Denver coughed to remind them that they weren't alone.

'It's so much easier to pass for normal with you people these days. Just check out the top ten videos online. Doesn't matter if you can't remember a thing about politics, as long as you have pop culture references to hand. You're all about the memes,' Marlowe explained.

'We're easily pleased, all right,' Jem agreed.

'Those tattoos,' said Martin, pointing at his own forehead. 'You use them to help find each other, every time you're, what, reincarnated, yeah?'

Marlowe nodded. 'Gold star. They've been pretty much first order of business every time we take a new body for centuries now. Really useful to know you've got one distinguishing mark to ask about when you're looking for someone who could be any age, any colour, and you don't even know if they're Arthur or Martha. God, I'd love to be a girl one last time.'

Denver looked at him askance, and he broke from his reverie.

'Oh, like you never enjoyed having a dick,' he said, dismissing her glare with a wave. 'Anyway. It gets easier to find each other every time, what with the media and whatnot. I guess we wouldn't need to draw on ourselves at all now. Just create an account on Warblespace, or whatever. Boom. Your society is finally starting to become comfortable for us, and it's nearly time to go, if Augie's right.'

'Those... powers must make things easy, though, surely?' Martin surmised. 'I mean, if you don't find yourself in some wilderness like Augustine was saying.'

'That never happened to me. You, Den?'

Denver shook her head. 'He insists it used to happen to him all the time, but can you imagine how unlucky that makes him? Who were all those people who were so isolated?'

'Probably weren't. Probably every one of them was on the outskirts of town, and the dickhead just walked in the wrong direction.'

'Maybe.' Denver giggled. 'Anyway, Martin, what powers of persuasion we have are only useful up to a point. I can only hold hands with two people at once, and if we're holding hands, they probably like me already, don't you think?'

'And those looks you give people?'

Marlowe waved dismissively. 'The looks are weak sauce by comparison. People get used to the eyeballing. Then you end up with the whole business of people pretending to still be in your thrall or whatever, thinking they can go around stabbing you and so forth. It's fine for a quick business deal, making people give you offices and whatnot, but it's not something to rely on for lifelong devotion. You've got to earn that stuff. Or pay for it, at least.'

'Looks fade,' quipped Denver.

'Never yours, sweetheart, never yours,' said Marlowe.

'Watch this one,' Denver told Jem. 'He's a player.'

Marlowe fixed Jem with a stare, arching an eyebrow and licking his lips, before breaking into a broad smile.

'I'll try to bear that in mind,' she muttered, frowning.

'Thing is, anyone can learn those techniques, in theory,' Marlowe continued. 'I mean, sure we had to spend a ton of years up a mountain, but it's only a matter of time before some prick puts the whole thing on the net for you to download. Then nobody will look anyone in the eye ever again. Or hold hands.'

Jem determined that she would wait a moment or two before releasing Martin's fingers, if only to reassure herself that she wasn't being made to do it.

'So what's with the numbers?' asked Martin, beginning to relax now, and pointing to his forehead once more. 'I thought maybe they were your ages, to start with.'

Denver laughed. 'You can't have thought much of us.'

'How many tattoos we've had,' said Marlowe, matter-of-factly.

'So, how many bodies you've been in, then,' said Martin.

'That's a much bigger number.' Marlowe chuckled.

'Lives, I mean. Obviously. How many lives you've taken over.'

'All right, yeah. If you want to put it like that. All the lives we've so heartlessly commandeered since the monastery. That's when we started counting.'

'88,' mumbled Jem, looking at the comparatively low figures written on the heads opposite her.

'Yeah, Augie gets through 'em, all right.' Marlowe scratched his head. 'Gets bored, gets depressed, gets crazy, gets dead. It's kind of an insult to us, if you stop to think about it. The trouble we go to, to find that prick every time.'

Jem let go of Martin's hand and leaned in toward Denver, as best she could manage in her unorthodox chair, ending with her elbows and chin resting on the table.

'Hey, what was that about Augustine's real life? I got the impression you know more than he does,' she whispered, conspiratorially.

Denver leaned forward and answered in clipped tones, 'that's none of your fucking business,' before sitting back once more.

'Oh. Sorry,' said Jem in a voice she herself could barely hear, and she shrank back, feeling suddenly cold.

**

Ray stood outside the doors to the top floor, panting, gripping his thighs. He had been so incensed when he had left Barbara Pappa's office, he had quite forgotten that he and exercise had been estranged for some years. He had charged up the first two flights. Then he had stomped up the next two. He had wheezed his way up the next four, and then he had taken a little break and briefly considered giving up, letting gravity win, and retreating. Four storeys further up, he had stopped again, and battled similar thoughts. He had barely made it up the remaining eight flights. He was still very much angry, but much of his fury was by now directed at the firm responsible for maintaining the long-broken lift whose sealed doors had taunted him at every level. He had also had the opportunity to vent some of his rage by launching a horrific torrent of abuse against a vacuum cleaner he had fallen over several floors lower down.

Now Ray stood, catching his breath, and feeling the muscles burning in his legs. He tried to gather his thoughts; what was he actually planning to say to these people? Barbara had displayed a complete disregard for his rank by not even consulting him before sending Jem up here, and the idea that she was happy in principal for Jeremy to go too was the final straw. She had bypassed him completely, and she had made it perfectly clear that she would take his entire team from him, if that was what these people wanted. The whole meeting had been deeply emasculating.

'If you've got a problem with it, you can talk to them yourself,' she had said.

'I might pop up for a word,' he had smiled meekly, adding a pathetic 'thanks, Barbara,' as he had backed out of the room and quietly closed her door behind him. As he had walked away up the corridor and headed for the stairwell, he had already begun to dwell on his meek exit. By the time he had reached the fourth floor, he had reinterpreted the whole scene to better reflect his heroic stance. By the seventh floor, aided to some degree by the decrease in the quantity of oxygen reaching his brain, he had more or less convinced himself that he had caused quite a stir in his meeting with the CEO.

'I might pop up for a word,' he had roared furiously in this new version of events, adding a sarcastic 'thanks, *Barbara*,' with a sneer, as he had stormed from her office, slamming the door violently behind him. Yes, that was more like it. And he was fairly certain that he had shouted 'YOU COW' from the corridor. There was still a small chance that this had only happened in his head, but if it had actually been out loud, he was pretty sure she would have heard it. Barbara had messed with the bull, she had gotten the horns, and there was an end to it. She would only respect him the more for reminding her that *the manager* began with *the man*. They were both professionals, and consequently he knew that neither of them would ever mention this terrible, and only partially fictional, blazing row again.

Now, with his heartbeat and breathing both gradually becoming regular once more, he focused on the reflection of his sweating, purple face in the small reinforced glass window before him, and allowed himself a more accurate recollection of his humiliation. As the unwelcome reality stared back at him, he finally remembered that he hadn't brought up Ian's contract issue, the whole reason for having gone to see Barbara in the first place, at all.

'You arsehole,' he told the face, even as he licked his fingers and patted down the brown short-back-and-greying-sides hair which framed it.

He remembered how cowed he had been by Manny the previous day. How ready he had been to give him everything he wanted, just because he was shiny and ill-defined, and his voice seemed not to be attached to his body. Just because he represented these people, whoever they were.

'You total pussy,' he told the ruddy complexioned face.

Ray was surprised as the face retreated from him and turned away. He realised that the door was now open, and a fat bald man who appeared to have appallingly thick cataracts stood before him in a fluffy white bathrobe, a cigarette dangling from his lip.

''fuck did you just call me?' asked Augustine.

***

Ian Gerald Peterson peered into the gloom. The windowless store room was lit by a single bulb, which dangled between high shelving units and consequently only illuminated a very small area to any appreciable extent. Entering the room from the bright harsh glow of the strip lighting in the Sales Department was like venturing into a crypt. The temperature seemed to drop immediately as he stepped into the darkness.

'Hello?' he ventured.

There was no response. He stepped further into the room, still holding the door open on its spring.

'Hello?' he tried once more.

Nothing. He stretched as far as he could while still holding the door with his fingertips, craning his neck to look down the next aisle of shelving. He still couldn't see far, and certainly not far enough to locate the storeman he had been assured was somewhere within. Eager to preserve the rectangle of light from the doorway, Ian raised his right leg behind him and hooked his foot around the edge of the door, hopping forward slightly on the other foot and freeing his hand.

'Stone me, he's doing ballet now,' came the muffled voice of Tim from Sales, somewhere behind Ian.

Reluctantly, he returned to standing on two legs, and the door slammed shut behind him. He allowed his eyes a moment to adjust to the low light and hazarded a couple more steps. He peered to his left, down the second aisle of five, a dark path between tall grey metal shelving units. At the end of this canyon of paper reams, parcels and long-since-obsolete computer peripherals, he thought he could make out something that might be human, just standing there.

'Hello?'

Still nothing. Gathering himself with a deep breath, Ian began slowly down the aisle. He passed typewriters, dot matrix printers, and laptops the size of suitcases, all covered in small round stickers of various colours from the many years of stocktakes they had seen. As he drew nearer to what was now definitely a figure, he could see that it stood facing away from him, into the corner, motionless. What little light that was emitted by the single dangling bulb in the next aisle was almost entirely blocked from here by the fully stocked shelves.

'Hello?'

Ian edged ever closer, no longer hearing anything but his own heartbeat. He could now make out that the figure was wearing a light blue shirt and was balding with a ring of cropped dark hair. It could only be his namesake, Ian Peterson. He reached out tentatively towards

Ian Peterson's back as he took the final steps towards him. Ian Gerald Peterson considered the possibility that Ian Peterson had somehow died standing up, and that he was about to disturb a corpse. He thought about the storeman suffering some kind of heart failure, and using his dying breaths to prop himself out of the way in this corner, thus bravely storing himself as his final act. There was honour in this, thought Ian Gerald Peterson. He visualised Ian Peterson collapsing to the floor as he touched him. He thought about the many questions the police would have for him about moving the body. As soon as they took his name, it would take them seconds to determine a motive. Tapping this shoulder could change his life. He almost withdrew, but he knew it was too late. Everyone in Sales had seen him go in there. He would be implicated either way.

Now close enough, Ian Gerald Peterson stretched out his trembling hand to the still shoulder of Ian Peterson, and as he did so, felt two large hands come firmly down on his own shoulders.

'CAN I HELP YOU?' shouted Colin from Stores as he gripped Ian Gerald Peterson, who let out an undignified shriek. Colin had stealthily emerged behind Ian from a narrow and particularly dark gap in the shelving normally reserved for squeezing between the aisles, but equally well suited to hiding in.

Ian Peterson wheeled around from his position in the corner, laughing hysterically.

'Oh man. That was the best one ever,' he said, as he wiped his eyes, while Ian Gerald Peterson stood clutching his chest and saying 'Jesus' repeatedly.

'You all right, chief?' Colin asked, slapping Ian's back.

'You bastards. You bastards,' said Ian, still catching his breath.

'Yeah. You're fine,' asserted Colin. 'Right, I'm off down the shop. Do you need any crisps, E?'

Ian Gerald Peterson was appalled to hear the name he shared with the storeman being abbreviated to a vowel that was entirely absent from its spelling.

'Nah, you're all right, London. See you in a bit,' replied the clearly-still-living Ian Peterson from Stores.

Colin left the room still chuckling, and seconds later the Ians heard a roar of laughter from the Sales team next door.

'Why do you call him London?' asked Ian Gerald Peterson, now recovering, and nodding in the general direction of the Colin's booming laugh.

'You know, "London" Colin,' explained Ian from Stores.

Ian Gerald Peterson looked at him blankly.

'*London Colin*,' sang Ian from Stores halfheartedly, to the tune of 'London Calling' by The Clash.

As the four syllables involved happened to be on the same note, it wasn't entirely clear to Ian Gerald Peterson that he was being sung to. He remained confused, and made no effort to conceal this with his expression.

'He's a cockney, all right?' said Ian from Stores at last, shaking his head. 'You kids. Bloody hell.'

Ian Gerald Peterson nodded sagely.

'Well?' said Ian from Stores.

'Sorry?' said Ian Gerald Peterson.

'What can I do you for?'

Ian took a moment to collect his thoughts, having largely forgotten why he had come down to Stores. He spent this time staring blankly at the other Ian with his mouth agape.

'Oh,' he said at last, playing for time, and then stood staring slack-jawed at Ian from Stores for a while longer.

'Bloody hell, we didn't break you, did we?' asked Ian Peterson, snapping his fingers in front of Ian Gerald Peterson's face.

'Broken. I need a new mouse. My mouse is broken,' said Ian.

'All right mate, we can do that,' said Ian from Stores cheerily.

After a few minutes listening to the other Ian whistle show tunes, Ian had a nice fresh boxed mouse in his grasp, and had dutifully signed for same.

'Very funny,' said Ian Peterson, glaring at the docket.

'Sorry?'

'Don't take the piss, mate. Sign your own name,' said Ian Peterson, flapping the docket under Ian Gerald Peterson's nose. 'Cheeky cock. Bloody hell, at least put Mickey Mouse or something.'

Ian's heart sank at this development. His name-nemesis didn't have the faintest idea who he was.

'Are you interested in home brewing at all?' he began.

***

Back downstairs, Ray was fuming. A trip to the kitchen for a nice strong mug of coffee hadn't helped him to calm down as much as he had hoped. He was, if anything, more agitated. He sat at his desk and ruminated on the erosion of his power base. He was now presiding over three empty seats, and had been made to feel small by both Barbara Pappa and a strange American-sounding man who had quite frankly reeked of booze. He didn't even properly remember what had happened with the American, but he had decided for the moment not to concern himself with this apparent gap in his recollections; the return of the memories would most likely only have made him more furious. He had, of course, always been aware of his place in the food chain, but this awareness had, for the most part, existed in the abstract for much of his time with the company. Shiny men who talked inside one's head aside, he had rarely, if ever, been made to feel inferior to his superiors. His ego urgently needed to be pumped back up.

On an instinctive level, Ray knew that the only thing to do here was to kick downward. He scanned the office, looking for underlings whose spirits he could sap in order to replenish his own. Slim pickings. No Keith, no Martin, and no Jem. Ollii and Thom, he had no direct control over, so chewing them out would have to be preceded by an awkward and lengthy conversation, in order to attempt to convince them that he was in any position to chew them out in the first place. He suspected that they would win that argument simply by pretending not to understand what he was saying. He could scarcely pick on Guy Mange, as he was a visitor to the country, and that placed certain duties, both custodial and ambassadorial upon Ray's broad shoulders. He could perhaps belittle Ian Gerald Peterson, but talking to Ian Gerald Peterson might involve Ian Gerald Peterson talking to him, so that was out of the question. In any case, Ian wasn't at his desk for some reason. Will wasn't really an option, as he was always on top of things, and in any case, there was something about his perpetually cold, blank expression that Ray found unnerving. It was as if the lights weren't on, but some *thing* was most definitely home. Rays eyes flitted across to Jeremy. Ah, yes. Jeremy, he could play with.

Ray performed his timeworn and honed manoeuvre of striding purposefully past Jeremy's desk at a pace that might, if observed in the peripheral vision of his prey, suggest he was leaving the office, before wheeling round and creeping up behind the hapless coder. He hovered over him momentarily, preparing to strike. From the corner of his eye, he could see the two testers shaking their heads disdainfully, but they were not important. In a way, that was the whole point; only one person was important in this room by any reasonable assessment of salary or job title, and nothing mattered but this moment; the moment Ray's hands would come down and grip the shoulders of Jeremy Starwars, and he could feel fully in charge of his own destiny once more. So keen was he to ensure a simultaneous slap of both shoulders, that Ray felt almost paralysed by the anticipation.

Down came the hands. Ray felt Jeremy Starwars lift in his seat and heard him bark slightly with the shock. He watched as Jeremy removed his oversized headphones, dropped them on his desk and instinctively clicked his mouse, turning on the music he hadn't been listening to. Ray listened as *White Riot* blared out from the discarded headphones until Jeremy fumbled his way to the pause button. Ray forced a chuckle. This was a near-perfect disruptive opening, but in his heart of hearts he knew that anyone in the office could have accomplished almost as much. With his ears covered, and his admirable tendency toward paying unwavering attention to whatever was on his monitor, Jeremy was an easy target for a good startling. On one occasion, Ray had observed the entire team quietly wheel themselves into a seated semicircle behind Jeremy before he had turned to notice them, all aping his deep frown of concentration.

'What?' asked an exasperated Jeremy.

Ray put his game face on as Jeremy lifted his head to meet his gaze. Solemn. Eyebrows every-so-slightly raised.

'Mister Starwars. All ready for the show?'

'I will be,' lied Jeremy Starwars.

'Not done yet?' asked Ray, entirely on an out-breath. A carefully rehearsed mixture of shock and exhaustion. The pretence of impatience, with just enough edge to make it clear that it masked genuine impatience, with just a hint of ire. A perfect reading. Ray almost believed it himself. In fact, had he dwelt on the ever-expanding timescale for Jeremy's project a little more before coming over, he probably wouldn't have needed to fake either impatience or ire. This wasn't about getting himself all worked up, though. It was about getting somebody else all worked up. It would almost certainly affect his performance, were he to put himself in the position of actually caring about all the things his senior position called for him to claim he cared about. That was just middle management, chapter one.

'Do you want it done quickly, or do you want it done right?' Jeremy asked half-heartedly.

'Are either of those options even on the table?'

Jeremy swallowed. Neither option was strictly feasible. At this point, he was fairly certain that he couldn't even deliver on the third choice, 'would you like it done wrong?' and it was certainly too late for 'do you want something else?'

He decided to just wait for Ray to speak again. Sometimes a dogged determination to wilfully interpret every question asked of him as rhetorical would draw confrontations to an awkward but hopefully insignificant conclusion.

Ray was uncertain as to whether he should be expecting a response to his barbed comment, but he was enjoying the edgy silence his stony glare appeared to be engendering, and decided to maintain it. Nothing was said by either combatant for nearly a minute, before Ray became uncomfortably aware of the sound of his own breathing. A ripple of panic struck him. He knew that the next stage would involve devoting much of his concentration to properly regimenting his respiration, and worrying that his lizard brain might refuse to resume the job on its usual semi-autonomous basis once he grew bored with it. He didn't have time to be taking on duties like remembering to breath in and out. He was a busy man.

'What do you have left to do?' he asked, jiggling his leg to distract himself from the functioning of his lungs. His keys chinked in his pocket.

'Tidying up, and some documentation,' said Starwars, automatically.

'That's what you said yesterday. I would have thought you might have finished one of those by now.'

Jeremy decided that this was another point at which saying anything might harm his case. He had neither finished nor started either of these things, as in the absence of any working code, he had nothing to tidy up or document.

'Well, I think you should concentrate on the tidying up now. The documentation you can finish off after the demonstration tomorrow morning,' said Ray.

This was the very rock face of management. He was effecting change in somebody's work schedule, and it felt good.

'Right,' said Starwars, hoping that it was the magic word that would make Ray disappear, so that he could get on with the business of tidying up nothing for tomorrow's demonstration of nothing. He drew some comfort from the fact that there was still one more night between him and the horror; one more chance that he might go peacefully in his sleep, and avoid it all.

Ray stopped shaking his leg and shifted his weight. Now that he had given instructions, it would be an inappropriate use of his time to stand around watching them being carried out.

Jeremy saw his project manager begin to look like he was about to leave, but instead of the relief he had expected to feel, there was something else; he was gripped by the feeling that one last opportunity to save himself was about to drift away. He had wasted much of the last two days daydreaming about conversations with Ray in which the demonstration had to be cancelled. The conversations had started in a hundred different ways, most of them involving outrageous lies about enormous magnets, or war injuries. Some of them had taken place over the phone; from another country, or while calling in a bomb threat. When worked through, many had ended with awkward questions about what he had been doing all this time. But there was one scenario he kept coming back to; the one in which he told *the truth*. Not *his* truth, obviously, that would be ludicrous. The truth about the demonstration being something of a waste of valuable company time. Not for the obvious and very real reason, but because of all the absentees. Could it work in real life? It had worked on at least the last ten dry runs in Jeremy's head. He saw Ray's eyes flick towards his own desk. Last chance. He was going to do it.

'Ray?' said Jeremy Starwars hesitantly.

Ray raised his eyebrows slightly in response, his game face still very much in effect and his jaw beginning to ache a little as a result.

'I was thinking,' Jeremy continued, 'that maybe, what with Jem and Martin *and* Keith not being here…'

He paused for a 'yes, and' from Ray, but none was forthcoming. He looked at the storm gathering in his project manager's face and, hoping that it might perhaps just pass overhead and hit somewhere else, he ploughed on.

'Well, that maybe we should postpone the demo.'

Jeremy Starwars felt his head going numb. He had actually said the P word. Surely all his pretence was about to unravel. Perhaps running straight out of the building was still an option. The element of surprise might give him a head start.

'Just so we don't waste company time, repeating things over and over,' he added, tilting his head from side to side for emphasis.

Ray's face didn't change.

'Just for a bit,' Jeremy added, his mouth now bone dry.

Ray quietly filled his lungs, fully aware that the slight flaring of his nostrils would cast the perfect note of contempt across his otherwise-still game face. Then he breathed out through his mouth, producing a moaning sound he imagined would adequately portray the disappointment he should probably be feeling at this point. He kept his gaze fixed on Jeremy, watching his face fall and his eyes dart this way and that, all the while continuing to breathe out. Then he realised that he was becoming light-headed and gasped.

He quickly regained his composure, and was fairly certain that Jeremy hadn't noticed the slight lapse.

'I see,' he said, and tutted.

'Do do do do doo,' he added.

His team member's head was down, his eyes looking up in supplication. This was all that Ray could realistically ask for.

'You have a point,' he said at last.

Jeremy Starwars raised his head, trying not to betray any emotion that might lead to further questions.

'We'll give them a few more hours to come back down. Let's have the demo after lunch, at two. Change the booking for the meeting room.'

Jeremy blinked. This was a very short stay of execution, but it was better than nothing, and perhaps he could still fall under a truck of some sort at lunchtime. Then he frowned as he realised that he would have to spend most of the hourlong break setting up his computer in the meeting room.

'Mail Barbara as well. She said something about coming along,' said Ray over his shoulder as he walked away. 'Thank you, Mister Starwars.'

Jeremy grunted an acknowledgement and returned to his screen, and the blank document he had been working on for the last hour.

Ray sat down at his desk once more, strangely unsatisfied. It had been as if Jeremy Starwars had no spirit for him to feed on in the first place. He had drawn little sustenance from the encounter. He was still deeply perturbed and felt a hollowness within him. What else could be done? He looked at his monitor, but just an empty spreadsheet gazed back. There was nothing to settle his busy mind there. He wondered whether another mug of coffee might take the edge off.

'You wanted to talk about what work I had lined up?' said Robert Smith, now stood before him, clutching a pen and a few sheets of A4.

'You really are too good to me, Mister Smith,' said Ray, and he smiled broadly at the unwitting goth.

***

Martin lay awake in the darkness of his makeshift bedroom, staring at the suspended ceiling and counting the tiles. He thought of his considerably more homely flat, and wondered whether it had been burgled yet. This is something he would often consider while sitting at his desk downstairs in the office, but it seemed altogether more plausible as a possibility now that his curtains had been open for two days. The two lights he had put onto timer switches for security purposes would presently be helpfully illuminating the electrical goods in his ground floor property like a shop window for any passing ne'er-do-well. He didn't have a pet, but he imagined a starving hamster anyway. The plight of this hypothetical creature seemed easier to worry about than his current situation. He thought of his presumably faithful notional pet gradually slowing down on its wheel, before dismounting with a small cough and curling up sadly in its empty food bowl. Occasionally pausing to remember that the skin-and-bones Fluffy didn't actually exist was a minor comfort, but a comfort nonetheless. All his belongings could easily be stolen or on fire at this point and some maniacs might very well be planning to nail him to something, but at least he knew for certain that nobody was buggering his hamster in a satanic ritual, because he didn't have one.

'Advantage Priest, I think,' he muttered and sat up.

Sleep wasn't coming any time soon. He would have watched something on his phone, if there had been any kind of signal in the building. Or indeed if Manny hadn't taken the phone, along with the clothes he had arrived in yesterday, for safekeeping. He got to his feet and retied the complimentary airline kimono he'd been provided with to sleep in. Staring at his reflection in the window, he bounced a bit on the balls of his feet and punched at the air.

'Oh yes. I flap like a butterfly,' he said, unimpressed with his form.

He scratched at the more bristly areas of his crew cut and frowned, noting that the light was accentuating the ginger in what he generally told people was brown hair, if pressed. He walked over to the window for a proper word with the reflection that had made such a cruel mockery of his shadow boxing prowess, but refocused on the car park when he got there. In the dim glow of the security lights he could see that it was still mostly filled with cars. Where did all these people get off, leaving their cars in a private car park for days on end? He couldn't even see his own old banger from here, having had to park up alongside an outbuilding yesterday because of these dicks taking all the spaces. He could make out Jem's *supermini* though. She was always able to get the same space, between two bay-straddlers, as she had the only car that could fit into it. Lovely Jem. She had come to his rescue. She hadn't let him stay in her room tonight though. 'This is the office. It's too weird.' She had said. 'I suppose you're right, in a way,' he had graciously admitted. 'Now bugger off, so I can push that filing cabinet against the door and go to sleep,' she had declared. It had seemed ungallant to try to convince her that she wasn't safe on her own. Cad-like, even. In any case, he was well aware that she was by far the braver of the two of them, and he'd probably just have ended up spooking himself. Still, he had paced to his door and back at least ten times since returning to his room, deciding each time that she was probably happily asleep by now and not to bother her.

Footsteps.

Martin turned to look at the tiny reinforced glass window in his door, dimly illuminated by the light outside the toilets. Could she have changed her mind? The footsteps were getting closer to the door. He quickly got back into bed and put his hands behind his head, in order to appear nonchalant. As the sound drew ever closer, he worked on his best '*I've been expecting you*' face; one eyebrow raised, and a *Mona Lisa* smile, or his best approximation. The vague silhouette of a head moved across the small window. Martin was struck by a fear that his look might come across less like '*I've been expecting you*' and more like '*I am evacuating myself in my kimono,*' and straightened his expression. The handle turned on the door. Martin felt the need to clear his throat, but he was now uncertain whether to pretend to be asleep, so it was too late to do so. The door swung open and what he saw caused him to breath in sharply and take to an immediate fit of coughing, thus solving that dilemma at a stroke.

'Hello Martin,' said Keith.

9

SOMETHING UNDER THE BED

Jem tiptoed up the corridor, cursing her bladder. She ducked as she passed the window in Martin's door. This had just been a quick toilet visit, and as far as he was concerned, she was still safely barricaded into her room and snoring. That was still the plan. She didn't want to get into that discussion again tonight. Straight back to the room. Cabinet back in front of door. Lie awake until dawn listening to the screams of the voices in her head. It was still a good plan. As she reached her own door, however, she could hear Denver's voice coming from the darkened lab at the far end of the corridor. She held the door handle for a moment, but suddenly here was a plan C, seemingly custom-made for the insomniac; *become a superspy*. She couldn't make out much of the conversation from where she was. Knowledge is power, she thought, and gingerly padded onward.

As she reached the point where the corridor met the lab, she hugged the wall, breathing as little as she could, and listened.

'And what exactly are you going to do with that?' said Denver's voice, sounding calm and measured, as ever.

Nothing but a grunt in response. Male-sounding, so Augustine or Marlowe, Jem assumed.

'Would you like me to look after it? I can put it somewhere safe until morning.'

Another grunt, and the sound of a palm slapping down on one of the workbenches.

'Fine. Be like that. But know this; we're so close now. If you off yourself again, I'm not going looking for you, and neither will Marlowe. We'll go back without you.'

'Fuh,' said what must by process of elimination have been Augustine, and he emitted a gurgling laugh.

Jem heard a tutting Denver walking away from the conversation, both tuts and footsteps seemingly drawing closer. She flattened herself against the wall and held her breath, hoping that Denver wasn't headed for the toilets.

'Seriously. We can and will find it without you,' Denver reiterated, and Jem slowly breathed out as she watched her come into view and head for the door to the stairwell, opposite the corridor and some forty feet away.

Five taps on the keypad, and Denver opened the door, went through, turned slightly and pulled it closed behind her. Then Jem went cold as she saw Denver, now in silhouette in the lit stairwell, stop at the window in the door and just stand there, apparently looking straight at her. Jem couldn't make out Denver's features, and tried to convince herself that she was staring somewhere else. Where Jem stood was in near darkness, but the dim glow from further down the corridor now left her feeling terribly exposed. Jem was at least thankful that this was happening after her visit to the toilet, rather than before. Her head was screaming for her to run, but her body was frozen to the wall, as she waited what seemed like minutes for Denver to open the door again, to walk directly across the lab to her and tell her that she wouldn't be able to let her live now.

And then Denver was gone. Jem slid down the wall until she was sat on the floor, hugging her knees. *She had just paused at the door, that's all. Everything is fine and I'm still a superspy.*

The clink of glass against bottle, bottle against table, told Jem that Augustine was still sat at a workbench. From her lower vantage point, she peered around the corner. Three benches down, she could make out a hairy pair of legs in furry slippers. She wiggled her toes, annoyed that she hadn't been provided with a pair herself, to go with her cheap complimentary airline kimono. She was about to abort her top secret mission and return to plan A, when Augustine struggled to his feet.

Realising that she was within crawling distance of a workbench, and not wishing to be caught cold once more, she eased herself around the corner on her elbows and knees, making her way underneath the bench, the central riff to the *James Bond* theme playing on a loop in her head.

As Augustine made his way down the lab, leaning on furniture and coughing, Jem could see that other than his slippers, he was wearing nothing but the fluffy dressing gown she and Martin had seen him sporting during the day, and that he had apparently lost the belt with which to tie it closed. He stopped to drain the last drops from the whiskey bottle he was clasping, and from beneath her bench Jem stared out at a scene of full-frontal nudity. She may not have learnt a great deal so far during this mission, but she had at least discovered that Augustine was circumcised. *A clue*, she thought, and pictured herself with an enormous magnifying glass, dispassionately studying the dangling member of the puzzled drunk.

She watched as Augustine staggered to the stairwell door, his dressing gown hanging lower on the right hand side and swinging, as if there were something heavy in the pocket. He tapped the keypad numerous times before finally succeeding in getting the door open, headed out through the door and disappeared from view. He had left the door open. Jem had a couple of seconds to consider going to wake Martin so that the pair of them could make a run for it, before she heard Augustine howl as he slipped and fell down the stairs.

Jem sat under the workbench for a few minutes, waiting to hear Denver come to Augustine's rescue, but all was silent. Cautiously, she made her way over to the door and peered out. From her viewpoint in the safety of the dark, she could only see the first few steps of the flight leading down, and if Augustine was sprawled stricken anywhere, it wasn't on those. She was going to have to bite the bullet and step out into the light. Light was anathema to the superspy, but needs must when the Devil drives. She noted a push-button switch in the hallway as she edged out, but thought better of using it. Slowly, she leaned over the banister, wincing as it dug into her ribs, and looked down to the next level. There lay Augustine, motionless, at the foot of the flight, his head at an awkward angle. And lying beside him, a few feet away, was a gun.

***

'Don't take this the wrong way, but aren't you dead?' Martin said at last.

'Do I look dead to you?' asked Keith as he walked over to sit at the foot of Martin's bed.

Although his wounds seemed to have been cleaned, they were all still very much present. His right eye hung slightly lower than the left as he turned to offer Martin a proper look at his face. Martin was grateful for the dim light in the room as he looked at Keith's misshapen head.

'I don't know how to answer that without hurting your feelings.'

'I don't mind you being a doubting Thomas, but please don't stick your fingers in my wounds,' said Keith, gently patting the now-concave right side of his head.

'Does it hurt?'

'Not now, no. It did at the time.'

'I'll bet. Bloody hell.'

'Don't worry about it,' said Keith, popping his roaming right eye back up into its socket with his index finger as casually as one might push a pair of spectacles up the bridge of one's nose. 'What's done is done. I'm not planning on sticking around for long anyway. This'll do.'

'So… are you a zombie now?'

Keith took a moment to consider this.

'If that helps. I am pretty much reanimating a corpse here, I guess.'

'OK. As long as I know.'

Martin thought about just how OK this wasn't, while Keith stared impassively at his colleague's eyes darting left and right.

'I'm not going to eat your brain,' he said at last, breaking what had become an uncomfortable silence.

'Right. Good,' Martin responded immediately, breathing out.

'Barely a snack there anyway.'

Martin showed the zombie software developer his middle finger.

'Well, really,' Keith continued, 'I'm a little insulted that you were my replacement. I'd have thought they would send Will, at least.'

'Thanks very much. I'm not too happy to be here, either.'

'I'm sorry, but come on, though. An analyst? You've got to admit, that's not right.'

'It was Ray's choice. They just wanted *anyone*, OK? I don't think anybody up here cared about your coding skills.'

This gave Keith pause for thought.

'Fair enough,' he said at last. 'I was never really clear on what they were trying to achieve up here anyway.'

'I'm sorry for speaking ill of the dead,' said Martin, and Keith seemed to brighten up a bit, insofar as a corpse could do so.

'Well quite. Show some bloody respect.'

Martin still wasn't a hundred percent certain that he wasn't asleep, but he thought he was handling the situation fairly well, all things considered.

'So what made you want to crucify yourself? I mean, Augustine told us his story, but I have to say, it didn't make me reach for the nails.'

'I still can't believe they just took that as read.' Keith shook his head and smiled, and his eye drooped a little again. 'They haven't the faintest idea what's going on here, Martin. They're children.'

'They seemed fairly clued-up to me. Have you seen their lab? Have you seen Manny?'

'Manny?' Keith tutted. 'You see? *This* is why I wouldn't bother eating your brain.'

'You're not impressed by Manny, then? Not impressed by the blurry man-shaped mirror with the booming voice?'

Keith shot Martin a sneer that caused his eye to drop out of its socket entirely. He cursed quietly as he pushed it back in.

'Of course I'm impressed by Manny. It's amazing. But they didn't make Manny, they just think they did. If you've seen their lab, surely you can see how ludicrous the idea is. They're dreaming, Martin.'

'Marlowe did say they'd forgotten how they did it.'

Keith performed what appeared to be a grotesquely exaggerated wink, and Martin was unable to mask his concern.

'Sorry. That was supposed to be a blink. Some of my face isn't working, as you can probably imagine,' explained Keith. 'Ah well, at the end of the day, I had to get out of here somehow. Personally, I wouldn't have used a hammer. This eye thing is annoying. Still, it's just possible he didn't know I was coming back.'

'Jesus.'

'No, but I understand the confusion,' said Keith, holding up his left hand to show the hole through his wrist.

'Oh please. Put it away,' pleaded Martin, turning his head away.

'Sorry. I didn't think you were the squeamish type. Destot's space, that's called,' said Keith, tapping proudly at the hole. 'Bones all around it. Supports your weight brilliantly. Some people would go for the palm. Amateurs. Still no idea why he did it at all, but I suppose I should be grateful for having the use of the hand.'

'So Manny did this to you?'

'One of them did. I suppose he thought he was doing me a favour. I did want to get back.'

'Back to what, the mothership?'

'I didn't belong in this body. He pulled me out.'

'What do you mean he pulled you out? You mean your soul, or something?'

'I'm going to go with *animus*. Slightly less loaded.'

Martin rolled his eyes. Keith had become considerably more hifalutin, postmortem.

'So what was that like? Having your anus pulled out?'

'Well,' said Keith, refusing to be baited, 'you know that feeling you get sometimes when you're drifting off to sleep and you suddenly feel like you've just been dropped on the bed?'

'Yeah. Yes, I do,' admitted Martin. 'I'll never get used to that. Someone told me once it means your heart stopped for a minute.'

'Well, imagine having that dropping feeling long enough to get used to it.'

'How is your brain still working? If you don't mind me asking.'

'Have a look.'

Keith turned so that Martin could look directly into the hole in his skull. Martin largely declined this offer, choosing instead to pull a disgusted face. He couldn't help taking a couple of little peeks though, just to see whether anything was moving in there, but everything seemed still.

'Sorry,' said Martin.

'Don't worry about it. I'm not using much of it any more. Motor functions, audio and visual, that's about it. Think of this body like an avatar.' Keith gave him a moment to consider this before helpfully adding, 'or puppet, if you like.'

'Piss off, I know what an avatar is.'

'They really should have sent Will.'

'I truly wish they had. So you're somewhere else right now? Your *animus*, I mean.' Martin air-quoted the word 'animus' as he wasn't ready to say it without some evidence of sarcasm.

'I am,' said Keith. He paused momentarily before adding, to himself as much as to Martin, 'Consciousness. I should have just said consciousness.'

Martin stroked his chin.

'So where did you go? Where was that important to get to, that it was worth dying for?'

'Birmingham,' said Keith.

***

Jem knocked again. She could hear movement and some mumbling coming from behind the door. Clearly she had woken him, and she briefly felt bad about this until she remembered that the drunken man she had just stolen from could wake up at any moment. Assuming, of course, that he wasn't dead. She was fairly sure that he hadn't been dead.

'Just a second,' she heard Martin say.

She was trying to peer through the small pane of safety glass in the window of the door, but all she could make out was darkness, and even that was wobbly.

'Come on,' she hissed, hopping from foot to foot and waggling the door handle. She would give him a count of three, and then she was going in regardless.

'Enter,' boomed Martin in his best headmaster voice, and Jem hurried in, shutting the door behind her.

Martin was lying on his bed, hands around the back of his head, with an odd look on his face.

112

'Are you all right?' asked Jem.

'Nothing. Fine. What?'

'You look like you're having a bowel movement.'

'What? *Nonchalance*. This is nonchalance,' Martin pleaded.

'Whatever,' said Jem, sitting down at the foot of the bed, careful to adjust the position of the item nestling in the pocket of her complimentary kimono as she did so.

'Hello,' said Martin, pulling one hand from behind his head for a little wave.

'Hello.'

'Well, here we are then.'

'Martin?'

'That's me.'

'I don't think I want to be alone tonight after all.'

'Bit smothering,' said Martin with as aloof a face as he could muster, 'but I suppose I could indulge you, under the circumstances.'

After play-acting being taken aback, Jem replied, with a glower, 'Oh, if I smother you, you'll stay smothered, boy. You'd *better* bloody indulge me.'

Martin smiled, but then remembered something that might prove to be a dealbreaker in this situation, and sighed.

'Hold that thought. In the interests of full disclosure, I should probably tell you something first.'

Jem drew back.

'I've got something too, but you go first,' she suggested, immediately imagining what awful experiments and/or STD tests might have been done in the laboratory down the corridor during the previous day.

'There's a zombie under my bed.'

Jem sputtered and pulled her feet up onto the bed, in mock horror.

'Save me,' she said, in her best southern belle accent, clutching her toes.

Martin met her gaze with a blank face and slowly nodded. Jem's smile faltered, and she dipped her head towards the floor to investigate. The first look was tentative and achieved little. She came back up with a slight giggle and clutched her forehead to steady herself from the rush

113

of blood. Then cautiously she leaned down again. She stayed down a couple of seconds longer this time, and gave her eyes a chance to adjust. This time she saw it. She pulled her head back up in panic.

'Jesus Christ, Martin, why have you got a corpse?' Her mind raced. Was this Augustine, back for his gun already? No. No, he almost definitely hadn't been dead, and even if he was, how could he have gotten there ahead of her? And what kind of question was that to be asking herself?

'It's Keith,' said Martin, keenly aware that this was no explanation.

'Keith.' She gave herself a moment to gather her thoughts. 'Why have you got Keith's body in here?'

'Well, you'd turned me down...'

'And why is it naked?' Jem continued her perfectly reasonable line of questioning.

Martin's face froze. In all the excitement of meeting a zombie and trying not to stare at its wounds, it hadn't even registered that it was a nude zombie. He knelt down and peered under the bed for confirmation. He came back up with a perturbed look and sat back.

'Why haven't you got any clothes on, Keith?' said Martin, in as carefree a tone as he could muster.

No response came from below. Jem hugged her legs and squinted at Martin in disbelief.

'And why are you talking to it?' became Jem's follow-up question.

'Keith, come out now, mate. She's seen you.'

No response.

Jem realised her eyebrows could go even higher, and raised them accordingly, maintaining a constant glare at Martin.

'He's just being a dick,' was the best he could manage.

The glare continued. If time wasn't a factor, she would happily have plucked both eyebrows and drawn them back on even further up her head.

'God damn it,' sighed Martin.

He got off the bed and onto his hands and knees. He reached under the bed, grabbed Keith's arm and pulled, saying, 'Come on Keith. Game's over.'

There was no cooperation from Keith, and the arm just flapped back down.

'For fuck's sake.'

Martin dragged Keith's dead weight out from under the bed by his wrist, getting to his feet and backing up as he did so. Keith's head thudded against the leg of the bed and bent slightly sideways during what was otherwise a fairly fluid movement. Martin dropped Keith's arm and looked down at the motionless body of his colleague. Jem dismounted the bed and tiptoed over to Martin. She gripped his arm as they both surveyed the scene.

'Jesus, Martin.'

'I know what this looks like,' said Martin. He paused briefly before adding, 'What does this look like?'

'Look what you've done to his poor wrist. And his head,' said Jem, putting a hand over her mouth as she caught her first glimpses of Keith's punctured wrist and brain, and his unnaturally relaxed eye.

'He was already like that when he got here.'

'But *why* is he here, Martin?'

'Look, I didn't undress a body and drag it back to my room, if that's what you're thinking. He walked in. He walked in like that, and we had a chat. Then you knocked on the door and he hid under the bed. Simple as that.'

'Well, I knew there'd be a perfectly reasonable explanation.'

Martin nudged Keith's torso cautiously with his foot.

'Keith.'

He gave it a slightly harder push.

'Keith.'

This time a proper stamp with his heel.

'Keith.'

'MARTIN,' said Jem, and he became aware that she was squeezing his arm. 'Show some bloody respect.'

He stopped, although in his mind he had on his army surplus boots from home, and was now kicking merrily away.

'Sorry. I'm sorry,' he said, 'but he really was walking and talking before you came in.'

'Well he's not doing much now.'

'No.'

The pair of them stood in silence for a moment with their thoughts, gazing at the distressed corpse before them. Martin's thoughts were largely of jumping up and down on it.

'I can help you put him back,' said Jem eventually. She would be the supportive partner, she had determined. They would get through this unpleasantness together, and Martin's proclivities, whatever they were, could be worked through in therapy. Or never spoken of again, for preference. Being left for a man, she could possibly laugh off at dinner parties as a funny 'typical me' story in ten or twenty years. If said man was also rotting, however, that might be pushing things.

Martin smacked his forehead with his palm.

'I didn't take him from anywhere,' he said quietly, still holding his head.

'OK. All right. But if you *had*, where do you think you might have found him?'

Martin turned to look at Jem, speechless.

'You know, hypothetically,' she said, wearing her best helpful face, and adding, 'like in that *O.J.Simpson* book.'

Martin shook his head.

'Well, he can't stay here, can he?' said Jem, throwing up her hands in despair.

Then Keith sat up, and Jem's hands came rapidly down again, to muffle the piercing shriek that she found to be emanating unbidden from her mouth.

'Sorry,' said Keith, turning to look at Martin. 'I went to the toilet.'

'You dirty bastard,' said Martin, breathing out in relief.

Jem was gripping Martin's arm and saying 'shit' repeatedly.

'Oh, I don't mean under your bed,' said Keith, to clarify matters. 'I left the body for a bit while it wasn't going to be doing anything. This is tiring.'

'What's he talking about?' managed Jem, as she felt her heart's lurching bids for freedom begin to subside.

'Keith's an avatar now,' said Martin.

'Oh. Is that right?'

'Oh yes.'

'Not a zombie, then.'

116

'If that helps,' said Keith, unhelpfully.

'Why aren't you wearing any clothes, you freak?' asked Martin in an accusatory tone.

'One of them must have cleaned me,' Keith thought out loud as he looked down at himself. 'I hope it was Denver. Anyway, I'm working a corpse here. It didn't even cross my mind to dress it up.'

'Fair point,' said Martin, uncertain whether it really was a fair point, without any appropriate reference.

'Shit,' murmured Jem again.

'So,' said Martin, 'what was under my bed was absolutely a zombie, and he's just forgotten his clothes because he's a massive pervert, not me. I trust this witch trial is at an end.'

'I need to sit down,' Jem announced, and did so.

Keith patiently took her through everything that he had previously explained to Martin, who interjected occasionally with quips he hadn't had the presence of mind to produce the first time around.

***

This was all quite a lot to take in for one night. Jem sat in stunned silence for some time, before remembering the heavy item she was cradling in her lap, hidden in the pocket of her kimono. It wasn't a wandering animus, but it was surely still noteworthy.

'I've got a piece,' she announced.

'Charming. Well, you know where it is,' said Martin.

Jem paused only briefly, accustomed as she was to the workings of Martin's mind.

'No, I don't need a *piss*, you cloth-eared arsehole. I've got a *piece*. A *gun.*'

She gingerly drew the small pistol from her pocket and placed it on the bed between them. Martin's head bobbed a few times as he looked from gun to girlfriend and back again.

'Why have you got that then?' he asked. He was trying to sound matter-of-fact, but his words were coming out a little squeakily.

'Augustine left it lying around. He was completely pissed, so I took it.'

'Right. Why?'

'Because he's a lunatic, Martin. You saw him today. He's not all there. And now he's hammered too. No offence, Keith.'

Martin was leaning forward, pulling a face that betrayed a brave struggle with comprehension. Jem puffed in exasperation.

'Look, I just thought it might be nicer for everyone if the drunk mentalist wandering around in nothing but an open bathrobe wasn't armed. So sue me.'

'Open?'

'That's what we're focusing on? Yes, open.'

Martin paused for a moment.

'Could you see his…'

'Oh, yes.'

'I see.'

'Quite the night of it I'm having,' she said, nodding across at Keith, still sat upright on the floor.

'Dead ones don't count,' said Martin.

He threw a pillow into Keith's lap, all the same. Keith didn't react.

'I can't believe you've been looking at Augustine's cock,' said Martin, turning back to Jem.

'Are you jealous?'

'No. I didn't want to see it.'

'Oh, you're bigger. All right? Can we move on?' said Jem, rolling her eyes.

'I wasn't asking,' said Martin with a fake cough and a grin. 'It's what you do with it, anyway.'

'So I hear.'

'He *wasn't* doing anything with it, was he?'

'I wouldn't be the least bit surprised, Martin,' said Jem, tapping on the gun from which the conversation was rapidly drifting.

'So, basically, what you're saying is, you saw a pissed, wanking fruitcake and you thought you'd just nick that off him.'

'That's about the size of it.'

'And you don't think he's going to come looking for it.'

'Well, if he does, we have a gun, don't we?'

'Apparently so. Is it loaded?'

Jem looked down at the small pistol.

'There's no spinning thing on it,' she observed. 'I don't know. Check.'

'Is the safety on?' asked Martin, not keen to pick it up.

'I don't know,' said Jem, adding after a moment's consideration, 'shit, Martin, I've had that in my pocket. I could have blown bits off myself.'

'Your best bits, too.'

'Thanks,' she said, punching him hard in the thigh. 'Really flattering. Twat. How do you put the safety on?'

Martin rubbed his leg and stared at the gun.

'I don't know.'

'Oh, for God's sake.'

'What? I'm an analyst. There's very little gunplay.'

'Well, you said you wanted a gun, and I got you a gun. Ingrate.' Jem gritted her teeth.

'Did I? So I did. In that case, I love it. Thanks, genie.'

'I can tell you don't really love it,' Jem pouted. 'Go on, take it back and exchange it for some stupid game instead. I don't care.'

'Well, if you've kept the receipt.'

'You haven't even touched it, you little bitch,' Jem taunted him. 'Go on, it won't bite.'

'You're still talking about the gun, right?'

'Pick up the gun,' she whispered, narrowing her eyes.

Martin considered the matter.

'I'm not sure I want my fingerprints on it. What if he's already used it? You know, on people?'

'Then we definitely need it. Keith, do you know anything about guns?'

Keith was still sitting quietly on the floor, his legs out in front of him. Though they now supported a pillow, they hadn't shifted from where they had been left when Martin had dragged him out from under the bed. No response or movement came from him.

'Not again,' said Jem.

'Please let me kick him properly this time,' pleaded Martin.

'He only went for a wee a few minutes ago. His bladder's smaller than mine.'

'I don't really get it. He reckons he's in Birmingham, pissing all over the place,' said Martin, shaking his head. 'Mind you, I've never been dead, so what do I know?'

'It's not the afterlife I imagined,' Jem agreed. 'What's Birmingham, anyway? Is that like paradise, or something?'

Martin shrugged.

They looked at Keith, his milky eyes wide open, pupils fixed and faded.

'Is he still looking at us? I can't tell,' whispered Jem.

'It's hard to say. His eyes are pointing in different directions.'

'What if he doesn't come back this time?'

'We go and get Manny, I guess. He can dispose of his own victims.'

They found it increasingly difficult to take their eyes off the lifeless, broken body of the former database engine specialist. Jem reached for Martin's hand.

'I've never had someone I properly know die before,' she whispered.

Martin took Jem's hand in his, careful to avoid brushing the gun sat between them, and there they sat, in quiet contemplation.

'Is that a mousegun?' said Keith, and Jem and Martin both jumped.

'Jesus,' said Jem, catching her breath.

'Stop doing that,' pleaded Martin, clutching his chest. 'Next time, we're burying you.'

Jem coughed and pulled the blanket around herself.

'Sorry,' said Keith, getting to his knees to study the pistol. 'It *is*. These are great.'

'I should have known you'd be a *Soldier of Fortune* weirdo. It figures,' said Martin with a sigh.

'I used to go to a shooting range with my dad, as a boy. And I still hunt to eat now, sometimes. Or I did.'

'You've got a flat in the centre of town, haven't you?' Jem narrowed her eyes.

'I live by the sea, close to some woods. Let's not get into that now.'

'All right. Yes, please. Let's not,' she agreed, looking at him askance. 'And you know how to use one of these?'

'Oh yes.'

120

'To shoot mice?' Martin looked for some clarification.

'No, just targets,' said Keith, unfazed by the question.

'Small, living targets,' muttered Martin.

'I've got back into shooting in recent years. Rifles, though. Just hunting for food, you know. We try to be as self-sufficient as possible. I suppose I *am* a bit of a survivalist now.'

'Not a great one though, mate, with respect.'

Keith gave Martin what he hoped was a quizzical look.

'Not very good at surviving. You, know, being dead and all.'

'Martin,' Jem scolded him.

'Oh. No. This is all since then,' said Keith.

'Have a proper look,' said Jem, handing the pistol to the zombie, like it was the most natural thing in the world.

'It's a semi-automatic. Really nice and compact. I think they just call them mouseguns because it's a cute name for them,' explained Keith, fondling the mousegun.

'So, to be clear,' said Martin, 'my girlfriend has given you a semi.'

'You are such a twat,' declared Jem, shaking her head.

'This is loaded. Where did you get it?' asked Keith, still keenly focused on the small gun.

'It's Augustine's.'

'Really? Interesting. Does he know you have it?'

Jem hesitated.

'No,' she said at last. 'He doesn't.'

'Well, he's probably going to want it back. You should hide it. The suspended ceiling maybe?'

'That's actually a good idea,' said Martin, staring upwards. He struggled to his feet, the mattress bowing beneath him, and motioned to Keith for the weapon.

'Is the safety on?' he asked as Keith passed it to him.

'No, there's no safety on those,' said Keith. 'Long trigger pull, though.'

'Bloody hell,' whispered Jem to herself, looking down at her lap. 'Be careful, Martin.'

'Should I?' said Martin, with more than a hint of sarcasm.

Standing on the bed, he was easily able to reach high enough to push up a ceiling tile and rest the gun carefully on the next one along. He gently lowered the tile back into position and smiled smugly at Jem and Keith.

'Safe as houses,' he said, stepping down from the bed and patting his hands together in recognition of a job well done.

Then he noticed the dust and debris that now littered his bed, tutted, and brushed it briskly onto the floor.

'That should be fine,' said Keith. 'I mean, with the right equipment, that would take about five seconds to find, but he wouldn't know how to use it.'

'If you say so,' said Jem, still unsure.

'Right,' said Keith. 'I should be off. Things to do.'

'You're pretty busy for a corpse,' noted Martin. 'What are we supposed to do?'

'For now, just do what they tell you. Don't worry, it's all in hand. Let it play out.'

Keith performed another grim-looking wink. Jem shot Martin a troubled look.

'Don't worry, it's supposed to be a blink,' Martin reassured her, blinking demonstratively as he spoke.

'No,' said Keith. 'That one was a wink. To set you at ease.'

'Oh. Well thank you then, Keith,' said Jem queasily, and hoping to ensure that it didn't happen again, she nodded, adding, 'mission accomplished.'

'Yeah, thanks for that, mate,' Martin agreed.

'All right, I'll let you get some rest, and take this body back to where Manny stashed it,' said Keith, getting to his feet and heading for the door. 'Don't worry, everything is going to be fine.'

Pausing briefly to poke his head into the corridor and listen, he waved to his former workmates and headed off, closing the door quietly behind himself.

'I'll bet he *did* shoot mice,' said Martin.

'Oh, stop it,' Jem chided him.

'Well, I mean. He's definitely the type. All those tattoos. What with him *and* Will, it's a wonder the lot of us haven't been massacred before now.'

122

'Will *is* a worry,' Jem had to admit. 'Keith's alright though, isn't he? Deep down? He's our friend. Our special dead friend.'

Martin furrowed his brow.

'Hey, you know you were saying you'd never had someone die?'

Jem nodded.

'Well, I have. A mate gassed himself in his garage. I *think*. I think that's what happened.'

'Sorry, sweet. Were you close?'

'Well, here's the thing. I know we were. But I can't remember when, or where.'

'Oh.'

Jem was uncertain what to say.

'I can't even remember his bloody name. All I know is what happened to him, and that he was a top bloke. Oh, and I think he had a weird accent. Can't remember where he was from, though. It's like everything else is gone. Do you think I'm going gaga?'

Jem took his head in her hands and kissed his brow.

'There, there, brain. No. I'm missing things too, I know I am,' she reassured him. 'It's this place. Come on, now. There's enough weirdness here to be getting on with.'

Martin stared up at the ceiling tile that was now supporting a firearm.

'Is that really safe?' he wondered out loud.

'Keith the wonder corpse seems to think so,' said Jem after a yawn. 'Try not to think about it now. We should really get some sleep.'

After they had pushed a desk in front of the door and cuddled up, Martin told Jem about his non-existent hamster, Fluffy, and together they thought of all the awful things that weren't happening to it, until they drifted off.

FRIDAY

DELETE

10

CHOP CHOP

Thom waited patiently for Ollii to get out of the car before saying 'Good mornings Olive, a-gah-gah-gah-gah-gah,' in his best Popeye voice. The impression was poor, and Ollii's expression was one of pity.

'Are you alright? Do you need me to call someone?' he replied, after a respectful period of silence had passed.

'I'll live. Nice night with the Janicide, mate?'

'My evening with Janice was just fine, thanks, if it's any of your concern.'

'She didn't forget anything major this time?'

'What you on about?'

'She forgot something pretty big last time,' Thom snorted.

'What?'

Ollii was nonplussed. Thom's face dropped, and he stood staring into space, frowning.

'Seriously, are you having a stroke, or something? Should I be getting help?' asked an unconcerned Ollii.

'Shit. Shit, now *I* don't remember. That's weird. It was something stupendous, anyway.'

'Sounds it.'

Thom continued to be troubled by the missing memory of the missing memory.

'Oh my God, it was something massive, I swear.'

Ollii shook his head and they both headed towards the office.

'Hey, I've got a picture of her, if you want to see,' he said, delving into his pocket for his phone.

Thom cheered up at once.

'There's literally nothing I'd like more.'

They paused at the door as Ollii ran his finger repeatedly across the screen of his phone, occasionally eyeing Thom suspiciously and making a great play of shuffling through the many photos he didn't want him to see. Thom stamped his feet, trying to keep warm.

'There. Pretty special, eh?' Ollii passed his phone to Thom with pride, having first locked the screen to make it clear that he wasn't inviting him to flip through his entire album, as many people were wont to do in these situations.

'She looks like a keeper,' declared Thom.

'Cheers, mate.'

'No, I mean she has massive hands,' said Thom, passing the phone back with a grin.

'Dick.'

Thom spluttered with laughter as he tapped in the key code and pushed open one of the big glass doors, deeply pleased with himself. His laughter quickly mutated into a fit of coughing.

'Choke, you bastard,' said Ollii, gleefully.

As Thom cleared his throat, they both stopped in the hallway to wave at Tracy Ireland, in mid-call at reception. She winked in acknowledgement.

Ollii peered in through the glass door at the ground floor, past Tracy and down the corridor.

'Have you seen much of Ian and Colin lately?' he asked Thom, as he watched several fellow workers wandering between offices carrying mugs. Through the soundproof glass he could see a hive of displacement activity silently making itself look busy.

'Ian was at the pub last Tuesday lunch. Colin I've not seen for weeks. I've heard him though, obviously,' said Thom.

'Obviously. Last Tuesday? Where was I?'

'You were off with that stomach bug, remember?'

'Oh yeah,' said Ollii thoughtfully. 'Nasty business.'

'Bullshitter,' grinned Thom. 'You said you had a migraine.'

128

'What? Oh, yeah, yeah. Sat in the dark all day, I was.'

Thom was shaking his head and smiling.

'Nah, you *did* say stomach bug,' he revealed. 'You cave too easily under questioning, mate. You want to shape yourself.'

'Twat.'

Thom leaned towards the staircase, but Ollii didn't move from the doorway.

'Are we doing some work today, then?' said Thom, pointing his thumb up the stairs.

'We should get them down the pub this lunchtime. Get a decent gathering. Remember how big our pub posse used to be?'

'Yeah. It used to be a complete nightmare waiting to get served.'

Ollii turned away from the glass door and towards Thom, a puzzled look on his face.

'What?' said Thom.

'Who *were* all those people?' asked Ollii.

Thom dismounted the staircase and stood stroking his chin, now looking equally confused.

'Well, there was Lee, who used to sit across from Starwars.'

'Oh yeah, Lee,' said Ollii, now also having a good chin-stroke. 'He buggered off to America, didn't he? To some course at MIT?'

'Yeah. Lee majors in robotics now.'

'Nice. Oh, there was Kevin.'

''Zero degrees' Kevin?'

'Yeah, that's what reminded me. Was anything on that guy's CV true?'

'I don't reckon. What happened to him, anyway?'

'I thought he failed upwards. Got kicked upstairs.'

'What do you mean?'

'You know, when it's not easy to sack someone, and you recommend them for promotion instead, to get them out of your way.'

'That explains a lot. Or it would, if there was anyone actually working on the floors above us.'

'Oh yeah. Huh.' Ollii paused, bemused. 'Don't know what made me think that. Must've been sacked, then. Who else?'

They stood for a moment, rubbing their chins, looking blankly over one another's shoulders.

'Was there someone from Sales?' hazarded Thom.

'Obviously, but they never sat with us.'

'Not from Accounts.'

They both snorted.

'Well,' Thom sighed, 'if you don't think about it, they'll probably all come flooding back. Come on, slacker.'

He started back up the stairs, and this time Ollii reluctantly followed. They stopped once more on the landing outside their floor, while Thom tapped at the keypad. The door buzzed and he pushed it open with his foot. He turned to see his workmate motionless once more, staring up the next flight of stairs, frowning, his mouth agape.

'What now?' asked Thom, impatiently.

'Nothing,' said Ollii, after a time, and they headed on into the office.

'For fuck's sake,' muttered Thom, as the door swung shut behind them.

***

Jeremy Starwars sat at his desk, feeling faint and cursing his fortune. Not only had he not passed peacefully away during what little sleep he had managed to have, but he had singularly failed to be involved in a multiple vehicle collision on his way to work. Up until the point at which he had entered the building, calling in sick had seemed such a blatant act of dereliction as to simply not be an option, but now he sat imagining that phone conversation with Ray, during which he would likely have been offered summary dismissal, in a far more positive light; he would at least have been at home. Instead, he was there in the office. He was actually there, and in a few short hours he would have no alternative but to demonstrate nothing to his peers, his project manager, and his CEO. There would be anger, and incredulity, and perhaps some exasperated laughter. All the respect that his workmates had once had, that he had built up when he still had some small understanding of what he was doing, would evaporate in an instant. And then he would be invited to leave the premises.

People might throw things as he walked away. Most of the team probably had rotten fruit in their desks, purchased in weeks gone by during well-intentioned but ultimately doomed bids to cut down on the mid-morning crisps and somehow live forever as a result. Jeremy had certainly made several such bids, and the crinkled, blackened, furry proof was right there, in his top drawer. Jeremy pulled the drawer open, and surveyed the contents. When the time inevitably came to empty out his desk in disgrace that afternoon, there was little there that he would actually want to take home with him. The plastic surprise tat from around a hundred chocolate eggs, of course he would keep. The ironically collected bubble gum trading cards depicting characters from Australian soap operas were also too important to leave behind. Were he to be leaving under happier circumstances, he would probably be sorting through both these collections and leaving the swaps, but what with the atmosphere of extreme enmity, name-calling and perhaps even spitting that he was imagining, that would probably be inappropriate. Particularly after all the anticipated questions along the lines of 'what have you been *doing* all this time' had been asked. No, he would simply scoop everything into a plastic bag, along with the assorted copper change, of which there must have been at least a fiver's worth. Not the decaying fruit, though; he would probably leave that. He suspected that some of it might have become quite strongly adhered to the bottom of the drawer by now, in any case.

He closed the top drawer, and slid open the deeper one beneath. It was the work of a moment for Jeremy to establish that this contained nothing but project folders and the minutes from hundreds of meetings. The minutes had some nostalgic value, but only when viewed in the company of the workmates who, he was certain, would shortly want nothing more to do with him. The drawer was also the overnight resting place for his enormous headphones, but those were currently on his head, silently warming his ears and cheeks. He pushed the drawer shut once more.

Turning to the surface of the desk itself, there were three browning apples that had been nearly ready to go in the drawer and be forgotten about, and a *Dilbert* desk calendar. He determined that he would take the latter; there were many days left in the year, and even allowing for the possibility that he would never again fool someone into employing him, he did at least have a desk of sorts at home upon which it could sit.

Jeremy imagined that it would take no more than five minutes for him to collect these belongings and be on his way, provided he wasn't being pushed and kicked as he did so.

None of this was getting his code-tidying done, or indeed the weeks of non-existent work that needed tidying. Jeremy looked at the clock in the corner of his screen and saw that half an hour of the morning was already gone. Soon, Ray would be coming over to ask if he was all ready for the demonstration again. He picked up his mug and headed off to get another coffee and hide in the kitchen for a bit.

He hefted the mug. He would probably keep that, too.

11

BUSY BUSY

Jeremy Starwars realised with creeping horror that he had just spent twenty minutes deciding upon a comfortable seating position. He felt more relaxed, or at least marginally less panicked, with his feet up on the base unit of his computer. However, this meant having his knees pressed against the underside of his desk, or bending his legs awkwardly and painfully to one side. This had made little sense to Jeremy, who distinctly remembered being able to cope with sitting in a chair on thousands of previous occasions. There were many skills he felt he could struggle through life without, but sitting down was most definitely not one of them. He had stood up several times and attempted to adjust his seat using its baffling array of levers, but the base would go no lower, and altering the angle of the back support just caused it to dig into his ribs. Finally he had wheeled himself backwards until his legs were straight, and he had sighed with relief. Then he had discovered that he could no longer reach his keyboard, his mouse, or, more importantly, his coffee mug.

'Oh, for fuck's sake,' he had said as he stretched forward in vain with both arms.

'Problem, Mister Starwars?' Ray had enquired from across the room.

'Nothing. Slow,' Jeremy had responded, thinking on his feet even whilst almost horizontal. 'The compiler's slow. This build's taking ages.'

Complaining about the available tools was a reasonably good way to quickly end the conversation, as there was little to be said on the matter; machines and software were updated according to the vagaries of budgetary surpluses, rather than actual need. Jeremy watched Ray shrug and return to whatever it was he did during office hours. The truth, so rarely an option in exchanges with Ray, was definitely not applicable here. 'My work is too far away' was certainly not a complaint that would have sat well with Jeremy's project manager.

With some degree of resignation, and the option of actual resignation ever-present in his mind, Jeremy Starwars had returned his feet to the ground and pulled himself forward, adopting the straight-backed posture that experts in ergonomics had erroneously insisted was best for the spine. His head had felt heavier in this position, like a concrete ball teetering on a spike. *This must be what full concentration is supposed to feel like*, he had told himself. *This is how one accomplishes things.*

Now he sat, staring in disbelief at the clock in the corner of his screen. It was break time already. Most of them were many years out of school, and there was no playground to go to, but 'break time' was still what they called their daily midmorning outing to the nearby corner shop.

'Shop shop shop,' said Robert Smith, now stood beside Jeremy in his frock coat, rapidly tapping one foot like a rabbit alerting others to a circling hawk.

Jeremy turned to look at him, and saw, behind him, the two testers getting their coats on. Every fibre in the being of Jeremy Starwars told him to get up and join them. He hadn't missed a shop trip in a very long time, barring illnesses real, imagined or invented, and he feared the consequences for his sanity if he did so now. The visit to the shop broke the morning up perfectly into acceptably proportioned periods of inactivity. Not to go now would leave little excuse for not achieving something, but unfortunately, today, achieve something he must. Every minute lost now, he would surely regret come the afternoon, as he stood speechless in front of a blank whiteboard.

'Can't. Too much on,' said Jeremy Starwars, the words sticking in his throat.

'Such a keener,' said Robert dismissively, turning then to join Thom and Ollii.

Jeremy watched sadly as they sauntered off. Their jeans and trainers reminded him that it was Casual Friday. For employees who had joined more recently, this held little meaning, as the office dress code had long since been relaxed, but old-timers like Jeremy would always make a special effort to be extra scruffy on a Friday. Not today, though. Today Jeremy was dressed like a man intending to stand in front of management and demonstrate nothing. He was in his best suit trousers and a freshly unwrapped shirt, which had probably been quite 'in' when it had been purchased for him by his mother several Christmases ago. His feet were tightly bound within his least comfortable but shiniest shoes, and he was almost overcome with grief at the unfairness of it all.

He took a swig of coffee, realised that it had gone cold, and went off to the kitchen, where he boiled the kettle several times while staring out of the window. He thought about what exciting fire-damaged or factory-returned products might be in the window of the small electronics shop that lay on the route to the general store. He wondered whether any new magazines might be on the racks. Several very similar periodicals were always in stock, with names like *Have a Rest*, *Them's the Breaks* and *Tittle-Tattle*, and each would feature exciting and inspiring headline stories such as 'I married my grandmother's rapist', or 'a fifty pound growth brought us together'. Each magazine would also have at least one example of what Jeremy and his colleagues termed 'grief porn' emblazoned joyously on its cover, with numerous exclamation marks. This would normally relate to a dead or at the very least decidedly moribund baby, or a winning lottery ticket lost in a house fire. Every editor seemed to use the same modelling agency, and as a consequence the same faces would appear again and again, marrying rapist after rapist, and giving birth to a seemingly endless stream of horrifically deformed children. Jeremy thought about the laughter he was missing as everyone gathered around and pointed at the cheerful, brightly coloured display of all these examples of desperate misfortune and terrifyingly poor judgement. Then he thought about how everyone would shuffle along the aisle to the refrigerated section, with its selection of sandwiches and pastry-based products, some of which would reliably be several days beyond their use-by dates. The record stood at over a month. At this point, Jeremy realised with some dismay that as well as foregoing his mid-morning snacks, he would now have no sandwiches for lunchtime. He put an extra sugar in his coffee, hoping that it would help tide him over.

By the time Jeremy Starwars returned to his desk, everyone was already back from the shop, enjoying their crisps and playing with the small plastic novelty items that had come with their chocolate eggs.

***

Between the gaps in the open blinds Jem could see Augustine through the boardroom's glass wall, sat slumped forward with his head face down on the table. The room was dark, the roller blinds on the windows still being down. She was uncertain as to whether his presence there proved him to have survived his fall the previous night, or whether he had simply been found and dumped in there by way of temporary storage. These people did, after all, seem to be in the habit of leaving corpses lying around. She squinted, straining to detect any sign of breathing in the dim light. Hearing Marlowe approaching, she quickly span to face him, attempting to defuse any potential accusations of snooping with a look of concern.

'Do you think he's alright?' she asked. 'He looks a bit ill.'

'I wouldn't worry yourself on his account, Miss Pepper. He's pretty much indestructible. Do you mind going and playing somewhere else for a bit?'

'Of course,' she said, and ambled off as slowly as she thought she could get away with, hands linked behind her back like some folk memory of a patrolling policeman. Looking over her shoulder from halfway across the lab, she saw that Marlowe had already gone into the boardroom and closed the blinds. Frustrated not to know for sure, she had to rely on the churning feeling in her stomach for information, and that was telling her that the previous owner of her gun was almost certainly still alive.

***

136

'Seriously? This early in the day?' Marlowe tutted as he walked along the boardroom's back wall, tugging open the roller blinds on the windows one by one.

Augustine hissed in response to the light suddenly flooding the room.

Marlowe bent to speak into the ear of his colleague, still face down on the table, eyes screwed tightly shut.

'Oh, we're a vampire now, are we?'

Detecting a barely audible response, Marlowe leaned in closer.

'Your what? Your brain? What about your brain?' he asked loudly.

'Migraine,' repeated Augustine weakly. 'Migraine, you insufferable prick.'

'Oh. Shame,' said Marlowe, smiling as he straightened up once more. He slapped him twice on the back and told him, 'it's a beautiful day.'

Whistling cheerfully, he began to make his way back around the large table.

'It's today,' murmured Augustine.

Marlowe stopped in his tracks and frowned.

'What?'

Augustine sighed. With a gargantuan effort and a huge accompanying groan, he managed to roll his head to rest on his right cheek. The cool pine effect surface offered him a brief soothing reward, and this new position granted his chin a little room for manoeuvre. With his eyes still tightly closed, he said again, 'it's today.'

'What is?'

Augustine swallowed loudly, and smacked his lips in preparation for further elucidation.

'It,' he said.

'Good. Helpful. Well, I've got a few things to be getting on with.'

'It's here. I can feel it. It's here, and it's going to happen today.'

'Shit. You're serious.'

'You need to lock this place down. Keep it here. Find it. So close to this all being over.'

Marlowe looked at the clock on the wall and saw to his dismay that it was just past one o'clock.

'We'll get right on that, then. Just as soon as everyone gets back from the pub.'

Augustine grunted and began to drool.

***

Having deliberately left the office slightly before the hour, in order to avoid getting stuck in a queue for drinks, Thom and Ollii had found themselves staring at an unmanned bar. Unmanned, but not undogged, as the owner's colossal German Shepherd, Simba, was stood on his hind legs, resting his front paws on the other side of the bar and staring back at them. Under different circumstances the two testers would have been banging coins against the brass fittings and shouting 'shop' to draw attention to their thirst, but Simba was as tall as either of them when stood rampant, and whenever either of them stepped too close, he would break off from panting to lick his lips in an unnerving manner. A further problem was presented by the fact that most of the brass fittings appeared to have been stolen since Thom and Ollii had last been in.

Leaving aside the ambiguous threat from the enormous dog, the Happy Cutter was, by and large, a relaxed and peaceful pub during daylight hours. This, and the fact that it was only around the corner, made it the local of choice for almost everyone from the office, and indeed from the industrial estate generally. After night fell, however, it was an entirely different proposition. 'You will never find a more wretched hive of scum and villainy,' as both Thom and Ollii were fond of saying in their best Alec Guinness voices.

A small crowd was stood nervously eyeing Simba by the time the landlady, Trisha, slouched into view. She rolled her eyes as she saw the queue.

'Gordon,' she screamed.

Simba emitted a small whine and dropped down behind the bar, disappearing but for an alert pair of ears.

'What?' came a muffled voice from somewhere else in the pub.

'People are waiting,' shouted Trisha.

She flashed said people a sympathetic 'what can you do' smile.

'I'm changing the barrels,' came the faint response.

Trisha tutted and asked the Sales team, who were by now stood to

138

the right of Thom and Ollii, what they fancied.

'For fuck's sake,' muttered Thom, as he watched them flout the 'first come' rule without a second thought.

The trio from Sales were served mercifully quickly, as they all opted for bottled beers. They then made their way to the pool table, where, after inserting some coins, they discovered that the cues and all the balls had been stolen. Another brief exchange with Trisha followed, during which she assured them that Gordon would be able to retrieve their money when he came back up from the cellar. Tim from Sales said that he didn't have any attachment to those particular coins, and that two pounds from the till would be perfectly acceptable, but this suggestion was met with a blank stare from Trisha, who simply restated that Gordon would be up from the cellar shortly.

'Now, what can I get you, lover?' she asked Thom.

The words were cheery enough, but they were coming out of a face that was clearly exhausted with the whole business.

There followed a sequence of beer requests that each resulted firstly in hissing taps, then more shouting at a distant Gordon, until finally Thom settled for a pint of foam that he would shortly discover tasted strongly of pipe cleaning fluid.

'I'll have the same,' said Ollii, now desperate to sit down.

'We had a turf war going on in here last night,' said Trisha matter-of-factly as she poured him his portion of soapy foam.

'Come again?'

'The Boot Boys and the Eagles, going at each other again,' she explained, with a shake of the head. 'They had machetes this time. I told them "not inside," but do they listen?'

Thom and Ollii came independently to the conclusion that no, they probably didn't listen.

'They'll get us closed down. Little toerags. Anyway, do you boys want to enter the raffle?' she asked, producing a tattered and yellowing book of cloakroom tickets. 'Help little Mutya get her operation?'

She gestured over her shoulder, in the general direction of a cork board filled with yellowing Polaroids of assorted red-eyed drunks. While Thom squinted at the board, searching for anything resembling a sick child, Ollii was already giving up and handing Trisha a pound coin.

'They're two quid,' she informed him. After a brief pause, he gave her another pound, and she tore him off a salmon-coloured number 375. The ticket appeared to bear the stains of much dog saliva.

Trisha and Ollii then both stared at Thom.

'Oh for… OK,' he said, reluctantly producing his wallet and acquiring number 376.

'Ooh, different colour,' Ollii breezily pointed out. 'Would you say that was blue, or green?'

Thom shrugged. 'Doesn't make much odds. I never win anything.'

'I think it might be cerulean. That's a colour, isn't it?'

'Are you broken, mate?' Thom shook his head as he stuffed the small paper rectangle into the special compartment of his wallet he reserved for receipts he fully intended to one day shred.

'Just trying to stay positive about what's happened to us.'

'It has been an ordeal,' Thom had to agree.

'Same for you, lover?' said Trisha, peering past them and grasping a pump handle.

'Yeah, I'll have some of that,' said Robert, having just arrived, and only now taking a first doubtful look at the froth his friends had just purchased.

By now the pipes had cleared, however, and he received a perfectly acceptable looking pint. He smiled smugly, as Thom and Ollii looked on in annoyance.

'Entering the raffle?' Trisha then asked Robert, hopefully. 'Help send little Keisha to Disneyland?'

'I thought she was having an operation,' said Thom.

'Oh, yeah. That's right,' Trisha confirmed. 'Poor love.'

'Mickey doing it, is he?'

She blinked at him.

'Sorry, I don't have any more cash on me,' said Robert.

He patted his thighs by way of demonstration. A distinct jingling sound came from the pockets, but the conviction with which he was patting seemed to win the day. She shrugged, and stowed the ticket book somewhere under the counter. Thom muttered something about wishing he had thought of that, and then they all watched Simba pad off down the hall with the book in his mouth, having immediately gathered it from its resting place.

'Bless him,' said Trisha.

'When's the draw, anyway?' Ollii asked her.

'The what, love?'

'The draw. For the raffle.'

'Oh. Oh right, yeah,' she said as she turned and left the bar, twirling her index finger as though just remembering something terribly important.

'Fuck's sake,' mumbled Thom. 'Don't even know what the prize is.'

'One pound, probably,' suggested Ollii.

Robert sniggered into his pint, and the testers followed him to a table. Ollii amused himself by lifting his feet in an exaggerated fashion from the disturbingly sticky carpet as he walked.

'I had a such a weird dream last night,' announced Robert Smith as he sat down.

Thom shook his head. 'Oh, here we go. You need to cut back on smoking that stuff.'

Ollii was more positive. 'I love these. Go on.'

'I don't remember what led up to it, but I had this tiny foetus, right, but with this adult sized brain.'

Ollii was already giggling.

'And I had it in a big envelope,' Robert continued, 'and I was trying to find somewhere to prop it up, you know, where the cat wouldn't get it.'

'You haven't got a cat.'

'I haven't got a foetus in an envelope. It's a dream, mate.'

'So you claim.'

They sipped their beers thoughtfully.

'So, what happened?' asked Ollii, with Thom immediately pulling a face and shaking his head at him.

'I don't know, I woke up. It's really frustrating. I can't stop thinking about it. I mean, where would you put it? It was a card-backed envelope, but it was really difficult to balance, you know? With the brain poking out the top and everything.'

'I'm sure.'

'I feel really bad for the little guy.'

'Well, you would, wouldn't you.'

'Jesus,' muttered Thom.

'Didn't there used to be a telly in here?' asked Robert, looking around.

'There were about ten a couple of months back,' said Ollii, pointing out several empty shelves.

'I'm surprised the pool table is still here,' said Thom.

'Innit,' agreed Ollii.

'Didn't the boys from Stores want to come and play today?' asked Thom, gazing at the oil slick rainbow in the unpleasant fluid in his glass.

'Oh bollocks, I knew I'd forgotten something,' said Ollii.

'You dipstick.'

'Oh well. They're not missing much. Hey Bob, do you remember who else used to be in our pub posse? There were loads, weren't there?'

'Were there?' said Robert doubtfully. 'We're missing a few today, I guess. Martin and Jem are upstairs, and Starwars is busy shitting himself in the meeting room. That guy is headed for the clock tower with the rifle any time now, I'm telling you.'

'At least he's not swearing at his work for not compiling this week.'

'Ha. Yeah. He's just given up pressing the button, I reckon.'

'Fucking build!' said Thom in a frantic-sounding high-pitched voice, imitating an irate Jeremy Starwars.

'Oh come on!' said Ollii, doing the same voice, and shaking his fists at the heavens gleefully.

After a brief giggle, he realised that he had become sidetracked, and resumed his line of questioning with Robert. 'Anyway, I meant the old posse. I'm talking about the guys who used to work here, like Lee.'

'Who?'

'Lee. Come on, you remember Lee.'

'You've lost me. Describe him.'

Ollii frowned.

'Thom, help me out. You remember Lee.'

Thom thought for a moment.

'Did he have a tache?' he finally ventured.

Ollii blinked a few times as he processed the question.

'Shit. I've no idea.'

Robert looked on, nonplussed.

'He sat opposite Starwars,' said Ollii, holding his hands up in defeat.

'Oh right,' said Robert, 'I remember somebody used to sit opposite Starwars, I think.'

'Well done. That's a lovely story. Yeah. Well, him, anyway.'

'Don't remember anything about him. Think I'd have remembered a tache, though.'

'He went to America.'

'Good for him,' said Robert, shrugging.

'Anyway, it doesn't matter. He's one of the ones we *do* remember.'

'Sounds like it,' said Robert, taking a long sip of his untainted beer.

'Fuck's sake. Who else did we get this morning?' asked Ollii, exasperated.

'I think that was it,' said Thom.

'There was about thirty of us some days,' said Ollii, shaking his head.

'There might have been thirty people, but I don't reckon we knew them. Just because they're in the same room as you, it doesn't make them your mates, mate,' reasoned Robert.

'D'you want any meat, blue eyes?'

A heavily perspiring man in a leather coat and bottle-bottom-thick glasses had come over to their table and was addressing Thom. Thom considered pretending not to have heard what was potentially some kind of sexual threat.

'D'you want any meat, blue eyes?' the stranger asked again, in a husky voice that seemed to be teetering on the edge of a large scale bronchial attack.

Thom glanced across at his workmates. Both were smiling, eyebrows raised, keenly awaiting his response. He turned to look at the man, who was thrusting a bulging carrier bag at him. Dark purple patches showing through the plastic suggested that he did indeed have a large quantity of raw meat to offer.

'No, you're all right mate. I've got sandwiches,' said Thom,

143

knowing full well that he had already eaten his sandwiches in the morning to allow more time for lunch.

The man paused to exhale slowly and loudly, fixing Thom with glaring eyes distorted and enlarged by his thick lenses. Thom met his gaze, determined not to betray his sandwich untruth with some careless telling movement of the pupils.

'Nice fried up, blue eyes. Lovely for your tea,' said the man at last.

'No. No, I couldn't, really.'

The man stood a moment longer, still breathing heavily, before sighing, and turning to leave.

'Sorry mate,' said Thom.

'Oh, I didn't realise he was your mate,' said Ollii, grinning, once he was sure the man was out of earshot.

'I thought it was his dad,' said Robert.

'You should have offered him a seat, Thom. We wouldn't have minded,' said Ollii.

Thom clutched his sides and mimed a belly laugh, sneering throughout, before dropping his arms limply to his sides and adopting a slack-jawed look of exasperation.

'What,' he enquired of his friends, 'the fuck?'

'That was special, even for this shithole,' observed Robert.

'Why didn't he ask you?' asked Thom. 'He didn't even go over to the Sales lot, did he?'

'I don't know, you tell us. He's your mate,' said Robert.

'Yeah, blue eyes,' added Ollii.

Thom looked over at Tim, Habib and Bronwen from Sales, sat next to the defunct pool table. Habib had clearly witnessed the attempted meat transaction, and smiled back, shrugging. Thom spent much of his remaining lunchtime worrying what quality he might have about himself that marked him out as a purchaser of dubiously sourced meat. Ollii and Robert made various suggestions as to the true contents of the plastic bag, ranging from roadkill to clinical waste, but Thom couldn't shift his paranoia at having been the only one asked.

The Sales team sat and watched as several more people came over and haplessly inserted coins into the pool table, not deeming it to be their place to intervene, and feeling progressively better about their own loss in the process. Trisha informed each of them in turn that the fate of their money was in the hands of the otherwise-engaged Gordon. Unfortunately, the barrels were clearly proving difficult or unwilling to change, as Gordon never did emerge from the cellar before everyone had to leave.

***

Jeremy stood in the meeting room, hunched over a projector, his back aching. The power lead was plugged in, the video lead was connected to the laptop he had diligently spent the majority of his lunch hour setting up and copying everything onto. The little black switch on the back was turned to the '1' position. What more did it want from him? As a last resort, he looked over at the wall to see that it was not switched on at the socket. He cursed whoever was responsible for this latest inconvenience as he walked over and bent down to rectify matters.

'Pow,' said Jeremy as he flicked the switch, imagining a freak power surge hurling him across the room, but no such merciful release was forthcoming.

He stood back up, and briefly saw silvery sparkles dance before his eyes. He fantasised that perhaps some kind of cerebral event might be about to put him out of his misery, but the lights quickly faded, leaving only the familiar combination of light-headedness and headache he always experienced when he hadn't eaten for a few hours. He checked the clock on the wall to see that he still had ten minutes before the nominal beginning of the end. Perhaps there was still time for him to at least lose consciousness. Jeremy began to consider pretending to have passed out. He pictured everyone slowly filtering into the meeting room and just sitting down, him all the while lying there on the floor, holding his wireless mouse in his outstretched hand, as if he had fought bravely to carry on against overwhelming medical odds. He thought about Ray finally coming in, and asking where Mister Starwars was.

'Down there,' someone would say, and they would point at the spreadeagled Jeremy Starwars.

'Get up,' Ray would suggest.

And then Jeremy would face what he considered to be the greatest ever test of his character; whether to get up and go through with the demonstration, passing off his little lie-down as nothing unusual, a preparatory exercise of some kind, or to show true courage, to have the strength of his convictions and remain prone until either an ambulance was called or people began to kick him. He pictured himself sitting in the ambulance, sharing a joke with the paramedics and asking to be dropped off at his flat. He realised that they might consider this an imposition, and that he would probably need to provide a sweetener of some sort, but Jeremy knew for a fact that there were several ten pound notes in his wallet, having visited the cash point on his way home the night before.

He looked up at the clock once more. There were just five minutes to go. His flight of whimsy was now a serious consideration. It was likely that the meeting would be delayed a little by people floating in late from the pub, particularly on a Friday, but Will would be punctual, possibly even early. If Jeremy was truly thinking of being found in a state of collapse, the window of opportunity for actually lying down and positioning himself comfortably yet dramatically was shrinking rapidly. He couldn't see himself swooning in company; he simply didn't have the acting chops for the job. It would just be embarrassing.

He thought about what lay before him were he to follow the more conventional path of actually giving his demonstration. His plan of action had been to simply project the original specification diagram that he had been given at the outset, and point at bits of that for a while until people hopefully drifted away; preferably without asking any taxing questions, such as 'yes, *and*?' His only real backup strategy would be to project the website for the third party software that he had been so certain early on would be straightforward to work with, and take them all through the bulleted list of useful features it offered, that he had been hoping to incorporate. If he could just talk this afternoon about what he had been asked to do, and what he had originally intended to utilise in order to do it, and everybody could just take it as read that he had actually accomplished any of it, everything might be fine. He could simply sneak the laptop home and by some miracle figure it all out over the weekend, and make it all true. Unfortunately, there was a reasonably strong chance that he would be asked to show it all working, given that this was the stated purpose of the demonstration.

He checked the clock again. Two minutes to two. Will would be coming through the door any second.

Jeremy Starwars heaved a sigh of resignation, and lay down on the floor, clutching his wireless mouse.

12

WORK WORK

Ray returned promptly from his customary Friday lunchtime pint and crossword to find an email notification awaiting him. Had the message been from anybody else, he would have wandered off to obtain the vital first coffee of the afternoon prior to reading, but this was from Barbara Pappa, and marked urgent.

A brief wave of panic passed over Ray as he considered the possibility that he hadn't merely thought about calling Barbara a cow the previous day, that perhaps it had actually happened. Perhaps she had been considering her response this entire time. Whatever the case, an urgent missive from the CEO was an unusual occurrence, and one which demanded his immediate attention. He clicked with a degree of trepidation.

'ALL STAFF MEMBERS' began the email. The realisation that it had been sent to everyone came as something of a relief.

'MEETING. PLEASE ASSEMBLE AT RECEPTION AT 2:00PM' it continued.

'BNP' it concluded.

Barbara Natalie Pappa had employed the triple initial sign-off ever since her promotion to upper management, believing it to lend her a certain gravitas. As far as anyone could work out, she remained blissfully unaware of the extreme right wing organisation that also bore her initials. Nobody had ever broached the subject with her, as everyone who had noticed also found it highly entertaining. Quite by coincidence, when Barbara had first risen to the rank of chief executive officer, one of her first acts had been to insist that everyone celebrate St George's day. She had considered it a little too self-aggrandising to call for a party in her own honour, but had nevertheless felt the need to camouflage an event of some kind in the trappings of whatever was closest on the calendar. Consequently, the first meeting called by BNP had been in an office temporarily bedecked with patriotic bunting and little iced cakes with red crosses drawn on them. Several members of staff hadn't known Barbara's middle name, and had, as a result, found the party very unsettling. These days, however, the celebrations were an established tradition, and everyone enjoyed taking photos of each other amid the sea of St George's crosses in order to send to friends and family with accompanying messages such as 'At BNP meeting. LOL.'

Ray looked up to see Will and Ian getting up from their desks. They had clearly already read the email, thus denying him the opportunity to announce something. He followed them to the stairs, where they met Thom, Ollii and Robert on their way up. He waved them downward.

'Meeting. Downstairs. Now,' he said. It wasn't a proper team announcement, but it was better than nothing.

The returning trio complained about not being allowed to put their coats away first, or indeed to urinate, but Ray was insistent and tapped the part of his wrist where he had once worn a watch, a practice which he had given up immediately upon acquiring his first mobile phone. He considered the clock facility on the phone to have rendered the watch redundant, and in any case, he had never enjoyed the way it had made his wrist smell by the end of the day. He saw Robert and the two testers in much the same light as his watch, although they had, at least, never caused his wrist to smell.

***

'They've definitely gone,' declared Jem as she opened the door and walked back into Martin's room.

She found him sat on his bed, clutching his chest.

'Knocking. Ever heard of it?' he asked momentarily, after exhaling demonstratively.

'Sorry. Were you having a wank, or something?'

He feigned shock. 'How very dare you. You're sure they left?'

Jem nodded. 'We've been abandoned. Not even a bloody note. Unbelievable.'

'I'm getting it out, then,' said Martin, stepping up onto the bed.

'You'll wear that thing out.'

'You're so funny. You should be on the telly,' deadpanned Martin, glaring at her.

He reached up into the ceiling and what his hand came to rest upon made his blood run cold. Tiling. Just tiling. No gun. He scrabbled around, feeling nothing but polystyrene tiles, and the metal framework holding those tiles in place.

'Shit,' he informed Jem, looking down at her, his eyes bulging.

'Don't even joke about that,' she advised sternly.

He shook his head.

'Oh no,' said Jem.

'Oh fucking yes,' confirmed Martin.

'Was that definitely the right tile?'

'You saw me put it up here.'

'Keith must have moved it then. He's the only other one who knew.'

'We'd better fucking hope so,' said Martin, frantically lifting other tiles and reaching into different sections of the suspended ceiling.

'Right,' said Jem, beginning to pace the floor. 'Right. Right. Let's keep calm.'

'Keep calm and think of Fluffy,' suggested Martin, groping around blindly above himself.

'What would Fluffy do. What would Fluffy the hamster do.'

'Fluffy wouldn't exist,' said Martin, sighing and withdrawing from the suspended ceiling empty-handed. He looked down at Jem, and tried to shape his forlorn expression into a reassuring smile.

And with that, he was gone.

***

Jeremy lay on the meeting room floor, worrying that he might fall asleep. Feigning unconsciousness might become untenable were this to

150

happen. He doubted that he would have the presence of mind to maintain the pretence immediately upon being woken up by whoever found him.

The carpet tiling was irritating against his cheek now. He suspected that for some days after he got up, he would probably be very rosy on one side of his face, and have skin with the texture of an orange peel. He wondered whether he had any carpeting at home similar enough to the tiling to even things out, but it seemed unlikely.

Jeremy was beginning to lose the feeling in the hand that was gripping his wireless mouse. He thought about whether he should be holding it quite so tightly, given that he was attempting to give the illusion of a light coma, rather than rigor mortis. He decided to take the risk of slightly relaxing his fingers. This was something that could realistically happen with a person in his presently undiagnosed condition, he surmised. The mouse made a faint clacking sound as it slipped from his palm onto the nylon fibre tiling. Jeremy held his breath for a moment, suddenly afraid that he might have given the game away. Nothing. All was quiet. He had gotten away with it, and now his hand felt very slightly more comfortable. The once more motionless Jeremy Starwars silently celebrated his small victory.

Having had his nose to the carpet tile for some time now, he was becoming keenly aware of an unusual odour. With a frisson of panic, he realised that it was from the chemical agents that were regularly used to clean the tiles. He was mostly likely becoming high now, he imagined. Jeremy Starwars pictured himself in the weeks that would follow his probable sacking, sat on a park bench, huffing on a bag full of the cleaning fluid to which he would by then most likely be hopelessly addicted. The thought that he would at least have a hobby to occupy his upcoming abundance of free time seemed something of a comfort.

He had lost track of how long he had been lying there, as he had failed to position himself such that he would be able to sneak a peak at the clock on the wall. He would actually have to sit up to see it, and knowing his luck, that would be just the moment at which somebody would come in. It seemed to Jeremy as though a considerable amount of time had passed. He was certain that he *had* heard the meeting room door open briefly and close again, but he had heard no footsteps in the room itself, just the muffled sound of other doors opening and closing one by one. Then those noises too had stopped, and he had been able to return his full concentration to the sound of his own blood pumping in his head. It had just been somebody looking for somebody else, he had persuaded himself. This had all been a while ago, and he was beginning to think he had imagined, or even dreamt it. He considered the possibility that he might have drifted off at some point, and missed everyone coming in. Was it possible that everybody was already in the room, quietly waiting for him to get up? He thought back to that time when he had been deep in concentration at his desk, entranced by the rhythms of a *Public Enemy* album, and everybody in the office had been sat behind him the whole time. He remembered how they had all maintained their frowns and continued to study his monitor when he had finally turned around. Could they be doing something similar right now? He couldn't risk looking. To look would be to reveal himself to be conscious, and then this potential audience might become an *actual* audience. As long as he didn't blink first, they would continue to exist in a quantum state; only to be resolved upon viewing. *Schrödinger's audience*. Jeremy Starwars resisted the temptation to smile, and continued to lie stock still on the carpet tiles. He was still very much in control of this situation.

***

Jem sat on the floor of her makeshift bedroom and wiped her eyes. She was aware of having spent some considerable time crying hysterically, but as she blew her nose on a wad of toilet paper she had earlier liberated from the Ladies, she realised that she could not for the life of her remember what it had all been over. This troubled her greatly. Could it have been that the sheer inexplicability of this wave of emotion was what had set her off? Was she simply unable to cope with her current circumstances, trapped up here alone?

No. There had been a gun. There had been a gun, and she had put it in the suspended ceiling, and now it had gone. It had gone, and she had overreacted. That was it. Looking up, she could see the space where she had slid the tile to one side while she had been desperately scrabbling around for it.

She sniffed and rose to her feet, cursing Ray for ever having pointed her out to Manny in the Wednesday meeting. It had been true that there was little for her team to test while everybody was waiting for Starwars, but that was scarcely her fault. Because of the ineptitude of others, she had been forced to stay for days with sinister people whose agenda was oblique at best, and as if that wasn't enough, she had spent a considerable period of time having conversations with the dead. This wasn't how her week was supposed to have panned out. She had been just getting back into drawing, for a start. She pictured the mostly blank pads and freshly purchased markers strewn across the kitchen table in her flat. Her flat. She remembered with a sinking sensation that her landlord was supposed to be coming over that evening for an inspection, and she wracked her brain to think whether there was anything embarrassing lying around. Not Albert, at any rate; he was safely in the drawer of her bedside cabinet, along with his spare batteries. After a moment of panic, it struck her that it actually felt good to have something mundane with which to occupy her mind. She sniffed and smiled, reminded vaguely of something someone had once told her about an imaginary pet they used to pretend they had; how they'd manufacture concerns over its welfare, just so they would have a fear over which they could have complete control, that they could pull the rug out from under whenever they elected so to do. Fluffy. That was its name. Fluffy the hamster. She struggled to recall who might have told her about this non-existent rodent, but ultimately had to settle upon the likelihood that it had been a long-forgotten schoolfriend.

***

Everyone was gathered in reception, looking puzzled. They spread along the corridor, each trying to find a patch of wall to lean against. Barbara Pappa beside the reception desk, arms folded, Tracy, her right hand woman, to her left. Her eyes darted between her members of staff, with a hint of nervousness that few had seen before, save for the veterans who had survived the redundancy rounds of the last recession.

'We're for the chop, I reckon,' said Ian Gerald Peterson from Programming under his breath.

Tim from Sales nodded gravely.

'Chop chop chop chop chop,' said Will from Programming, chiefly for his own amusement.

'Don't look great, does it?' said Colin from Stores.

'Bollocks,' said Ollii from Testing and Support.

Thom from Testing and Support said nothing, but pouted a little and raised his eyebrows, having not yet really formed an opinion about the proceedings.

Ganesh from Accounts also remained quiet, but in a manner which he hoped suggested the kind of underlying knowledge of events that he felt a man in his position should probably have had. He had no such underlying knowledge. He was aware of a cash flow problem, but it was the same cash flow problem that had existed when he had joined the company, and it was one that had always been dealt with via the straightforward means of always withholding payments to suppliers for at least four months, and pleading poverty at every pay round. He had been unable to improve the situation, but neither had it deteriorated. There were no gaping holes in the finances that he was aware of. The only real mystery Ganesh from Accounts had encountered during his time there, was that of a series of peculiar gaps in the employee numbering system, something that he had only noticed recently. He was aware that there had been redundancies over the years, but this was different; these numbers appeared never to have been used, as if they were being kept in reserve, or had perhaps been considered unlucky by his predecessor. In addition, it seemed to be catching, as two of the jumps in the numbering had occurred on his watch. This despite the fact that only five people had been taken on after him. He had made enquiries with the company that produced the payroll software, but he had yet to hear back.

Ganesh from Accounts turned his head to look at Corinna from Accounts. She was similarly taciturn. This was good. They should be showing a dignified, united front here. She was, if anything, doing an even better job of looking in possession of privileged information than he was managing. Was it possible that she *actually* knew something?

Corinna from Accounts turned and flashed him the briefest of smiles. He returned the favour instantly, and quickly looked away. Perhaps she *did* know more than him. This was maddening.

Corinna from Accounts turned back to look straight ahead once more, and contemplated the coworker she had just caught leering at her. This was typical, she thought; people were always falling for her. If anything, she was surprised that it had taken this long for Ganesh to succumb to the old Petro charms. Not that she had done anything to encourage him, of course. She resolved to be cooler towards him for a while. It would be a shame if things were to become unprofessional. Their room was awfully small to be housing an atmosphere.

In addition to these thoughts, Corinna from Accounts wondered what was going on.

'Chop chop chop chop chop,' said Will from Programming.

'Children. I'm sure it's not as bad as you think,' said Ray from Programming (Management), folding his arms and imagining the kind of settlement he might receive.

'Is everybody here?' asked Barbara in her loudest voice, standing on tiptoes with one hand to her forehead to mime herself peering past all those assembled, despite her modest height making this a physical impossibility.

Everybody stopped mumbling and looked around at the people in their vicinity.

'I think so, Barbara,' said Ray, reasserting at the same time that he was on first name terms with the CEO. So was everybody else, but he was *entitled* to be, and it felt only right and proper to remind people of that fact.

'Right,' said Barbara hesitantly, and she turned to whisper something to Tracy, who then picked up her phone and spoke a few short words into it.

'They're on their way down now,' Tracy informed Barbara solemnly, after hanging up the phone.

'OK, if I could ask you all to be patient for a little longer,' said Barbara, once more using her big voice.

'They're coming down to sack us in person,' said Habib from Sales.

'Been nice knowing you, Beeb,' said Tim from Sales.

'You too, buddy,' said Habib from Sales.

'Get a room before I vomit all over the pair of you,' suggested Bronwen from Sales.

'She looks serious, doesn't she? Tracy,' said Ollii from Testing and Support.

'This all looks a bit terminal, mate,' said Thom from Testing and Support.

'Shit, man. What if they actually make us do work in our next jobs? I'm not ready for this.'

'Don't worry about it. Everywhere is the same,' said Robert Smith from Programming, sagely.

'Severance package,' said Ian Gerald Peterson from Programming, rubbing his fingers together, thinking that this could perhaps be his big chance to turn *HomeBrew-HomeBrew* into a full-time going concern.

Ray from Programming (Management) tutted.

'Chop chop chop chop chop,' said Will from Programming.

A man and a woman walked into reception, wearing business suits and dark sunglasses, and everyone went quiet. The man nodded to Barbara, who went over to the door and began tapping at its keypad.

'Chop,' said Will.

'Is this everyone?' asked the man, surveying the scene. His gaze lingered on Will, who was still in the midst of saying 'chop' a few more times under his breath.

'I believe so, apart from whoever you have upstairs,' said Barbara, finishing her tapping and returning to stand at the reception desk, hands clasped in front of her.

'I checked the floor above. All the offices, the meeting room, the bathrooms. All clear. Everyone who's here, is here,' said the woman.

'Good enough. OK, good afternoon, everybody,' began the man. 'I'm Marlowe, and this vision of beauty is Denver.'

He motioned to Denver, who batted her eyelids in a response masked entirely by her sunglasses.

'We're from upstairs,' she explained, 'and we're very sorry for not having introduced ourselves before now.'

'As your owners, we've been very lax in that regard, but we've been so terribly busy,' said Marlowe, pulling a sad face.

156

'Still,' said Denver, 'we're here now, and we'd very much appreciate all of your help with our little investigation.'

Looks were exchanged in the crowd.

'And to that end, we're going to have to ask you all to stay quite late,' said Marlowe.

A brief rumble of white noise erupted from those assembled, composed almost exclusively of tuts and swearing. Denver lifted her sunglasses, just for a moment, and the hubbub faded.

'I'm afraid this overtime is mandatory,' she said, calmly.

'The doors are locked, and the shutters are down, people,' said Marlowe. 'The weekend starts here.'

Looking around at the faces of his team, which were currently displaying feelings ranging between troubled and outraged, it suddenly occurred to Ray that Jeremy was missing.

'This is bullshit,' said Bronwen from Sales.

***

Augustine stood in the ladies' lavatory, struggling with a bow tie in front of a mirror. He had decided to scrub up for his grand entrance in there, as the room had far nicer furnishings than the Gents, and the floor was considerably drier. His trusty bathrobe and jeans lay strewn across a wicker sofa whose designer had probably hoped that it would find its way into a nice conservatory. Three whiskey bottles, two empty, one full, stood by one leg of the sofa, in testament to the time Augustine had spent gathering his thoughts and strength prior to shaving. As a consequence of this preparation, his hands had shaken very little throughout the process, barring the odd spasm, and certainly less blood had been drawn than he had feared would be the case. The single sheet of toilet paper clinging to his left cheek was handling that small matter admirably. This was another advantage to his choice of lavatory; a more absorbent class of sheet altogether than was to be found in the Gents.

The off-the-peg dinner jacket Augustine had ordered from the Internet fitted surprisingly well. His recent diet of takeaway food and spirits had punished him only slightly, a hastily assembled piece of expansion equipment constructed from a couple of paper clips having been sufficient to allow him to more or less fasten the trousers. It was only after persuading said trousers to stay up that Augustine had realised that he had forgotten to request some dress shoes. As he looked down at the fluorescent green sandals that he was apparently stuck with, he wondered whether they might perhaps be marring the ensemble.

Returning to the suit, he ruminated over where he might put his gun; whether it might spoil the line of his trousers, or cause his jacket to hang awkwardly. It was at this point he realised that he was no longer in possession of his firearm, and his mood began to worsen. He picked up his final bottle and began to dwell upon the matter.

13

BANG BANG

Denver, Marlowe and Barbara had stepped into the downstairs meeting room to talk, and from the reception area could be seen but not heard through its thick glass walls. Any relief that those assembled in Reception might have felt about discovering that their jobs were not, as most had supposed, on the line, had dissipated rapidly to be replaced by confusion and anger.

Some, however, were keeping calmer heads. Will was among them.

'Oh, human rights, blah blah blah,' he reasoned. 'We'll get double time for this if it goes into the weekend. What else would you all be doing?'

This was largely met with the shaking of heads.

'Phones are down,' said Habib, returning from the Sales room.

'The doors to Stores are locked,' called Ian Peterson from Stores, on his way back from the far end of the building.

'What the fuck?' asked Bronwen, throwing her hands up in exasperation.

This was taken to be rhetorical by those around her, which angered her further, as she had in fact been hoping for an answer of some kind.

'I can't get a signal,' said Tim, looking up at his phone, which he was holding aloft.

'I've never had a signal here,' said Corinna, to no-one in particular.

'I've sometimes managed to get one bar in the toilets,' Ganesh suggested to Corinna.

'Firstly yuck, and secondly what would I be doing in the mens' bogs?' said Corinna.

'I'll give it a go, mate,' said Tim, heading off down the corridor.

'Seriously, never call me on the toilet,' Corinna told Ganesh firmly.

'I would never…' stammered Ganesh, hurt by the suggestion.

'The shutters ain't moving,' yelled Colin from another room.

Thom and Ollii were at the reception desk, attempting to capitalise on their influence with Tracy.

'Come on, Trace,' said Ollii.

'Yeah, come on Tracy Ireland. We need international rescue,' said Thom.

Tracy folded her arms and sat back in her chair.

'If I had a pound for every time somebody had cracked that, I wouldn't be behind a reception desk, that's for sure.'

'Oh please, Trace, I need to call Janice,' pleaded Ollii. 'We had plans tonight.'

'Sorry, sweet pea. Me and Barry had plans too. Everybody had plans, but I'm telling you, there's no outside line.'

'I thought it was quiet,' said Thom. 'Didn't I say it was quiet?'

'When did they say they were coming to fix it?' asked Ollii.

'Give us a chance, it only went down at lunch. Barbara said it was a fault outside, and they were sorting it,' said Tracy.

'Can I use your email then?' asked Ollii. 'Please.'

'It's all on the same pipe, lover. Everything is internal only at the moment.'

'So they've locked us in and cut us off. This is freaking me out a bit, mate,' said Ollii to Thom.

'Don't panic, *Mister Mainwaring*,' said Tracy, trying to keep things light.

'We don't like it up us,' said Thom.

'That's not the way I hear it,' said Robert Smith, lounging in one of the reception area's five comfy chairs.

'Are you not worried, at all?' asked Ollii, turning to stare at him in disbelief.

'What?' said Robert, sitting up. 'Sorry, I wasn't really listening.'

'You never cease to amaze me, Bob,' said Thom.

160

'Thanks, mate,' said Robert.

'Where's Jem?' asked Ian Gerald Peterson, sinking into a seat next to Robert.

'Don't know,' said Thom.

'Did she ring in, Trace?' asked Ollii.

'Not to me, sweet pea,' said Tracy.

'Where's Starwars?' asked Ian, continuing to look around.

'Don't know,' said Thom.

'I don't reckon he came down, you know,' said Ollii. 'Was he at the pub?'

'Nope,' said Robert. 'He was pissing about with a laptop, last I saw of him. For his demo.'

'Maybe he did a runner,' said Ian.

'I wouldn't put it past him. The only demo I can see that bloke doing, is one against getting up in the morning,' said Robert.

'Ooh, hark at Mister Pot,' Ollii chided him.

'That's a bloody good name for him,' said Thom, smirking.

'I meant pot as in kettle, Trace,' Ollii explained, not wishing to be the cause of a random drug test.

Having not really been listening, Tracy elected to shake her head while smiling. Her husband Barry was frequently on the receiving end of this practised response.

Looking at no one in particular, Robert dropped his jaw in mock horror, leaving his mouth to hang open for a moment before making a play of snapping it shut with the back of his hand.

'This isn't much of a BNP meeting,' he complained, after observing the small crowd milling around in the corridor for a moment. 'Where are all the red and white balloons?'

'The halitosis bombs?' Ollii grinned.

'God, yeah. They stank so bad when they popped. I think whoever filled them used their arse instead of their mouth.' He thought for a moment before adopting a look of concern. 'It wasn't you, was it, Trace?'

'What, chuck?'

'Nothing. Doesn't matter.'

'Where's Ray, then,' asked Ian, still not settled.

161

'Are you taking a register or something? Bloody hell.' Thom shot him an incredulous look.

'Actually, he's got a point,' said Ollii. 'Where did Ray go? He was screaming at everyone to stay calm a minute ago.'

'Gone to the bogs to wring the piss out of his trousers, probably,' suggested Thom.

'*Thomas*,' Tracy reproached him sharply.

'*Sowwy Twacy*,' he said, pouting.

'He is kind of useless, though, Trace,' said Ollii.

'That's your *boss*,' said Tracy, doing her best to appear appalled at this disregard for rank.

'He's not the boss of me,' Ollii declared indignantly.

'Jem's our boss,' explained Thom. 'Ray's just like some odd, lonely bloke who hangs round our desks sometimes.'

'Yeah, he's like a weird smell. He's only in charge of these losers,' said Ollii, pointing to Robert and Ian.

'Ray is Jem's boss, and that makes him your boss too,' said Tracy, folding her arms.

'Please don't tell me you fancy him, Trace,' said Thom, leaning over the desk. 'That's not it, is it?'

'Ewww,' said Ollii.

'I'll bang your heads together in a minute, the pair of you,' said Tracy, blushing.

***

Jeremy Starwars continued to lie on the meeting room floor. So far, this was going much better than he had expected; he had yet to demonstrate nothing, and he hadn't had to explain himself to a medical professional either. And all the while, the clock was ticking the afternoon away, leaving less and less time in which his demonstration could take place. He couldn't see the clock, but it felt to Jeremy as though a couple of hours might have passed.

With his ear to the tiling, Jeremy could hear something of a commotion coming from the floor below. This had been going on for some time, but he had been uncertain as to whether these sounds were normal, not having previously spent any great amount of time lying down in the office. It certainly felt as though there were more swearing than he might have expected. He had always assumed the people downstairs to be far more content with their lot, in general, than either himself or anyone he worked with on the first floor. From his more usual seated position, he rarely heard anything but laughter coming from below. Upon reflection, however, he noted that this laughter had always identifiably come exclusively from the booming voice of Colin, the cockney storeman who worked with the other Ian Peterson. Jeremy considered the possibility that the loudness of this one man might have given him a skewed perspective on the mood of those at ground level. It could perhaps have been that everyone other than Colin was constantly angry or upset, and that Colin himself was either filled with a particularly cruel and hateful quantity of schadenfreude, or was clinically insane. Deep down, Jeremy had always suspected the latter of anyone who seemed especially happy.

Whatever the case, downstairs was a world with which Jeremy rarely had cause to interact, so he was glad of the distraction that these sounds of unrest were granting him from his own darker thoughts. Every so often, however, he would hear one particular voice that would make the hair stand up on the back of his neck. Every time he heard it, he became more certain of his identification. It was Ray. He was sure of it; Ray was downstairs. This meant, above all else, that Ray was definitely not sat at the meeting room table staring down at him scornfully. In fact, it seemed increasingly likely to Jeremy that he was alone, that there wasn't a crowd silently waiting for him to get up, and that nobody had thus far spat on him. All those sensations had merely been bits of him falling asleep.

Everyone was downstairs. It all made sense now. That was why Jeremy was hearing so much unhappiness coming through the carpet tiles; all the anguish come from up on his floor. The migration of so much combined ennui had even engulfed poor Colin; Jeremy could now make out the sound of him moaning about some blinds not working. They had practically made him one of them already.

The question of everyone's presence downstairs was less important than the fact that they weren't upstairs, waiting for Jeremy Starwars to start his demonstration. There was nobody else in the meeting room, and it was seeming increasingly likely that there was nobody else on the first floor. Jeremy agonised for a few moments longer, and finally risked opening his left eye. His right eyelid was partially in contact with the scratchy tile material that had been causing such irritation to his cheek and ear, so he had no intention of opening that, until he had moved his head. As his eye adjusted to the light, Jeremy looked out across a dense forest of artificial fibres. He couldn't see much from his viewpoint, mere inches from the ground, but there were clearly no feet under the meeting room table. Unless everyone was stood on their chair, there was genuinely nobody else in the room.

Jeremy tried to lift his head, but was reminded by a sharp pain in his neck that it was going to be necessary to first roll onto his side. He did so with great discomfort, and in the same movement peeled his sweaty, reddened face off the carpet.

He was definitely alone. He rolled onto his back to relieve his aching right arm of supporting duties. As some mobility returned to his hands, Jeremy repeatedly clenched and released his fists in an effort to restore the flow of blood. Gradually and painfully, he managed to straighten his neck enough to be able to point his head forwards. He felt the right hand side of his face, presently creased and wrinkled; a perfect, if slightly sticky, mould of the surface of the carpet tiling, complete with a ridge from where two tiles hadn't quite met correctly.

Jeremy's back complained vehemently as it lifted him into a sitting position. He strained to look up and finally see the clock on the wall that he had been picturing spinning round in his mind's eye throughout his holiday on the floor, hoping and half-expecting it to be nearly home time.

The clock read twenty-five past two.

'Oh for fuck's sake,' said Jeremy Starwars.

***

Everyone had now more or less separated into two groups, sorted by floor. The programmers and testers, feeling very much the visitors, had occupied the front-of-house comfy chair area. Only Will still stood among the downstairs people, failing to feel any more out of place with them than with his own workmates.

Tim returned from the toilets shaking his head.

'Nope. Nothing,' he said, looking at Ganesh, who pouted to display his disappointment.

'Worth a shout,' Tim added, not wishing him to feel bad about the failure of his suggestion. 'Definitely worth a shout.'

'Took you long enough to check,' remarked Bronwen.

'Yeah, well, I took a strategic dump,' explained Tim.

'Unbelievable,' said Bronwen, gaping at him.

'What? What if these fruit loops lock the bogs next? You don't know.'

'He's actually got a point,' said Corinna, and she headed off down the corridor.

'Oh, bloody...' began Bronwen, before following Corinna, determinedly staring straight ahead, so as not to meet the eyes of her fellow salespersons.

Tim grinned broadly, and watched as she walked away.

'Good turn out, bud?' Habib asked Tim, euphemistically referring to his colleague's recent bowel movement.

'Excellent turn out, mate,' he responded.

'Why do they do that?' Will asked the group.

'What's that mate?' asked Tim.

'Go to the toilet together. Women, I mean,' Will clarified.

He was already regretting asking the question, as he knew it to be hackneyed, and had no particular interest in the subject. He did have a lot of questions related to women, but given the fact that he hadn't yet bothered trying to find the answers on the Internet, he felt that they probably weren't worth raising in public.

'I really don't know, mate,' said Tim. 'Maybe they need the chit chat so they can go.'

'Shit chat,' offered Habib.

'Nice,' said Tim, and the two salesmen bumped fists.

Ganesh thought back to Corinna's disgust at the idea of being phoned from the toilet, something he would never in a million years have considered doing, and pondered the double standard. He imagined her sat in a cubicle shouting at Bronwen through the divider, '*No, no, no. Shut up. You're on the toilet. You can't talk to me.*' He smiled to himself. It would never happen. But now he realised that she was no longer shouting, and he was just thinking of his coworker sat in a toilet cubicle. She was kicking the door open and smiling that smile she had shown him a few minutes before. He broke off from his reverie, a little unnerved.

'You all right mate?' He realised Tim was speaking to him.

'Nothing. I wasn't… What? I'm fine, thank you,' said Ganesh, straightening his tie.

***

The downstairs Gents was like some parallel universe version of the one on Ray's own floor, he thought; almost identical, yet somehow alien. He sat in its equivalent of Trap Two, listening carefully to make sure that Tim was gone. Rarely had he felt the pressure of leadership as he did at this moment, on this unfamiliar toilet. His troops were out there, waiting for him to fix whatever this was, relying on him to make everything right. He had to be strong. He had to be their rock. Most importantly, he had to rise above the feeling of panic that had gripped him since the doors had been locked.

He couldn't explain this feeling of unease, but suspected that his subconscious mind remembered more of his experience with the sinister, drunken American on the top floor than it was prepared to share. He couldn't shake the notion that there was something terrible up there, that he was now trapped in the building with it, and that it was coming for him, and for his people. He clenched his fists and determined that he would direct these fears into useful action.

He stood up to wipe himself, and was shocked to see that there was nothing in the bowl. He felt a chill run through his stomach, as if he were in the presence of something supernatural. Ray gathered himself as he pulled up his trousers, and toyed with the notion of not flushing, in the circumstances. There were, after all, just a few sheets of relatively clean paper in the bowl now, the result of a couple of exploratory wipes. He might be able to exit more discreetly, without the attention-grabbing noise of the cistern. Then he considered the possibility that someone might come in immediately after him, see the contents of the toilet and assume that he had been sat in there crying. He depressed the flush button decisively and left the cubicle.

As he washed and dried his hands, Ray noted the light coming from the frosted glass of the window in the end wall. The window backed onto a narrow alleyway between themselves and the neighbouring tyre yard. This was the far side of the building from the car park, and Ray struggled to remember whether he had ever actually looked at it from the outside, and whether there were shutters there. In any case, clearly none were currently down. He walked over, pulling his keys from his pocket. He searched through them until he found the proud status symbol of his rank; the small key that fitted every one of the building's window locks. Many had tried to argue that the key should simply have been left on the hook provided for it, on the office wall, where everybody could get at it, but Ray saw that as a basic dereliction of duty. Custody of the window key was his responsibility, and his alone. Now, finally, all that hard work was about to pay off. This tiny key, which would have been useless to anyone at this moment had it been hanging on a wall upstairs, or, as seemed more likely to Ray, had it been stolen or accidentally swallowed by one of his team, was instead fulfilling its destiny by unlocking the lavatory window before him.

Returning his keys safely to his pocket, Ray slid the lower pane upwards and was disappointed to see a steel mesh appear beyond it. Of course. This was why there was no shutter. Ray reached through the window, and, poking his fingers through the mesh, grasped it with both hands. He tested its strength by attempting to pull it back and forth, but there was little give. Pushing his head out of the window as far as the mesh would allow, he could see precious little gap between the wall and the security frame.

Ray gingerly withdrew his head, straightened up, and released his grip on the mesh. He stepped back a little and stroked his chin, staring at the mesh barrier and pondering whether there might be any bolt cutters in the building. He snorted at the ridiculousness of this idea. He was middle management, and he should get a proper grip on himself. He should head back out there and wait to talk things through with

Barbara. His first reaction should certainly not be to try to break out through a toilet window. He shook himself down, and went to close the window. No matter how ludicrous it seemed at this moment, it was still a potential alternative exit strategy, and he didn't want to draw undue attention to it.

As Ray reached up to pull the pane back down, an enormous-eyed sweaty face hove into view, pressing itself against the other side of the mesh, and causing him to jump back with a start.

'D'you want any meat, blue eyes?' asked the face.

***

Bronwen and Corinna exchanged glances, having returned from their toilet break.

'Go on,' Corinna urged Bronwen with a nudge.

'This is just a thought, right,' said Bronwen, quietly addressing the group gathered in the corridor. 'I'm not saying we should, right, but what if we set off the fire alarm?'

'I'm listening,' said Tim, thrusting his hands into his pockets.

'You think they're going to just open the doors and tell us to assemble in the car park?' asked Habib, making it abundantly clear that he didn't think that this was what would happen.

'No, maybe not. But it might make the shutters go up, don't you think? Like, isn't there some kind of automatic failsafe for those things? You know, to stop us dying?'

'I doubt it,' said Ian Peterson from Stores, rubbing his chin.

'You'll be lucky,' boomed Colin.

He chuckled, as he so often did, but there was a detectable drop in the levels of enthusiasm in his laughter. Ganesh looked at him and wondered whether this might be his version of despair.

'OK, I grant you they might not have thought about us burning to death when they fitted the shutters, but at the very least, the alarm would bring the fire brigade out, wouldn't it? They'd have to let them in, and us out, wouldn't they?'

'And then there'd be lovely firemen,' added Corinna.

Ganesh tried not to react to this. He could have been a fireman, he felt sure, if he'd had a mind to.

'I think we should give it a go,' said Tim.

'The firemen tipped it for you, didn't they?' asked Habib, grinning.

'Just trying to line you up with something for the weekend, Beeb.'

'Sorry, pardon my French, but what the fuck are you doing?' asked Bronwen.

She was addressing Will, who was now tearing paper he had obtained from the photocopier in reception into strips and piling them up on the floor.

'Making the fire. Can't see any wood to chop. Chop chop chop.'

She glowered at him and pointed to the small red box on the wall above his head.

'We're not actually torching the place, you bloody idiot.'

Tim tutted and attempted to break the glass with his elbow, which he instead caught on the corner of the box. He went off down the corridor swearing.

'Oh, for pity's sake.' In a single movement, Bronwen swiped her right shoe from her foot, stepped across to the wall and put the heel straight through the glass and onto the button.

Nothing happened.

'Seriously?' She raised two hands and one block-heeled leather shoe in defeat.

'Perhaps it's a silent alarm?' suggested Corinna.

'Yeah, that's a great idea,' laughed Habib. 'The building's burning down, but don't tell anyone. It's a secret.'

'Well, I don't know.'

'Now I think about it, didn't Tracy just phone through the last fire drill we had?' said Ian Peterson.

'Bloody hell, I think you're right,' bellowed Colin.

'That thing's probably not even wired up,' said Will, gathering up his paper kindling. 'They probably just glued it to the wall.'

'You should put your shoe back on,' Ganesh advised Bronwen. 'There might be glass.'

'Yes. Thank you, Ganesh,' she replied, but in such a tone as to ensure that he would know to infer no actual gratitude on her part. She folded her arms and glowered into space, now forced to wait for an appropriate interval before slipping her foot back into the shoe, rather than appear to be slavishly following what she considered to be at best obvious and at worst patronising advice.

Tim walked back to the group, rubbing his arm.

'Well, it was worth a shout, mate,' he reassured Bronwen. 'Definitely worth a shout.'

'Right. Next?' She stood akimbo, one leg still lower than the other, like a jug in the process of being poured.

***

Jeremy Starwars felt more like an intruder than ever, as he walked cautiously through the deserted office. He stooped to look under and around office furniture as he went, reminded of his compulsive need to check under his bed as a small boy. It was unlikely that his colleagues were hiding from him, but he imagined how foolish he would have felt if they were, and he hadn't taken this minimal precaution. As he peered through chair legs and beneath work surfaces, he countered any embarrassment he felt by reasoning that anyone watching, and waiting to laugh at his nervous behaviour, would presently have to be crouched in the foetal position under a desk. They would surely have as many questions to ask of themselves, as they would of him.

He reached his own chair without incident, after completing his cursory search of the office. Remaining standing, he tapped the shift key on his keyboard and his screen slowly lit up.

Jeremy observed the small red flag sticking out of a mailbox with a number one on it, in the corner of his screen. Here, almost certainly, was the explanation for everyone's absence. He reasoned that he couldn't read the mail that this signified without clearing the graphical notification, at which point he would no longer have plausible deniability on his side. There was always a chance that the mail was requesting his presence downstairs for a relocated demonstration of nothing. Perhaps his presentation had been moved to allow room for a larger audience. For a moment, Jeremy considered the possibility that everybody's parents might have been invited. As matters stood, he could claim not to have received any message, and to have been waiting in the meeting room, in good faith. The longer he could maintain this indeterminate state, the fewer the hours in which his demonstration could take place. He stepped quietly away from his desk.

Despite this rigid adherence to the small, red, flag-shaped details of his cover story, curiosity still gnawed at Jeremy Starwars. He tiptoed across to Robert Smith's desk. The desk was similar to his own, except for the black tinsel taped around the monitor, and the two comic action figures that stood guard on either side. The screen itself was displaying an animated flyover of what looked like the cover of Joy Division's *Unknown Pleasures*. The rest of the office tended to allow their screens to rest in standby mode when they left their desks, but Robert always seemed determined to find something for his computer to be getting on with, while he was otherwise engaged. Jeremy gave Robert's mouse the gentlest of taps with his fingernail, as if concerned that incriminating prints might be taken. The screen saver ended, and he was annoyed to see the same notification of unread mail appear. No good. Clear the 'unread' status of somebody else's mail, and his plea of ignorance would unravel, just as surely as if he had been foolish enough to open his own in-box.

He sidled over to Will's more spartan desk, and deftly performed the same mouse flick. Will's in-box became visible as the screen brightened, and Jeremy was able to read the request for everyone's presence at the BNP meeting downstairs. He felt slightly sick at the realisation that he was now a full three quarters of an hour late for whatever was happening.

To his horror, Jeremy now heard the distant but familiar sound of the tapping of the entry pad at the other end of the office. He couldn't see the door from where he was, and so was unable to tell for sure how panicked he should now be. As his mind raced, there didn't seem to be a scenario that would result in relief, regardless of who came through the door he now heard scraping open against the carpet tiles. The absolute best he could hope for was the cleaner, and he was uncertain as to whether her discretion could be relied upon.

He looked across at the meeting room, which lay between him and the door, obscuring his view of whoever was approaching, and cursed himself for having risen from the safety of its floor. It was already too late to run back in there, and pretend never to have left. If he were to be seen now, all efforts to feign ignorance would surely come to nothing. Jeremy Starwars ducked down and scuttled under Will's desk.

Jeremy was relieved to hear a single set of feet walking from left to right, rather than towards him. Whoever they were, it sounded like they were headed for the toilets. Perhaps somebody had simply found themselves caught short on their journey up or down the stairwell, and had popped in accordingly. Not wishing to be caught making a dash for the meeting room, Jeremy decided to fish the uncomfortable array of electrical plugs from underneath himself, and wait it out.

The world beneath Will's work surface was markedly different to the pristine asceticism above. As Jeremy tucked his knees to his chest, he saw that his trousers were covered in the debris from what must have been months' worth of crisps, biscuits and pastry products. For the briefest of moments, Jeremy Starwars believed this to be the worst thing that had ever happened to him. Now that he was in a position to properly inspect the floor, he could see that there was an almost perfect circle of crumbs and flakes surrounding the normal position of Will's chair. It reminded him of the rings of Saturn, and he idly wondered whether the planet might be occupied by a race of spectacularly messy eaters.

Jeremy's stomach churned as he heard several doors open and close in the distance. This person hadn't merely needed to relieve his or her self, unless they were now marking every room as their territory. It sounded like they were looking for someone. This was the second search Jeremy had heard this afternoon, and it was becoming increasingly difficult to convince himself that he wasn't the quarry. Matters had progressed too far for him to adopt any course of action other than one of continued concealment. He pulled Will's chair towards himself by one of its five wheeled plastic feet for additional cover, wincing as his finger got caught in the caster.

He heard footsteps moving this time from right to left, and swallowed hard at the sound of yet another door opening. He knew that the unknown searcher was now looking into the meeting room. He could no longer claim to have been in there the whole time. The door closed, and the footsteps began to grow louder, and closer, pausing after every few steps. Jeremy realised that they were checking under the desks, just as he had done. He felt as though he might pass out. The only way he could conceive of this situation resulting in less than immediate humiliation and dismissal, was if this were to prove to be Will approaching. He strained to imagine himself shouting 'boo' and the pair of them laughing, but all he could see in his mind's eye was a mixture of confusion and disgust on Will's face, closely followed by the rapid unravelling of Jeremy's career.

No way out.

They were close now, having paused again mere steps away. Jeremy considered the merits of binding his wrists with his shoelaces and claiming that his current location had been forced upon him by a burglar, but there simply wasn't time. He felt suddenly very cold.

No way out.

He closed his eyes, on the off-chance that when he opened them once more, he would be in his own bed, that this would all be over.

'You need to stop what you're doing,' asserted a voice that sounded unexpectedly close to Jeremy's head, which he promptly banged on the underside of the desk.

He opened his eyes, unsurprised to find his sub-desk circumstances unchanged. What did surprise him, was what appeared to now be standing the other side of the chair's star-shaped base. Struggling to focus, he realised that he was looking at a pale, naked, hairy pair of heavily tattooed legs.

***

Ray looked at the heavily perspiring man, whose nose now partially protruded through the security mesh in a fleshy diamond. The man gazed back, his greatly magnified eyes barely blinking behind inordinately strong prescription lenses.

'Nice fried up, blue eyes, lovely for your tea,' said the man.

'Thank you, no,' said Ray hesitantly.

The meat man breathed loudly at Ray through the mesh.

'Which is it, blue eyes, thank you or no?'

'No, thank you. No, I mean. Thank you. Thank you but no.'

'What are you having for your tea, blue eyes?'

'I—I don't honestly know.'

'Meat.'

'Probably not,' said Ray, glancing around the room, as if to demonstrate his present lack of cooking facilities.

'Probably meat?'

'Not. Probably not.'

'Meat. Probably meat.'

'Jesus,' muttered Ray.

'I don't want any meat. Do you understand?' he said loudly, enunciating every syllable and shaking his head demonstratively.

The man just stood there, his eyes fixed on Ray, who in that moment hoped that the mesh was as strong as it had seemed.

'You'll get hungry soon enough, blue eyes,' said the man eventually, and he pulled his nose out of the mesh to leave.

'Wait,' said Ray.

'Perhaps I'm in a hurry now, blue eyes.'

'Please. Could you take a message to someone for me?'

The man eased the end of his nose back into the mesh.

'There's a portable cabin in the car park with *security* written on it. I need you to go there, and tell them that our shutters have gone wrong, and we want them to use their keys and pull them up manually.'

The man stared at Ray.

'He'll need to unlock the doors too. Did … did you get that?' asked Ray.

'I've a terrible memory since I got out, blue eyes. You'll have to write it down for me.'

'Since you… right. OK. Do you have any paper I can write on? I have a pen.'

Ray produced a silver ballpoint from his shirt pocket and clicked it.

'That's a nice pen, blue eyes.'

'It does the job. Do you have some paper? A receipt or something?'

'Write it on some money, blue eyes.'

'Oh. OK. Fine,' sighed Ray, looking through his wallet. 'Will a fiver cover your trouble?'

'The meat is twenty pounds,' said the man, holding his bag up

174

against the mesh, its contents visibly spreading like blooming bruises against the plastic.

'I don't want … OK, OK. Whatever,' said Ray, rapidly scribbling his plea for help across the Queen's purple face and holding it out towards the window.

'Cash on delivery,' said the man, not attempting to take the banknote.

'What?'

'Meat first, then money. That's how we do the business, blue eyes.'

'Right. I can't come to the door right now, though. Can you just leave it outside? I can get it later.'

'I can't take your money until the meat is in your hands, blue eyes.'

'Look, I can't open the door. That's what the message is about. Once the security man opens the shutters and unlocks the doors, then I can collect the meat. OK?'

'No, blue eyes. Meat first.'

'The door is locked.'

'The window is open.'

'Yes, but there's a mesh, isn't there?'

'The meat can go through the mesh, blue eyes.'

Ray blinked. He refocused from meat man to mesh, to meat man again. The mesh was blackened by pollution and streaked with the faeces of numerous birds. He looked at the bag, with its loosely identified masses of questionably coloured flesh.

'Right. Give me the meat.'

The man proceeded to force some very dark-looking fillets of what may have been poultry through the mesh. Ray watched as each piece flopped onto the window sill, scarred by its journey and leaving bits of itself on the security grille. Then the man moved on to some light brown cuts, which Ray decided to assume were bovine in origin. These were considerably larger than the previous items, and the man was struggling to push them through.

'These need working through, blue eyes. You're going to have to pull them,' he advised.

'What is all this? Should I ask?'

'Mister Silver. Practice,' explained the meat man, waving a

dismissive hand.

'Practice? Jesus, is this from a vet?' Ray retreated a little.

The meat man shook his head.

'Mister Silver practised, then all meat for me,' he explained.

'A butcher then, yes? A trainee?'

The meat man shrugged, and then tapped at the beige clump hanging from the grille.

'Pull, blue eyes, pull,' he insisted.

Ray did as he was told, and, coping bravely with the ever-growing smell, he assisted in pulling the better part of four clumps of meat through the mesh.

Finally, the man pushed various items of offal through the steel screen. For these, he no longer required Ray's assistance, as they easily squished through several holes at once. They dropped, readily diced, on top of the other meat, sometimes bouncing from there onto the lavatory floor. Ray kicked the straying lumps to the skirting board.

The man looked down at the pile of distressed meat on the window sill, and then up at Ray.

'Do you want the bag?' he asked.

'No, I'm good,' said Ray, and he watched through a diamond grid now reddened and thick with ribbons of flesh and gristle, as the man shrugged, and crumpled the bloodied bag into a ball and popped it into the pocket of his leather coat.

'Twenty pounds.'

Ray handed him the folded banknote through one of the few holes in the mesh that wasn't now caked in meat.

'You'll tell the security guy what's written on there now, yes?'

The man tapped his nose with the note and grinned at Ray before turning and disappearing from the window.

'You're too good to me, sir,' Ray called after him.

He waited a moment for a response, which wasn't forthcoming, then slid the pane back down. As the window closed, it cleaved the pile of meat, putting the finishing touches to what now looked like the scene of a horrific accident in the workplace.

Ray strode out of the lavatory, and back up the corridor to where the Sales and Accounts staff were still skulking.

'Right, ladies and gents. Sorted. I sent a message,' he said, smiling proudly.

They all stared at him, their faces aghast.

'Jesus Christ, Ray. What have you done?' asked Bronwen, backing slowly away.

Ray stood and looked upon the awe of the underlings, now all bowing their heads before him, and saw that it was good. They continued to look at his red hands, and his shirt and trousers, now blood-spattered and flecked with small pieces of meat.

Ray's own team looked on from Reception, mouths agape.

'Where's Ian?' whispered Olli to Thom.

***

The owner of the naked legs waited patiently while Jeremy tried desperately to think of reasons why he was under Will's desk.

'I'm not hiding,' he assured the legs.

'You'll need to put whatever you're working on down there to one side.'

'It's just... these plugs...'

'The people upstairs have been looking for you.'

'Really? I thought I heard some doors opening and closing earlier, but I've been very busy preparing for a presentation.'

'They've been looking for a little longer than that.'

'Oh,' Jeremy gulped. 'I was going up to see them, honestly, but I was supposed to finish my project first.'

'Seriously. You wouldn't believe how long they've been looking for you.'

'I'm sorry. I didn't get the email. If there was one. I wouldn't know, I haven't checked it in hours.'

'Please come out from under there, Starwars. We have to talk, and I have things to show you.'

Jeremy looked at the bare feet before him, and the black wavy lines inked on the calves which they supported. One of the feet turned itself sideways and tapped impatiently, and in what was surely an optical illusion, it seemed that he could now see light shining through a small hole behind its ankle, above its heel.

'I'm not sure if I can see your things right now. Could we do this after the weekend?'

'Come out. This is beyond important.'

Jeremy realised that the naked legs weren't just going to walk away. With a sigh, he rocked himself forward onto the soles of his feet, pushed Will's chair out of his way, and waddled, squatting, out from beneath the desk. He saw the naked legs backing away to make room for him as he went. Once clear of the work surface, he raised his head a little.

'Genitals,' he said, before he could stop himself.

'Right. Sorry, I keep forgetting.'

Jeremy looked up a little higher.

'Keith. Naked Keith, for some reason. Hello.'

He struggled to his feet, trying not to look at the naked Keith, and sat down in Will's chair.

'Oh, for fu…' said Jeremy, realising that he was now eye level with Keith's penis, and resolving to stand.

He now caught his first proper glimpse of the caved-in head and popped-out eye of his colleague, turned, and threw up onto Will's keyboard. He gripped the desk to steady himself.

'Are you OK?' asked Keith.

'Fine. No, it's… I'm having a difficult day. Lovely to see you,' gasped Jeremy, electing to carry on looking at his newly liberated breakfast.

'I'm sorry. I must look a sight.'

'No. Lord, no,' insisted Jeremy, continuing to look away. 'This is nothing to do with… You look great. Well, not great. All right. Normal. A good average. If I was that way inclined, though. You know. The tattoos are looking—God, I never realised you had so many. They're still not going to make you a Maori though, you know. Why haven't you got any clothes on?'

'Sorry,' said Keith, and he wheeled over the chair that had once been his, in order to cover the modesty of what had once been his body. 'OK. I guess we should probably address the elephant in the room.'

'It's not that big. Probably. I don't know. I didn't look.'

'I think you know I'm talking about my head being shaped like the Apple logo.'

'I really hadn't noticed.'

'Really. How about my wandering eye?'

Jeremy briefly attempted eye contact, something he found difficult at the best of times, and was unnerved to discover that he now couldn't manage it in one go. He sat down again, and looked longingly at the underside of Will's desk, remembering the time he had spent there with all the fondness one might reserve for some beloved childhood holiday.

'It's OK, Starwars. This isn't some plastic surgery gone wrong, that I'm trying to be brave about. I am aware of what I look like. You're not going to hurt my feelings. I got hammered. I was nailed against a toilet wall. I died. I got over it.'

Jeremy attempted to gather his thoughts, his head swimming from a combination of panic and hunger. His now entirely empty stomach seemed to be causing a variety of temperatures to radiate through his body in rapid succession. He was seized by a nagging notion that Ray could burst through the door at any moment, demanding that he begin his presentation at once. He tried to keep the invading dread occupied with the idea that he might be able to use his naked, battered-looking workmate as some kind of distraction, leaving at least a portion of his brain to concentrate on more immediate concerns.

'Right. The first two things sound like they happened at some sort of club, and I'm fine with that. You live your life how you want to, more power to you. Struggling with the next bit. Was this a hate crime? Did someone... you know, bash you?'

'Oh, shut up, you tit. Look.'

Keith thrust his stigmatised wrist under Jeremy's nose, and then hooked his left leg around the back of his chair, resting the foot on the seat in order to point at the hole above the heel.

'Nailed.'

Jeremy then slavishly followed Keith's index finger as it rose up to sternly indicate the demolished areas of its owner's head.

'Hammered.'

Jeremy swallowed and nodded, concentrating with all his unblinking might on Keith's good eye.

'Dead,' Keith concluded, moving his spread palm in front of himself in order to indicate the general area in which he was presently decomposing.

Jeremy nodded again, increasingly proud of himself for how long he was maintaining eye contact this time. He made a mental note to always focus on one eye, regardless of who he was talking to, and used his newfound confidence to offer an alternative diagnosis.

'You're still surprisingly active, though, considering. I think you might want to seek a second opinion. Have you even seen a doctor? You should. That's the first thing I'd do in your condition. Well, after getting dressed. You should put some clothes on, and see a doctor.'

'Are you finished?'

'I've said my piece, yes.'

Jeremy lost concentration and accidentally looked at the bad eye again. He broke off from his manly stare and turned his attention towards his own knees.

'OK. I'm alive. Whatever. We'll deal with that later. I need you to come and look out of the window.'

Jeremy had long dreamt of the day that he might be asked to look out of the window in an official capacity, rather than merely as a cautious enthusiast, but this nude and badly distressed database programmer didn't have the rank to offer him a proper change of job title. In an ideal world, his excellent window work would be spotted by upper management and rewarded with a permanent post, with immediate cessation of current duties. This, however, was not an ideal world. Scanning the vomit-strewn desk beside him, Jeremy noticed Will's neatly folded emergency jumper, resting in his in-tray, only slightly splashed. He picked it up and thrust it in Keith's direction, while continuing to avert his gaze.

'Here,' he said, shaking the argyle-patterned v-neck.

Keith took the jumper and swiftly fashioned it into a knitwear apron by tying its arms behind his back.

'Happy now?'

'I truly wish it were that easy.'

Jeremy got up and followed Keith to the window, trying to ignore his still-exposed buttocks, now framed in a peek-a-boo fashion by woollen

180

wear.

'Look. Look out there. Tell me what you see.'

'Is there any way we could do this in the meeting room?' asked Jeremy, joining Keith at the window, and being careful to stand on his good side. 'It faces the same way, and I'm supposed to be preparing this thing.'

'Don't worry, no one's coming in here any time soon,' Keith reassured him.

'Oh,' said Jeremy, surprising himself at how easily he believed his workmate, and convinced that no good could come of pressing him further on his knowledge of the situation. 'OK, a blue sky.'

'Down a bit.'

'Trees. Rooftops. Seagulls.'

'Lower.'

'The security bloke sitting in his hut with his weird man doll. Some cars.'

'Lots of cars. How many, do you think?'

Jeremy shrugged and took a guess, 'a couple of hundred, counting the ones round the back of the hut?'

'And how many people work here?'

Jeremy paused to think.

'Fifty?'

'It's less than thirty. Might even be less than twenty, by now.'

'Tough times, I suppose.'

'They are. That's not my point. Do you know who all those cars belong to?'

'One or two. I can see mine. And Jem's is in its usual place. She's the only one who can get in there.'

'One or two. I can do a bit better than that,' said Keith, pointing down into the car park. 'Let's start with the BMW 3 series; that's Clive's. Old guy. Used to be head of Accounts. He's on the board. Next to that, with the old Jag, we have Philippe, from Canada. From Marketing. Paid more a year in insurance than he did for the car. The blue Audi next to that belongs to Suzy, also from Marketing. The people carrier is Clare's. She's Camberwell's PA. *His* grey Audi is round the front, by the way, in the bay next to Barbara. The BMW 5 series is Kevin's. He's head of strategy on the 5th floor. Rose through the ranks incredibly fast. You must remember Kevin. Zero Degrees Kevin. Huge bullshitter. Used to work with us on this floor.'

Keith turned briefly to face Jeremy, who was still staring blankly at the cars, before continuing.

'Stephen. Sam. Tara. Naomi. Vikram. My car. Stefan.' He ran through the names in quick succession now, punctuating them by stabbing at the window with his index finger as it moved from left to right. 'Am I ringing any bells here at all?'

Jeremy screwed up his face in what he hoped looked like concentration, before hazarding, 'I think I may have met Micah.'

'Who?'

'Micah?' Jeremy repeated the name hesitantly.

As Keith realised the source of Jeremy's confusion, he attempted a disbelieving sneer, immediately cursed his lack of facial control, and slapped his palm to his eyeball to hold it in place. As it happened, the palm slap appeared to Jeremy to be a quite natural response. This impression faded however, the longer he left the hand in place.

'My car. I said "my car". As in, the car belonging to me.'

'Oh. Sorry,' said Jeremy, managing a little chuckle. 'I don't know any of those people, then.'

'I've seen them all recently. In an old painting, at any rate. The people are long gone. Do you know where that painting is, Jeremy?'

Jeremy Starwars shook his head.

'It's in Birmingham.'

Jeremy took a moment to consider this.

'Alabama?'

'What?'

'Birmingham, Alabama?'

Keith paused, still holding his hand to his face.

'I can't tell if you're joking. Are you joking?'

Jeremy shook his head once more, puzzled.

'I thought it would still have had some resonance. I thought it would at least have lasted a while longer than that.' Keith sounded taken aback. 'OK. All right. We'll stick a pin in that and come back to it.'

Keith fell silent, and after a spell, Jeremy became unnerved by this, realising that his colleague was not merely quiet, but entirely motionless. He started at the sudden awareness that he couldn't see Keith breathing.

'Hello?'

'Sorry,' said Keith, finally moving his head once more, 'they were changing my catheter.'

Jeremy decided that his eyes had been playing tricks on him, and resolved not to look at Keith any more than was necessary to meet the bare minimum requirements of politeness. The quick, jerking, stabs at eye contact he was so practised at would be more than sufficient, particularly given the window-gazing with which he had been tasked, and to which he now returned with renewed vigour.

'Sorry,' Keith said again. 'Where to begin? Right. All right. There are lots of worlds, OK?'

He didn't wait for confirmation that this was OK with Jeremy Starwars.

'There are lots of worlds, and they're all layered on top of each other, like pancakes. Or sheets of paper.' He slapped his palm upon a ream of appropriate props piled next to the printer beside him. 'Yeah, that's better. Imagine the world is a sheet of this copier paper, all two-dimensional, and it's sat in the middle of this ream, all three-dimensional. Then imagine there are another couple of dimensions to the paper, and you've got it.'

'I've heard of the theory,' bluffed a nodding Jeremy, remembering to chance a fleeting look at, if not strictly into, Keith's good eye.

'OK,' said Keith, although Jeremy thought he could detect some measure of doubt in his tone. 'The world's much bigger than this paper, of course.'

'Of course.'

'And the ream is really tall. *Really* tall.'

'Load of sheets.'

'So many sheets. Now imagine… have you got a bottle opener?'

Jeremy searched his pocket, and produced a keyring, from which dangled a miniature penknife. He folded out the small bottle opening attachment.

'Oh, not one of those. A corkscrew, I mean.'

'Oh. Then, no.' Jeremy snapped the hooked implement shut, a little annoyed at this waste of his time.

'Maybe you can visualise it without me actually doing it.'

'Yes, perhaps.' Jeremy was quietly confident, considering himself to possess an imagination that was powerful, bordering on the overactive.

'Imagine a corkscrew going right through that ream.'

Jeremy shook his head. 'Were you actually going to ruin all that paper, rather than just say that?'

'You seemed distracted. Visual cues help, sometimes.'

'Thanks. Maybe I'll set fire to something during my presentation.'

'Maybe.'

Keith trailed off. Jeremy once more found himself staring at his pale and silent colleague's chest, and once more he felt a small wave of panic break over himself as he saw no signs of respiration there.

'The corkscrew passes through a single point in each sheet of paper,' Keith said at last, and it occurred to Jeremy that his lungs seemed to be expanding and contracting purely to pass air through his larynx, and for no other purpose.

'Now think about drawing on the paper. Completely covering it, starting from that one point. Then imagine that hole in the paper is a single point in time and space for a whole plane of existence,' Keith continued. 'Think of that point like a seed for some unique crystal. The point could be anything, anywhere, anytime.'

Jeremy shrugged, fairly certain that he could get away with just saying that he'd thought about this.

'OK.'

'In this plane, on this planet, it's you, Jeremy.'

Jeremy spluttered. 'Are you telling me I'm a beautiful and unique snowflake?'

'I'm telling you you're responsible for one. Mostly, I guess the corkscrew seems to go through something fixed. Maybe some places the paper never even gets drawn on, but here it's in flux. It looks like everything hangs off your consciousness.'

Jeremy adopted a look of what he imagined to be understandable scepticism.

'This world revolves around you. All the history, all the wars, all the

184

geography, all the geology. It's all been building up to you, it all radiates from you.'

'Oh. Right. Well, that's nice, isn't it?'

'And you're fucking it up.'

'Oh.'

'For everyone.'

'Right.'

'You shouldn't entirely blame yourself, of course. I mean, look at you.'

'Of course. What do you mean?'

'You know how you worry about things, and rather than addressing them head-on, you try to pretend they don't exist, ignore them and hope they'll go away, and somehow everything just seems to work out for the best anyway, like it was silly to be worried in the first place?'

'I suppose. I'm always worried about something though. That's normal though, isn't it?'

'A lot of that stuff is normal. What isn't normal is how things always work out for the best. That's not how it is for everybody. Every time you deny something until it gets better, things change radically around you to make that happen.'

'You're telling me the universe reshapes itself to suit me.'

'That's what I'm telling you.'

'Bollocks. Why am I so fucking miserable all the time then?' Jeremy surprised himself with his blurted admission.

Keith became static once more, while he considered this.

'I don't know, Jeremy. Maybe you should get some exercise. See a doctor, or something. The point is, things and people that are inconvenient to you are getting lifted right off your sheet of paper and dropped onto the next one up.'

'You reckon my problems are magically going away, all by themselves?'

'I'm not saying you've actively chosen the life you have. My God, imagine the paucity of ambition.'

'Thanks a lot.'

'I'd say it's reactive rather than proactive, and I'm sure you're not doing it consciously, but anyway, it's like you're twisting the paper, and putting crinkles in it. Then they're poking into the next sheet and shearing off. The analogy is breaking down a bit. Are you sure you don't have a corkscrew?'

'Leave the paper alone. That thing's always empty when I need it, and I hate having to go down to Stores,' said Jeremy, sighing. 'Keith, this all sounds like the ramblings of a man who's recently suffered a massive head trauma.'

'All those cars outside belonged to people whose only crime was to expect something from you, directly or indirectly. They all worked here, and now they're all gone. Whole floors of this building are empty because of you hoping they would go away.'

'And they're all in this Birmingham now,' said Jeremy, stroking a long imaginary beard on his chin.

'All buried long ago in Birmingham,' said Keith, nodding. 'Your biggest achievement, or at least I hope it is. A city of over a million people just disappears and gets forgotten about. Pulled out of existence here, and jammed into history on the next plane. What you've done down here is nothing to what you've done up there.'

'What do you mean?'

'Down here, I'm guessing you left a crater in the Midlands, and history worked round it, doing what was supposed to be done there elsewhere…'

'You're saying the Midlands Event was me?' Jeremy interrupted.

'The what?'

'The big crater in the Midlands. The one you're talking about,' said Jeremy, staring at Keith and blinking as though he had been asked what shoes were for.

'Remind me?'

'How can you not know? It's massive. Happened about 500 years ago. They think it was from a meteor bursting in the air, or something. You must know. It's like a huge quarry. Every British science fiction show ever made was filmed there.'

'That'll be where Birmingham is supposed to be.' Keith nodded. 'You got given a big bespoke system to write for the council, realised you were out of your depth, and I think you just lost it, and shut down. And then you denied the whole city all the way out of this reality.'

186

'When is this supposed to have happened? I don't remember any council thing. I've been working on the report generator for months.'

'That was supposed to take a few days here and there, while you were dealing with the stuff for Birmingham. Think about it. There's a lot of time here you can't account for, isn't there? More than usual, I mean. I remember we all had inventive time sheets. But to have taken that long to finish plugging in some third party library code. Come on.'

Jeremy grimaced. It probably shouldn't have taken him this long to finish what Keith was making sound such a small task, but he definitely should have at least started it by now.

'There's more to it than you might think,' he said, well aware that presently, there was considerably less to it than there should be.

'Is there, though?'

Jeremy shrugged.

'You don't remember all this, because everything here has reshaped itself around you. If I'd been here, I'd have forgotten it all too, and you've no idea how bad that would have been for me,' explained Keith. 'Jeremy, one way or another you have to stop what you're doing. The people waiting for this presentation of yours could be next.'

'What do you mean, if you'd been here? You are here.'

'Well, yes, but I'm dead, aren't I?'

'Stop saying you're dead. You're clearly not dead, or you wouldn't be in a position to tell me that you were dead,' reasoned Jeremy.

Keith thought for a moment, and then said, 'right. See for yourself. I'll come back in five minutes.'

With that, he quit his broken body and let it fall to the office floor, his head striking the plastic collection tray jutting from the printer behind him on its way down, causing it to make a twanging sound.

By the time Keith returned five minutes later, as good as his word, and sat up, Jeremy was in no doubt as to the mortal state of his workmate. After trying repeatedly in vain to find a pulse, stopping intermittently to practice on his own wrist, he had spent much of the intervening time panicking, and wondering how to dispose of the body. He had attempted to pick him up by the feet a couple of times, but had found him surprisingly cumbersome to drag. He had decided, in any case, to give up once Will's jumper had begun to ride up against the carpet. Being found in charge of a corpse was one thing; being found apparently undressing one was another thing entirely. The dead man twisted his head, now in a worse state than ever, towards a shocked and recoiling Jeremy and asked, 'well?'

Jeremy could only nod in response, robbed temporarily of the power of speech. The pair sat in silence on the floor for a short while, Keith gradually learning from experience, as he was, that people required time to acclimatise themselves to the facts of his condition.

'Are you OK?' asked Keith, eventually.

Jeremy nodded once more.

'Are you?' he asked in return. 'Of course not. Sorry.'

'Don't worry about it. Really. I'm just a late developer.'

Jeremy could tell Keith was delighted with his quip, and managed a feeble laugh out of politeness.

'I suppose it's good that you can joke about it all,' he mooted.

'Well, it all happened so long ago. I got over it.'

'Apparently. And the rest of it? That was all true as well?'

'Yes, Jeremy. This whole reality hangs off you.'

Jeremy considered this information. He had lived his entire life burdened with the constant, almost unbearable feeling that he was letting people down. The idea that there might that whole time have been a genuine reason for this, appealed to him greatly. The overwhelming majority of his self-loathing had always been focused on this enormous mental burden having been merely an illusion he was too weak to shake off. Now there was a possibility that he had been sensing something real all along, that there really might be an appallingly unfair weight arbitrarily heaped upon his shoulders by an uncaring universe. And it felt good.

Jeremy Starwars smiled, and, if only for the briefest of moments, felt relaxed. It was truly a rare feeling, and he wanted to luxuriate in it.

Keith observed the change in Jeremy's countenance, and frowned, as best he could.

'I hope you're not going to get a complex over this,' he said.

Jeremy laughed.

The left hand side of Keith's mouth curled into a half smile at this, the right hand side lifeless but stretched by the activity. Then it fell once more, his lower lip drooping slightly where his facial control was most limited. He held his ill-secured eyeball in place with two fingers as he dropped his head.

'Jeremy, about the people upstairs.'

'Yep?'

'They're here to find you.'

'So you say. They're not doing very well so far, though. It's not like I've been hiding.'

'Well, it is a *bit* like you've been hiding, though, isn't it?'

'No, I was… I had to sort out those plugs.'

'Fine. Anyway, they don't know who they're looking for yet. And they won't, until they actually see you do something extraordinary.'

'Right. Well, just so you know, I probably won't.'

'You will, Starwars. Trust me. And when you do, some other people are going to come for you.'

'Some other people. How do you know all this, exactly? How do you know they're after me, if they don't even know?'

'Because it's already happened for me. I watched the other people leave to go and get you.'

Still basking in the fleeting glow of something approaching contentment, Jeremy had decided to take all this in his stride and largely ignore it, on the assumption that it would all turn out to be nonsense. The worst thing that was happening here was that a colleague was explaining the plot of some film he had just seen, behaviour which he would generally prefer to quietly get angry about later on, by himself, in his own good time.

'Oh, fine. You're from the future. That was the missing piece of the puzzle for me. Everything makes sense now. And what did these other people do, when they *came for me*?' He made his hands into claws, gripping the air in front of himself and wriggling his fingers in order to dramatise the latter part of the question.

Keith shrugged.

'I don't know. They didn't come back. I'm absolutely sure the plan was to stop you, though.'

'Stop me.'

'Stop you.' Jeremy watched as Keith did a little dramatisation of his own, drawing his index finger across his throat. Whatever this film was that Keith was presently spoiling, Jeremy didn't think it would be his cup of tea at all.

***

Shareef sat in his portable cabin with Frankie, watching the afternoon game shows on a small portable television, as he did most weekdays.

'*Spirited.* Eight, Frankie. Beat that,' he said triumphantly, tapping a pen against his teeth.

Frankie remained silent, facing the window. The contestants on the television programme revealed that they had both found the same seven letter word, 'striped', on this occasion.

'Seven? Rubbish,' said Shareef, momentarily very pleased with himself before realising that there was only one 'i' available, thus invalidating his effort.

'Rubbish,' he said again, glancing over at Frankie, a little embarrassed not to be admitting to his error.

It wasn't as if Frankie would have made fun of him. Frankie was, after all, a tailor's dummy dressed as a security guard. Nevertheless, Shareef was loath to show any sign of weakness in front of his one member of staff. Frankie was a trusted assistant, making the cabin look occupied, and the trading estate guarded, whenever Shareef wasn't there. Break-ins would still occur, and cars would still be stolen, but the dummy couldn't be expected to give chase. Shareef could only assume that Frankie was successfully acting as a deterrent to the many other crimes that doubtless weren't happening in his absence.

'Numbers round,' he noted with a sigh. 'We don't do those, do we, mate?'

Shareef rose, and turning to the cabin's small kitchen area, lifted the kettle to check it, before switching it on. He dropped a tea bag into a mug on which was written the name 'Frankie'. The mug had sat gathering dust for a year, an idle folly, until Shareef had one day broken the mug upon which 'Shareef' had been written.

'Borrowing your mug again, mate,' he explained to his plastic companion.

Frankie said nothing. His staunch refusal to complain left Shareef feeling a twinge of guilt, as he looked at the mug he had purchased as a birthday present for the dummy. He briefly considered scratching the name off and writing his own in its place, but just thinking about such a betrayal made him feel a little queasy. Frankie's inability to move, to think, or to sense anything, implied a great deal of trust on his part, that his friends would do right by him. Shareef reached for a teaspoon and resolved once more to buy a new mug at the weekend.

A thump at the cabin window caused him to jump and drop the spoon into Frankie's mug with a clatter. He turned, almost disappointed to see that the dummy wasn't clambering to its feet. Instead, a man in thick glasses was stood outside, palms flattened against the glass, peering in at Frankie.

'Hey, blue eyes,' the man said to the dummy.

Shareef briefly considered letting Frankie handle this, and getting on with making the tea.

'Got something for you, blue eyes,' said the man, thumping on the pane.

Now that the man had moved his hands, Shareef saw that he had left what appeared to be two bloody hand prints on the window. He looked over at the expandable baton, resting in the corner, which he had purchased on-line after a recent spate of rioting elsewhere in the country. He wasn't strictly supposed to keep such a thing at work, but, as with Frankie, he felt better just knowing it was there.

'Are you shy, blue eyes?' the man asked Frankie. 'Big man like you, in your nice uniform.'

As the man hammered on the window again, Shareef turned down the television and opened the cabin door. The meat man saw him, slapped his palms against the window once more, and offered Frankie a mean glare, before ambling over. He stood at the foot of the breezeblock steps leading up to the cabin, his eyes level with Shareef's name badge.

'Sheriff. Are you the sheriff, blue eyes?'

'I'm Shareef. How can I help you? Are you hurt?'

'Am I hurt, sheriff? I am. Blue eyes hurt my feelings,' said the man, pointing to the window from which Frankie was staring out at him.

'I'm sure he didn't mean to,' smiled Shareef, folding his arms and glancing over at the dummy.

'The uniform changes some people, sheriff. I know. I saw it inside.'

'Shareef.'

'Sheriff. Sheriff blue eyes.'

The man nodded, and exhaled slowly and noisily, his mouth hanging open.

Shareef saw that the man was sweating profusely in his big leather coat, though the afternoon was mild.

'Are you OK? Your hands…'

The meat man looked at his hands, coughed, and wiped them with a handkerchief.

'I had some lovely meat, sheriff. Blue eyes bought it.'

'Frankie? I don't think so. He doesn't eat meat, mate.'

A puzzled Shareef pointed across the cabin. The man blinked behind his chunky lenses.

'Blue eyes,' he explained, gesturing over his shoulder.

'Right,' said Shareef, becoming impatient. 'What do you want?'

'I've got a message for you, sheriff. From blue eyes.'

'OK.'

Shareef unfolded his arms and leaned against the door frame in such a way that he could surreptitiously reach the handle of his baton. He waited for this 'message', trying not to appear tense. The man just stood there, breathing heavily, for what seemed like minutes.

'Well?'

'What can you give me for twenty pounds, sheriff blue eyes?'

'What?'

'I can't just give it to you, sheriff. That's not how we do the business.'

'This isn't a shop. Look, I've got shit to be getting on with, mate.'

'Getting on with meat. You have meat? I have a bag.'

'No, I … we don't have any meat.'

'I had meat.'

The meat man sounded mournful. Sighing, he reached into his coat. Shareef tightened his grip on the baton. He relaxed a little as the man pulled a banknote from an inside pocket, but seeing the red stains on

192

the note ensured that he maintained his guard.

'Blue eyes wrote the message on here, sheriff. If you want the message, we have to do the business.'

'Can't you just read it to me?'

'My eyesight isn't what it was, sheriff,' said the man, his eyes owl-like behind the heavy lenses.

'Let me read it then.'

Shareef reached out awkwardly, the fingers of his other hand still over the concealed night stick. By now, this was more to prevent the embarrassment of it toppling noisily to the floor, than to maintain its readiness as a weapon.

'Didn't come down in the last shower, blue eyes.'

The man backed away slightly, gripping his money with both hands, and eyeing Shareef with suspicion.

'Forget it, then. You're wasting my time, mate,' said Shareef, waving the man away.

'I'll show it to blue eyes,' said the man.

'Good. Whatever. You go back and see blue eyes,' said Shareef, closing the cabin door.

Back inside, he shook his head, and put the kettle on once more. There was another thump at the window, but this time he didn't bother to turn round. The kettle boiled almost immediately, and he poured the water onto the still-waiting tea bag.

'Have you got that now, blue eyes?'

Outside, the man waited a moment for a response, tutted, peeled the banknote away from the security cabin window, and walked away. Frankie continued to stare out, watching the meat man depart, ever-vigilant while his companion stirred the tea.

***

'We heard you swearing earlier, Bronwen.'

'I'm sorry. You'll have to pardon my French. Is this a disciplinary thing?' Bronwen looked over her shoulder at Barbara Pappa, who pretended not to have heard the question, and tried to make this state of affairs as clear as possible by frowning and looking through the blinds into the hallway, as though witnessing something unacceptable. She tutted and shook her head to emphasise the severity of the imaginary activity, aware that Denver and Marlowe were also now staring at her.

Raising his eyebrows in a facial shrug, Marlowe turned his attention back to Bronwen.

'There's no judgement here, Bronwen. We're just interested in why you were so upset.'

'Oh, right. Well, I don't like being told I can't go home on a Friday afternoon. This is my time.'

'And how does that make you feel?'

'Pissed off, if you want to know the God's honest truth.'

'You want to change your situation.' Denver phrased it as a statement, while posing it as a question.

Reminded of the theme to Minder, Bronwen half sang, half sighed a little of it.

'I'm sorry?'

'Nothing. An ancient TV show. You probably wouldn't know it. You're not from here, are you?'

Denver glanced across at Marlowe, cocking an eyebrow, before enquiring, 'why do you say that?'

'Oh God, I just meant your accents.' Bronwen was flustered. 'I'm not a white supremacist or something.'

Denver raised her sunglasses and stared impassively into Bronwen's eyes. Her demeanour changed in an instant.

'Oh God, you look so lush. How do you get your lashes like that? I wish I could wear that colour lippy. I'd look like a ghost, and you look amazing. Drop dead gorgeous.'

Denver dropped the glasses back down onto her nose, and Bronwen clapped her hands to her face in embarrassment at the gushing words that had just come out of her mouth. She so very much wanted these people to like her.

'I've seen enough,' said Denver after a moment's further observation of the discombobulated salesperson. She was addressing Marlowe, but Bronwen took it as a dismissal, and began to rise from her chair, head bowed, her brow furrowed in confusion.

'One other thing, Ms. George.'

She looked up from her shoes at Marlowe, who had smiled throughout the interview, in a friendly fashion that had in no way put her at ease.

'The guy covered in blood out there. What's his deal?' he asked.

'Ray? He said something about having sent a message,' she replied, surprising herself at how forthcoming she was being, and yet somehow unable to hold back.

'I think he's done something horrible in the toilet,' she blurted.

Marlowe sniggered. Denver quickly concealed a grin with a disapproving eye roll directed towards him, and cleared her throat.

'You said a message?'

'Yes.'

'For us?'

'I don't know. Perhaps.'

'OK. Well, it's been lovely to meet you, Ms. George.'

She saw a fresh and encouraging warmth in Marlowe's smile now, as he held his hand out to her. She took it to shake, and her knees buckled. *We were friendly. We were so nice. We didn't talk about anything special. There's nothing to worry about.*

She gave them a little wave and a simper as she left the room, ignoring Barbara entirely and closing the door carefully behind her.

Denver turned to Marlowe as he span in his seat beside her.

'Who do you want to see next?'

'I'm interested in this blood-soaked messenger and the one who says chop all the time. They're both pretty scary.'

'Yes. I'm guessing Chop Chop saw whatever it was that the other one did. We know for sure they haven't cut Augustine up, do we?'

'He's still upstairs, putting on the Ritz, as far as I know. Maybe we should check the toilets though, see what this guy's smeared on the walls in there.'

Marlowe took one more spin in his chair until he was facing Barbara Pappa.

'Babs, can you go get Jack the Ripper for us?'

She stretched open a gap in the blinds with thumb and forefinger, and peered out into the hallway at the blood-spattered man to whom she assumed they were referring.

'That's Ray Ciscombe.'

'Ray. Death Ray. I like it. Can you ask him to come in?'

Barbara opened the door.

'Oh, and then go take a look in the Gents,' Marlowe called after her. 'Don't do any cleaning in there, though. We might want to see what he's done.'

'I won't,' she muttered over her shoulder, before sternly scanning her staff lining the walls in the corridor, looking for the slightest hint of a chuckle or a grin.

Once Barbara had gone, Denver cocked her head toward Marlowe.

'If this Ray is making people disappear, doesn't it seem likely that he's doing it by rather conventional means? I'm not sure he's what we're after.'

'Stands out, though, doesn't he? And who's to say, maybe sacrifice is part of how it works. Maybe he feeds off it.' Marlowe shrugged.

'I remember the old stories about the city, before they had electricity, how they would offer up virgins to the forest,' mused Denver, stroking her chin. 'They would tie them to trees out at the Junction at dusk, and by morning they would be gone.'

'Taken by the wolves.'

'Of course.'

'And why did they do this, exactly? I don't remember much about Birmingham.'

'Oh yes. I forget how young you are.'

'I was. Now, who knows? I'm older than Augustine, anyway. Poor bastard never knew it at all.'

'It's strange to think about it, after all these years. But you're right. Poor little Augie.'

'Poor little Augie.' Marlowe sighed. 'Let's not dwell. He's still a pain in the ass old fart here. So, why off the virgins?'

'They gave them up to ask the gods of the forest to make their people fertile.'

'And did it work?'

'In a manner of speaking, I suppose it did. They were getting rid of everyone that nobody wanted to have sex with.'

Marlowe spat a mouthful of coffee onto the table and Denver

196

chuckled.

***

Barbara walked up to what she calculated to be arm's length from the gore-spattered Ray, careful to maintain eye contact. His face was smeared with crimson from what she hoped had been forgetful rubs, rather than some kind of primitive warpaint. He offered her an affable smile and she took a step back. It crossed her mind to consider which members of staff she hadn't seen that afternoon, and she found herself suddenly gripped by the strangest notion that many people were missing, though she knew that couldn't be true. She cleared her throat in as authoritative a fashion as she could muster.

'Ray? Can you join us please?'

'Certainly,' he replied.

The 'us' had been instinctive, ingrained; the result of years spent subtly insinuating herself into higher echelons. Barbara knew she wasn't truly part of the upper strata in the room she had just left, but the idea that some people might think she was, made her feel somehow more secure. If enough people believed, it might just be enough to make it true. She pointed Ray in the appropriate direction, to make it clear that she didn't in fact want him to follow her to where she was next headed. There followed an awkward exchange of 'after you' gestures before he finally conceded and passed her. Then she turned and hesitantly peered down the corridor, to the corner around which the toilets lay awaiting her attention.

***

Jeremy Starwars sat rubbing the freshly bruised shin on his left leg, whilst kicking out at the abandoned vacuum cleaner on the stair landing with his right.

'Bloody cleaner,' he moaned. He looked up at Keith. 'I hope Jem appreciates this. I could have been out the window, down the fire escape and gone by now.'

'I'm sure both she and Martin will be very grateful.'

'Who?'

Keith stopped and stared at him through the gloom of the stairwell.

'Oh, Starwars. Not him, too.' He broke off, seemingly exasperated. 'Jeremy, you know that thing where you go upstairs and forget what you went up there for?'

'Only too well.'

'I really need for that not to happen with you now.'

Jeremy shrugged, rose, and patted himself down, and they carried on up the stairs.

'So if everything hinges on me, does that mean there's no free will? For everyone else, I mean.'

'Good question. All I can say is, if I don't have free will, what the hell do I think I'm doing here, trying to influence you now? Maybe all this is just something that happens. Maybe you just do what you do. For that matter, maybe things are supposed to move between planes like this. Perhaps all our choices are illusions. I don't think it helps anyone's cause to think like that though, does it?'

'I don't know. Maybe it helps lazy people. I think it might help me.'

'But if everyone started thinking there was no free will, wouldn't they all just give up? Stop striving for anything?'

'If they were right, then what choice would they have?'

Keith paused on the stairs for a moment. Jeremy had already grown to hate these pauses, as when Keith stopped moving, all pretence of life fled from him.

'I suppose you're talking about entropy, and that does seem to be built into the system,' said Keith, as he began to ascend the stairs once more.

Jeremy nodded sagely. He had no idea what Keith might be referencing, but the dead man seemed to be crediting him with some sort of insightful remark, and he had no intention of disillusioning him.

'As I say, pointless to think like that, though,' said Keith. 'We've got to do what seems right in the circumstances in which we find ourselves, don't we?'

'Whatever passes the time, I suppose. Keith, can you do me a favour?'

'What's that?'

'Wave your arms around when you stop to think. It creeps me right out when you just turn into a corpse like that.'

'You want me to do a hand jive whenever I'm thinking?'

'Yes, and just whenever you realise you've stopped moving, if that's not too much trouble. Just flap them about a bit.'

'Do I have any choice in the matter?'

'Let's assume you don't.'

'Fine. You're the Axis, I guess.'

'Damn straight. I'm the what, now?'

'The Axis. That's what they call you now in Birmingham. Among other things.'

Jeremy considered this for a moment.

'And who makes their world turn? Who's their Axis?' he asked, not keen to know the other names by which he himself might be known.

Keith jerked his arms around spasmodically for a moment, and Jeremy stepped back, slightly startled.

'It's a chamber in a big cave. It's called the Bull's Arse.'

'Right,' said Jeremy, dejectedly.

'Were you hoping it would be another you?'

'No. Maybe. A bit. Thanks for the arm thing, though.'

'There are bound to be other yous on other planes, but everything is different on that Earth. Well, it was until you put Birmingham there, anyway. They're the only humans there, as far as they know. They've gone where they most needed to go, for fuel, food and minerals, but it's not easy when there are so many more trees. When you think of all the great European explorers, they had it easy by comparison. All the big lands they discovered had largely already been deforested by the people who actually lived there. This planet is mostly untouched. The Brummies have barely made a dent yet. Just getting to the coast of Britain must have been tough for the first generation. It was full of wolves, for a start.'

'I see. And what are Brummies?'

'The people of Birmingham. Jesus, you really don't have any recollection of a whole city? I still can't get over it.'

Jeremy shook his head, while trying to look as sombre as possible. He imagined this to be the least he could do. They took the next flight in silence, with Jeremy ruminating upon the information he had been provided so far by his dead colleague. As they reached the landing, the next point to jar with him percolated to the surface.

'What did you mean, 'first generation'? If what you're saying is true, I can't have put them there more than a few weeks ago.'

'Oh, it's only days ago for you. But how long do you think it took them to even begin to fathom the science involved in communicating with this plane? Or to theorise how they came to be where they were to start with? The people I've met, the people I've lived with for over sixty years before they figured out how to put me back in this body one final time, are essentially from your future. It's an entire civilisation. They're over five hundred years on from the people you sent there. Most of *those* people didn't make it past the first decade. When you just drop a city into a dense forest, where it suddenly has to cope with having no power stations or farms anywhere, bad things start to happen pretty quickly.'

'Well, I didn't mean for anything bad to happen to anyone,' said Jeremy. He was, however, speaking very much in general terms, as far as he was concerned. He was surprising himself a little with the detachment he felt regarding the fate of these so-called 'Brummies', but lowered his head to feign contrition anyway. Somewhere at the back of his mind, he was still clinging to the notion that although he now knew himself to live in a world that contained zombies, he didn't yet know for a fact that zombies didn't lie.

'Sixty years?' he said, after dwelling on matters a while longer.

'Thereabouts, yes. I've got a family there, and everything. Did you not notice I'd picked up an accent?'

'Well, I noticed you were talking funny, obviously, but I didn't like to say anything. I thought it was because of your injuries.'

Keith cast him what he assumed to be a half-smile. However, having selected the paralysed corner of his mouth to turn up, his face remained in an unaltered grimace.

'Ta very much for your discretion, I'm sure.'

'And kids? You? Jesus.'

Jeremy scratched his head, and Keith gave him a nod of confirmation.

200

'They're grown men, now, with bald patches and ear hair of their own.'

'Wait, aren't you already married?'

Jeremy imagined that he could detect a hint of indignation on Keith's face as he turned to respond. He knew that he didn't take enough interest in the lives of others, and it often came back to bite him in conversation.

'No, I'd just been living with... with...' Keith became unnervingly still once more.

'Sophie,' offered Jeremy, helpfully.

'...Susan for a couple of weeks. I'm sure she moved on just fine.'

'I'm not sure she would have, mate. You've only been upstairs a few days.'

'Of course, I forget. Well, she will. She will,' said Keith, talking more to himself than to Jeremy.

'Hold on though, how the hell could you remember all those cars after sixty years?'

'I may have bluffed on a couple of them, but I studied some recordings we have before I came back this time,' said Keith. Seeing Jeremy's eyes narrow, he quickly added a dismissive 'I'll tell you about them later.'

'Oh,' said Jeremy, dissatisfied, but already distracted by the next question popping into his head. 'Well, why are those cars even there? I mean, if the people don't exist here now. I mean, this Birmingham place is completely gone, isn't it?'

He was gratified to see Keith's arms flap as he waited for a response.

'Birmingham was a special case, I hope,' said Keith at last. 'You hadn't had any direct contact with the clients, so I'm guessing whatever angst or resentment you had going on there was completely unfocused, and you just took it out on the whole place. Whatever the case, you ripped out a lot more history with that than you would taking out a person. Anyway, reality seems to close the gaps you leave in as simple a way as it can, so artefacts get left behind all over the place when you wish someone away. They end up with different histories attached to them, or plain abandoned like those cars. I doubt they're even registered to anyone now.'

Jeremy considered the possibility that some of the people might have had children prior to disappearing, and wondered whether they too might have become abandoned artefacts, or whether he might simply have made their existence impossible. He couldn't see an answer that would make him happy coming from questioning Keith on the matter, and it struck him as being a good point to stop speaking. They were, in any case, nearly at the top floor.

***

Ray looked at his palms. The red on them seemed now to have taken on a darker brown hue, and he felt that wiping them on his trousers could only make matters worse. They would have to take him as they found him. He took a deep breath, and made sure that he had finished saying 'do do doo' before he pushed down the meeting room door handle and went in.

Marlowe and Denver were sat at the other side of the table. Marlowe smiled and beckoned Ray in. Anyone who wasn't looking for it wouldn't even have noticed the downward glance as he did so, or the briefest of frowns playing across his brow, but Ray caught it all. There was no question that his being covered in blood had not escaped the man's attention.

'Come in. Take a seat. You'll forgive me if I don't shake hands. Ray, isn't it?'

'Yes. I've spoken with Manny before. He probably mentioned me?'

'No.'

'Oh. But Barbara will have filled you in on my role here, I'm sure. I'm in charge on floors one and two.'

'We're in charge on all the floors, Ray. And there's nobody on floor two. You know that, right?'

'Of course.' Ray did know this, and he wasn't sure why it was relevant.

'Seems strange that you should claim dominion over an empty floor, Ray, don't you think?'

'Well, it's there when I need to expand the department.' Ray was thinking on his feet, and finding the experience exhilarating. He narrowed his eyes and studied his twin reflections in Marlowe's sunglasses.

'Or perhaps it was there, and then you shrank the department.'

Ray smiled. 'I think I'd remember something like that.'

Marlowe and Denver exchanged a look which Ray took as a sign that they were impressed with him. This was going really well.

'Maybe you would. Don't feel bad about Manny not singing your praise, though. We don't talk to him a whole lot.' He turned to Denver once more. 'Where is Manny, anyway? I haven't seen him in a while.'

She frowned and her eyes flicked up behind her shades, as though trying to read memories directly from her own impeccably maintained eyebrows. 'I suppose he's been working with Augustine.'

'We should keep closer tabs on that guy. I feel like he's got a whole other agenda going on sometimes.'

'Augustine?'

'No, Manny. I'd be happy if Augie had any kind of agenda at all.' Marlowe turned back to Ray. 'Sorry, man. You don't want to hear about us. Let's talk about you. Who did you cut up out there, Ray?'

'What? No one.'

'That's not your blood though, right? I mean, if it is, please say. I'd hate for someone to bleed out in here. It's not great for morale.'

'No, no. This? This is just from some meat.'

'Meat?'

'Yes. I missed lunch.'

'I see. So you were hungry, you got some raw meat out of the fridge, and you went and chowed down in the toilets.'

'I—Yes.' Ray followed Marlowe's eye line and looked down at his own heavily stained trousers. 'I suppose I should have used a napkin.'

'There's a whole lot of things you should have used, Ray. You normally eat on the shitter?'

'I didn't want to have to share it. As I said, I missed lunch.' Ray feared that he wasn't portraying himself in the finest of lights here, but the message had to be protected. A hint of a frown flickered across his face as it occurred to him that the security guard was taking a long time to respond to said message.

'Makes total sense to me, Ray. Honestly. And when Barbara comes back from the Gents, she's not going to tell us she's just found a member of staff strangled with their own guts, and I WILL KILL AGAIN smeared on the walls in there?'

'I don't know why she would. I did maybe spill some of my lunch though, I think. I'll definitely clean it up before I go home. When can I tell my team they can expect to go home, by the way?'

'What was the message, Ray?'

'Nothing. What? Nothing. What message?'

'Were you trying to scare us?'

'What? No. No, of course not.'

'Barbara tells us you've served in the Territorial Army, Ray. You've killed before, right?'

'No. God, no. I was a Drill Sergeant. The worst I ever did was make people drop and give me twenty.'

As he spoke, Ray thought he detected disappointment on their faces, and a part of him longed to invent some combat experience for them there and then. Marlowe sighed.

'Right. Let's get a proper look at you.'

***

Great Birmingham: The Year of Unity 474

Talisha Designer had been unable to look away from the display since the spherical probe had winked back into existence atop its slender perch in the cave. Now, finally, it was showing the welcome rectangular glow from an open portal in the globe, helping to illuminate the passage of two figures heading down the suspended walkway. Talisha exchanged relieved looks with Sandeep Programmersdaughter and Harrington Barber, and they rose from their consoles, gratefully discarding the headsets that had slowly scored sweaty grooves over their ears and into their cheeks during the preceding two hours.

They watched, almost in disbelief, as the hatch opened with a hiss and Captain Sevita Minister and Commander Kush Accountantson stepped out, grinning, rejoining the team as though they had simply popped down to the canteen.

Talisha hurried forward and hugged each of them in turn. She held on to Sevita as she stepped back from their embrace, and looked at her, beaming broadly. She had rehearsed so many lines with which to welcome them both back, over the many nights she had dreamt of this moment, but now that it was here, the best she could do was to sputter a laugh and feel the tickle of the tears rolling down her cheeks.

'It's OK. Maybe you'll get rid of us next time,' Kush reassured her, with a rub of the shoulder.

'You've lost weight,' she managed after a moment, still focused on Sevita.

'And he found it,' Sevita replied with a smirk, nodding over to Kush, who patted his stomach with pride.

He walked over to where Sandeep and Harrington were hanging back respectfully, and wrapped his arms around both their necks, pulling them in to plant kisses on their foreheads.

'All right there, big fella?' asked Harrington, his voice semi-strangulated.

'Totally bostin, mate. Just another day at the office,' Kush replied excitedly. 'How long has it been for you? Like we thought?'

'You've been gone ninety minutes as far as we're concerned, almost on the dot,' Sandeep informed him.

'Right, right. Shit, man, we've been gone a month.' Kush took a deep breath and exhaled slowly, releasing a seemingly interminable letter F, then shook his head before pulling the two engineers close once more. 'Ah, I've missed you, boys.'

'Give over, man, I've barely had time to eat a sandwich since I last saw you,' said Harrington, pulling himself free from the co-pilot's grip. 'And I'd like to keep that down.'

Kush used his freed hand to tousle Sandeep's hair before releasing him to straighten it once more, rolling his eyes and tutting as he did so.

'I want to be fully briefed about that sandwich later,' Kush warned Harrington, waving a finger in his face as he turned back toward Talisha.

Harrington shook his head in despair as he straightened his tunic.

'It was a pretty good sandwich,' he admitted, looking temporarily lost in nostalgia. 'Peaceful.'

'We think we saw Augustine,' said Sevita with a wide-eyed smile, clasping Talisha's hand as she told her.

'That poor bastard,' said Harrington.

'Bloody Dudley. That's unbelievable,' said Talisha, ignoring her hairy engineer. 'How did he look?'

'Like a tramp,' offered Kush. 'Worse than the Hancocks I've seen.'

'Really. So much worse,' agreed Sevita. 'Oh, Tal. That boy wasn't taking care of himself at all.'

'You didn't see the other dreamers, then.'

'No, he seemed to have gotten separated from them. Don't know what happened. I wish we could have spoken to him.'

'Sandy has some ideas for that.'

'I do,' confirmed Sandeep, directly into Sevita's ear. She turned with a start to see him stood at his console across the room, waving smugly.

'Thermoacoustics,' said Talisha, proud of her protégé. 'It's quite neat. He's changing the air pressure next to you by altering its temperature. We think it might be possible to use it down there outside the probe.'

'That's amazing,' Sevita conceded. 'If you microwave my head, I'm going to kick your arse inside out though, Programmersdaughter.'

'Don't microwave Captain Minister's head, there's a good boffin,' said Talisha.

'Ma'am.' Sandeep acknowledged the request, tapping a finger to his forehead.

'I still can't believe you've actually been down there.' Talisha stared at Sevita, unblinking.

'I went too,' Kush reminded her, folding his arms.

'Yes, I gathered that from the fact that you walked into a room and came out an hour and a half later with a massive beard,' Talisha told him, her gaze still fixed on Sevita.

'And here's us calling Augie a tramp,' said the captain, sniffing her armpit and casting a smile at Kush. 'We must stink. I can't even tell any more.'

'You smell fine,' lied Talisha. 'We'll try to get a bigger water reserve in there. It's not like we're short of the stuff here. How was the head?'

'Oh, it stank so bad. Whatever chemicals you gave us to flush that bloody thing, double it next time. I don't care how much it makes my eyes water. Or if Sandy can think of a way for us to dump all our poo in the other world, that works for me too. It's not like they'd notice.'

'I think a pooping probe is beyond us for the moment. We'll put a decent pump and an enzyme tank in for next time. It'll save space anyway. Might even be able to get some energy out of it. Are there a lot of waste bags to come out? I suppose there would be.'

Sevita nodded, a mixture of revulsion and embarrassment on her face.

'You know, no matter how many of those things you collect, it never turns into a fun hobby, like you might think.' She cradled her forehead in her palm. 'I can't believe you gave us transparent bags.'

'I'm so sorry, Veet,' said Talisha, covering her mouth and suppressing a giggle.

Sevita glowered at her.

'If I see my piles of carefully packaged shit on that *Brum's Biggest Hoarders* show, you're going to get a hoof in the foof, Ms Designer.'

'Fine talk from our nation's hero. This is what a month with Kush has done to you.'

Kush was indignant.

'What about what it's done to me?' he boomed in their ears from the device at Sandeep's console. 'The horrors I've seen. The ointments. The Pads. The waxings.'

'The waxings. The waxings,' he repeated, clearly thrilled by the authority that the address system was lending his voice.

'Will you please switch him off?' Talisha requested, and Sandeep duly obliged.

'Oh, I do like that, Sandy,' declared a beaming Kush. 'I'm going to make pronouncements like a prophet one hundred percent of the time when I'm using that.'

***

'Feeling better?' Talisha watched her gallant crew of two file into her office, freshly scrubbed and changed.

Harrington sat, arms folded, on the end of her desk, seemingly unaware of how much this annoyed her, while Sandeep fiddled with a box in the corner.

'Human again, just about,' said Sevita, nodding.

'Call me what you will, I bloody love a bubble bath,' declared Kush, relaxing into a swivel chair and sighing.

Talisha leaned forward at her desk, keen to crack on.

'So anyway, where did you pop initially? Anywhere near where we figured?'

'More or less exactly where Deep Probe One popped,' said Sevita. 'I recognised the hill straight away. I've seen the footage enough times.'

'Like we thought.' Talisha stabbed at the desk with her index finger. 'It moves a bit, but the Axis is still anchored to the planet's surface, just like the cave. It doesn't matter when you arrive, you'll pop somewhere on the route to the origin.'

'Well, we were certainly grateful not to find ourselves in deep space. That would have been a very boring month. No offence, Kush.'

'None taken, I'm sure.'

He had a quick spin in his chair.

'I'd hope you would have spent it plotting star and planet movements,' suggested Talisha. 'Still, I'm glad we don't have to sit working out when things are going to pass through a fixed point.'

Kush managed to stop the chair with him facing in almost the right direction. 'It does all leave us knowing where but not when, though.'

'That's up to the team studying the dream recordings. If they can find you on there somewhere, they can work out the gap until the day they all ended. Then we can put you there, near enough. Did he get a proper look at you? Augustine?'

'I don't reckon. He looked half cut. Plenty of others did, though.'

'Do you know how you looked to them?'

'It was weird.' Sevita frowned. 'It was obvious they could see us, from their reactions, but… We must have seen ourselves dozens of times in reflections in windows before we figured out it was us. Then we went right up to a mirror, and focused on it, and we could just see the mirror.'

Talisha looked puzzled. 'I'm not following. So, no reflection then?'

'Vampires. I knew it. I'm going to give you such a staking,' said Harrington, pointing accusingly at Sevita.

'In your dreams, buddy. No, we could see the mirror in the mirror. And the mirror in that mirror. You know? Like when you point a camera at its own monitor.'

'Like an infinity mirror, then. I've got one in my bathroom.'

'You do surprise me.' She gaped at him mockingly. 'Anyway, it was only when we pulled right back that we started to make out the shape. We were a floating ball, maybe two foot wide, fuzzy at the edge, and light just bounced off us.'

Talisha nodded.

'Sounds about right on shape and dimensions for the probe. I think, down the line, we can give you a much more useful shape, project something that'll let you properly interact with the environment, but baby steps for now. I didn't know for sure what the light would do. Thought it might bend round. It's really encouraging that it reflects. It sounds like you can have a genuine presence there.'

'It would be useful if you could make people a little less terrified to see us.'

'We have something for that, too. The box Sandeep is patting over there. His team has been playing with it for a while.'

'And what does that do?'

'It allows whatever is within its vicinity to insinuate itself instantly into your reality,' Sandeep explained enthusiastically. 'A reason for its presence, for its existence, even, will appear immediately obvious to those around it. We call it the Plausibility Field Generator. P.F.G. for short.'

'Well, that all sounds reasonable.'

'It should do. It's been switched on since before you came in.'

Sevita scratched her head and regarded the small, plain, unprepossessing, plastic box.

'So we can just have that with us in the chamber, and the people on the other plane will just view the probe like a particularly unusual uncle, or something?'

Sandeep shrugged. 'Whatever best fits the scenario, within reason. I mean, you're still going to look odd, but it should mean no crowds chasing you with pitchforks. It should work great with the probe too, because that punches a bit of a hole in time around itself, as well as space. This should fill that nicely with a little back story. The Axis seems to do something similar, but on a much grander scale. I suppose nature hates a void.'

'Wait. You say you've been working on that thing, but if it works like you say, how do you know that's true?'

'Good point. I'm convinced I helped create it, but I guess there's every chance it made its own way here.' Sandeep shot the box a wide-eyed glare. 'Either way, I guess it's working, at least. You'll have to ask me again once the field fades.'

'And it won't do anything to us? It won't make me suddenly start believing Kush's fairy stories about his love life?'

Kush made a 'W' shape with his fingers, to save him the trouble of saying the word 'whatever', and presented it to Sevita with a tired stare. She made an 'L' shape with her own fingers in response, and brought it up to her forehead.

'I know you are, but what am I?' asked Kush in a singsong voice and switching his fingers from a 'W' to two 'V's.

Sevita assumed the question to be rhetorical, and shook her head with a smile.

'No, it'll be fine. We'll mount it on the shell, and it'll project outward,' said Sandeep, ignoring the exchange.

'It'll be fine,' he said again, uncertain as to how convincing he had sounded the first time.

'It'll be fine,' Talisha agreed.

***

The buzzer woke Jem from her reverie with a start. With a quick shiver, she was back in the moment. Something was happening, at last. She had lost track of how long the people upstairs had left her alone there with nothing to do but search in vain for a gun she now suspected she might have just dreamt of having in the first place. Finally, someone was coming to see her, perhaps to tell her that it had all been a terrible mistake, that she wasn't needed up here after all, and that she should just go back downstairs.

She stood up from the bed and adjusted and retied her kimono, wrapping it tightly around herself, having been unable during her explorations to locate the clothes in which she had arrived. She straightened her hair in what faint reflection the window offered, cleared her throat indelicately, and left her makeshift boudoir.

Hugging the wall as she approached the mouth of the corridor, it was with some relief that Jem recognised the partially blurred faces in the window of the main door. She jogged over, beaming with delight at the sight of a slacker and a zombie. As she waved through the glass at them, she realised that she couldn't remember the last time she had seen Keith. She knew he was dead, and she knew that she had spoken with him since his death, but she could only remember him as being alive and a little unpleasant. This was troubling, but then, she reasoned, there were any number of issues she would need to work through with a professional of some kind, if she ever got out of this building again. And it was good to see Jeremy. He had come for her, just like he had reluctantly agreed. She wondered how his demonstration had gone.

Jeremy knocked on the pane, and pointed to her left, directing her towards the keypad. Jem's hand went to her mouth as it became apparent that her visitors weren't going to be able to simply tap the pad on their side and let her out. As she returned her gaze to the pair waiting on the other side, and pondered whether she could pick two people in the building less likely to be able to kick down a door, they both began tapping at the window impatiently.

'I don't know the code,' mouthed Jem, and she performed an exaggerated shrug of her shoulders, pulling the saddest face she could muster.

It was difficult to effectively communicate the situation through the toughened safety glass window in the door, and she thought her face must appear just as distorted as those of the two panicking, shouting people on the other side.

She didn't know the code, and having the pair of them, wide-eyed and pointing at her, poking at the glass, wasn't helping anybody. She was taken aback at how quickly they seemed to have fallen apart over her present inability to let them in. Keith was unavoidably at least fifty percent wide-eyed at all times now, but his good left eye currently looked as manic as the one bobbling in its stricken socket.

'What?' she mouthed, cupping her hand to her ear more for display purposes than practical ones.

They both repeated their cries, and this time Jem tried to focus on Jeremy's lips. Another finger point, and something 'you'. Charming.

Augustine was practically on top of her by the time she realised that the first word had been 'behind'.

***

'So, Will, is it?'

'Last time I checked the certificate.'

Will realised he had come dangerously close to a joke, and this made him a little uneasy. Humour was an awkward and unpractised sphere. He fixed the man in the dark glasses with an unfocused stare.

Marlowe studied him for a few moments before breaking into a broad beam.

'Wow, that's a pretty intense gaze you've got there, fella.'

'Sorry,' said Will, remaining expressionless, and turning his head instead to glare at the woman, who was also wearing sunglasses.

'I see what you mean. Gosh,' said Denver, offering Will a friendly smile.

'Right? Looks like he's trying to erase us with super-vision, or something.' Marlowe snapped his fingers. 'Eyes back on me now. You got superpowers there, Will?'

Will paused before offering his reply.

'Not that I know of.'

Marlowe leaned toward him over the table. 'Yeah, but would you tell us if you did?'

Will remained impassive. 'I probably wouldn't tell anyone.'

Marlowe wagged his finger at him, and sat back. 'This one. This one.'

'Hard to read, isn't he?' Denver was frowning behind her shades. 'What are you thinking about, Will?'

'Three children that died when a treehouse collapsed the other day in

212

Luton.'

'I'm sorry?' Denver was taken aback.

'It was awful,' Will informed them assuredly.

A perfectly executed piece of social interaction; information offered, and an appropriate opinion expressed. He was so pleased with himself that a brief smile crept across his thin lips before he remembered to adopt a more funereal countenance.

'Oh, my,' said Denver, and seemingly lost for further words, she turned to Marlowe to continue.

'OK, Mister ice man,' he began, as he cracked his knuckles, 'Tell us about your boss. Whose blood is he wearing?'

Will shrugged.

'You don't seem at all troubled that he looks like he's hacked somebody up.'

He shrugged again, pointing out that, 'it wasn't me.'

'Well, there's that. There's that. There's always a bright side.' Marlowe drummed his fingers on the table. 'There's no-one here you'd be upset to hear was missing?'

'If they were here, they wouldn't be missing.'

'Good point,' Marlowe conceded with a little sigh. 'And is anyone missing, that you're aware of?'

Will shrugged for a third time.

'OK, Shruggy Shruggington. It's the glasses, I think. These glasses are getting in the way of us properly bonding. They're coming off, we're going to gaze lovingly into each other's eyes, all nice and friendly like, and you're going to answer one more question for me.'

'All right.'

Marlowe slowly and deliberately removed his glasses, his eyes locked on Will's throughout the manoeuvre.

'Is this making you feel uncomfortable at all, Will?'

'No. Was that the question?'

Marlowe glanced over at Denver, before fixing Will with an intense glare once more. Will noted that Marlowe's eyes were bloodshot, and watched with vague interest as his pupils adjusted to the light.

'Have you made anyone disappear, Will?'

'Once, when I was six.' Marlowe's eyebrows rose. 'They were only behind the curtains really, though. Mum and Dad said they didn't know how I'd done it, but looking back, they must have done. They must have. They weren't that stupid. Even at the time, it seemed far too easy a way to impress people. A cheap trick. The whole experience just left me feeling hollow. I lost interest in magic shortly after that.'

'You don't like magic.'

Will's inquisitor let out a loud sigh of exasperation, and pinched at the bridge of his nose. Denver touched his shoulder and leaned in to whisper something to him.

Will tutted quietly to himself. He couldn't abide whispering, considering it to be the very height of rudeness. He watched as Marlowe nodded and took in whatever he was being told so secretively.

Marlowe turned back to Will, and with a beckoning gesture, took his hand in both palms. *We just had a bit of a chat. Everything is fine. There's nothing to worry about. You can't even remember what we asked you. Just boring admin stuff, really.* The unchanged expression on Will's face told him that he was wasting his time. He released Will and raised his hands in defeat.

Denver removed her own shades, and asked, 'Will? Can you look at me for a moment?'

He obliged, and she observed him silently for a moment.

'Thank you, Will. I don't have any more questions. Marlowe?'

'Me neither. Thanks, Will. Can you go join the others for now?'

They watched him leave the room.

'Nothing,' said Denver, her voice betraying a nervous excitement. 'That's either a man with no empathy at all, or he's something more. I think we may have found what we came for.'

'I think you might be right,' he responded, and she realised that for once she could see something other than a grin on his face. She wasn't sure if it was relief or worry.

***

'We should get in there,' asserted Keith, as he and Jeremy stood peering through the small window in the office door at the scuffle underway on the other side.

Jeremy leapt into action, and mounted a shoulder-barge attack which caught the door entirely by surprise. Somehow, however, the door resisted this assault, and Jeremy was left with an immediate and profound sense of regret over the pain he now found himself to be in. He gripped his shoulder and upper arm in various places, trying to remember whether the various bumps and protrusions he could feel had been there before. Panicking, he felt the other shoulder for confirmation, before realising in the process that his hand and arm were moving freely. With relief, he wiggled the fingers on the end of the limb he had briefly suspected to be shattered beyond repair. Jeremy had no formal medical qualifications, and had a tendency to believe himself to be a likely candidate for any affliction he had ever read up on, but he was reasonably certain that as long as you could wiggle, you were basically all right.

'If you could stop fondling yourself for a minute, you might want to step back.'

Seeing that Keith was now wiping what appeared to be a particularly filthy handgun on Will's jumper, Jeremy obliged.

'Where did…'

'You know. You just don't want to know.'

A strong smell of excrement assailed Jeremy's nostrils as Keith pointed the gun at the lock. He fired twice, the reports high-pitched and deafening as the sound bounced around the stairwell. Jeremy, his ears ringing, continued to hug himself as he watched his allegedly deceased colleague kick open the door, so recently his worthy wooden adversary, but now splintered, ragged and defeated.

Jeremy could now see Jem framed in the doorway, lying on the floor and rising to her elbows, as Keith entered the office, leading with his gun arm. He watched the gun fly from Keith's grasp as Jem's dinner-jacketed assailant appeared from the right hand side of the doorway, blindsiding the over-achieving corpse, gripping his wrist, and punching him to the ground. He witnessed Jem, scrabbling to become reunited with the weapon she had once stored in her suspended ceiling. He saw the fluorescent green sandal-clad feet of the otherwise-smartly-dressed man first kick the gun away from her, and then kick her squarely in the head. His eyes flicked across the room to the firearm, now lying beneath a desk several metres away, and back up to see Jem tumbling over and coming to rest at the wall. He watched as the gun stopped being far away, and his hand became filled by its now warm barrel. He observed as he strode into the office and rained down blow after blow upon the head and shoulders of the man in the dinner jacket. He continued to watch as he turned the small gun around in his hand, palming its now reddened grip and sliding his forefinger into its trigger guard. He saw himself point it down at the man now alternating between trying to get up, and collapsing once more onto his back, waving and laughing.

Jeremy heard Keith shout something that he would later reflect upon as having sounded like 'do it'. He definitely heard the man in the dinner jacket say 'at last', just as he felt his finger pulling back the trigger.

The first bullet tore through both of the man's hands, raised as they were, one in front of the other, palms splayed as a final line of defence, for want of anything else behind which to hide. The second went straight through his forehead. He went limp, the back of his head hitting the floor with a crack which, to Jeremy, seemed louder than the pistol. His arms came to rest outstretched, palms facing upwards, revealing the two perfectly centred wounds that had just been inflicted upon them.

Jeremy Starwars continued to point the gun until he felt certain that the man had stopped moving, at which point his arm fell trembling to his side. He continued to stare at the now still face of Augustine, and fancied that he saw a hint of serenity in its slack jaw and relaxed features. Any sign of fear or surprise seemed to have departed, perhaps dislodged as skull had met thinly carpeted concrete.

Keith rose once more, seemingly unhindered by his fresh injuries, and unconcerned by the fact that his wandering right eyeball had now disappeared from his face entirely. He knelt down beside Augustine's body and lifted its left arm by the wrist.

Assuming this to be an attempt to locate a pulse, Jeremy asked, 'anything?'

Keith gave no immediate response, and instead dropped the left arm, waddled around the corpse on his haunches, and picked up the right.

Jeremy saw now that he was studying the wounds in Augustine's palms. His colleague looked up at him with his remaining eye and gave him what seemed like a smile from the more active half of his face.

'What's black and white and red all over?' he asked.

'What?' said Jeremy, more in stunned reaction to the question than in reply.

'This guy,' revealed Keith, pointing downward. 'Do you know what you've just done?'

'I had to,' said Jeremy Starwars. 'Didn't I?'

'That's not what I mean.'

'I don't know. It all happened so fast. Did I... did I just murder someone?'

'Yes, Jeremy,' Keith reassured him, 'you murdered the shit out of someone.'

'Oh God. Oh Christ. What was he, anyway? A waiter?'

Keith's laughter in response to the question was sincere and unforced, but the monotone sequence of staccato 'ha' noises that emerged from his dead throat sounded deeply sarcastic.

'He did wait a fair bit, yes. His name was Augustine. Don't worry about it. He'd had a good innings.' Keith's tone became more serious. 'How did you get the gun, Jeremy?'

'I don't know. Jesus. I went and picked it up, I suppose. The whole thing is a blur.'

'No,' said Keith, getting to his feet. 'It was way over there, under a workbench, and then the bench was gone, and the gun was in your hand, while you were still in the doorway. And he saw you do it. And that's how they found you.'

'Your jumper's gone crooked,' said Jeremy absent-mindedly, as he backed towards the nearest swivel chair, shakily turning it just in time for the seat to meet his rapidly descending posterior, and leaving him sat sideways. He barely looked away from the waiter that he had just killed. Jeremy was unsure as to whether he was actually in shock now, but he was already pondering the social niceties of the situation, and he felt that looking haunted and staring wide-eyed at his prey was the least he could do. He felt, more than usual, as though he were acting; nothing seemed especially real at that moment. Best, for the time being, to simply try to meet whatever expectations he imagined others might have for his behaviour.

Keith adjusted his jumper-cum-apron to restore his modesty, and continued to look like a cryptic crossword enthusiast unexpectedly faced with an entirely new setter and an unnumbered grid.

From the edge of the room, Jem moaned. In the wake of becoming a cold-blooded killing machine, Jeremy Starwars had entirely forgotten about her. Hadn't his insane fury been ignited entirely by her peril in the first place? Why had he not immediately raced to ensure that she was all right? He couldn't tell whether guilt or awkwardness was the more prevalent feeling in his mind as his eyes briefly flitted to see her clasping her head. Listening to her quiet-but-repeated profanities as she became acquainted with what was clearly a severe headache, Jeremy felt it best to stay in character, face frozen, staring at his victim. From the sounds, he pictured Jem rolling over, and beginning to struggle to her elbows and knees. While this was taking place, he realised with creeping dread that he was no longer focusing on the body; This Augustine was just a blur. Would this be noticeable to the others? Would they spot the change in his eyes if he refocused now? Perhaps staring at nothing was more appropriate anyway; it was just so hard to tell. He had no frame of reference for his actions beyond a liking for thrillers. He decided that it was best to just stay as he was and not move a muscle. When Jem saw him like this, there would be no need for explanations or excuses as to why he hadn't tended to her. If anything, all the sympathy would be directed towards him. He imagined how entirely broken he must now look, and wrestled with an urge to smile.

'Jem. Back in the land of the living. Good, good,' said Keith encouragingly. 'You're probably in shock. Starwars certainly looks like he is. Nice cup of tea will help. You should probably pop the kettle on.'

'Fuck off,' suggested Jem, still on her elbows and gripping her head like she was attempting to threaten it into submission. It was some minutes before she was on her feet and vomiting over the corpse of Augustine.

'Here,' said Keith, helpfully removing and throwing Will's jumper for her to clean herself up.

'Thanks,' said Jem dubiously, catching the garment that had been

218

serving as Keith's woollen loincloth, and trying to remember which side of it had been facing outward.

Unable to be certain, she turned the jumper inside out prior to wiping her face thoroughly with it, reversing it once more before returning it to Keith.

'That smells like shit,' she noted.

These actions appeared to take an eternity from the perspective of Jeremy, as he strove valiantly to remain a statue of a troubled man. Finally, Jem came over and waved her hand in front of his face. While he pondered whether or not to draw a line under his catatonia and acknowledge her, she leaned in, inches from his face, and peered into his determinedly defocused eyes. He was vaguely aware of Keith talking away in the background, but everything was just white noise while he could feel her breath rolling over his cheeks. Tinged though it was with the scent of vomit, he felt as if he could bathe in its warmth forever. Jeremy Starwars decided that this huge, looming, blurry face, most likely filled with concern for his wellbeing, was the most beautiful thing he had ever almost seen. And still, he didn't respond. He was now afraid to move, for fear that it would cause her to withdraw all the sooner, and never come that close to him again. After a few more precious seconds, the big face became smaller anyway, and now she was snapping her fingers in front of him. When would come a believable moment for him to wake from his torpor? He felt certain that slapping would commence shortly after snapping failed. Should he wait to be slapped? His mind flashed back to happy times spent lying on the floor of the meeting room, and thoughts of paying off friendly ambulance men. It had all seemed so simple then.

'Ow,' he found himself saying, as the sting of her first slap worked its magic. It had flown in far sooner than he had anticipated.

'Oh. Oh, I'm sorry, was that hard? I didn't mean it to be hard. Your poor face,' she said, gently rubbing his cheek with the same palm that had just battered him senseful.

With several long and deliberate blinks, Jeremy began to look with fresh eyes at this vision of mildly violent loveliness, smiling and caressing his head, and almost immediately caught himself attempting to look down her kimono. Reasoning that erratic eyeball movements could very easily be symptomatic of his emergence from a catatonic state, he proceeded to flick rapidly between lovely face and shadowy cleavage, before quickly concluding that he was failing singularly to take in either, and that his eyes were beginning to hurt in the attempt. He squinted and pinched the bridge of his nose, and as he looked up once more, realised that Jem had straightened up and was rubbing the small of her now arched back. Jeremy Starwars found this to be an unreasonably sensual sight with which to be greeted after battling his way so bravely out of an admittedly fictitious fugue state.

'Bugger, that kills,' said Jem, before embarking upon a small coughing fit.

'Jesus,' she croaked, once her lungs had decided to go back to something approximating their normal respiratory duties.

She turned her attention once more to the poor, stricken Jeremy Starwars.

'Sorry. Are you OK now, sweet?'

'Think,' said Jeremy, deciding that whole sentences should probably be beyond a person in this stage of his condition.

'You killed the baddie,' she observed, glancing as briefly as she could over to Augustine. 'That's pretty hardcore, Jeremy.'

'Hurt you,' explained Jeremy, struggling to get to grips with the grammar of the bewildered, and panicking that he might be descending into Hulk-speak. He watched as her jaw dropped a little, and her hand went instinctively to the reddened and bruised side of her face. Then all at once, she was hugging him.

'Aw, come here,' she said, giving him a final squeeze, before planting a kiss on his forehead and releasing him. 'My hero.'

Jeremy Starwars dropped the arms, his stupid arms, which had got as far as stretching pathetically, grasping nothing, having failed entirely to envelope her, to draw her closer, to reciprocate the hug in any way. He felt certain that this had been one of the greatest moments of his life, and still he had found grounds to hate himself. He stared at Jem as she walked to the window, rubbing her head, and surveyed the outside world, seemingly deep in thought. Perhaps if he just stared hard enough, with sufficient intensity, she would turn around, come back and hug him again. It was the only way, Jeremy reasoned, to make up for the years of neglect, all that time he had spent not noticing this angel in his midst. Yes, he would glare at her with what would obviously come across as a burning desire, and not at all lecherous or sinister, and she would understand, and there would be an unspoken something between them that he could seek to nurture at a later date.

After a moment, Jem turned back from the view of the trading estate and the residences beyond, and Jeremy felt certain that he had compelled her to do so. He watched her lips part to speak, and then looked deep into her eyes as the brow above them furrowed.

'Are you sure you're OK?'

A pinkish blur passed twice between her eyes and his, and Jeremy became aware that she was waving at him. He attempted a reassuring smile, as a prelude to explaining that he was just fine, but before he could speak, his head was jerking forward, and the breath with which he had intended to make words was leaving his mouth in a single sharp exhalation.

'Puh,' he said, and he felt a stinging sensation at the back of his head. It was as though he had been suddenly struck.

'KEITH,' he heard Jem shout. Was there panic in that voice?

Episode. Stroke. Grand mal seizure. Tumour. Cerebral hemorrhage. Diagnoses flashed rapidly through Jeremy's mind. There was no time for grammar or reasoning, as he rapidly fired through multitudes of half-remembered medical articles, blog entries and televisual dramas. Everything he had ever read about, or seen, relating to malaises of the brain, and had consequently expected to experience for himself at some point thereafter, he saw now all at once, as he frantically pattern-matched. In the cold light of day, none of the possibilities appealed to him greatly.

'And you're back in the room.'

Cheeks suddenly cold. *Sudden blood loss from the ears, perhaps.* Floor going away. Head lifting once more. *Sense of balance gone because ear canals full of blood?* Now he was looking at the half-collapsed face of Keith, telling him that it was sorry, but that it needed his full attention. *Hearing unaffected.* His cheeks were being gently patted by the same cold, dead hands that he now realised had been holding his face, and raising his head.

221

'You didn't need to bloody twat him.'

'It was supposed to be a gentle smack. It's what he needed though, honestly.'

'Oh, you're medically trained as well now, are you, Doctor Death?'

'He had to snap out of it. We need him thinking clearly, and the quickest way is the only way, right now.'

Jeremy breathed out in three short puffs as he rode out the wave of adrenalin, now fully alert.

'You arsehole,' he declared, and the working half of Keith's mouth smiled briefly, before his chin took on a more urgent jut.

'Right. We're on a fairly tight schedule from now on. They'll be looking for you, Starwars.'

'I thought they already were.'

'Not them. Team Manny. Deep Probe Two. They came because of this, because this is when the recordings start running out. They were able to pop anywhere along a line through history that lead up to today, but no later.' Keith paced as he spoke. 'And this is when they saw your face.'

'Who saw me? Are those cameras on?'

'No, no, no. I mean, yes, the cameras are on, and yes, you probably will want to erase the footage of you shooting an unarmed man in the head at some point, but that's not it. The main thing is that *he* saw what you did.' Keith was pointing at Augustine.

'Shit. Shit.'

'Look, you haven't really killed him.'

Jeremy took a series of little looks at the body, no longer wanting to take it in for too long in one go.

'There's a hole in his skull, and he's not moving,' he said, summing up his assessment.

'There's a hole in my skull. I won't deny it's a setback, but it's not the be-all and end-all.'

'Oh, the jury's going to love that. Fine. I don't know why I was bothered. I didn't kill anyone, I just made a little hole.'

Keith stopped moving, in the way that made Jeremy's flesh crawl.

'I hate it when he does that,' said Jem.

Jeremy nodded.

222

'It just makes me want to cover his face with something.'

'I sometimes wanted to cover his face with something when he was still alive, to be honest,' Jem admitted.

'I heard that,' said Keith, becoming animated once more. 'All right. Listen. Augustine, Linda and James, they were three children in Birmingham. They didn't know each other there, but they did here, when they dreamt. They would inhabit whatever body was available to walk around in, and they would somehow recognise each other whenever they met. By the time the journalists found out about it, they were already starting to work out ways to leave signals for each other, and prepare things to make it easier for themselves in their next lives, the next time they slept. By the time the scientists got hold of two of them, they had essentially lived many lives, and they remembered everything. From the things Linda and James were able to tell them about this world, they started to realise that it was a real, solid place, and that it wasn't on their planet. That's when some of them began to rethink everything that didn't make sense about their own history, and they started to put two and two together.'

'About me.'

'Eventually.'

'What about you?' asked Jem, her brow furrowed.

Keith waved a pale, cold palm in her face. 'Please. Maybe later.'

Jem cursed under her breath, her head still hurting a little too much to push the matter for the moment, and Keith continued.

'Anyway, the research team wasn't satisfied with having to interpret this world through descriptions from a couple of teenagers, as helpful as they tried to be. Why would they be, when they had dream recorders?'

'Is that what it sounds like?' Jem's eyes were lighting up.

'Probably. You plug the dreamer in, record their brain activity, then you play the recording back into someone else's brain and they experience the dream. Rachel and I tried it with each other one time, at a hotel. Never again. Holiday ruined. Best to stay out of loved ones' heads.'

'I knew that could be done. I had a massive argument about it with...' Jem frowned, and paused for a moment before conceding that her memory had failed her. 'Well, with some boyfriend or other. That's weird. I remember a stupid blazing row, but not who it was with.'

'Perhaps you dreamt it,' offered Jeremy, and he received a silent, sarcastically mimed belly laugh in response.

'Anyway. Jeremy. Listen,' said Keith, trying and failing to snap his fingers. 'So, they recorded them a couple of times, and it worked. They could see this world, or this world as it was a few thousand years ago, at any rate. It took them a while to find Augie. Linda and James did what they were told, and tried to persuade him to come forward when he was awake, but he didn't seem to understand what they meant. He didn't know where they kept disappearing to. It seemed that he only knew this world.'

'Always asleep. Coma?' Jeremy was trying to look like he was paying attention. He often used this as a defence mechanism against being made to listen to people's rambling stories twice, whether he was listening the first time or not. He stroked his chin, and nodded earnestly.

'Right. Coma. So Doctor Hancock, he was the guy in charge of the research team, he told Linda and James to stay around Augustine, and he had them drugged to keep them under, to keep them here. Monitoring their dreams the whole time, of course. Then the team set about recording every coma patient in Birmingham, until they found the one seeing the same things as Linda and James. And when they finally did find him, of course, they knew straight away why he didn't know anywhere but here.'

'Why?'

'Because he was an anencephalic baby. Born without a good portion of his brain.' Keith made a sweeping motion with the side of his hand against his forehead to try to suggest a more misshapen skull than the one he was sporting. 'He'd never been conscious for more than a couple of seconds.'

'Jesus,' uttered Jem, slack-jawed, staring down at the smartly dressed corpse Augustine had formerly inhabited. She was fairly sure she didn't believe the vast majority of the story she had just heard, but her stomach was saying otherwise.

'Once they had all three, that was when they really started to get greedy. They thought these kids were leading them to something specific, and they didn't want to miss anything. So they made them sleep all the time. When their hosts died here, it would wake them, but only long enough for Hancock to have them put back under again. And so it went, until the day they all stopped dreaming, and the Hancock Recordings were complete. It was fifty years before Tal Designer found another way in, and started to make sense of them.'

'Host?' Jeremy was pointing at the body, still not eager to look at it.

'Yes. You did kill somebody. All right. But you didn't kill Augustine. He was dying anyway, somewhere else.'

'And is that supposed to make him feel better? That this is just some innocent bloke? Nice one, Keith.' Jem cast him a withering look.

'The guy was already dead the moment that baby possessed him. Believe me.' Keith did his best to sound convincing, though he still felt doubtful repeating the claims Kush Accountantson had tried to impress upon him.

'So Linda is Denver, and James calls himself Marlowe,' Jeremy frowned and stroked his chin some more. 'How did Augustine know his name? Did the other two tell him?'

'I don't know if they knew about him. He didn't have a name there. I suppose because he hadn't been expected to live. He named himself, really. It was the research team that filled in his paperwork, when they took possession of him.'

'Took possession?' Jem was aghast. 'Where were his parents?'

'They never found them. I doubt they looked very hard, though. He was found abandoned outside a hospital in the first place.'

'God. Poor thing. So how are they dreaming this? We are *real*, aren't we?'

The corpse she was asking went still for a moment before responding.

'I'm as sure as I can be. I guess it's some kind of quantum entanglement thing.'

Jem raised an eyebrow, and Keith for once balked in the face of scepticism. This really wasn't his field.

'Oh, all right, I don't know. I'm bluffing,' he confessed. 'Birmingham is hundreds of years ahead of us. Whatever the case, their consciousnesses can only be in one place or the other. If their hosts stopped living here, they'd wake up there. In a panic, normally. Then they were simply sedated, and put back to possess some other poor sod. I've seen footage of it happening again and again, especially with this guy. You're not the first person to kill *him* by a long stroke. He just rubbed people up the wrong way, I think.'

'He's a baby,' Jem reminded him, glowering as she did so.

'Yeah. Go figure. Well, they can be annoying, can't they?' As he spoke, she stared at him, unconvinced at best. He attempted a smile with the few facial muscles he had at his disposal. 'Ah, you'd understand if you were a parent.'

'God, I hate when people say that.'

'Sorry. I used to, as well. I don't always catch myself.'

'Where do the camera feeds go?' asked Jeremy.

'Don't worry about that now. I shouldn't have mentioned it. Quite honestly, if you get charged with anything, it'll be posthumously. Deep Probe Two is here somewhere, and one way or another, it all ended today.'

Jeremy had stopped listening, busily engaged as he now was in looking around at the walls and quietly cursing wireless technology for the lack of obvious traceable clues as to where the camera output might be getting recorded. Jem, on the other hand, was still paying close attention.

'Why do you keep going all past tense?' she asked.

Keith waved his arms around. 'Because I saw them leave to come here, years ago. I mean, I wasn't there, but I watched the broadcast. Everyone did. It was like the Moon landing. They've been to their Moon too, by the way. It was really neat. They sent one probe up with a printer. That printer printed other printers, and robots, and between them, they built an entire base out of powdered Moon rock. All solar powered, of course. All the Brummies had to do was wait.'

'And they didn't say what they did when they arrived?'

'What, the astronauts?'

'Shut up about the Moon, Keith.' Jem glared at him. 'This deep probing thing, what did they do here?'

One of Keith's shoulders shrugged.

'They didn't come back, and with the probe gone, and no more dreamers, that was more or less an end to it all. Tal was devastated. She carried on pretty much alone, with very little support. She refused to just let go. It was years before she figured out another link, how to send someone after them.'

'And you were someone.'

'I was the only one, as far as I know.'

'Special,' she said, waving jazz hands at him in a way that suggested she might think otherwise. Keith raised a single eyebrow in his attempt to show mock surprise and indifference at this display.

'Why am I still here?' asked Jeremy, having decided to temporarily suspend his investigation into the cameras.

'What?' Jem sounded exasperated.

'If Manny already knows about me, if he's already seen my face, why has he waited this long?'

'They,' Keith corrected him patiently. 'They've waited because they couldn't touch you before you'd appeared on the Hancock recordings. If they don't see you in the first place, they don't come back to stop you. You see?'

Jeremy frowned and dropped his head as he considered this explanation. He looked up through his eyebrows at Jem, who was poking her bottom lip out, seemingly having arrived at a temporary truce with her own bafflement.

'So where is he now?' he said after a moment's further deliberation.

'They. They're probably asleep, waiting it out somewhere until the time the other two recordings are scheduled to end. Any issues with causality will be out the window after that. All bets are off then, and you can see what they're capable of.' He pointed the crushed side of his head at Jeremy, who instinctively put a hand to his own head, as if to protect it from the idea of harm. 'They're not on this floor, I take it, Jem?'

She shook her head.

'You do mean the shiny fella, right?'

'I do, yes.'

'I don't think so. Mind you, I didn't know this guy was still here,' she admitted, pointing a thumb at the deceased.

Keith flung his arms around once more, before declaring, 'I think it's time to go down and talk to the dreamers. Is there a phone handy?'

14

KEITH

Great Birmingham: The Year of Unity 492

Talisha stopped and closed her eyes to concentrate fully on breathing in the sea air, and listening to the gulls, and the tide crashing against the rocks far below them. She felt heat against her cheeks, and the weight of her long grey ponytail as the wind tugged at it.

'Are you all right, Professor? Do you need to rest?'

'Thank you, Seth, I'm fine. It's beautiful, isn't it? I'd forgotten.'

The young assistant puffed and shrugged.

'Yes, I suppose. A spot of sunshine always is. You spend too much time indoors, hidden away in that bunker you call a lab, if you don't mind me saying so.'

'I'm out now, aren't I?' she replied, her eyes still closed, trailing off into a mumble. 'Never bloody satisfied.'

'Did you remember to put sunblock on when we were in the maglev?'

'Yes. Shut your face. I'm trying to have a moment, here.'

They stood in silence briefly, Talisha soaking in her surroundings and allowing nature this rare opportunity to visit her senses, while Seth repeatedly checked the time. Then he held his thumb to his ear, and his little finger to his mouth, in the manner in which one would mime a request for another to phone, said 'office' and proceeded to make a call. Most chose the added convenience of retinal and cochlear enhancement, but Seth persisted with the less invasive digital implants; with those, he at least retained the option to ignore a caller.

'The place hasn't burned down during your short absence, I take it?' asked Talisha, once he had completed his brief conversation and thrust a now cold hand into his coat pocket.

'They make me check in every so often to reassure them that I haven't left you in a ditch somewhere,' he said, sniffing. He peered down at the rocks pointedly before adding, 'or pushed you off anything.'

Talisha smiled wryly as she watched him shake a stone from his shoe, and then blow his nose.

'You look more ready for the ditch than I do. I hiked all the time, you know, when I was your age.'

'I jog around the campus sometimes. It's nice and flat. Built for people.'

'You want to be outside, but not too outside, is that it?'

'It's possible to take the air without clambering over rocks like some kind of mountain goat. I enjoy having ankles that work.'

Talisha opened her eyes once more and looked to the heavens for inspiration.

'Perhaps you can just manage to help an old lady up a hill to see her friend before your fragile little legs snap.'

'Yes, Professor.'

They carried on up the hill, a warm breeze coming in off the sea to help them on their way. Seth repeatedly steered his charge to the centre of the path, away from the long grass, which he insisted would be teeming with ticks.

'Nearly there.' He tried and failed to mask his impatience to be at their destination, so that he could begin to prepare himself for the long walk back to the maglev. 'His path is just as bumpy as the rest of this ridiculous hillside, so please take my arm. I'd sooner not have to carry you out of here.'

Talisha obliged and they made their way up the makeshift dirt path to a large arc of glass frontage embedded in the hill. They paused on the modest patio in front of the enormous windows, Talisha turning to look out at the giddying view down the hill and out to sea, while Seth scanned the property for a door.

'Let's hope he hasn't changed his mind about seeing me, now,' mused Talisha.

'It's a good thing we came at it from below, or we'd never have found the place,' Seth complained. 'I mean, what is he, a badger?'

'He has strong opinions about making as little environmental impact as possible. Where he's originally from, they made a bit of a mess of things.'

'Well, he's had an impact on the soles of my boots, today. I wish he'd at least chosen to live closer to the station, and the town.'

'Tell him about it, not me,' said Talisha, her face breaking into a broad smile.

They watched the man they had come to see bound toward them across the atrium and effortlessly slide back one of the huge panes to greet them.

'Tal Designer. Welcome. You look well.' He put his arms tentatively around her, patting her lightly on the back.

'Thank you, dear. I'm sure that's not true.' As he released her, she looked Keith up and down, holding her palms out in mock shock at this craggy, heavily bearded and unkempt version of the reedy young man she had found lying naked on the floor of her probe, all those years ago; the man the nanobots had somehow made in his own image.

She made an effort to straighten his shirt collar.

'Come here. You look like nobody owns you.'

'Give over.'

'You look tanned and healthy, though. I'll give you that.'

Keith offered a limp wave of dismissal before looking down at himself.

'I made myself a board and took up surfing. Rachel hates it, convinced I'm going to kill myself. But it keeps me fit.'

'Surfing. You'll have to tell me what that is,' said Talisha, with little intention of pressing him on the matter. 'This is the young man who does for me, by the way. Keith, Seth. Seth, Keith Byrne, the man from nowhere.'

She waved a hand between them as she made the introductions, stretching her fingers as she landed on Keith, as though suggesting that he were several times larger than her assistant.

Keith shook hands with Seth, who explained that it was a pleasure to meet him. Keith begged leave to doubt it.

'I hope you're looking after her. She's one of this world's few true geniuses, you know. Any world, really.'

Talisha rolled her eyes at this.

'Yes sir. I'm aware. I do my best,' said Seth.

'Good. Good. Come in, both of you.'

Keith stepped to one side and held out a hand to indicate the direction in which his visitors would have to walk in order to pass through the door and enter his home. In terms of the information being relayed, it was a redundant gesture for anyone who had prior experience of doorways, but he did it all the same; guests were rare on his hill, and he was keen to appear welcoming. Talisha had developed something of a shuffling gait since the last time Keith had seen her, and this gave him enough time for his arm to become tired in its horizontal pose, and for him to gradually lower it at what he hoped was a respectful rate.

'Surprisingly cosy,' Seth remarked as he looked around the sizable atrium.

The bulk of Keith's home was on two levels, set back further into the hill. The atrium itself housed generously proportioned cooking, dining and sitting areas. Seth tried not to let his gaze stop noticeably on the large glazed gun rack he had just spotted beside the staircase.

'It's all about the design. We have more or less the same temperature all year round, and the energy cost is negligible,' Keith explained.

'You know we aren't short of energy, though, right?' said a sceptical Seth. 'Why bother with all this, if you don't mind me asking?'

'Look out there.' Keith nodded at the expansive view afforded them by one entire side of his property. 'It's perfect, isn't it?'

Seth looked out at the hill rolling down into the bay, the sun sparkling on the waves, and the islands beyond.

'It's nice, yes,' he was forced to admit.

'Wouldn't look better with power cables criss-crossing it, would it? Or with an oil rig in the bay?'

Seth couldn't see how any of these things would be necessary in a world that had fusion and induction coils, but thought it best to simply nod quietly at the hairy man.

'It's a lovely home,' said Talisha, stooping to pick up a stuffed animal toy from the slate floor. 'You and Rachel must be very proud. Is she here?'

'She's at work. She teaches at the school in the village. Mike and Bobby go there, so it's handy, if a little embarrassing for them.' He looked up at the sun, apparently sizing up its position. 'They'll be a few hours yet.'

'I wish I could have seen them.' She stroked the toy, a confused smile playing across her face as she studied its long stripy tail.

'Do you like Lemmy? I made him myself, he's not printed.'

'He's really cute. So fluffy. Um. What is he?'

'It's rabbit skin. He's supposed to be a Lemur.'

'Right.' Talisha made no attempt to conceal the fact that the word meant nothing to her.

Keith shook his head and grinned.

'I don't know if they exist here or not. I always liked them, though. He's Bobby's favourite. Always has to be there at the door, waiting for him.'

'Right. I'm sorry, Lemmy. I'll let you get back to work.'

Talisha patted the toy and returned it to its sentry duty on the floor, turning it carefully so that it had the best view of the world outside. Her assistant stared at it, and scratched his head.

'You still have the tattoo, then,' she said, looking at Keith's left forearm, smiling and shaking her head. She nodded for Seth to look at the symbol. 'He was in such a rush to get that thing drawn on himself, when he first arrived.'

Keith raised his arm to look at the symbol as though seeing it for the first time.

'I remember drawing it so many times at the hospital, trying to make sure I would remember it right. In truth, I still don't know if it's the same.'

'I've never understood the appeal of those things,' said Talisha. 'Pictures are for walls.'

'Doesn't it move?' asked Seth, a look of bafflement on his face.

'It's like a talisman,' said Keith as he continued to gaze at the vaguely circular icon with its criss-crossing internal lines, through the sun-bleached hairs on his arm.

He recalled how much the black ink had once stood out against his pale nascent skin, in comparison to the bronzed and weathered hide from which it now fought to contrast itself. He visually traced the lines, compelled to follow a path that ran through each one in turn without revisiting any. It was a ritual he must have practised thousands of times, but he still found it pleasing that he remembered the route without fault. He felt a little queasy at the very idea of forgetting. Becoming suddenly aware that nobody was speaking, he put his arm quickly to his side, a little embarrassed, and hoped that his reverie hadn't been lengthy. He was already convinced that Tal's assistant had taken him for an eccentric hermit, and gazing lovingly at his own arm for any period of time wasn't going to help matters.

'I still vid every now and then with Sandy and Harry. They always remember my birthday.' He air-quoted the word with a smirk. 'Do you see much of them?'

'Sandeep is Vice-Chancellor Programmersdaughter now, as you probably know. I'd have no funding without him, I'm sure, but we don't speak often. He's so busy with administration. Such a shame. I can't imagine he doesn't miss the work. Harrington I haven't seen in years. We just don't move in the same circles any more. Gave up the sciences altogether, didn't he?'

'He paints now. His hair's so long you can't tell which way he's facing unless you look at his feet. He had a big exhibition in Moseley this year. Sold quite a few, I think.'

'Good for him. Good for him.'

Sensing a lull in the conversation, Keith clapped and rubbed his hands together.

'Let me get you both some tea, and you can tell me about the big breakthrough.'

***

'Have they gone down?'

234

Keith picked at the run-off from one of the candles while his wife walked back to the dining table.

'Little sods.' Rachel sat down, smiling. 'They're finally settled, I think.'

She looked to the enormous windows, and the dark sky outside. Clouds had rolled in across the sea and hidden the field of stars to which they were so often treated as they ate their evening meals. She drew a square in the air with her finger, uttered the word 'curtains', and the world outside was gone, replaced by the image of huge, deep red drapes, gently billowing in a non-existent wind. Keith had argued long and hard for real curtains, but the scale had proved prohibitive for the use of natural material, and the ability to watch films on his windows had eventually won him around. Not that there was much that interested him coming out of Birmingham's film industry, but the windows recorded all that occurred outside; sometimes he would sit in the living area looking out at an incredible storm that had happened months before, or watching Rachel and the children play on the patio on a bright Summer's day, while they were away at school in gloomy Autumn.

'So,' he said, briskly dismissing the wax from his fingers, 'what do you think?'

She frowned.

'I don't know how you can trust her. She's already lost at least one team, that we know of.'

'But I wouldn't be here without her.' Keith reached across the table to hold her hand. 'I'd never have found you.'

'That doesn't mean she won't make you disappear again. Why can't she leave well enough alone?'

'She lost someone important, you know that. With the chamber gone, she was left with no way of knowing what happened. For all we know, all this is still in danger. The Axis could still be out there, ready to take it all away. She's devoted years to trying to find another way in, and now she finally thinks she's there. Wouldn't you want to know?'

'Why can't she go look for herself?'

'I'm the only link left. I wish she could have stayed long enough to see you and explain it all properly. She can put *me* back in *me*, that's the only way it'll work.'

'So she claims.'

'Trust me, if she could go, if there was a way she could see Sevita again, she would do whatever it took. They've put other people there, research volunteers, but only for an instant. They snare on a consciousness, just catch glimpses, and then snap back here again.'

'What's that like for the people they're snaring?'

'Tal says it's probably like the sudden jolt you feel in bed sometimes, when you're drifting off.'

'I've heard that's your heart stopping.'

'Really?' Keith tried not to look concerned as he considered the many times he had experienced the sensation. 'Well, not that, exactly, but like that. The point is, I'm the only one who's going to be able to stay there. Because it's my own consciousness.'

'You sound like you've already made up your mind.'

'It would be one night in the city. You could come with me, take Mike and Bobby to a show. You know how they love the plays in the village. They'd go mad for a big production, especially Bobby. I'd just be asleep for a bit, see everyone I used to know, wake up, and we'd be back home again before you knew it. All expenses paid.'

Keith looked at her and thought he could almost see the words 'oh, you've got it all figured out, haven't you?' forming behind her eyes. He realised he might be pushing too hard.

'But if you don't want me to do it, I'll tell her no.'

Rachel held her head in her free hand and closed her eyes.

'Simple as that,' Keith added.

'Is it. And how do you figure that?'

'What do you mean?' he asked, guardedly.

'Firstly, she's the closest thing you have to a mother, and secondly, it's where you came from. If you're going to sit there and tell me all I have to do against all that is to say "no", I'm here to tell you that's horse shit.'

Keith sat back, not knowing what to say.

Rachel gave herself a moment before sweeping her hair back and meeting her husband's gaze.

'Do you miss them?'

'Who?'

'You know. Everyone. Everyone from *there*. Do you miss them?'

Keith's eyes darted every which way, as he searched frantically for the correct answer.

'No,' he said finally.

Rachel raised an eyebrow.

'No?' he said again, realising too late that this time he had made his response sound like a question.

'It's all right if you do, you know.'

She shook her head as she spoke. She often did this when they talked, and after seven years of marriage, Keith was no closer to working out whether or not it was deliberate. Either way, he now had no idea what either of them wanted.

'It's not like I have to give her an answer right away,' he said at last.

Rachel sighed for so long, it occurred to Keith that his spouse might be deflating.

'I know you're going. Just promise me you're coming back.'

***

'Just try to relax. I know it's not easy with all the equipment.'

Keith wasn't sure if he was closing his eyes, or the drug the nurse was administering was rendering him blind, but Tal's closely attentive face was blinking on and off. She seemed, to him, to be calm enough. Any concern in among the wrinkles looked to be friendly rather than betraying any lack of confidence. Of course, that could all have been the drug as well, stripping away his powers of judgement as it eased his anxieties. His head was being held in a vice-like grip by the helmet he had been told was designed to pass magnetic pulses through his skull, so it was difficult for him to ascertain whether anything else in the room was struggling to exist in the way Tal now seemed to be. A sensation akin to his brain being tickled made him want to squirm, and brought him close to laughter. Then all at once, no more glimpses of her face, or the lights in the ceiling above it. No hint of red through eyelids, if they were indeed closed; just darkness. Enveloped in black, with a sensation of being liquid, rippling, a wave running repeatedly from toe to head. He anticipated the next wave, relaxed into it, and was gone.

***

Light. Instinctively, Keith put a hand to his forehead to shield his eyes, before realising that they weren't hurting from the glare. They were already fully adapted to their surrounding conditions; it was he, sat behind them, who needed to adapt. The next thing he became aware of was a strong smell of perfume. Keith wondered whether he might be having some kind of seizure.

'Yes, Mister Byrne?'

This was a male voice. Not Tal, not the nurse. Somebody new was in the room. Keith's ear canals informed him that he was no longer lying down, but sitting now, and with this sudden update on his alignment came a fleeting impression that he was lurching forward. As he rode out the sensation, he discovered that his right hand was raised. He lowered it, trembling a little, noting that there was no longer an intravenous tube protruding from the wrist to which it was attached. He was at a large table, functional rather than grand, and in another room entirely. He knew this table. Looking up, he recognised the people sat around it, although he felt certain that he would be unable to remember all of their names.

'Sorry. Nothing. Sorry. I thought I was going to sneeze,' he told Ray, and having done so, realised that he remembered not just the man's name, but much else about him. He smiled goofily before he could stop himself, tickled at the very idea of being so delighted to see him. 'Don't mind me. Go on.'

She'd done it. He was actually there, among all his old workmates, and none of them had the faintest idea that he was now masquerading as himself. There was a man sat next to him that he didn't recognise at all, in a spotless linen suit, and he realised now that this was the source of the perfume. The name 'Guido' popped into his head from somewhere. Something like that. Perhaps he did remember him, a little.

Perched on the meeting room table in a failed lotus position and clearly uncomfortable, Ray dropped his head and exhaled loudly through his nose, as though struggling to summon the will to continue.

'Do do doo,' he said, tapping his fingers on the pine veneer before abruptly pointing at another attendee sat a couple of places down from Keith. 'Mister Starwars. You were about to tell me when I can have my report generator.'

'I don't remember saying anything,' said Jeremy Starwars.

Ray wagged his finger and smiled at a joke he wasn't sharing with the group. 'Ah, but you were about to.'

'Right. Well, it's nearly there. I can see light at the end of the tunnel.'

'It's about time you moved towards the light. When can I have it?'

Keith looked at Starwars, who by this point looked like a rabbit caught in headlights, and the colour appeared to be draining from his face by the second. He scanned the other faces around the table, noting that they were mostly looking down at notepads, or into their own laps. Keith thought back to these meetings, and realised that he had never noticed how little eye contact occurred during them. Suddenly aware that he might be studying his workmates too closely, he turned his attention determinedly to the notebook he now realised lay in front of him. His brow furrowed. He was barely able to read the scrawl that he assumed to be his own writing. Helping Mike and Bobby with their own penmanship in recent years had lead him to achieve a level of legibility in which he now took some pride. People hardly wrote by hand any more, but Keith had taken great pains to convince his children that the dying art was important, and worth preserving. Looking at the paper before him, he was confident that he could do better with his foot.

'Within the next few days,' said Starwars, sounding as though he had given the matter considerable thought.

'Oh, fine. Will I see something by Friday, then?' Ray continued to press him.

Keith looked back at Starwars, who was saying 'next week,' and nodding in a manner clearly intended to inspire confidence.

Ray paused, staring into space, as though checking this information against a calendar which only he could see.

'OK. Good,' he decided, after some consideration. 'Good stuff,

Mister Starwars. We need to get this stuff out of the way. Birmingham is looming. Right. The lovely Ella, how have you been keeping yourself busy this fine week?'

Ella, it transpired, had been unable to keep herself busy at all, owing to the continued lack of a report generator from Starwars. She seemed genuinely annoyed, and Ray restated the assurances of Jeremy Starwars that her wait was almost at an end, suggesting that she come and see him after the meeting to figure out something to do in the meantime.

Next, someone called Will, of whom Keith had little memory, spoke of a similar discontent over the unfinished report software, before suggesting quite strongly that some naming conventions or other needed to be discussed. Ray told Will that perhaps they could do this the following week.

Keith watched as the meeting continued, relieved to realise that he had clearly already spoken before he had arrived. He had no idea what he had said, but some of the words that he could decipher on his notepad hinted at what he might have been working on. He considered the possibility that he might be called upon to do some actual work while he was there, and the thought sent a shiver down his spine. He hadn't written a line of code in the last twenty years, since waking up in Tal's chamber. The notion of a programmer was entirely redundant in Great Birmingham, as for many generations the computers had designed and programmed themselves. Scientists and creative types tended to simply describe what they required, and those with the biggest ideas either sought out those with the greatest descriptive skills, or referenced and tweaked existing concepts, bolting them together in new ways. The computers could even bring these ideas into physical existence, through printing. On occasion, if a printer wasn't large enough to accomplish the task at hand, it would print the components for a larger printer, and forward the job to that, once it had been assembled. Keith had once visited the printer that had constructed the chamber in which he had been found, and marvelled at its cathedral-like stature. As a tip of the hat to his second place of birth, he had ensured that the glazing for his home was printed there, but dipping his toe into the world of wish fulfilment architecture had been the limit of his involvement in design and development for two decades. Just being spotted trying to remember where the letters were on the keyboard, was likely to attract suspicion. He would have to find an excuse to get upstairs and make contact with Deep Probe Two as soon as possible, assuming that the timing of his visit was correct, and it was there. He felt a little frisson of panic at the thought that he might be days, weeks, even years too early, before remembering what Tal had told him about the extraction process, how it was all under his control. He could go home at any point, and leave himself there to get on with whatever he was supposed to be doing.

'One last piece of any-other-business, gentlemen. And lady,' said Ray, and Keith began to listen properly again, noting that everyone else had also perked up. Glancing at the clock, he realised that he had passed the time while pretending to attend with just as much skill as any of them, and thought that he could perhaps stand in for himself quite well after all.

'Barbara's asked me to send someone up to help the people upstairs.'

Nobody else had been talking, and yet it seemed to Keith that the room had become quieter anyway. Perhaps everyone was now holding their breath. Whatever the case, this was perfect, he thought. *Wait. Lady?* Keith was suddenly aware that there was only one woman at the table. *Jane. Jan. Jen. Jem.* Jem, that was it. Jem, who was in charge of the testers. She was there, but where had the angry woman gone? Where was Ella? He was sure that nobody had left the room, despite his daydreaming. He felt the blood drain from his face at the thought that he might have just witnessed a removal. She had been sat between Jem and *Malcolm. Marvin. Martin.* Of course, Martin. Now they were sat together, with no empty seat between them. He knew that he hadn't dreamt her. He remembered admiring her drive, and her obvious work ethic, but she appeared to have stopped existing without being missed by any of those remaining. Keith now had the unshakable feeling that the Axis was there in the room with him, and a strong suspicion as to who it might be. He was filled with a renewed sense of urgency. His hand was up almost before he had thought to raise it.

'Mister Byrne. Are we about to sneeze again?'

'No, I'd like to volunteer to go upstairs.'

Keith could almost feel the ripples of shock emanating from the others as they all took furtive glances in his direction. Nobody, however, was speaking up to dissuade him from this apparently heroic stance.

'What about the full workload you were talking about earlier?'

Keith frowned and looked down at his notepad, still unable to comprehend much of it.

'Oh, that. That was mostly bollocks. I'm not really busy.'

Ray narrowed his eyes and cocked an eyebrow. From what Keith could remember of his job, what he had just said could very easily be true. He looked at Ray with a hopeful smile, and watched his facial movements as he struggled to weigh this public display of insubordination against his relief at avoiding the potentially ugly scene of having to nominate someone himself.

'That figures,' said Ray, settling upon a half-smile that he hoped would convey an unfazed nonchalance. 'It's a good job you're taking the minutes and can correct all that, isn't it?'

'Absolutely.' Keith scrutinised his notepad once more, in the light of the new and disturbing information that he was supposed to have been taking minutes. Now that he looked closer at the squiggles near the top of the page, he could make out what might have been names. He wondered whether Ella was still among them.

'OK. Thanks, Mister Byrne, you lying bastard. Type up the minutes first, and you can head on up after that.'

'Great.' Keith picked up the ballpoint pen that had been lying in front of him since he had arrived, and tapped it against his teeth. He would have to ask everyone to reiterate everything that they had said, but he knew they would all be happy to do so. Revised versions of events were generally preferable to those that actually took place in these meetings, he remembered that much. What he didn't remember was several of their names, but he felt certain that he could wing it.

Within the hour, several pages, which in all likelihood bore little resemblance to anything that had been said during the meeting, had been written and attributed to what were, for the most part, the attendees actual names. Keith had suspected that one or two of the responses he had been given upon asking his long-term colleagues who they were, may have been intended as sarcasm, but his recollection of the popular culture of the time was hazy at best. As a result, a newsreader and a particularly murderous soap star had been credited with some of the more insightful contributions of the day. To Keith's discomfort, he was thanked thrice more by an increasingly sincere Ray, and then he was finally on his way upstairs to look for Deep Probe Two.

***

Keith had been with the people upstairs for almost a full twenty-four hours before they had finally introduced him to their highly reflective assistant, Manny, who they believed themselves to have somehow invented. Not that the intervening time had been uneventful, by any means; he had, after all, met all three of the dreamers. Denver had been very friendly. Marlowe, he had felt a little less at ease with, however. All had seemed well, until they had shaken hands. For some reason, he couldn't help but feel that Marlowe was eyeing him with suspicion from that point onward; he had even removed his pretentious dark glasses, seemingly the better to glare at him. Denver and Marlowe had argued in hushed tones shortly thereafter, and Keith had felt certain that the bone of contention had been in some way related to him. They had certainly been careful to step away from him. Augustine had joined them late in the morning, and they had once more whispered among themselves before introducing him to Keith.

Augustine had struck Keith in turn as threatening, malodorous, half-dressed, threatening again, and finally as mentally ill. Keith had striven to remain polite at all times, however; the man had clearly been through much, in what had, by all accounts, been an extraordinarily long life. Keith had been very pleased with himself for the way in which he had managed to appear believably sceptical of the man's tales of meetings with historical figures, and indeed his allusions towards actually being several others, and yet sympathetic when he had spoken of his many desperate attempts to leave this world by whatever means necessary. Keith had long known about the trio's multi-millennia-long wait, and Tal's probes had encountered them on multiple occasions, as they had followed the crooked path that the Axis had traced through time for them to follow, and that Doctor Hancock had insisted that they pursue. What he hadn't been prepared for, was to witness the scars that this long an existence had apparently wrought on the man from whom the other two seemed to take their lead. It was clear to Keith that Denver and Marlowe had coped considerably better than Augustine during their stay, and initially, at least, he had taken this as a sign that he was the weakest of the three. As their conversation had continued, however, Keith had begun to appreciate the vastness of the hidden reserves of strength this man had been forced to bring to bear, across his many lives.

Augustine had proved an unwilling recipient of any sympathy on Keith's part, however, and had appeared to consider the very idea to be insulting. He had suggested to Keith that he clearly didn't know who he was talking to, and that he should learn 'some fucking deference'. He had then advised Keith that he should fear him, at which point he had raised his sunglasses for the first time since they had been introduced.

Keith had been surprised, and a little nauseated by what Augustine had revealed, and he had struggled to conceal his pity. He had realised almost at once that this was not the reaction that was expected of him, but by then, it had been too late, and Augustine had got up and left the room without a further word. As the door had swung shut, however, Keith had caught the start of a conversation with either Marlowe or Denver in the hallway.

'I think it might be him,' he had heard Augustine say.

Now, at last, after what had been a lonely but filling takeaway in the quarters with which they had provided him, Keith stood back in that same boardroom, having been led there once more by Marlowe. He was confronted with an area that a man of average height might occupy, with only vaguely discernible edges, betraying its shape purely by reflecting its surroundings. He struggled initially to resolve what he was looking at in the dim light afforded by the single working strip light.

'Hello, Keith,' said the area.

Keith was taken aback, as the voice seemed much closer than its source.

'I'll leave the pair of you to get acquainted.' Marlowe flashed a smile and left, closing the door behind him.

Keith stared at what he now realised to be his own reflection on the surface of the man-shaped hole in the room.

'Deep Probe Two?' he enquired hesitantly.

The blurred shape seemed to take a while to respond.

'Please call me Manny,' it said at last.

'I know what you are.'

Another pause.

'It *is* you, isn't it? You're the one we found in here. How can that be?'

'Tal—Professor Designer sent me.'

'Tal?'

'Am I speaking to Captain Minister?'

'Yes. Sevita, please. Yes. You've seen Tal? You've spoken to her?'

'Yes. She misses you very much.'

'I miss her too. So much. And me. Shh. One at a time or it gets confusing. She's well?'

'She's fine, yes. Older now, of course.'

'What? What?'

'Sorry, I should start again. And I'm talking to both of you, aren't I? Is Commander Accountantson there too?'

'He is. Hello. Yes. Call me Kush. What do you mean, she's older?'

Keith cursed his stupidity.

'I can't say too much. Just… this is a later mission.'

'Are—Are you saying we don't make it back?'

***

Keith slid the catch across on the cubicle door, and sat down gingerly on the loose toilet seat. He smiled to himself, remembering now the poor state of repair that had always been the hallmark of the building when he had worked there. Even before the people upstairs had taken over, the management in general, and Barbara in particular, had always seemed to view the dilapidation almost as a badge of honour. Their philosophy had it that wear and tear were the hallmarks of a company hard at work.

This had also been the sole cubicle equipped with toilet paper. For once, he had been thrilled to discover that it was of the cheap, industrial pack variety. The sheets were long and dense, and he surmised that the ink wouldn't run particularly.

He pulled a few sheets from the roll, and felt a brief moment of panic as he reached for his shirt pocket and found nothing there. He patted his trousers, and was thankful to feel the shape of the pen he had taken from the meeting room. Upon arriving upstairs, he had been relieved of his mobile phone, for reasons of security that he had been assured he would understand, or he might have considered simply leaving the note on that. Thinking further upon the matter however, as he tapped the pen against his teeth, there was every chance that he wouldn't look at the phone straight away, and in any case, he was sure that he would have struggled to remember how to use it. No, an old-fashioned physical note was best. He wrote swiftly, pausing several times to curse under his breath as the pen went through the paper and left ink marks on the beige cargo trousers he had been surprised to find himself wearing.

KEITH

I'M SORRY TO PUT YOU IN THIS POSITION, BUT YOU'RE UPSTAIRS NOW. YOU'VE ALREADY MET EVERYONE, SO YOU SHOULD EITHER PRETEND TO KNOW THEM, OR TELL THEM THAT YOU PASSED OUT ON THE TOILET AND FORGOT THEM ALL AGAIN. THEY'VE GIVEN YOU A ROOM TO STAY IN. IT'S WHERE THE KITCHEN WOULD BE IF IT WAS DOWNSTAIRS, IF THAT MAKES SENSE. YOU'RE HERE TO DO SOME WORK FOR THEM, BUT THEY HAVEN'T ACTUALLY SAID WHAT THAT IS YET. I'M SURE YOU CAN HANDLE IT.

JUST KNOW THAT YOU'RE NOT IN ANY DANGER, AND IT ALL WORKS OUT FOR THE BEST IN THE END.

A FRIEND

PS FLUSH THIS AS SOON AS YOU'VE READ IT.

PPS I'M WRITING IN CAPITALS BECAUSE I SAW YOUR HANDWRITING EARLIER, AND IT MADE ME QUESTION YOUR READING LEVEL.

Keith was actually writing in capitals purely because he was working with toilet paper, but he couldn't help having a small dig, hoping it might at the very least offer some small spur to self-improvement. He still felt a twinge of guilt at leaving himself like this, but he'd done what Tal had asked of him, and this wasn't his problem any more. More importantly, he had a deadline, to leave before Birmingham did. Tal had been worryingly vague about the consequences of being present for that event. He impaled the length of paper on the small jacket hook on the cubicle door, and sat back down to admire his handiwork. The note would be the first thing he saw when he woke up. All that remained was to go home.

Keith stood up and bent over until he was looking at the toilet from between his legs. He grimaced at the yellowy-brown streaks he could see on the enamel from this vantage point. He felt the veins rising on his forehead, and waited in this position until his face felt like it was glowing. Then, after breathing out as fully as he could, he swiftly rose to his full height and extended his arms above him, just in time before everything went black.

He awoke not knowing how long he'd been out, his vision blurred. He could make out a flickering strip light overhead. No friendly nurse was hovering over him, and Tal's face was nowhere to be seen. As his surroundings began to come into focus, his heart sank. He could see the note he had left himself, still hanging on the door. He was still in his old workplace, still in the toilet cubicle. Only now he was lying in a twisted heap on the floor, which he had come to regret not having had the foresight to mop. He winced as he went to stand up. His back had clearly struck the toilet seat on his way down. He rubbed at the sore area, and became aware, with no small amount of horror, that the back of his shirt was very damp. Half of him hoped that it was blood, but when he checked, and then sniffed at his palm, his worst fears were confirmed. Tutting, he struggled to his feet, and back to the matter at hand. Why was he not back in Birmingham? Tal had assured him that losing consciousness would be sufficient to pull him back from this body. This was precisely why he had been careful to stay awake all night. He reasoned that he had, perhaps, just not been out for long enough. He started pulling paper from the industrial-sized roll. This time, he would at the very least fall onto a dry floor. Having dealt with the remaining puddles that his shirt had thus far failed to soak up, and having stuffed the resultant wad into the bowl, he found himself looking between toilet and roll once more. After a few moments of consideration, he began unspooling the entire roll. Once done, he possessed, as he had hoped, a sizable quantity of paper, which he heaped onto the toilet seat, draping as much as would balance over the front. Happy that this makeshift padding might at least spare him *some* further bruising, he bent over once more.

He came to in the toilet again, his back sorer than before. The paper hadn't helped at all, and he was still no closer to being reunited with his wife and children. He held his throbbing head, and tried to gather his thoughts. Having recently passed out on two occasions, he found this endeavour to be like swimming through treacle. He couldn't for the life of him fathom why this wasn't working, why he wasn't home. All he could think to do, in his diminished state, was to try again. The only minor tweak he could conjure up was to pad himself instead of the toilet. He stuffed all the paper into the front and back of his shirt, until he looked like he was wearing a fat suit, all the while calling himself an idiot for not thinking of it in the first place. In the space left at the bottom of his note, he added a further postscript.

PPS SHIRT FULL OF TOILET PAPER. FLUSH THIS TOO (SEVERAL FLUSHES OR WILL BLOCK).

Then down, up, and out like a light for the third time.

He woke up to a face, like a welcoming light at the end of his tunnel vision. His first waking feeling was relief. This was quickly dispelled when he recognised the face as his own. Confusion came next, as the

248

face came into sharper focus, and he saw that it was framed by a shape he couldn't reconcile as being that of his own head. As his peripheral vision gradually returned, the blurred edges of his reflection became clear to him, and he knew that he was staring into Manny, as it in return regarded him.

'I'm still in the office, aren't I?'

'You're in the toilets. They sent me to find you, when they realised how long you'd been gone. I found your feet sticking out under the cubicle door. I had to remove the door to get to you.'

'There's a note.'

'It's gone. Don't worry. Are you all right?'

'No, I'm not. I can't get back. Tal said I just had to lose consciousness, and the link would be severed, but I'm still here. I'm still here in this fucking toilet.'

'Calm down. Why didn't you just wait until bedtime?'

'I don't think I could. I had to keep myself awake all night to avoid going back too soon, so I thought, and now I'm knackered. Anyway, they're going to tell me what I'm supposed to be doing here soon, and if I'm not gone before they do that, I won't know what I'm supposed to be doing here. I didn't want to leave myself in the lurch like that.'

Manny paused to consider this.

'But you were leaving a note anyway.'

'Oh, shut your face. I'm a bit discombobulated here. I just want to know how to get back. Who am I talking to, anyway?'

'This is Kush. Veet's taking a nap. Between you and me, I think the air in here is getting to her.'

'Hello, Kush. I've got a family waiting for me, and Tal waiting to hear from you two. What am I going to do?'

Keith's reflection looked at him silently for a moment.

'I don't know how much the dreamers told you, but I don't think sleep is going to cut it.'

'I'm not like them. Am I? What are you telling me? I'm stuck?'

'I know what you need. Wait here.'

Keith peered out from the cubicle and watched the man-shaped reflection of the lavatory step around the corner of the end stall, and out of his field of vision. He heard the door to the Gents swing open and then click shut. He thought about the ramifications for the version of him that was supposed to be there, in this body, if his consciousness were to be trapped there permanently. It would mean that he had essentially died in that meeting room, scrawling on a notepad and probably bored senseless. Keith slumped against the edge of the stall wall between Traps Two and Three, feeling sorry for himself.

A few minutes passed before he heard the squeak of the door spring, and Manny was stood before him once more, now brandishing a hammer.

'You'll barely feel it.'

'Fuck, no. No.' Keith pushed himself up the stall wall a little in his efforts to back away, before falling sideways into the door-less Trap Three.

'Honestly, this will totally free your mind. Your consciousness will have nowhere else to go, and you'll be back with Tal within the minute.'

'I don't want to die. I don't want *him* to die. There has to be another way.'

'There really isn't. Anyway, he's already dead. You know that. Where do you think he went when you arrived? Whether you stay or go, he's not coming back. Tal must have explained this.'

Manny drew closer.

'She didn't. Maybe this is different. You don't know. Stop. Wait.'

'Seriously, Mate. This is what happens now. Tell her we sent our love.'

'No. No. Stay ba—'

Then there was nothing but a bright light, and a deafening ringing. In the distance, a muffled voice was saying that it was really sorry, that he should stay still this time. The bell rang once more, and the light exploded into a million colours Keith had never seen before. One after another, they flashed and were gone, and the high-pitched whine dropped in tone and stuttered into silence.

Kush looked upon his work and marvelled at how easy it had all been. The detachment the probe afforded him from the world beyond made everything seem like a game. Veet didn't see things the way he did, though; she became too immersed. He felt certain that had she been conscious, she wouldn't have been able to commit to what had needed to be done. She wouldn't even have allowed him to practise on the animals outside.

Keith had only uttered one further word, just between the hammer blows, and Kush would ponder its significance for some time as he was nailing his corpse to the wall, cleaning up elsewhere, and getting his stories straight for Marlowe and Sevita respectively. He couldn't be absolutely sure, given the damage he had done to the man's face with his initial swing, but he thought that Keith had said 'Susan'.

15

MISSING PERSONS

Marlowe stretched back in his chair, arms behind his head, as the door opened.

'OK Babs. Who's missing?'

Barbara Pappa thought this informality with one of the owners quite jolly, and allowed herself a little smile as she tapped her pen on the clipboard.

'From Tracy's list of who turned up this morning, we have four people who don't seem to be on this floor at the present time.'

'Four? Damn, Babs. We just ask you to assemble your staff in one place, and you lose four?'

Barbara's smile faded.

'Well, I'm counting the two who are upstairs helping you. Keith Byrne and Jemima Pepper. I'm surprised you haven't sent Keith back down, actually. Didn't I hear that he wasn't working out?'

Marlowe and Denver looked at each other, and then back to Barbara.

'Don't worry about Keith, Barbara,' Denver reassured her. 'We have three upstairs, though. Is Martin one of your four?'

'Who?'

'Martin Priest.'

Barbara's brow was furrowed as she ran her pen down two columns on one sheet, flipped to the second and checked the remaining column printed there.

'Nope. We don't have any Martins. We did have a Mark up until last month, but he was only a temp.'

Marlowe and Denver exchanged glances again.

'Interesting,' said Marlowe to his fellow dreamer. 'Wonder why it took him.'

'All right, we won't worry about that for now,' suggested Denver, hurriedly. 'Who else is missing?'

'Ian Peterson, and Jeremy Starwars.'

'Didn't we already talk to Ian Peterson?' asked Marlowe.

'Yes, we've had him in already,' Denver agreed.

Barbara paused for a moment.

'Sorry, we have two.'

'Not four?'

'Pardon?'

'Two missing.' Denver looked confused.

'No, two Ian Petersons.'

'Two Ian Petersons,' Marlowe sought confirmation, as he tapped his fingers on the table.

'Yes. Two Ian Petersons.'

'And you've lost one.'

'There's one missing,' clarified Barbara.

'Well, what do you propose we do about that, Babs? Just interview the other one twice?' He turned his palms face up, as though ready to catch her response.

'The missing one is Ian Gerald Peterson,' she offered. 'From Ray's department.'

'Death Ray? I don't hold out much hope for your boy Ian, then.'

'You think… that mess in the Gents?' Barbara was appalled.

'Let's not jump to conclusions,' said Denver.

'Ritually gutted, cut up, and flushed bone by snapped bone, probably,' suggested Marlowe, getting into his stride, and grinning. 'That sick fuck.'

Her face whitening by the second, Barbara peeped out between the blinds at Ray, who stood nonchalantly in the corridor, looking to her as though he had not a care in the world. She even thought she saw a sly smile play across his lips. She let the blinds snap shut, turning away for fear she might vomit.

Denver was keen to change the subject.

'What about this Jeremy Starwars?' she asked.

'Well,' began Barbara, only to be interrupted by a knock at the door. She opened it just enough to partially reveal Tracy Ireland's face in the crack.

'Sorry to bother you, but I've got Jemima on line four.'

'I thought the phones were down.'

'Internal calls are still working. Would you like to take it in here?'

'Yes, thank you, Tracy. Put her through, please.'

'Oh,' said Tracy, as Barbara closed the door, assuming the next word would have been 'kay.'

The three of them turned their attention to the unusual triangular-shaped telephone at the end of the table, toward which Barbara now walked.

'It would be best if I take it, I think,' said Denver.

'It's a conference phone, so there's no handset.'

'Yes, if you could leave us for a moment, Barbara.'

Barbara tried not to look crestfallen. 'Do you know how to operate it? It's a bit different from the desk phones.'

'Thanks Babs, we do have a meeting room upstairs.'

Marlowe sat with his mouth agape in such a way as to suggest that it would only close again once Barbara Pappa had departed. She made her way back to the door, hesitating after turning the handle.

'I'll see if I can find Ian while you're doing that, shall I?'

'If you could, Barbara. Thank you,' said Denver, courteously.

'Toodles,' said Marlowe, with a slight wave of his fingers, as she left the room.

He and Denver then sat and listened to the distant ringing of phones in various other parts of the building as Tracy attempted to locate the extension number for the meeting room.

***

'Wahey. Look who it isn't,' said Thom.

'Bit late, boss,' said Ollii, glaring at Jem and tapping his wrist, despite not having worn a watch since childhood.

254

'Have you just got up?' asked Thom, looking at Jem's attire. 'Nice jimjams.'

'Who's the monk?' whispered Robert.

Jem, Jeremy and Keith filed into reception, as Denver ensured that the door was safely closed behind them, secure in the knowledge that no one had seen her operate the keypad. Keith's crushed skull was shrouded beneath the hood of a fluffy white towel robe Augustine had discarded in the upstairs Ladies, and the sunglasses he also no longer had use for successfully concealed the fact that Keith was down to one eyeball. For the moment, at least, the stares directed towards him were quizzical in nature, rather than nauseated.

'I think you'd better follow me straight through to the meeting room, Keith,' suggested Denver, her voice still mellifluous and calm, betraying neither shock nor stress. Resurrection was scarcely new to her, although for someone to return in the same body most certainly was.

'Is... is that my jumper?' asked Will, as Keith walked past, still clutching the heavily soiled knitwear.

'Will. Yes, I'm done with it now,' said Keith, handing the garment to him. 'Thanks so much.'

Eyeing the hooded man suspiciously, Will failed to notice the dampness and additional weight of the jumper as he draped it around his shoulders for safekeeping. He continued carefully to watch the unlicensed pullover borrower until the striking woman in the business suit had followed them into the meeting room.

Bronwen was also watching the cowled figure, and from her vantage point, she caught the briefest of glimpses of him removing his hood before the door had completely closed. A small gasp escaped her mouth before her hand could rise to cover it.

Will began to sniff demonstratively.

'Can you smell that?' he asked nobody in particular, and nobody, in turn, responded.

'It's stronger down here,' he continued, as he headed off towards the Sales Department.

Tim and Habib observed the unworldly programmer vigorously pursue the mystery scent that he alone was experiencing, darting this way and that between the workbenches, and as they did so, Bronwen sidled across to them.

'Did you see that?' she whispered excitedly.

'Yeah,' said Tim. 'Imagine working with that every day.'

'Not that weirdo, you dick head,' she hissed, 'the guy in the bathrobe. His bloody head was caved in.'

'What you on about?' Habib turned briefly away from the spectacle of Will in the distance, holding his jumper to his face, inhaling deeply, and then throwing it to the ground in apparent shock.

Bronwen clicked her fingers, gesturing furiously for them both to pay attention and bring their heads closer. Her whispers were now having to compete with the distant booming laughter of Colin, who was sat in Sales with his compatriot Ian, watching Will's fear and disgust as he further investigated the horrors of his tainted sweater.

'It was the wrong bloody shape,' breathed Bronwen, alternately making convex and concave shapes with her hand around her own head. 'He'd taken a right beating, I'm telling you.'

In unison, the three members of the Sales team turned to stare at the blood-spattered figure of Ray, who winked back at them, quietly pleased with the attention.

***

While Will was entering the Sales Department behind her and sniffing loudly, Barbara was standing in the doorway to Stores, inspecting the dimly lit room.

'Ian?' she called, hesitant to step into the shadowy, shelved netherworld. Some of the broken computer parts and dot matrix printers she could make out in the gloom certainly seemed old enough to be haunted.

Ian Gerald Peterson waited in silence, concealed in the gap between the shelving from which he planned to exact revenge upon the people of the stores for terrorising him the previous day, or at the very least to pass the favour on to some other unsuspecting victim. He quite reasonably assumed the shout to be for the Ian who actually worked among those shelves, and equally reasonably continued to lurk out of sight. He had been there for some time, and was proud of the way he had become inured to his dark surroundings and had stopped dwelling almost entirely upon what might lie in their more Stygian depths. There was an old-fashioned forty watt bulb burning away, and this source of light had helped to ground his darker flights of fancy as he bided his time. And now, while the CEO was holding the door open, a shallow pool of brightness from the Sales Department provided further illumination.

Barbara jumped a little as the other Ian called 'yes, Barb,' from behind her.

'Can I help at all?' he added.

'Is there anyone back here?' she asked, gesturing into the shadows.

Ian Gerald Peterson wrestled briefly with the idea of responding, but reasoned that she was definitely talking to the other Ian Peterson at this point, and that it would be rude to butt in. It would also betray his position to the person he least wished so to do.

'Shouldn't be…' began the storeman, before becoming distracted by thunderous laughter from his colleague Colin.

Similarly intrigued by the sight of Will dancing around his jumper, occasionally lifting or poking at it and making various noises to indicate distress, Barbara idly reached for the light switch and extinguished the forty watt bulb.

Ian frowned in the darkness, and tried to console himself with the fact that he still had the light from Sales to tether himself to the world of men.

Barbara stepped away from the door, allowing the spring to perform its function and swing its heavy wooden charge closed.

In that moment Ian Gerald Peterson hated the spring, as much for its smug certainty of purpose as for plunging him into complete darkness with such gleeful haste. He stood firm, however. He would wait, and he would strike, and his nemesis would quake in fear before him, and he would be victorious. He still had the voices from outside to remind him that he had not been swallowed whole by some hellish leviathan.

'Just push in the button in the knob, if you would, Barb,' said one of these voices, and Ian listened in despair to the single click from the lock and the continued reverberation of Colin's hooting.

'So, you're back, then,' said Marlowe at last.

He had been scrutinising Keith across the table for some time, and now removed his sunglasses and leaned forward.

Though he had pulled back his hood upon entering the room, Keith retained his own eyewear. Fortunately, his cranial remodelling hadn't changed the position of either ear, or the bridge of his nose, all of which still served to support the black wraparounds admirably.

'Can't seem to keep away.'

'All right. I'm going to come right out and ask it. I hope you aren't going to take this as rudeness, Keith, but what are you?'

'That does sound a little rude.'

'I mean, we dismissed out of hand that you could be what we were looking for when you died upstairs. Are you one of us? Are you a dreamer?'

'You might say.'

Denver slid an elbow onto the table and rested her chin against her palm as if to suggest boredom. 'Will you be removing those glasses, Keith? It feels a little impersonal talking to you through them.'

'That's a little rich, if you don't mind me saying so, young lady.'

Her eyes narrowed briefly at this; present condition aside, her body here was clearly older than that of the overconfident young cadaver before her.

'Do you recognise these shades, by the way?' Keith spoke low as he continued, in a disinterested tone that matched the front she was presenting.

Marlowe's smile fell away as he turned to look at Denver, her eyes widening as they darted briefly to meet his gaze. She swallowed and gave a shallow and solitary nod, her head still supported on her hand.

'I take it he's dead,' said Marlowe, as matter-of-factly as he could manage.

Keith stared at him in silence, wondering whether he would in fact have cut a more imposing figure without the glasses. As a corpse, his ability to maintain eye contact without blinking was going to waste. Still, preserving some mystery felt good in itself, and it seemed to be unsettling them enough. There was also the question of the now empty socket. These people hadn't struck him as having weak stomachs, so to reveal it might merely serve to display a weakness of his own.

'So, we're all on the same page now?' he asked, when he felt that he had waited long enough.

He had thought that he would struggle to remember his lines and their timing, but both seemed to flow naturally from him. He wondered idly whether changing his actions at this point was even an option, or that in the event that he were to divert from the recordings, both them and his memory of them would be instantly altered. Perhaps whatever he did now would seem right, and fit with the peculiar brand of déjà vu he was now experiencing. He didn't want to risk going too far off-book, but he thought it might be worthwhile dipping his toe in the water in some way, just to check.

'Lemmy the lemur,' he enunciated carefully, after some further consideration.

The dreamers raised their eyebrows and looked to one another in mild confusion. Keith fancied that he could now recall seeing himself saying those words during the final recordings, while reasoning that his mind could easily be playing tricks on him. If his memories were accurate, not only was he not tied to a script, but he had a means to send messages to his younger self, for receipt soon upon his first arrival in Birmingham. The brief heady feeling that came with this realisation was immediately followed by more paranoid thoughts; if he could send potentially life-changing advice or cautions to the young Keith, could he know for sure that Talisha wouldn't have edited the recordings prior to presenting them to him? For now, he decided not to press the issue further. Even if he was free to alter events at this point, there was too much that he didn't want to risk changing.

'I don't know what that means,' said Denver, plainly.

'You don't need to,' Keith reassured her, waving a hand in what he hoped was a calm and dismissive fashion, though it looked to her as if he were frantically batting at some unseen wasp. 'You just need to know that I know you, and what you are, Linda.'

Denver recoiled at the name.

'So you really are from there, then?' Marlowe could barely close his mouth as he spoke.

'Yes, James.'

'Have—Have you seen my parents?' asked Denver.

'They're very proud of you, Linda. As yours are of you, James. And I can't tell you how pleased Doctor Hancock is with the work you've done here.'

Keith spoke the truth, for he had no idea how pleased Hancock had been. Talisha's breakthroughs had come decades after the man's death. He was careful to speak in the present tense, though, and to him, this little white lie seemed a kindness. The last thing these young people needed was to be informed that they were long gone, and that he had seen their final moments on both planes.

'We're not done, though,' said Marlowe, sniffing. 'We haven't found what we came here for.'

'You don't need to worry about that any more. It's in hand.' Marlowe looked uncertain until Keith added, 'Thanks to you.'

Keith was getting a kick out of viewing this familiar scene from another perspective. He had, for example, had no idea that a small smile might return briefly to Marlowe's face at that point. His recording had merely shown him to stare fixedly at Keith's face, seemingly impassive. The only real hint a viewer would get of the dreamers' emotional responses during this exchange would lie in their occasional furtive looks to one another for reassurance. Keith began to appreciate now how much of their experience on this plane was missing from Hancock's recordings.

'He's really not coming back, then?' Denver was outwardly serene, but there was a tremor in her voice as she added, 'Augie, I mean?'

'No. His dream's over.'

Keith pictured footage he had seen many times, of the assembled doctors and technicians shaking their heads, and the various apparatus surrounding the infant being switched off.

'Is that why you're here? Do you mean to end us too?' She seemed distant as she breathed out the words, as though she had already gone.

'Are you going to send us home?' whispered Marlowe.

Keith looked into his eyes, and saw the tears welling there.

'There's one more thing you need to witness. Then you can go when

260

you're ready.'

***

'Mister Starwars. Nice of you to join us,' Ray boomed as he strode over to the latecomers.

'And Mistress Pepper,' said Jem, leaning this way and that, waving her hands in front of her face as if to suggest a fear of having become invisible.

Her test team grinned as Ray continued to ignore her. She threw up her hands in defeat and plonked herself beside them in one of the comfy chairs reception had to offer. She was surprised to find her pique fading almost immediately in the face of the sudden comfort, and decided to relax into it forthwith.

Jeremy was preparing to lie extensively to Ray about broken projectors, malfunctioning laptops and all manner of other technical obstacles he might heroically have been battling against upstairs, when he noticed the unusual amount of dried blood on his project manager.

'Is that—,' he got as far as saying, before Tracy Ireland stepped between them, tutting.

Jeremy watched in delight as she spat in a handkerchief and began attempting to clean Ray's face, while he fended her off as best he could.

'Not here,' he mumbled in protest.

Jeremy looked over, slack-jawed, at Jem and her test team, who were engaged in fist-bumps and saying things like 'told you.'

Once Ray's face had been wiped to Tracy's satisfaction, it had turned from red to purple. He was ready to reassert his dominance over those present. He was desperate to feel normal again.

'So, Mister Starwars,' he began, while giving his face a quick once-over with his own handkerchief to ensure that no spittle remained, 'talk to me.'

Jeremy felt sure that Ray was making a deliberate point of standing well within his personal space. He could feel hot breath from middle-managerial nostrils assaulting his forehead. Looking at the ground was next to impossible at these close quarters, and he quickly realised that staring down at Ray's trousers for any length of time simply wasn't an option, regardless of the unusual matter that he could see them to be caked in.

'Um,' said Jeremy Starwars.

Turning his head to one side felt awkward too. This was absurd, he thought. He had killed a man since he had last spoken to Ray. If Keith was to be believed, he had the power to make people disappear. It was preposterous that he should be so cowed now. He would lift his head. He would raise his head, and he would look his project manager straight in the eye. He would simply tell the truth, and there would be an end to it. Or perhaps the act of staring at him would activate his powers. Either way, he thought it likely that Ray's head would be exploding within the next few minutes.

Jeremy looked up. He saw in stark close-up the broken blood vessels blossoming across Ray's bulbous nose and purple cheeks. Fearing that only strangled squeaks might emerge from his mouth, Jeremy realised that he needed to clear his throat before the truth could set him free. At this range, he risked spraying Ray in phlegm, which he thought more of a closing statement than a gambit, so he brought his hand up awkwardly between himself and the man stood so threateningly close to him, to cover as discreet a cough as might be possible under the circumstances.

This duly accomplished, Jeremy opened his mouth to speak, just as Barbara Pappa approached.

'Ray, Ian Peterson is missing,' she asserted.

'Isn't he with Colin? I heard him cackling just now,' said Ray, reluctant to draw his gaze away from Jeremy, who he felt certain was on the verge of cracking.

Barbara was now standing facing Ray's profile as he continued to stare at Jeremy, who thought the pair of them now looked as though they were about to perform some sort of Abba tribute.

'Not that one. Your one.'

'Ian Gerald Peterson is missing?' Ray could barely get the words out without grinning.

'Yes. And I need to know what you know about it.'

Jeremy watched as Ray's comprehension of this conceptual

rollercoaster played out on his face. The upturn Ray was fighting at the corners of his mouth disappeared as his jaw dropped, and he finally turned to face Barbara. Jeremy was now peering directly into a shock of white ear hair.

'What?'

'He was here before we locked the doors, and now he's gone. You don't need me to remind you that you two have some history with poor industrial relations. I've had you both in my office on several occasions. And now, with this,' she blustered, waving at the stains and small fleshy lumps still clinging to Ray's clothing.

'What?'

'He did throw a mug of coffee over the guy the other day,' offered Robert Smith, receiving a brief but dark glare from Ray for his trouble.

'It was an accident.'

'I'm sure that'll be taken into account,' said Barbara measuredly. A thought seemingly striking her, she looked up the corridor to the nearest unoccupied room. 'Perhaps we could talk about it in Accounts.'

'No, the coffee. I mean the coffee was an accident. I'd sooner talk here.' Ray was keen to nip this, whatever it was, in the bud, and besides, he was gripped by the strangest feeling that she intended to lock him in there.

'If you're sure.'

'No, that's fine, Barbara.'

Jeremy panicked briefly as he felt a sudden tightness in his stomach, before realising that it was being caused by Jem pulling him away from the fray by the back of his shirt. He flumped down beside her in the last available comfy chair, where he received an amicable pat on the head and a cheesy smile, by way of acclimatisation. This was an altogether more agreeable environment, he decided, simpering back at his rescuer, and wanting at once to hold that gaze forever, to lose himself in her big brown eyes. He was certain that he saw a hint of a puzzled frown flash above those eyes before Jem turned her attention back to the main event. Embarrassed, Jeremy also turned to look up at the beleaguered Ray, and sat trying to persuade himself that looks could easily be misinterpreted. He told himself that she would quickly dismiss whatever she thought she had seen in his face as merely a product of her imagination, and if confronted on the matter, that's what he would tell her too. They would laugh about it. Jeremy thought these things, and then sat quietly hating himself once more.

'Alright. Well, there's no easy way to put this, so I'll just come right out and ask you. Is that Ian's blood?'

'What? No. What? No.'

'Then whose is it, and what did you mean when you told people you had sent a message?'

Ray sighed.

'I bought some meat when I was in the toilet.'

A single hoot escaped from Robert before he managed to clamp his hand over his mouth. Jem was struggling to stifle a similar outburst.

'I'm not sure I'm following you, Ray. Were you and Ian…?' Barbara trailed off, not even sure how to complete the question.

'What?'

'I'm not up on the slang. Cottaging? Is it cottaging?' Now bright red, she tried to maintain as earnest an expression as was within her power to produce.

Ray's own face was a portrait of confusion.

'What? You think—No. No, I bought some meat. Meat,' he said, emphasising the word, and directing her to look at his stained crotch with frantic hand gestures.

Realising that this wasn't helping matters, he picked a brownish fleck of flesh from his flies as quickly as he could and held it up for her to see.

'Meat,' he said again, by way of further identification. 'A man sold me meat, at the window. It was awkward to get it through the mesh, and that's how all this got on me.'

Barbara's eyes narrowed.

'Nothing more complicated than that,' Ray assured her.

'Oh my God, that's your mate,' whispered Ollii to Thom, who shushed him.

Suspicious of the sudden cessation of the giggling coming from the direction of the comfy chairs, Barbara caught this exchange, and turned now to the Test Department.

'Do you know something about this?'

264

'It's Thom's dad,' offered Robert.

'Fuck off,' proposed Thom, before quickly apologising to Barbara.

Ollii described their earlier encounter with the mysterious meat man, and his equally mysterious meat. Ray was quick to agree that this was likely to have been the same man.

'I can't leave you two alone for five minutes, can I?' Jem was shaking her head in admonishment.

'Hey, we didn't buy the meat,' Thom reminded her. 'Sorry, Ray, but seriously, mate. We've only been locked in for a few hours. How hungry can you be?'

Barbara was nodding. 'It's pretty weird, Ray. And Ian is still missing.'

He shrugged in response, like a petulant teenager. 'He's here somewhere.'

'Find him,' she instructed. 'Before I have to ask the police to.'

She walked away immediately after issuing her ultimatum, to make it clear that she would brook no argument.

'Fine,' said Ray, huffing and puffing.

He pointed down at Jeremy and instructed him not to go anywhere, before stomping off down the corridor. Denver, Marlowe and a once-more-hooded Keith were emerging from the meeting room as he passed by. Jeremy could hear Ray asking them if the room was free now, and whether he could book it. It was clear to Jeremy that he was deliberately speaking loudly for his benefit, and that the room was for him. He watched as Marlowe shrugged and from what he could lip read, appeared either to tell Ray 'go for your life,' or 'go fuck yourself.' The project manager's reaction suggested the former, as he strode onward to the Sales Department.

'Come on, you two,' said the cowled Keith as he followed the dreamers to the reception door. 'I don't think we have long.'

Jeremy didn't need telling twice, and rose immediately.

'Really?' said Jem, less enthusiastic. 'I just sat down.'

'Can we go now?' Thom asked the backs of the people assembled at the door.

'Just a few more minutes now,' said the one in the hood, without turning around. 'Then you can all go.'

***

As they reached the door to the offices on the first floor, Keith raised his hand for everyone to stop. Jem was surprised to see these people who had seemed so confident, now so meekly submissive.

'Right,' said Keith, and he appeared to be addressing her directly. 'Denver and Marlowe here are carrying on all the way upstairs.'

'OK. Bye.' She waved.

'You need to go with them.'

'What? Why?'

'They're about to let go of all this, and they need someone to bear witness to that. Wouldn't you want somebody with you too?'

'Let go? What are they going to do? Why me? I've just come down from there. Remember how you had to come and get me out?'

'Things are different now, trust me. Apart from anything else, the lock's been shot off the door. You're not getting locked in again, whatever happens.'

'But what about… you know?'

'What?'

'The other bit of shooting.' She mouthed the word. 'Do they know? I don't want to have to explain it. I don't really want to be there when they see it.'

'They know, and they're fine about it. Honestly.' Keith gestured to Denver and Marlowe for confirmation, and they both nodded solemnly. 'Just go with them. You have to be there, because you're the last face they see.'

His voice had dropped to a whisper now, but what it had lost in volume, it had gained in urgency.

'Are they going to…' Jem trailed off, and quickly traced a line across her throat with her finger, being careful to ensure that Keith remained stood between her and them to hide this action.

'Don't think of it like that. They just want to wake up.' Keith was careful with his choice of words.

'And I have to watch.'

'Trust me. I know you can do this. You're very comforting, honestly.'

'And she'll be safe?' Jeremy sought some reassurance. 'This is on these Hancock tapes? You've seen what happens?'

'She'll be fine. Really.'

Keith began to wave his arms around, and Jem stepped back.

'It's all right,' said Jeremy, shaking his head, 'he's just thinking.'

'You know what's weird?' asked Keith, after a moment.

'That,' suggested Jem, pointing at his flapping limbs.

'I have two memories of how the end of their recordings play out now. One with you, and one with Martin.'

'Who?' Jem whispered the question. The name disquieted her, and she had no idea why.

She saw Keith give a look to Jeremy that made her feel as though she were being excluded from some dark secret. Brief scrutiny of Jeremy's blank face, however, suggested that if he was involved in some conspiracy, he wasn't aware of it. She was uncertain as to whether this should be a cause for relief or further anxiety.

'Don't worry about Martin. He's not here, but you are. It can't be helped.'

Jeremy shifted his weight uneasily.

'Why do I feel like I should know that name?' asked Jem, not yet ready to let the matter rest.

'He was yours, and then it took him,' said Denver dispassionately. 'The thing that drew us here took him.'

In an instant, Jeremy's face had turned white, and he was throwing up in the corner, all over the fire extinguisher.

'Jeremy?'

He waved one hand behind him as he leaned gasping against the cold wall with the other.

'I'm...' he managed before vomiting again.

'Jeremy?'

'It's him, isn't it?' said Denver. 'Keith?'

'Well, shit,' said Marlowe.

'Thanks a heap, Linda,' said Keith. 'Can you and James explain this stuff to her up there? I need him straight.'

As Jem shouted at Jeremy for a third time, she failed to see Denver approach to take her hand. As their palms met, the fear and confusion drained from her. She cocked her head as she looked at the spewing Jeremy Starwars, now merely a casual curiosity. Nothing mattered but to go with the woman who had brought this serenity into her life. Denver walked her back to Marlowe, and the trio mounted the steps, and began to climb.

'Wait.'

Jem and the dreamers stopped on the stairs and turned back to Keith. Their bemused stares seemed to him to last a lifetime before he finally decided he had to say what he had to say.

'Rachel. Mike. Bobby. I love you.'

Keith appeared to have got every single one of their names wrong, but Jem decided to ignore this and just appreciate the sentiment. All was love. She beamed at him.

He waved them on, and with shrugs of shoulders they resumed their ascent. Jeremy stopped heaving and watched them, bleary-eyed, as he wiped his mouth. After a few more steps, Keith stopped them once more.

'Sorry. Wait. Sorry,' he said before pausing stock still once more. 'Tal, never let me see this. And never let them see me like this.'

He waved them on again, with further apologies, and this time watched in silence until they became obscured by the next flight.

'What was that about?' asked Jeremy Starwars after what he took to be a respectful interval.

Keith fell silent, while remembering to flail his arms around for Jeremy's sake.

'Huh. She never did show me,' he said after a time, and one corner of his mouth turned up.

***

Great Birmingham: The Year of Unity 492

Keith was sat up in bed in the recovery room, breathing heavily. Talisha mopped his brow and nodded to the nurse, who promptly left.

'Rachel and the boys are here. I've asked George to keep them in reception.'

'They're here? I can't face them yet.'

'They're waiting downstairs. Don't worry.'

'I can't... I'm not ready. She'll know something's wrong straight away. The boys, too.'

'Nothing's wrong. You're here. You're fine.'

'Oh, yeah. I'm here, I'm fine, and I've just experienced my own violent death.'

'Do you know how many times Augustine went through that?'

'What's that got to do with anything? This was my body. Have you been through it? No.'

'Well—'

'Right. Shut up, then.'

This was the first time Keith had ever raised his voice to her, and it immediately left him feeling even more nauseated. There had been protracted hysterical shrieking when he had awoken an hour earlier, but that had been vague and undirected. If Talisha was offended, she hid it behind a chastened look, and mimed pulling a zip across her lips.

After they had spoken further regarding Keith's premortem experiences, the conversation returned to the subject of a potential second visit.

'I'm sorry, Tal, but I told you what your psychopathic mate Kush did to me,' said Keith, shaking his head throughout. 'There's no way I survived that. There's nothing to go back to. You'll have to find another way.'

She squeezed his cheeks between her palms. 'Listen to me, Keith. I know that you do go back.'

'You keep saying that, but how? He smashed my skull in. You need to let it go.'

Talisha sighed and released her grip on his face. 'I know because I've seen it.'

'What?' asked Keith, after several moments spent fruitlessly attempting to interpret the statement, a sinking sensation all the while intensifying in his stomach.

'You're on the recordings. You're there with the dreamers at the end.'

Keith was speechless. Nothing he'd considered had been anywhere near.

'And yes, your head is a funny shape.'

He let out a small laugh, and tried to sniff it back in, hating himself for it. He really only wanted her to see hurt and anger on his face for the time being.

'You knew.'

'I'm sorry. I'm so sorry, Keith. Yes, I always knew that dying was how you were coming back. I promise I didn't know Kush was responsible, though. The dreamers thought you had killed yourself.'

'You told me all I had to do was sleep. You knew, and that's what you told me. Christ, and they knew too, didn't they? Kush knew?'

She nodded, unable to look him in the eyes. 'He knew what I knew, no more.'

Keith looked up at the ceiling tiles, his mind racing.

'What if the dreamers were right? What if Kush only killed me because of the recordings, and that wasn't how I was supposed to go? Maybe I did kill myself before.'

Talisha shrugged.

'What if? There is no "before". The recordings reflect what happened.'

Keith felt as though the sense of injustice was occupying so much of his brain, that it might begin to threaten the functioning of his other senses.

'Bollocks. If I'd known what was going to happen, I wouldn't have gone back. I don't go back, I don't go upstairs, I don't die. It doesn't happen.'

'I'm so sorry you had to go back,' Talisha said quietly. 'I'm so sorry. You had to go back.'

They fell into silence. Talisha sat with her head down, casting furtive glances at a red-faced Keith as he looked in any direction but hers, scanning for something to take it all out on. As the walls and metal fixtures looked too hard to punch, he opted for pounding at the bedding with his fists a few times, and he quickly found himself simultaneously kicking at the mattress with his heels. The bed was soft and bouncy, and he felt entirely ridiculous. The howl of frustration that sprang involuntarily from his lips only made him feel worse.

Shocked by the display, Talisha waited until Keith had been still for some minutes before she felt able to speak again. Her words were largely inaudible.

'What?' snapped Keith.

'How you were found always seemed strange,' she mumbled once more, uncertain as to whether he had heard her the first time.

'What? How was I found?'

'I suppose there's no harm in you seeing it now.' She sounded distant.

'Oh, great. What a treat.' Keith was trembling, pressure building in his head. 'Even if you could figure out a way back, you have the audacity, the fucking gall, to expect me to ever trust you again, you insane bitch?'

He stared at her, incredulous, as he watched the tears begin to roll down her cheeks. This woman whose big ideas, and even bigger nanobot-filled metal womb, had somehow given him this second life. He had made mother cry, and he found himself welling up. His weakness exasperated him, and he was relieved to see her turn her face away.

'I don't know why you should, Keith, and perhaps it won't happen for years,' she said, her speech punctuated by sniffles. 'Who knows how long it takes to work out how we do it. But I know that you do go back. You forgive me, and you help me one more time.'

'That seems pretty bloody unlikely.'

'I know.' She looked at him once more, and braved a smile. 'I know. I'm afraid you're just tied to all this. It's a part of what you are.'

'What I am. What I am,' he sighed. He realised that she was holding his hand, and wondered how long that had been the case.

'An idiot,' he decided, and a flicker of a smile betrayed him.

Talisha chuckled and gulped back a further sob.

'Take your time,' she said with a sniff, squeezing his hand. 'Rachel and the boys will be fine downstairs for a while. There are some great toys down in reception. No lemurs, but lots else. Another time, when you're feeling up to it, I'll show you the recordings. No more secrets. I'll show you your future.'

***

Jem stood back a respectful distance from the edge of the roof, watching Denver and Marlowe take the air on the raised ledge in front of her. Marlowe stretched out his arms and peered back at her.

'Not joining us? It's beautiful. Get up here on tippy-toes, and all you can see is the sky in front of you. All you can feel is the wind caressing you. It's like flying.'

'I'm fine where I am, thanks. Winds can change. It's an amazing view, though,' Jem called out over the breeze, and the sound of a flag flapping loudly nearby.

She remained surprised by just how windy it was up there, given what a still day it seemed down at ground level. She allowed herself briefly to peer down below the horizon, at the tiny roofs glinting in the sunlight, and immediately felt slightly ill. She took a step to one side, in order to better stabilise herself by slapping a palm down firmly on the top of one of the several long air conditioning units which littered the roof. The clattering sound caused Denver to spin round and step down from the ledge, clutching her chest.

'You'll be the death of me,' she said, puffing.

'Sorry,' said Jem.

Her apology was genuine, but it was nevertheless accompanied by a small grin, which she tried to cover with a hand as quickly as possible. It seemed strange to witness such an unguarded moment of panic, however brief, from this woman who had previously seemed unflappable. Jem tried to dismiss the thought of Denver simply falling off the roof in response to her having accidentally made a small noise, as she knew that she wasn't far from hysterical laughter of the most inappropriate kind.

It wouldn't do to forget what these people were up there for, and Jem was having some trouble working out the most appropriate level of solemnity for the occasion. She looked at Marlowe, still on the ledge, now balancing on one leg and making slow, gentle flapping motions with his arms. She tried to convince herself that she was watching a master practitioner of some graceful and meditative martial art, rather than a grown man doing an impression of a flamingo, and she was both surprised and relieved at how quickly the observation of his movement calmed her. As she watched, she idly noted that there was no vibration from the air con unit she was leaning against; no hum coming from any of the other units, either. All off. She thought back to the ridiculous timed lighting in the stairwell. Whatever else these people were, they were most certainly careful with their money. Still, they had at least gone to the trouble of finding and returning her clothes, during their brief stop-off on the floor below. She didn't imagine that a kimono would have provided much protection against the elements she was presently encountering. She shivered anyway, as she pictured the pair of them stepping dispassionately over their fallen friend's body, as though it hadn't been there. They hadn't reacted at all.

Jem didn't like the direction in which her thoughts were taking her, and determined that she should say something before the silence took control entirely. She blinked and focused anew upon the bird man.

'I've flown in dreams, that's enough for me,' she remarked momentarily, thinking this an apposite contribution.

Marlowe ceased flapping.

'Get out of here. I never have. You, Den?'

Denver shook her head and pouted. 'Where do you go to dream, Jemima? It sounds incredible.'

'I don't know,' said Jem, taken aback by the question. 'It's a pretty normal thing, I think. I mean, it's just bits of places I've seen, I suppose. Nowhere real.'

'You sure about that?' Still rock-steady on one leg, Marlowe stretched his arms out once more and stood cruciform against the blue sky.

Jem frowned.

'Of course. I mean, it doesn't feel real.'

'Uh-huh,' Marlowe called back, doubtfully.

Jem's brow became more furrowed. She could feel the wind beginning to go through her, and folded her arms. Not wishing to lose contact with the security of the air conditioning unit, she leaned awkwardly, in order to still be able to rest her other palm against it. These contortions failed to distract the dreamers from their line of questioning.

'Do you often return to places that are familiar to you? In these dreams, I mean.' Denver pointedly air-quoted the word 'dreams'.

'I suppose. Sometimes. There's a town with really tall old shops that I seem to end up in sometimes, and lately there's a student house I think I'm living in, with an art college nearby, that I'm enrolled in.'

'Frustrated ambitions, do you think?'

Jem shrugged.

'I wouldn't have thought so. I mean, I did go to art college. Not this one, though. These are probably just places I've seen on telly.'

'Perhaps.'

'Definitely.' She reinforced the assertion with a nod of the head. 'I mean, that's what dreams are supposed to be like, isn't it? Sort of collages of things you've seen before, somewhere.'

'Well, I don't know, Jemima. I've dreamt perhaps fifty lives, some of them from childhood, but it sounds like you know what you're talking about.'

'I can only talk about my own dreams, can't I? And, I mean, they're like dreams. You know? I think I know it's not real even when I'm there.'

'And what makes you so sure all this is real? I'm seeing the same rooftops you are, I assume, and to the best of my knowledge, I'm fast asleep.'

Denver gestured vaguely at their surroundings. Jem followed her hand briefly before snapping back to focus on her face. The wide open space seemed easier to cope with if she chose not to acknowledge as much of it as possible, for the moment. She moved her palm a little on the comforting steel surface of the air conditioning unit, in order to confirm its presence, to make it seem somehow more solid.

'I'm freezing my tits off, for one thing.'

'And you've never felt cold in a dream?'

'Not that I can remember, no. I don't think you can, can you?'

'I'm feeling pretty cold right now. You do accept that I'm dreaming, don't you?'

'I only know what you've told me.'

'But you've seen what we can do. You've felt it.'

'Yes, but…'

274

'And here you are, in the middle of our dream.'

'That's different. It's not like you're dreaming me, is it?'

'But if we're both dreaming this, couldn't you be, too? And the vanishings. Are those things that happen in your idea of reality? What about Manny? Does he fit in with your assumptions of what is real? Does he match your experience of the world?' Denver stepped a little closer as she spoke.

Jem bristled with the kind of irritation that she would normally reserve for an insurance claim form; there were too many questions here that she had no earthly interest in answering.

'I don't pretend to have seen everything. And I don't think you can necessarily believe everything you see, either.'

'And what of your boyfriend? Did you believe in him?'

'Jeremy isn't my boyfriend,' Jem blustered. 'We just work together.'

'No. Not Jeremy.'

'Who are you talking about, then?'

'Martin. You were very much in love, I think, before Jeremy took him from you.'

'What? Who?' Jem curled her lips at the nonsense.

'He probably didn't even consciously will it. I imagine you were the subject of a passing whimsy, and Martin was swept away to make room. If this is truly anyone's dream, it's Jeremy's.'

'I don't know any Martin,' insisted Jem. 'I don't know what you're talking about.'

'Oh, dear Jemima Pepper, still clinging to what's left of your reality, while it crumbles around you.' Denver shook her head and tutted as she walked towards her. 'And not even sure of the ground beneath your feet.'

Jem uncrossed her arms and straightened up, mumbling that she was fine. She only looked down briefly, to check that the safety of the air conditioner remained within reach, but when she raised her head, she saw that Denver had removed her sunglasses and was reaching out toward her.

'There's really nothing to be concerned about, is there?'

'No,' said Jem, and she took Denver's hand.

As she did so, she was engulfed by the warmth of a safety and a trust she hadn't experienced since childhood. And then came the sense of loss; every joke, every smile, every tender moment shared with Martin was returned to her in an instant, and she knew what had been taken from her. She felt a gentle tickling sensation on her cheeks as they became wet. She looked over to a blurry Marlowe, still on the ledge, arms still outstretched, but facing her now, and beaming, and she smiled weakly in return.

'There. It's fine,' said Denver. 'I've got you. Now come and show us how to fly.'

***

Ian Gerald Peterson felt his way along the shelving units, trying not to dislodge anything that might make a noise. He reached what seemed to be the end of the row, and waved his hand tentatively into the blackness beyond, trying to laugh off the irrational fear that something would immediately grasp it. When he found that nothing did, he moved left and took a hesitant step forward. He could make out a narrow but reassuring horizontal chink of light coming from what he took to be the top of the door to the storeroom.

Ian was still unsure at this point as to what he would do once he reached the door. He had heard the click of the lock, and thought it likely that trying the handle would yield little success, and he couldn't yet imagine himself hammering at it, and yelling for his release. The laughter from his enemies would surely prove unbearable. Any excuse he might put forward for his predicament would meet with derision, and how long might they wait, anyway, before even letting him out? However, this sole exit and single source of light enticed him beyond resistance, drawing him to it. Unable to recall with certainty whether there might be any low-lying obstacle such as a table between himself and the door, he moved gingerly toward it, hunched over with both hands in front of him, probing the darkness for anything that might block his progress. His fingers seemed to feel colder as he plunged them into the unknown, but he told himself that this was purely because he was causing a draught by waving them around.

It wasn't so much the fear of bruising a shin that informed his caution, as a desire to not make any unnecessary sound, to not be detected. And much though he told himself that it was by the haters outside that he didn't want to be heard, he couldn't help but feel that he had a more pressing reason to remain silent; the longer he stayed in the pitch black, the more convinced he became that he was not its sole occupant.

He jumped a little as his fingernails tapped against the door sooner than he had estimated, and he froze for a moment, listening. He could hear no booming laughter coming from the Sales room, nor any approaching footsteps, and he relaxed for the briefest of moments, before the notion that everyone might have left for the weekend began to gnaw at him. He pressed his ear against the rough varnished surface of the door and strained to detect signs of life without.

Nothing.

He swallowed and listened again.

The click of a door some distance away, perhaps Accounts, perhaps the meeting room, and some quiet murmuring, probably from the corridor between Sales and Reception. He fancied that he even heard some swearing.

He wasn't alone. *Thank God*.

A scraping noise from behind him caused him to wheel around, and he began to dimly make out sections of shelving across the room moving and distorting, from left to right. Then he saw what appeared to be a human face, silently moving closer, grey vertical lines shimmering beneath it, appearing to each side and radiating outward.

He wasn't alone. *Oh God*.

Ian found himself rooted to the spot, his heart pounding, as the face neared him. For the second time in recent days, he had a warm, wet feeling in his trousers, and this time he knew it not to be coffee. Or at the very least, it hadn't been coffee for several hours. As the trickling sensation ran down his leg, he realised that he recognised the face, and that it was a fun-house mirror version of his own.

'It is time,' said a voice far closer to Ian's head than any that could belong to the twisted face, which had stopped perhaps three feet from him.

At this point, Ian made peace with the fact that he was pissing himself. Had he not already begun to do so, he reasoned that he would surely have started now. Stood stock still, he began to feel a dampness in his right sock, and was faintly bemused that there was still a warmth to it, whereas his crotch and inner thigh had fast become cold and numb. As he gazed in terror at the look of disgust on the face floating before him, his arms and legs refused to respond. However, when he willed his toes to curl, whatever primal instinct was now in control permitted them to do so, perhaps reasoning that they were safely out of sight within his shoe. He felt a squelch beneath his sole, and, detecting no further liquid seeping in, decided that his bladder-emptying must have ceased.

'What?'

The word slipped quietly from Ian's mouth, surprising him, as he had not thought himself ready to speak.

'It must end,' the voice told him.

'I think I've stopped now,' said Ian absently. 'What?'

'Where is Jeremy Starwars?'

The question seemed to ease Ian's paralysis. As he brought his hand to his nose to wipe it before answering, he saw that the face produced a wavering hand of its own, in a similar motion. Ian waved his hand in front of the face, and the face did likewise.

'M—Manny? Is that—'

'Where is Jeremy Starwars?' repeated Manny.

'Upstairs,' whispered Ian, pulling at his trouser leg in stunned dismay.

'So did you check it, or didn't you?' said the door behind him.

'We're locked in,' mumbled Ian. He had been preparing to announce this fact to Manny, and now spoke it far too quietly for whoever might be beyond the door to hear.

'So basically, you're saying you didn't,' insisted the door.

Male and female voices bickered in muffled tones, and then there came a click, and the door swung open, illuminating Manny sufficiently for Ian to be able to see how horrifically apparent the large dark stain down his inside leg was, purely from a quick study of his own rippling reflection.

'Barbara Pappa. Racist Scum.' Manny acknowledged each of the liberators now stood in the doorway in turn, though neither could tell for certain which of them he was looking at, each seeing their own face in his surface.

'There, he's alive,' an indignant yet disappointed sounding Ray told Barbara, 'I trust this witch trial is at an end.'

He then sniffed the air suspiciously. Ian Gerald Peterson continued to face the other way, trying desperately to come up with excuses for his situation, his mind a blank.

'It must have been hell in there, Manny,' remarked Ray, still sniffing, and staring reproachfully at the back of Ian's head.

'I am most terribly sorry, Manny,' said Barbara.

'Take us to Jeremy Starwars,' demanded Manny of Barbara Pappa.

'He's waiting for me in Reception,' Ray assured him, patting at the air in a gesture designed to suggest that everything was under control.

'He's gone upstairs with your people,' said a better-informed Barbara.

She patted at the outside jacket pockets of her business trouser suit before inviting Manny to follow her. Ray trailed them both, silently mouthing some of the things he planned to say to Jeremy Starwars.

Ian Gerald Peterson remained in the storeroom, facing into the darkness, listening to the laughter now building in the Sales Department and pulling surreptitiously at his trouser leg, as the door swung shut once more behind him.

16

COMING UNSTUCK

'I didn't expect them to find us that quickly. I thought they'd go to the top floor first, and maybe panic about that murder you did for a bit.'

'Nice plan. Thanks. How long is that going to hold that... thing, exactly?' Jeremy was looking at the upended filing cabinet now blocking the meeting room door.

'I really don't know, Starwars. Just be grateful that the dream of the paperless office hasn't yet materialised. It looks pretty heavy, doesn't it?'

One of the drawers had slid open, and begun to vomit forth its cargo of long-forgotten files. Jeremy tentatively tried to push it closed with his foot, but several inches of displaced cardboard blocked its progress.

'I don't know. You pushed it over. Was it heavy?'

Keith shrugged his working shoulder.

'I couldn't tell. I suppose it was light enough for a corpse to move. There's not a lot else in here. We could move the table, maybe.'

'Is it worth it? I mean, isn't Manny just going to seep through the crack between the door and the frame anyway?'

'I think you've been watching a little too much television.'

'Well, bloody hell. Excuse me, night of the living Keith,' Jeremy blustered. 'I don't know the rules of whatever fantasy land you people inhabit, do I? Just do whatever you're going to do quickly.'

'It's you that's going to do it.'

Jeremy began scanning the windows for an escape route, wondering whether he could survive a jump from that height. Perhaps if he were to roll with it, like a paratrooper. A teacher at infant school had once complimented him on an excellent parachute roll.

'Starwars?'

The roll had been conducted entirely at ground level, during a game of rounders, having tripped over between bases. It was possible that the teacher had praised him to distract him from crying, but he genuinely hadn't skinned his knee, or anything. He looked at the car park below. Perhaps he could land on a car. Would that skin his knee?

'Jeremy?'

It was hard to see what was parked at the wall. If there was something tall down there, like a people carrier, that would be less far to fall. Would a broken leg hurt that much? He would probably ruin his trousers, and he'd only bought them the previous week.

'JEREMY.'

Jeremy jumped, and began to blurt.

'What? Look, what can I do? I thought you were going to sort this out. If you're relying on me, we're fucked.'

'Calm down. It's fine. You can definitely do this. You might even enjoy it. You're going to make a sigil.'

Jeremy took a few controlled breaths, hoping that from then on he wouldn't have to concentrate entirely on respiration as a consequence.

'I'm sorry, what? You want me to make a cigar?'

'A sigil, cloth ears.' Keith handed him a marker pen.

'Right. Of course. And what's one of those?'

Behind Jeremy, Keith could see the door handle being tested.

'OK, very quickly. Sigils are a way of telling the universe what you want through symbols. They focus your desires. Companies use them all the time. They build them into their logos. When you get millions of people looking at them, it only needs to be glances. It keeps them charged. Keeps them powerful. What's the logo on the big window on the front of this building, for example?'

'It's a weird squiggle. The people upstairs put it on a flag on the roof the other day, too.'

'Yes. Flags as well. If you want to invade a bunch of countries, it helps to get a load of people really invested in a flag first. They eventually cancel each other out, most of the time, though.'

'Whatever. Nobody knows what this thing's supposed to be. At least the company they bought out had a cheetah on theirs. You could tell what it was. This one's stupid.'

They both heard two knocks at the door.

'It's a sigil. These guys know all about this stuff. They've been here a long time, and they've used all kinds of magick to get them to where they needed to be.'

'A failing software house on a trading estate.'

'To find you.'

'And there's magic now. I suppose I should have expected it would come to this.'

'Magick,' Keith enunciated the second syllable pointedly.

Jeremy blinked.

'It still sounds like you're saying magic.'

'We just need a quick chat, Jeremy. Will you be long?' said a muffled voice from the other side of the door.

'I'm saying it with a 'k' at the end.'

'Right. And why are you doing that?'

Keith shook his head.

'It doesn't matter. Sorry. I just want you to put the end-of-the-pier stuff out of your mind. I'm not going to ask you to pick a card, and we're not going to saw anyone in half. Let's call it reality engineering.'

'Can we not? That sounds unbelievably poncey.'

'Wise up, Starwars. This is all about attitude. Look, you can make stuff happen, right? Change reality?'

'So you keep saying.'

'But you don't have any control over it. You're doing it all subconsciously. This,' Keith tapped the whiteboard, 'is going to give you that control.'

Jeremy looked at the marker he was holding. 'You want me to draw something.'

'Yes. It's going to concentrate your mind. Focus your will. You're going to send everyone to Birmingham with a drawing. Reunite the two planes, and end this.'

'Wait, shouldn't I just be bringing everyone that you say is missing back here?'

'You do that, and five hundred years of advancement are gone. All those lives lived, for nothing. And it's a better planet, Starwars. It's like this one, if *we* hadn't happened to it. They have clean energy. Everyone can be happy there. *I've* been very happy there. I've had a wife and two sons there.'

'No, they've blocked it with something,' said the muffled voice from behind the door.

'You're asking me to take a lot on faith, here.'

'What's the harm? If I'm talking shit, they'll be through that door in a minute anyway, and you can try to reason with them then, if you like.'

'Mister Starwars, you're trying my patience today,' said another muffled voice behind the door.

'If everyone's so happy, why would they want to kill me?'

'They're pulling up the ladder. They've seen this place through the dreamers' eyes, and they don't want you lot there, any more than they want to come back here. They like things how they are, and you're like some sword of Damocles dangling over everything. They know you could take it all away at any moment.'

'Jeremy? It's Barbara,' said the muffled voice of Barbara Pappa from behind the door.

'Look, You've got a chance to put everything right here, and I mean everything. If it doesn't work, you can always take your chances here. Most likely scenario, that door opens, Manny comes in swinging a hammer, and it's all over in seconds. Best case? You convince him to leave you alone, and your life carries on exactly like before.'

Keith received only a frown from Jeremy in response.

'I think you'd sooner take the hammer,' guessed Keith.

Jeremy remained tight-lipped.

'So let's do this first, yes?'

Jeremy looked at the scuff marks on his shoes. One more thing he hadn't gotten around to.

'Jeremy?'

'And all this hideousness will be gone, and we'll all just be happy?' asked Jeremy at last.

'Honestly,' said Keith after a short pause. 'It's paradise, and you can put everyone there with me, today.'

'Right,' said Jeremy Starwars, looking up, and wiping his nose in preparedness. 'Fuck it. Right. What do I do?'

'That's the spirit. OK. First you need to write what I want, what we want, in a nice succinct sentence. As simple as you can.'

'Is this like cosmic ordering? I think I've heard of this.'

'A bit, I suppose, if you like. Does that help?'

'Not really.'

Jeremy thought for a moment, before writing on the board 'SEND EVERYONE TO BIRMINGHAM.'

'Good.'

'And that'll be all right, will it? Everyone will fit?'

'Birmingham's what they call the planet. Everyone will fit. Just think of them as being in the same place, but somewhere else.'

'Oh, very helpful. And what will it do to you? Anything? I mean, you're already there, aren't you?'

'I'm there, yes. But I'm here, too. I have to be. I'm the link back to there. I'm the wire you're going to send everyone down. And it doesn't really matter what it does to me, anyway. I've not got long.'

'What? Don't be silly,' said Jeremy, trying to sound both surprised and supportive. Immediately after speaking, he became concerned that this might have come across as sarcastic, talking as he was to a heavily battered corpse.

'I don't mean this. Obviously, this hasn't got long. It's going to start rotting soon. I mean there. I'm a very old man, Jeremy. It's been years since I last sat up, never mind walked. I'm fed through one tube, and I piss through another. That's why I agreed to come back, when Tal's niece finally approached me, offering the chance to have control of my body again.' He flapped his arms. 'It's not quite how I'd imagined it was going to be.'

'I'll bet.'

'Well. It's still been nice. With Rachel gone, and the kids grown up, it beats staring at the ceiling. Mike's a fisherman now, you know. And Bobby's busy making a name for himself as an actor.'

'Right.' Jeremy found himself slipping very comfortably into the

284

role of not listening to the old man, now that he knew himself to be conversing with one.

'So proud of them both.' He waved his arms. 'God, I miss her.'

'I'm sure.' Jeremy slowly turned his head back to the board, as respectfully as he could. 'What now?'

'I'm sorry. Write it out again, but—I'm sorry.' More arm-flapping followed, during which Jeremy patiently waited, his marker pen hovering at the board. 'I'm sorry. Write it out again without the vowels.'

Jeremy sighed loudly and did so, and was left with 'SNDVRYNTBRMNGHM.'

'Right. Now wipe out all the letters that appear more than once.'

'What, so both 'M's go?'

'Yes. We're trying to simplify this as much as possible.'

After some deliberation, and more than a little pointing by Keith, Jeremy was down to nine letters.

'Right, you need to jumble those letters up, and make a little monogram out of them. Be creative. Make them different sizes, elongate bits, overlap them, whatever. The important thing is that it looks right to you.'

'Can I put them sideways? Why have you got your back turned?'

'This has to be personal to you. And yes, it doesn't matter how you turn them. They can look nothing like letters when you're done, the more abstract the better. It only matters that you know what this sign represents.'

'I can't shake the feeling that this is going to end in potato prints.'

'Maybe later, if you do a really good job on this. Concentrate on what you're doing.'

'Finished,' said Jeremy almost immediately.

Keith rolled his eye.

'You're sure?'

'Yeah.' Jeremy chuckled.

'Why are you... have you made it look like a cock or something?'

'A bit.'

'Well, don't *tell* me,' said Keith, exasperated. He turned his head a little to peek, and snorted. 'Very good. I hope you're proud. Well, I've seen it now. You'll have to do another one.'

'OK, whatever.'

Keith listened until the squeaking had ceased once more.

'Done?'

'Yeah. It looks fine. All decent.'

'Then all that remains is to charge it.'

'We're not going to wait forever,' said a voice from behind the door.

'Charge it? How do we do that?'

'You need to concentrate on it in a heightened state.'

'What do you mean, heightened state?'

'Some use sex, but that's not really on the cards here. You could crack one out, I suppose. I'll keep my back turned.'

There was a pause.

'Starwars? Have—Have you started?'

'What? What do you mean? I'm not doing *that*. That was a stunned silence, you perverted freak.'

'OK. I suppose getting in a bit of a panic would do. Shouldn't be a problem for you. God, now I think about it, you've probably been using sigils this whole time without knowing it. Staring at code you didn't understand, feeling sick with worry, and wishing various people would leave you alone. Does that sound about right?'

'That does sound familiar,' Starwars admitted.

He was shocked at the revelation that Keith had him so thoroughly pegged. He had been so certain all this time that he had been presenting an outward image of a man in complete control. Still, it felt strangely pleasant to be relieved of the burden of carrying the awful truth alone.

'God, that's it, isn't it?' Keith continued. 'A normal person wouldn't have the power to make those things actually happen, of course. You, though. You've charged a load of code up by focusing all your angst and self-loathing onto it, and you've turned it into some kind of loaded psychic weapon. Well played, universe. You've given godlike powers to someone with an inferiority complex.'

'I do understand most of the code. It just doesn't seem like it's ever going to fit, or do what I need.'

'Fine. You don't need to justify yourself to me, I don't work here any more. I'm dead in this town. Just focus your fear onto that symbol.

Really concentrate. You can do this.'

Two more knocks at the door.

'We're coming in.'

'This isn't working.'

'It has to. You have to make it work.'

'Nothing's happening. Should I feel something happening?'

'Shut up. Concentrate.'

A thought struck Keith, and he tapped at the laptop's keyboard to wake it, hoping that what he was looking for would be easy to find for someone who had only used such a quaint device once, briefly, in many decades. The knocks at the door were turning to heavy thuds as he scanned the desktop icons. A moment's fleeting glee at recognising what he sought, was replaced by horror at the realisation that his dead fingers weren't being recognised by the computer's touchpad, and he fared no better stabbing at the screen. Try as he might, he couldn't make the mouse pointer move to where it needed to go. Accessibility options for corpses seemed not to have been enabled.

Further thumps, and the door was beginning to give.

Keith looked down in despair, still managing to avert his eye from the creation on the whiteboard. Half his face lit up as he recognised what he saw lying at his feet. Snatching up the wireless mouse that had faithfully kept Jeremy company during his time feigning catatonia on the carpet tiles, he slid it across the table and clicked hurriedly. As he waited for the machine to respond, his arms flapped in an impatient nervous tic that probably would have manifested as finger drumming, had his control over the body been more complete. Finally, the development software presented itself, and he fired up the projector, hoping that it was still pointed in the right direction. He heard Jeremy take a step back as the whiteboard lit up, with the hated project now shining on top of his sigil.

'This is it, isn't it? The code you've been staring at all this time.'

Jeremy felt his forehead go cold. A screen full of the cursed keywords, constants and parentheses glared malevolently back at him, larger than he had ever seen them before. It all did something, but none of it what he had hoped. It was as though he had been nailing jelly to the wall, day after day, and had then been desperately cleaning up after himself, for fear that someone might see the mess. And here it was. The mess, on public display, for anyone to see what an idiot he had been. He felt sure that Keith would have seen it straight away for the drivel that it was. He knew that he was judging him now.

'Yes,' he managed to utter.

'Keep looking at the sigil, but try to take in the code too.'

Jeremy did as he was told, and immediately began to feel like something barely liquid, like a particularly thick and heavy porridge, was being pumped into his skull, leaving less and less room for his brain.

Keith moved as quickly as he could to prop himself against the filing cabinet, discovering at once that his weight made little difference. The door was about to open. There was just time for one last push.

'These people are coming in to see what you've been working on. Is it ready? Everyone's waiting for you, Jeremy. Everyone's depending on you. You need to understand that code now.'

He sensed himself begin to slide across the floor.

'You must know. It's obvious,' he lied, and then there was only time to shout, 'show them what it does.'

Jeremy listened to the filing cabinet scraping against the carpet tiles. He stared intently at the round and most definitely non-phallic squiggle he had formed from the letters of his request to the universe. He heard the screech of the wood against metal as the door's edge ground against its obstacle. He studied the variations in thickness of each stroke on the whiteboard, and every negative space they formed in between. Why wasn't this working? Why did he even think it should? Once again, he'd been assured something would be straightforward, and now somehow it would be his fault when it didn't work. This was so typical. At last he felt the familiar knot beginning to tighten in his stomach, and he welcomed it like an old friend. This was it. He recognised it now. This was his metamorphosis, his transformation sequence, his Hulking. *You wouldn't like me when I'm pathetic*. One more loud squeal from the doorway. Manny's voice was in both his ears now.

'Jeremy Starwars? What are you…'

And with that, Jeremy was alone, and listening to the cars crashing outside.

288

***

Great Birmingham: The Year of Unity 473

The first thing Keith noticed was that the smell had gone. The musk of Guy Mange was no longer invading his nostrils.

The next thing he became aware of was the absence of Ray toying with Starwars. No giggling in the background. There was no sound in his ears at all.

Then he realised that he could no longer see any workmates; no windows, no walls, no table, no notepad or coffee mug striking his retinae.

He no longer had the sensation of sitting in a chair. By this point, Keith had already decided that this really wasn't much of a meeting any more, and there was little point in his continued attendance. This was for the best, as it then occurred to Keith that he no longer had nostrils, ears, eyes, or a body with which to sit in a chair. He reasoned that this would significantly impact his performance both at work and at home. Susan certainly wouldn't be happy. She had some boxes for him to unpack, and he really couldn't see how he was going to manage that now.

This trying state of affairs continued for a while; precisely how long, Keith would later prove unable to recount. The absence of the senses rendered the marking of the passage of time difficult at best. After an unknowable period had elapsed, Keith began to feel once more. These feelings initially manifested themselves as a tickle that began in the very centre of his brain and radiated outward until he was eventually aware of being within a prickling shell in the once-familiar shape of a man. The unreachable itch coursed through this shape until a rhythm of some description began to establish itself, and Keith breathed again, gasping involuntarily with the first beat of his heart. Between this and the second beat, he saw a flash of himself in a mirror, and a red hammer coming toward him, seemingly from within this mirror. Upon later recollection, and the reliving of this moment in numerous dreams, he would fail to reconcile this image with any experience of which he was aware, and would therefore elect to put it down to some misfiring of the synapses.

'Um,' said a female voice.

Keith's eyes weren't yet offering any usable information; just a painfully bright, confusing flickering. Sounds, however, were beginning to fill his head. Everything seemed clearer than he remembered. These ears felt like his, but they were without the waxy build-up to which he had always been a martyr.

'Tal? What's wrong?' he heard another female voice say, from further away.

'We cleared the chamber, right? There was a security sweep.' The first woman again, a little closer now, and shouting.

Keith winced as the sound rang in his ears. Whoever these people were, they were far too loud.

'They swept through the whole place, then swept right out.' A man was shouting now, but at a reasonable distance, at least. An echo accompanied his voice. 'We're in a complete lockdown. Nobody here but us chickens.'

'Erm. Why?' The second woman was moving closer, clanging and creaking sounds marking her approach, and she was only slightly raising her voice now.

'Because there's some…' The first woman again. He could hear her footsteps as she walked away from him. Flat shoes. Rubber soles first on something like linoleum, and then squeaking against metal as she withdrew farther. She paused, and Keith heard her swallow, as crisp and distinct a sound as if the saliva were descending his own gullet. He detected the tremulousness in her voice as she added, 'there's someone lying in there.'

***

Jeremy clambered out through the window in the Accounts room, and stood blinking in the sunlight. He had found the remote for the shutters lying in the corridor where he assumed Barbara had been standing before he had sent everyone away. The altered key code for the front door had proved more troublesome. Jeremy had hoped to somehow be able to detect the most recently used buttons on the keypad, in order to narrow down the possibilities, but every button had turned out to be smeared in a mixture of finger grease and dried blood. It appeared that Ray had been trying many combinations while they had been upstairs, and the exterior door in the workshop had told a similar tale. The fire exit hadn't been any more useful; when Jeremy had eventually managed to prise it open, he had discovered a brick wall immediately beyond it. The unfortunate positioning of the small outbuilding which housed the generator hadn't struck him until that point. It was dawning on Jeremy Starwars that if the people upstairs had never turned up, the company for which he worked would probably have killed him eventually through criminal negligence. So it was, that he had come to seek out the window that looked out on the highest point on the sloping car park, in order to minimise his chance of injury, and then to work his way through a hex key set he had found in the workshop until he came across one that approximately fitted the lock on the handle.

As he stood in the car park next to three cars with crushed roofs, and took in the evening air, Jeremy realised that he had probably expected to be greeted with complete silence, and that those expectations were presently being confounded. Although there was no traffic noise, there was a repetitive thudding sound, and a fairly loud hum, which he took to be emanating from the idling generator. There was also birdsong, and this gave Jeremy pause for thought. He had sent away the people, but the animals had been left behind. Initially, this seemed to him to be a good thing for all the other species, having just removed the one at the very top of the food chain, but then he thought of all the pets presently awaiting their owners, and this saddened him. He considered the animals on farms. While some were undoubtedly receiving a stay of execution, others were waiting to be fed, or brought in for the night. In the distance he heard a dog bark, and wondered whether it was outside, or trapped in someone's kitchen.

At this point, it occurred to Jeremy Starwars that all the buildings were still there. He had noticed their presence already, as he was not entirely unobservant, but it had taken him this long to consider the fact that their being there with him also meant that they were not elsewhere with all the people he had sent to Birmingham. He had made an entire planet homeless. This was a slightly larger concept than he was prepared to deal with for the present, and he decided simply to hope that Birmingham was as advanced as Keith had claimed, and that it wasn't raining.

Jeremy walked slowly across the car park in the general direction of the security cabin, stopping occasionally to pry into the window of a car here and there. It felt odd to him to be this invasive of other people's privacy with such abandon. The idea that there was nobody watching would take some getting used to. He realised that he could break into any of these cars without fear of prosecution, but he resolved that at least for the time being, he would stop short of doing so. For the moment, the knowledge that he could was sufficient. Jeremy tried to remember the names of the cars' owners as he looked around, and was pleased to discover that he could recall five in his general vicinity. He realised that he had no way of knowing whether this was fewer than he would have been able to name that morning, or how long these memories might linger, but it was something. He hadn't forgotten everybody, at least not yet. The dog was still barking somewhere beyond the industrial estate. Jeremy wondered what would happen to him if he did finally forget everyone entirely. Would he forget himself, without reference to others? Would he still know that he was human? He reasoned that books must have been left behind too. Books would save him. Jeremy Starwars had never been a big reader, but he had always considered himself the kind of person who would be, granted the absence of distractions.

Jeremy wasn't sure exactly why he felt drawn to the security cabin, but he thought it might have been the sight of the tailor's dummy in the window. Another human shape. Approaching the steps of the cabin, it struck him that the sounds he was hearing had altered in an unexpected manner. Although the humming had become quieter as he had moved away from the generator, the accompanying repetitive thudding had remained constant in its volume. The thudding was coming from somewhere else. He turned, looking this way and that, seeking the source of what was now the loudest noise he could hear; for all he knew, the loudest noise there now was, anywhere. Finally, he looked up and saw the police helicopter.

Jeremy quickly passed through excitement, fear, relief and sorrow, as he briefly thought that he wasn't alone after all, panicked at the strong likelihood that he wouldn't get on with this other person, and then realised that the pilot had almost certainly just put the craft onto automatic, prior to being wished away. Jeremy hoped that they had not arrived in Birmingham at the same height at which they had departed Earth. The helicopter was hovering at a fair height, and Jeremy thought it to be above one of the large houses behind the estate. One of the properties surrounded by the nice tall pines that he couldn't see from any windows but those in the toilets when he was at work. It crossed his mind that there was nothing to physically prevent him from living in one of those houses now, barring perhaps the dog he could still hear barking. Jeremy thought about the many planes that would have been airborne across the globe at the moment he sent everyone away, and he began to feel nauseated. He determined that he had to assume everyone had arrived in Birmingham on the ground. He just had to. The alternative for everyone that had simply been upstairs in a building was too awful to contemplate. Keith wouldn't have simply let him essentially wipe out a sizable fraction of humanity at a stroke. He would surely have thought that all through. He would have known that everything would have worked out fine. Surely. Jeremy decided to take the opportunity to stumble backward at that point and sit down with some considerable force on the breezeblock steps leading up to Shareef's cabin, and reasoned that this was an ideal moment to indulge in a bout of uncontrollable sobbing.

After a time, Jeremy felt that he should pull himself together. If not for his own sake, then for that of the dummy watching him with obvious disdain from the security cabin window. Having gripped the breeze blocks several times during his outpouring of emotion, he unthinkingly wiped his hands on his pale slacks in a bid to remove the grit from his fingers. He instantly regretted this as he stared down at the oily, muddy streaks he had created. The rate at which he was falling apart surprised even Jeremy. Still, with the exterior of his trousers ruined, he now deemed his hands to be clean enough to risk delving into a pocket for a handkerchief. He blew his nose and struggled back to his feet. The helicopter continued to hang in the air and make its thudding noise at him. He marvelled at its stillness a while longer, before turning to investigate the cabin.

Although he was fully aware of the presence of the uniformed tailor's dummy, he still jumped a little when it appeared in the periphery of his left eye as he stepped inside. He saluted it silently and stooped to pick up the baton that was leaning against the door frame to his right. He hefted the jumped-up club in his palm, and told the dummy he didn't want any trouble. He sidled up to the mug of tea sitting on the small fold-down Formica table, close to where the dummy was leaning, and sniffed at it. Jeremy was proud of himself for deeming it to be half full, until he considered the fact that it was too cold to drink, and realised that he was now simply a pessimist overestimating wasted beverages. He raised an eyebrow as he read the mug.

'I'm sorry, deputy, but you're in charge here now,' he told the dummy. 'I hope you won't miss Frankie too much.'

Frankie the dummy remained taciturn, too polite to correct the stranger, and far too busy in any case with the business of carrying out his duty, staring into the car park. The portable television beside the mug was quietly displaying a black screen. Jeremy tried some other channels, and was delighted to find the closing credits of a film on his fourth or fifth attempt. Once the usual assortment of corporate logos had scrolled past, however, that channel too turned to silent darkness.

He turned off the set and settled down next to Frankie to peer out at the chopper, resisting the urge to put his arm around the faithful dummy, not wishing to push the boundaries of this new relationship. Together they sat and watched until, after an hour or so, the rotors stopped and the helicopter fell peacefully from the sky, and the dog began to bark once more.

***

Jeremy Starwars ran his hand over the whiteboard. It was pleasantly cold to the touch, and he found its blank expanse agreeable. It was filled to all four of its bevelled steel edges with possibilities, every one of which was thoroughly unexplored. He examined his palm as he lifted it from the surface, and noted that it was entirely unsoiled by the ink marks he imagined would have accompanied an encounter with an overworked board. He drew closer still, and stood facing it, losing himself in its featureless territory, and wondering how long it might take for one to develop snow blindness or pass out from such a pursuit.

A glance at the clock on the wall revealed the lunch hour to be over. He had passed the hour profitably, after paying a visit to the corner shop and discovering the alcohol shelves to be unattended. In point of fact, he had yet to find anything to be attended, but was unready to fully embrace this state of affairs and run riot across the globe. Apart from anything else, there were logistical concerns, given his inability to fly a plane or captain a boat. There was a significant amount of studying involved if he intended to pillage beyond Great Britain.

Time, in any case, to begin the presentation. Jeremy raised his fist to his mouth and cleared his throat in a demonstrative manner, as he turned to face the empty meeting room.

'Now then. I suppose you're all wondering why I asked you to join me here today,' he began, affecting the accent of a Belgian detective. He had wanted to add the phrase 'someone in this room is a murderer' to make his little joke clear, but at the last moment discovered that he couldn't get the words out, because it was true; there was indeed a murderer in the room. He offered a forced grin to each chair around the table, allowing a little time for any polite laughter to disperse.

'Some of you will be aware that I've been looking into getting a report generator integrated with our system. Well, more looking *at*, rather than into. Staring at, really. Staring right through, if I'm honest. This is probably a good time to turn the projector on.'

He leaned over the table and did so, excusing himself to the nearest chair, and then turned the dimmer switch on the wall until the room was in near darkness, other than the dim light reflecting from the board now doubling as a projector screen. Another good reason for not having used a marker on it.

'Ooh, spooky. Can you just push that door to, Rob?'

He waited for a moment, watching the narrow strip of light between door and frame at the far end of the room, before sighing, and saying, 'never mind, I'll get it. I'm closer.' He walked over, clicked the door shut, and was surprised at how much darker it suddenly was. Before his eyes could adjust, he had walked into one chair, and caught his elbow on the back of another. Alternately swearing and excusing himself accordingly, he felt his way back to the front of the room.

Jeremy dug into his trouser pocket and produced his house keys. After a moment spent sorting through the items among them, allowing the majority to drop and hang from the ring, he brought forth a small laser pointer.

'Pew! Pew!' he said, tapping a couple of times on its button, and causing a red dot to flicker on the meeting room table. After a moment's thought, he began experimenting with trying to elongate the little dot, by crouching at the edge of the table, and positioning the pointer as close as he could to its surface. Stopping himself, he exhaled through pursed lips and stood back up, nodding, to address the table once more.

'I'm losing the room here, aren't I? This is what I'm like. I'm easily distracted. I don't even need this pointer. There's a perfectly good one on the laptop screen I'm projecting right there.' He pointed offhandedly at the diagonal arrow now being shone on the wall behind him, and shrugged, returning his keyring to his pocket. 'I can control that with my phone.'

He slid his phone from another pocket and ran a finger across the screen.

'Now this is a massive distraction. Huge. Ordinarily, you'd be waiting a few minutes now while I checked my mail, but everything is a bit quiet on that front at the moment, as you can imagine. Even knowing there's nobody out there, it's taking every ounce of willpower I have not to fire up Warblespace and just sit here warbling into the void. I had over five hundred Flockers, you know, hanging on my every word. And have you played the games? I mean, it's no match for a dedicated console, but some of them are really addictive. I never told any of you this, but I actually have the fourth best score in the world on Dangleword. That's in the world. Think about that. Just from sitting out there on the toilet.' He gestured in what he thought was the right direction, changing his mind twice, and then looked mournfully back at the phone. 'I suppose I have the best score on everything now.'

'Right.' The arrow on the wall sprung into life, dancing across the grey screen, as Jeremy traced first circles, then his name in joined-up writing, and finally a giant penis, with just a fingertip on his phone. The arrow left no trace of these scribblings, and the large screen remained an impassive grey rectangle.

'That's supposed to be black,' Jeremy explained. 'This projector is shit, like all the equipment in this office. Anyway, a bad workman, and all that. It should still give you a pretty good impression of what I've accomplished in all this time, while I've been telling you all I was nearly done, week after week, meeting after tedious meeting.'

He made the pointer slowly and deliberately patrol the perimeter of the screen to give the room a chance to take in his work in its entirety.

'You might be considering asking me to hand off what I've done so far to somebody else at this point, to get it finished. If so, let me tell you that this screen also serves to show you everything I've understood over that same period. Don't get me wrong; there were times when I thought I might have grasped aspects of the third party stuff I was supposed to be bolting on. But every time I did, I realised that it was awful. Just complete crap, and at least five years out of date. I don't want to be making excuses, but it put me off a bit, to be honest. I felt like I was trying to dig my way out of a pit, and I was too proud to tell anyone I made a mistake in asking for a shovel instead of a ladder. So after a while I just stopped digging, and sat in the pit. And day after day, it seemed like more and more people were crowding around the mouth of the pit, blocking out what little sunlight there was, and just shouting down, asking me if I was done yet. And it just got darker and louder down there. Not very pleasant.'

Jeremy turned off the projector.

'There wasn't really a pit, of course. There was never a shovel. There was a spoilt, arrogant man-child in a cushy office job, is what there was. And there was never a time when I didn't know that. Never a time when I didn't hate myself because of it,' lied Jeremy Starwars.

He pulled up a chair and sat staring into the pitch black.

'And then one day, all the voices just went away. So that's it. You don't have any reports, and the project is stalled. And I'm the bottleneck. But if you'd just give me another crack at it, another couple of weeks, I really think I could do it, if I came at it from a different direction. And if I asked for a bit of advice here and there. I really think I could.' He was surprised at how easy it was to bare his soul in this effusive fashion, now that there was nobody around to judge him.

Jeremy Starwars sat in the darkness and waited, wondering how long it might take for his other senses to become heightened in compensation. He tried to breathe more quietly. The double glazing only permitted the highest pitched birdsong to penetrate from outside. He felt a warmth in his ears, countered by a slight chill in his hands. Jeremy slipped the hands into his pockets and tried not to concentrate on the ears, which somehow seemed to make his head feel heavier. He craned his neck in response to the ache he assumed would be there, given the newly conspicuous cranial weight. He felt a twinge both in his upper left arm, and its accompanying thumb. This disturbed Jeremy, and he focused all his attention on the right thumb, hoping to feel a similar sensation in that one, and therefore confound his grim initial diagnosis. Quickly he noted, with some relief, the same twinge; both thumbs reporting the same tingle, the same numbness at the tip. Perhaps just a minor circulation issue. Jeremy reasoned that he could do with getting more exercise. He slid down in his chair in order to put his lead-filled skull back, and take some of the strain off a spine he imagined to be twisting and buckling under the pressure. Jeremy closed his eyes, and pondered the numbness he now also detected in his lips. He performed an exaggerated shiver from his near-horizontal position.

A chair creaked. Reasoning that it must have been his own, Jeremy didn't stir.

There came a cough. Jeremy didn't remember having coughed. He smiled at the thought that he might be experiencing himself in the third person, and at the question of whether this might be more or less bearable than his normal viewpoint. He listened intently for further coughing, but it wasn't forthcoming. Only the sound of the shuffling of paper. Jeremy experimented with rubbing his sleeves against the fabric of the chair, in an attempt to replicate and explain this new noise. As he did so, with inconclusive results, he realised that he was experiencing a smell he hadn't previously noticed. A musky scent that he imagined might be given off by a rose that had been watered solely with sweat and orange juice for its entire life, was assaulting his nostrils. As

Jeremy cogitated upon this unexplained odour, he heard himself cough again, louder this time, again with no recollection of actually coughing. He tried a few sample coughs, his head still tipped back. These proved unsatisfying, seeming too deliberate, insufficiently visceral. Nevertheless, as he lolled in the chair, enjoying the cool freshness of the flecks of spittle now sprinkled over his face, Jeremy did note that the memories of each cough faded quickly. Without the droplets of saliva to offer some semblance of physical proof that coughing had taken place, it would be straightforward, he reasoned, to convince himself that none had. It seemed to him, in that moment, that memory was at best an imperfect means of establishing one's position in the world. He trusted his body telling him that he was slumped amid a mixture of hard edges and cloth-covered foam padding, which experience told him could only be an uncomfortable office chair. He accepted that he had to trust in his identification of physical properties as he experienced them. There seemed little sense in throwing all of his knowledge of the world out of the window; office furniture was surely a reality. But was this chair necessarily where he imagined it to be? Could he be certain of anything prior to this moment? He interrupted his own train of thought with another cough, this one involuntary and most assuredly his own, ejecting a string of saliva which had briefly troubled the back of his throat and now dribbled slowly from the corner of his mouth. As he considered pulling hand from pocket to wipe his face, he heard two knocks at what still sounded very much like the door his recollections told him featured at the other end of the room. He jumped a little, and opened his eyes. Still dark. No new information there. He closed them once more.

'Come in?'

The phrase certainly seemed apt, and like something he might have said in this situation, had there really been somebody at the door, and yet it sounded unusually feminine to his ears. Had he been a woman all this time, merely dreaming she was a man? Jeremy dug his hands further into his pockets. No, there were things down there to suggest otherwise. Perhaps he had imagined the higher pitch and girlish tone, or perhaps he was just detecting this character in his voice for the first time. It could simply be, he thought, that having his head tipped back in such a fashion was causing the effect. He resolved to experiment at once, and began repeating the phrase to himself. As it didn't immediately resemble what he had just heard, he deliberately made subsequent iterations increasingly high-pitched and camp.

'Come in?'

'Come in?'

'Come in?'

'Sorry, Barbara. I've got Vikram in Birmingham on line four. They're still not happy.'

A sigh.

'OK. Thanks, I'll take it in my office. It looks like we're done in here, anyway.'

A small grunt.

A scraping sound.

A click.

Jeremy Starwars decided at this point to stop saying 'come in?' with an affected accent and pitch. He was hearing too many things that were simply too hard to reconcile as having come from his own lips. He opened his eyes once more.

New information. The light was on now. Perhaps it had never been off. He only had his own word for that. He strained with a groan to lift his head and look forwards, feeling the gob begin to drip down his face under new instructions from gravity as he did so. He blinked a couple of times, but the room full of ashen-faced people seated around the meeting room table didn't seem to go anywhere.

Jeremy waved at his audience, and two of its members waved back; only Jem and Martin appeared to have properly enjoyed his presentation. They grinned from the far end of the table, and Jem offered two thumbs up to the event. Ella seemed less impressed, and next to her, Robert Smith was parting his hair in order to rub the sleep from his eyes. At the front sat Guy Mange, face on to Jeremy, and so close that their knees were almost touching. Ever the epitome of professionalism, his look of disapproval was barely perceptible, but it was withering nonetheless. The smell of distilled perspiration and tangerine peel that Guy had probably invested a significant amount of money and time in selecting, enveloped them both in a cloud that, if it had a mood, Jeremy would have deemed to be almost threateningly judgemental.

'I look forward to your minutes, Mister Smith,' said Ray, blinking as he adjusted to the light.

'What?' said Robert.

'If nobody has any questions, we'd probably better call time on this and get back to our desks, ladies and gents.'

'You heard him, back to the toilets,' said Martin, rising and stretching.

Jeremy stared at Will, as he too got up.

'I can't believe you're wearing that jumper.'

'What? It's cold,' explained Will. After further consideration, he added, 'You're a mental case. You want locking up.'

'OK, that's enough. Back to work please, folks,' said Ray, his voice raised a little but tempered with an intonation of exhaustion.

'On what?' said Will with a snort. 'I need a parser, and *someone* hasn't bolted it in. I mean, should I just do it myself?'

'We'll discuss it later. Go. Go.'

Jeremy watched with some satisfaction as Ray shooed him from the room.

Once everyone else had departed, Ray leaned in to whisper in Jeremy's ear.

'We're going to have to let you go. You know that, don't you?'

Jeremy nodded silently.

'OK. You should probably go and start packing up your things. We'll get something in the post to you tomorrow.'

Ray slapped his hands down on Jeremy's shoulders, and for once, he didn't jump. After the briefest of reassuring pats, and an 'OK, Jeremy,' Ray turned to leave the room. As Jeremy watched him switch off the light and close the door, he considered the weight of these final words. Just like that, he had been stripped of the rank of 'Mister Starwars'. Any piece of paper they sent him now was a mere formality.

Jeremy Starwars sat in the darkness, listened to the birdsong and smiled. For the first time in what seemed like forever, it felt as though everything was going to be just fine.